Spun Sugar
and
Bootblack

CHRISTOPH JAMES

Order this book online at www.trafford.com
or email orders@trafford.com

Most Trafford titles are also available at major online book retailers.

Printed in the United States of America.

ISBN: 978-1-4269-6085-7 (sc)
ISBN: 978-1-4269-6086-4 (hc)
ISBN: 978-1-4269-6087-1 (e)

Library of Congress Control Number: 2011903779

Trafford rev. 03/07/2011

 www.trafford.com

North America & international
toll-free: 1 888 232 4444 (USA & Canada)
phone: 250 383 6864 ♦ fax: 812 355 4082

Prologue
(Windsor Court)

"We perceive a great threat to the sovereignty and have every confidence in your abilities to render this great service unto us."

The Widow of Windsor nodded almost imperceptibly, signaling an end to the audience.

Branan Stoke strode across the courtyard, in an undeniable state of shock. Her Majesty's revelations were nothing short of astounding. He would have dismissed the allegations as pure fantasy, had they been relayed to him by anyone other than the Queen of England herself.

"Sweep north to the border of Scotland," she had instructed. "Take with you such men as you can trust, and speak to no one on this matter, save for Mr. Brown."

Spun Sugar and Bootblack

Scotland, 1864

-1-

Tamlyn moved stealthily towards the drift of quail and raised his weapon in the air with a swift spinning motion. Suddenly the ground beneath his nimble feet trembled, and the birds burst into flight with a flutter of wings.

"That's twice today that the ground has shaken," whispered the youngster. The birds had not flown out of Tamlyn's range. He raised his sling again and sent a smooth stone through the cool afternoon air. The projectile connected with a quail's head, knocking it from its roost. The small boy pounced on the stunned bird and swung it deftly to snap the neck.

Murdoch spoke excitedly. "Well done, now I'll show you how to clean your kill, and we'll eat, but first we'll find shelter.

Murdoch hung his short hunting bow from a shoulder and looked to the sky. "The clouds are moving in and it will rain soon."

"Look," exclaimed Tamlyn. "See how swift that crow is."

Murdoch cocked his head to squint at the black form winging rapidly from view. "You have sharp eyes, little brother. Not all who fly are what they seem. We had better return home under cover of the trees."

The two hunters emerged from the thicket of gorse and began to descend slowly towards the woods. Tamlyn walked behind his brother, who was whistling a soft tune. "Murdoch, how do you know when you've seen a real shape-changer?"

The older boy slowed his pace and placed an arm on his brother's shoulder. "Five claws," he said, thrusting his hand forward, "like the hand of a man. If you get close enough you'll know."

The young boy's eyes widened as he shook his head. "I hope I am never that close."

Murdoch urged him forward with a gentle nudge. "Not all shape-changers are evil. Mother once told me that some of the townsfolk believe Grandfather can take the shape of a large dog."

"I would laugh if I saw that," said a suddenly amused Tamlyn. "I could tell Grandfather that we sighted a rook today, and he'd bark and wag his tail." His laughter was answered by a distant clap of thunder. Murdoch peered at the darkening clouds and urged his brother forward again.

The black bird took note of the travellers as they entered the glade, two young hunters of no importance, hardly worth a mention in his report. He was to take notice of any movement of large groups, and these children certainly didn't fit the criteria. He flexed his talons—ten in all, five on each foot—and changed altitude as low clouds began to obscure the landscape below.

Some shape-changers, in most cases the villainous types, had long, involved names that didn't mean much to anyone but themselves. This swift and cunning creature was known as Domnash, his full name being Domnash Trelinka Vardekuzsh Miseritof Todemetris Azubar.

Domnash surveyed the winding river over which he now flew. The larger of the two falls was several miles ahead where the river widened. When he reached the first set of falls, he would rest for a short period. He had flown long and hard and would soon require food to renew his strength for the remainder of the journey.

The bird's keen eyes spotted a red squirrel near a small stand of trees to the left of the falls. The changeling's large talons gave him the ability to hunt like a hawk, swooping down on his prey and dealing quick and efficient death to the victim with his sharp beak.

Domnash, within seconds of the kill, undertook the transformation to his alternate form.

In the shape of a man his features bore a strong resemblance to his avian counterpart. The nose was long, narrow, and beaklike, and his eyes under heavy lids shone dark from deep in their sockets. Black hair like wet seaweed framed a pale angular face, falling to shoulder length, with a thin braid on either side that joined behind his head with a silver clasp.

Long-fingered white hands with sharpened nails hung from the sleeves of a loose blouse the color of charred bone under a tightly laced jerkin of dark leather. His breeches were a mottled gray material, similar in texture to his tall boots, which were fashioned from softened cowhide.

Domnash, like others of his kind, had a liking for shiny objects of rich color and luminosity. He wore a brooch above his heart that glowed a deep angry purple. The stone had been given in payment for one of many unconscionable acts of betrayal.

Autumn fog was gathering in the low areas as Domnash stepped carefully through the damp grass. The dark creature had eaten the animal quickly and was picking the small bits of raw meat from between his teeth with a splinter of bone. Then he angled his pocket watch toward the fading light with an impatient sneer.

"Dig me up a handful of that wild garlic," said Murdoch. The quail had been stripped and gutted. The older boy quartered the bird and dropped it in the small cooking pot that accompanied him on all his forays into the country. His rucksack also contained a well-made hatchet and a valuable l tinderbox. He had been careful to build the fire at the southern end of the clearing, as the breeze was from the north. The smoke would drift away from them and filter harmlessly through the trees, leaving little sign of their temporary encampment.

"You know," said Murdoch in a low voice, "these movements underground can bring forth many changes. I've heard tell of an entire village falling into a space between the cliffs and vanishing altogether."

Tamlyn's eyes widened. "Where would everything go? What is beneath the earth?"

"According to Father," the older boy replied, "there is nothing other than fire and death, but I've heard stories."

"What stories?" asked Tamlyn eagerly.

"Nothing that I care to mention just now" answered Murdoch, returning his attentions to the cooking. "Remind me tomorrow, in the daylight, and I'll tell you a story."

Tam handed his brother two plump cloves of garlic root and glanced nervously at his feet, half expecting the ground to give way. "Do you think we'll ever go to war?" he asked, changing the subject.

"I don't know little brother. Why do you ask?"

"Grandfather was in a war. That's how he lost his finger."

"Well," replied Murdoch, "it was a fight, certainly not a war." "When Grandfather was a young man, his family moved to our valley in search of a living. After his people had settled in and made a home, they were bothered by the English soldiers who were always making trouble for them, nothing like the nastiness of the old days, but still bothersome.

Murdoch stirred the fire and turned the pieces of meat. He continued, "The fight lasted for some time, and Grandfather killed the English captain, but only after the leader's blade had severed his index finger. Grandmother Vannah was quick to stop the bleeding, and grandfather carried on.

"What did they look like? The English, I mean."

"Father remembers seeing the troops when he was a boy about your age, but they are seldom seen above the border nowadays," Murdoch replied. "I've never seen them"—he gazed across the flames with a vacant look and dropped his voice to a whisper—"except in dreams. I've seen them in dreams."

"And what did they look like in your dreams?" asked Tamlyn.

Murdoch shook his head and smiled at his brother. "Just shadows ... but never mind, let's eat quail, and I have a skin full of cider to wash down our meal. Then we'll make our way back before nightfall."

For a while the youngsters ate without speaking, enjoying the woodland smells that mingled with the comfortable aroma of wild game, wood smoke, and fragrant clover. After carefully extinguishing the fire the brothers turned towards home and set out with an eye on the darkening skies.

"I'm going to pick some mushrooms for us," declared Tamlyn. He recalled that just before the falls where the field began to blend into the High Wood there was a patch of grasses that would yield the tastiest mushrooms for miles. The small fungi were more visible in the reflected light of evening, and Tamlyn would have had difficulty locating them earlier in the day.

By the time Murdoch and Tamlyn had skirted the edge of the woods and climbed the rise above their village, Domnash the shape-changer had been across the valley, back to the second falls, and was on the return leg of his flight, passing the travellers above the low clouds, just out of sight.

Back at the village, Ceana laid her weaving aside and quietly cursed the failing light. There were not enough hours of daylight to finish the tasks she had set herself. In any case, her eyes had grown tired, and she wanted a place by the fire. She shifted her gaze to a stand of dark trees that grew along a gradual rise to the left of her home. She sensed the return of her sons before they came into view at the crest of the hill.

Looking down from the trees, Murdoch smiled at the sight of his village. The fireplaces had been lit, and a smell of roasting meat reached them from below. Somewhere in the valley a piper was crying out the rhythms of an evening song, and a shooting star tore across the deepening blue of the night. Tamlyn was anxious to tell his father of the day's adventure and the meal of quail.

Charlotte emerged from the doorway and waved at her returning brothers. Charlotte was tall and strong for a girl. Her golden red hair fell down the length of her back, and her knowing eyes flashed with mischief. She greeted her brothers with an excited smile. "Father had visitors," she blurted, "two Englishmen from the south. It's all very secretive."

Murdoch looked concerned, and turned to his mother for confirmation. Tam's mouth remained open as Ceana spoke. "Your father will be back in the morning,"

"Is it true?" asked Tamlyn, studying his big sister's face for signs of deception.

"Yes," continued Charlotte, "one rode in on a large roan mare with the most beautiful saddle, and he almost fell from his horse because he carried a wound."

"Where is father?" inquired Murdoch, "and why would he help the English?"

"Your father and Uncle Caymus took them to Grandfather's for medicine." replied Ceana. Then she lowered her voice: "The injured one is named Fearghal." It appeared to all three children that their mother was concerned with the day's happenings and suddenly anxious to change the subject. "I want to hear about your day," she said, brightening and taking Tamlyn by the hand. "And I want some stones from the fire."

Tamlyn's adventures dwindled in stature next to the events that had transpired in his absence, but he helped his mother wrap some stones from the fireplace and told her all about the quail hunt. The large, flat stones would be wrapped in a blanket and nestled at the foot of her mattress.

Murdoch, Tamlyn, and Charlotte lived in a pleasant four-room stone cottage with a thatched roof, at the very top of High Street. Murdoch and Tamlyn slept in a small half room to the left of their parents' bedroom, and Charlotte occupied a smaller sleeping chamber to the right. Ronan and Ceana Macleary enjoyed life with their children in the little Scottish village, despite the creeping poverty that had swallowed up so many families. Dunradin's woollen mill had closed, and new roads bypassed them in favour of the larger towns to the east. Ronan had developed into a skillful smithy, not caring for botany and medicine, as his father Tyburn had.

Tyburn Macleary, for his part, was the nearest approximation to a doctor that the town had, and the old gentleman relied heavily on his knowledge of flora and fauna for the relief of most maladies. Murdoch enjoyed spending time with the old man when he could and was himself becoming educated in the practical uses of plants such as rose hip and opium poppies from the Far East.

As Charlotte lay on her mattress, she thought about the stranger Fearghal, visibly in pain from his injuries. He looked much like her father but taller, and darker in complexion, with a full-length woven jacket with a long opening at the back to accommodate riding and tall, well-worn boots. His hair was long and loose, peppered with much silver and gray. His lean, tanned face was in need of washing, and judging by the stubble on his high cheekbones, he had not bathed or shaved for several days. The stranger's eyes were coal black and intense. Overall, Charlotte found him attractive but also felt a cold sense of familiarity in the crooked half smile that he had granted her.

Tamlyn lay awake for some time, too excited with thoughts of soldiers and large horses to let sleep come easily. He'd gained no information from his sister except that the stranger Fearghal and his companion had entered the village on horseback, led by Uncle Caymus, and that Father had seemed very surprised and concerned at the visitor's appearance. The two men had wasted no time and left immediately with no explanation other than Ronan's promise to his wife Ceana that he would return in the morning or send word.

Tam closed his eyes and listened to the breeze as it caressed leaf and branch in a symphony of calming presence. He allowed himself to be taken away with the rhythm of the wind, ignoring his brother's quiet snoring. He had the uncanny ability to put himself at ease by entering a cocoon of silence that shielded him from the outer world, and before long he drifted off to sleep.

-2-

Tyburn removed Fearghal's jacket and slowly raised his patient's left arm. The Englishman winced with pain. "Your wound is treatable, and does not pose any immediate danger," said the doctor. "I have ointments that will cure and clean the wound, but you've torn a muscle in your side, and this will require stillness and inactivity for at least a fortnight—no travel and as little movement as possible. You are welcome to stay here of course, as is your companion, and if you take it into your heads to do otherwise, I will not be responsible for your lack of wisdom."

"Thank you," replied Fearghal. "We will accept your kind hospitality for the time being. However unforeseen events may force me to recover more quickly."

Tyburn Macleary merely nodded and motioned the four guests to follow him along a well-tended garden path towards a small pond. Despite the old man's apparent good health, he walked with the aid of a stout cane.

After his children were grown, Tyburn had moved to the country to practice his medicine. The stone cottage's original inhabitants were lost to history, and all that remained as a clue to their vocation was a low stone table towards the entrance of the garden. Rumours of witchcraft and demonic rituals were passed down through time, and no one in recent memory, save for Tyburn, had been willing to occupy the property.

Fearghal's companion, who had been introduced as Dafyd Kendrick, led the horse and its owner across the grass, preceded by the remaining members of the party. Dafyd was attired in a fashion similar to Fearghal and might have passed for him at a glance were it not for the difference in height and skin tone. Dafyd was darker and shorter, with a full black beard. This was understandable, given he was a Welshman.

Tyburn directed his guests to the table and pointed in the direction of the pond. "The water is good to drink for both man and beast," he said, with a bow towards Fearghal's horse. "It's very rich in curative minerals."

Dafyd led the thirsty animal to the water. "Is he to be trusted?" inquired Ronan quietly, referring to the footman.

"Yes, in all matters," replied Fearghal, "but please don't assume that Dafyd is my servant. My cousin may look like a simple foot soldier, and in fact this is how he prefers to be regarded; however, he is of a very distinguished lineage."

Fearghal then began a narrative on the recent history of their English neighbours, some of which was unknown to his hosts. Tyburn was perhaps more knowledgeable concerning the English, but even his eyes widened with some of Fearghal's revelations, the most startling of which was the confirmation of the existence of the fabled Teriz. Tyburn Macleary alone had heard the name, and it dwelt in the far reaches of earliest childhood memories, in the form of a frightening rhyme he could not quite recall. "They are a nasty-looking race of pale beings who have been around for centuries, for the most part keeping to caves and foraging for food under the cover of night. This is not to say that they are an unintelligent people, for in fact they are very advanced in a most conniving and cunning way."

Fearghal turned to Ronan and placed a hand on his shoulder. "I've returned with a warning for you and Tyburn, your lives may be in grave danger. Had it not been for the kindness you showed me as a child, I would be elsewhere today."

Ronan remembered well the day that Fearghal had left in search of his real father. Tyburn had raised the children himself, and until the day they left, the two boys had been inseparable. Such was Ronan's anger that he seldom spoke of the past, and before long Fearghal's name ceased to be mentioned. Ronan's children had no knowledge of their uncle's existence, and only Ceana knew the story that had been kept from her children. Tyburn, for the sake of his son's feelings, agreed to the decision to place the skeleton into the closet.

It was true, Tyburn had fought with an English soldier, killing him and losing a finger in the struggle, but behind the old tale lay many untold truths. The English soldiers that had been stationed in the hills behind the valley coexisted peacefully at first with the villagers of Dunradin. This changed in an instant, when a soldier in the regiment brutalized Tyburn's young wife Vannah as she washed her clothing at a stream. In his rage, Tyburn confronted the young man, and a vicious fight ensued between the two. The soldier, who went by the name of Dorian, was the stronger of the two. However, Tyburn's rage enabled him to throw his opponent to the ground, and he pushed his dirk through the young man's heart. In the throes of death the Englishman found a surge of strength and struck at Tyburn's weapon hand with his short sword, severing one of his fingers.

Months later, after Tyburn had fully recovered, his wife gave birth to a baby with curling black hair and olive skin. She convinced him to accept the child as his own, even though many of the villagers were aware of the boy's true father. Before long the child they named Fearghal was joined by two half-brothers, Ronan and Caymus. Tyburn's generosity had not extended to the English regiment, and fortunately it was not long before they were recalled to a post below the border.

"It warms my heart to see you again, brother" said Ronan, not able to recall the time when his remembrances of Fearghal had turned from anger to curiosity. "My last words to you were spoken in anger, and I've long regretted my thoughtlessness."

"What dangers have you come to warn us about?" interrupted Caymus. He was two years younger than Ronan and had spent less time with his half-brother. In truth, he did not share Ronan's love for this man, who had not managed to find a reason to return until now.

Fearghal, looking paler now, took a deep breath and said, "If I may speak to you at your convenience, I have an urgent matter to discuss with you and my brothers."

Dafyd stepped to his side. "Sit down," he suggested, guiding Fearghal to the stone table.

Fearghal settled himself and went on. "Father, here only you recall the name of the Teriz, and even to you it is no more than a name. They have dwelt beneath the ground for so many years that they've vanished from human memory in your part of the world. Many of the English, though, unfortunately have more knowledge of them than they wish to."

Fearghal went on to explain that the Teriz had been multiplying rapidly and were running out of space, forcing them to dig deeper into the earth, farther from the light of sun or moon. Fresh air was a luxury, and water had to be carried for great distances. "The Teriz are ready to emerge from the darkness. Over time a leader has arisen within the governing body of the Teriz, who is ruthlessly determined to secure lands above ground for his people." Fearghal went on to describe the men of the underground race, telling of their pale features and dull blue eyes. "Their hair is thin and white despite their age, and most of them are stooped from years of scrambling about in narrow tunnels and passageways.

"The danger you face," he continued, turning towards Caymus, "is an invasion of these creatures, who are bent on taking over any small, out-of-the way village with poor defenses."

Ronan suddenly had an uneasy concern for the welfare of his wife and children. "Are you suggesting that they will attack here, and how soon?"

"Within the month, or within the week," replied Fearghal, "which is why we have travelled here in such haste. We encountered a small band of the creepers, as they are sometimes called, some thirty leagues from here, but they were shifting to the west of you."

"We were lucky to escape with our lives" added Dafyd, who had remained silent to this point. "Fearghal was wounded in the defence of our companion, who succumbed to his injuries. Had we not stopped to bury him in a proper manner, we would have arrived a day earlier."

Caymus peered intently at the Welshman as if to measure the extent of his intentions. "How do we know that either of you are to be trusted?" he asked, shifting his gaze to meet his stepbrother's eyes.

Fearghal smiled tiredly. "You have not changed so much, Caymus ,and a man who questions all that he hears is a useful ally indeed. I ask humbly for your trust and will return it in kind."

The doctor took note of Fearghal's weariness. "It's time I dressed your wounds, and you are in need of rest and food. I imagine your brothers are still capable of hunting, unless at their advanced age the skill has been forgotten."

Ronan shouldered his bow and winked at his father before beckoning Caymus and Dafyd to join him. "I see you carry a sling," said Ronan to Dafyd, "a very useful tool for the hunt. My son Tamlyn is becoming an accomplished marksman with his sling."

"Indeed," replied the Welshman, "ammunition is always available, but it is not the easiest of skills to master. Do you find he has changed much? Your brother, I mean," he asked turning the subject to Fearghal.

"I think he is no longer afraid to speak his mind," said Caymus.

"We were all boys when he left," said Ronan. "It seems a very long time ago. Fearghal was not much for conversation; he and I would sit in silence for long periods of time. He was very affected by the passing of our mother, and it was she who told him of his father. In the end she wanted him to know."

"I would not have told him," insisted Caymus. "It has only caused hardships."

They had not travelled far when Ronan came to a stop and studied some droppings in the dirt. While he knelt for a closer look, Caymus turned his attention to Dafyd, raised his crossbow slowly, and pointed it in the stranger's direction. The lath was already cocked, and a bolt lay in place. "Don't move," he murmured, squeezing the iron trigger. The bone nut released the bridle, and a bolt whistled past the Welshman's upper arm and struck its target.

With a squeal, a large boar crashed to the ground several yards behind Dafyd. Caymus looked at the unshaken Welshman with surprise and wonder. Then he handed the stranger his bow and took a large gutting knife from his belt as he stepped past him to the kill. "We have fresh meat for our meal."

The young man studied the bow carefully, impressed with its efficiency. "Well done, brother," commented Ronan, with a glance towards Dafyd. "That boar was ready to charge."

"This is an impressive weapon," said Dafyd, "one that I have never used."

Caymus handed him the gutted boar in exchange for his crossbow. "I will explain the workings to you if you wish," he replied, as the trio of hunters retraced their steps to the cottage.

The boar changed hands again, and Ronan carried it ahead to prepare it for the spit. A thin stream of blood from the beast left a narrow trail along the path, that would within minutes be negotiated by a hungry bottle fly. "This," explained Caymus, "is in fact a composite bow made from layers of yew, horn, and sinew. It's glued and bound as you can see with eagle tendon, much stronger than any crossbow you may be familiar with. The draw length is short, so it needs a higher draw weight, but it's very manageable with practice. The advantage is that I can carry the bow drawn and need only drop the bolt into place when necessary."

"I see," said Dafyd, with a cautious smile, "and it performs well at the hunting of man?"

"This has not yet been determined," replied Caymus, "but if Fearghal's story is to be believed, I feel my weapon may be put to that test."

"Tell me, Dafyd, are you in truth a cousin to Fearghal, or is your use of the word merely a term of friendship?"

"Fearghal is a cousin, given that my mother was sister to his blood father, my Uncle Dorian. After the unpleasantness with my uncle, our family, for practical purposes, became outcasts. We were regarded simply as troublemakers, so we moved on, with the troops. I was a mere child and have no recollection of that time. Dorian's brother spoke of reprisals, but no man had the heart for it, understanding that your father's actions were justified."

As they approached the doctor's cottage, Dafyd resumed his tale. "Fearghal found us without much difficulty, as we were not a people in hiding and had lived just below the border for some years. Since that time we have become rather mercenary, a necessity brought on by the emergence of the Teriz. Fearghal has relayed some of this history to you, but our story goes much deeper." Caymus was warming to this soft-spoken stranger he had previously regarded with suspicion but held his peace. Dafyd stopped walking and turned to Caymus. "Many of us have resisted the Teriz, and we are a people divided. It's hard to know who to trust. Your father, however, is a very wise and influential man."

Domnash thrust his head forward and dropped his right shoulder, steering his sleek body into the cooling air current. The oxygen at this height was thinner than he preferred, and the large raven began his descent. A smoking chimney was visible beneath the thinning clouds, where a small stone cottage stood beside a shimmering pond. The hills behind the home were colored with the last remains of the day's light.

Far to the south, but still visible, there lay a semicircle of brightness.

Domnash turned again to the right and sped south, in the direction of the small village.

-3-

While everyone had their fill of the slow roasted game, conversation continued. "Well then," said Ronan, "to the matter at hand. You will recall that, since leaving the highlands, we are no longer a warring people and have spent many years at peace in our small valley. Do you suggest that the level of danger is such that we should abandon our village?"

"I think there are two options," answered Fearghal. "Flee or defend."

"And for what purpose," continued Ronan, "do these Teriz require our lands? They are not farmers or hunters, but scavengers."

"Indeed, scavengers and more," replied Dafyd, "whose hunger for new land would have them burrowing through your green hills like moles. I am for defence. These Teriz would foul your land with their tunnels and lairs. Our familiar plants, vegetables, and fruits refuse to grow where they have been.

"Their diet consists mainly of meats, some of which you would be most reluctant to consume. Their leader, or Messiah, encourages consumption of all manner of beasts and lives with a fear that his hoards will turn to cannibalism out of desperation. It's already been suggested that some have developed a taste for human flesh, but this cannot yet be confirmed. A large number of the lesser educated or careless perish from the scurvy every year, yet their numbers continue to grow."

"So this great leader of the Teriz is capable of fear?" asked the doctor. "And who is this leader, what name does he go by?"

"He is Euther de Faustine, but is chiefly known as Faustine,. He is a hero and prophet to his own kind, who has developed a cult of worship, by sheer will. The strength of his purpose would be admirable, were it not for his vile practices and deep hatred of anything that is not Teriz.

"Make no mistake: this Faustine is the essence of evil. Yet having said that, I believe with your help he can be defeated."

Fearghal shifted awkwardly in his chair and stared into the fire. Tyburn placed his fingertips lightly on his bottom lip and exhaled. "Evil exists in our world for one reason It is here to experience defeat, and for that very reason I will not run."

Ronan shrugged off an eerie shudder, as if an invisible shadow had flickered in the pool beyond the fire. "How," he asked, "do you propose we fight these potential invaders? We are few, and if you are to be believed, they are many."

"To begin with," suggested Dafyd, "we must think in terms of defence. I am told by Fearghal that there is a large wool mill beside the river, long abandoned."

"Yes, this is true," agreed Ronan, "abandoned by all save the rats."

"Perhaps," continued Dafyd, "we might transform this building into a center of defence and an armoury of sorts, assuming we are granted permission."

"Portus, the grocer, is, in a manner of speaking, our town magistrate," offered the doctor "and will surely tell you that the mill property rights belong to the town, which in essence belongs to the townsfolk. A town council meeting may be arranged, and in any event I would suggest that we apprise Portus of the situation as soon as possible."

"Of course," agreed Dafyd quickly. "However, I would caution against involving many people in this process. As I'm sure you are aware, too much knowledge can be a dangerous thing, and panic would serve no purpose."

-4-

Murdoch tossed in his sleep, turning from one side to the other and back. The young man was in the midst of a frightening dream, and he'd broken into a cold sweat. Somewhere above him a gaping mouth had swallowed the sky, and bat like creatures swirled inside the horrible opening, which was sucking him with dizzying force towards two rows of huge, rotting teeth.

The older boy rolled to his side again pulling the blanket from Tamlyn, who was curled up on the other side of the mattress. Tamlyn awoke, cold and somewhat annoyed at his brother. He had not slept for long and needed to pass water. The youngster stepped out the front door and rubbed his eyes. Judging by the position of the moon, daylight would not be long in coming. He moved clumsily toward a tangle of gorse and emptied his bladder. As he angled his head back and filled his lungs with night air, his eyes rose to the familiar grouping of elm trees at the crest of the hill. Tamlyn narrowed his eyes and tried to focus. There appeared to be a figure amongst the trees, silhouetted by the first hints of light from the new day. The boy had an uneasy feeling that he was being observed. He dropped his eyes to the village lights below. Glancing back to the trees, he could not tell whether it had been a trick of the night. The figure, if it had indeed existed, was nowhere to be seen.

He reentered the cottage and sat for a time considering his options for adventure today. He decided a walk down the hill to the town square was in order and chose the longer path, through a healthy stand of blackberry bushes. Half an hour later he arrived at the fountain in the center square, his cap filled with berries, and the sun had risen to a respectable height.

Padraic, the grocer's son, appeared from a shop entrance and waved to his friend Tamlyn. The youngsters exchanged smiles, and after Padraic seated himself, Tamlyn placed his cap between them and they shared the delicious fruit.

Padraic, who had never been able to speak, nodded between mouthfuls as Tamlyn recounted the mystery of the visiting Englishmen.

The mute's days were neatly proportioned, to the point of boredom, and his friend's arrival offered an opportunity to hear something other than the usual town gossip. "Father has promised to return this morning," said Tamlyn. "I hope he doesn't return alone."

Padraic nodded in agreement, with a smile that revealed the stumps of brownish teeth that were cleaned only now and then. His thick reddish hair, completely unfamiliar with brush or comb, stood out from his narrow head at all angles.

The prospect of seeing the English contained a degree of unfamiliarity that honed their excitement to a fine point. Padraic's father Portus had nothing good to say about his neighbours to the south. According to the big man, the English were nothing short of monstrous and should have been met with force at the border and quickly turned away on every occasion.

With the building of new roads, Dunradin had practically fallen from the map in recent years and even the government had lost interest in the village. It was as though the little town had been forgotten by all but its remaining inhabitants. In fact a pilgrim travelling north could not be blamed for shaking his head in surprise as this phantom village appeared suddenly off the beaten path. Despite being something of a ghost town, Dunradin was filled with happy occupants who were for the most part self-sufficient and had little or no need to leave the valley.

As Tamlyn spoke, Padraic took a straight length of willow from his pocket and cut through the supple bark a couple of inches from the top. He had already cut one end at an angle, and now tapped the uppermost section gently but with a concentrated purpose. Soon he managed to slip off the outer covering in one undisturbed piece, and laid it aside as he notched the bare portion with a deep groove.

He used his mouth to moisten the twig and then slipped the cylinder of green back on and blew through the mouthpiece, creating a sound not unlike the wail of a loon. Tamlyn laughed out loud at his friend's cleverness. Padraic handed him the whistle and retrieved a somewhat larger, more ornate version from his pocket.

The two boys played at imitating waterfowl for a time until Tamlyn turned in the direction of High Street and noted that his brother Murdoch stood at the top of the street, presumably looking for his younger sibling and perhaps curious at the source of the whistling. Tamlyn waved, and Padraic yawned widely and lifted a hand in greeting. Murdoch soon joined the young boys by the fountain.

Images from Murdoch's nightmare began to come back to him. Tamlyn studied his brother's face and remarked, "You must be tired. You spent most of the night thieving blankets."

Murdoch scratched his chin, "I dreamed of terrible things last night. I feel it's a sign or warning of something to come." Tamlyn's brows knotted in concern. "Something feels wrong, little brother, I have a bad feeling in my stomach, and I wish Father were here."

"He may return this morning," replied Tam, hopefully.

"Yes, I'm sure you're right," Murdoch replied with a smile, realizing that he would do well to not frighten his young sibling unnecessarily.

Secretly he was certain that events of some importance were being discussed between their father and the strangers, that would delay his return. "In any case," he continued, "I think we should go up on the ridge today and scout about. We might catch sight of our mysterious guests."

The brothers agreed that this would be a practical way to pass the day and soon returned home to tell Ceana of their plans.

"We're going to climb the ridge today and keep an eye out for Father," said Tamlyn.

"I'll join you," interrupted Charlotte. Plainly the prospect of seeing the strangers at close range held more appeal than her chores, which involved sewing and washing. "We can fish together below the falls."

The boys' duties were hunting and foraging for food, but they both relished an opportunity to explore the river with their sister. The road home from Grandfather's followed the deep river to the base of the falls, and with any luck they might intercept the travellers.

Ceana eyed her children with pride. Charlotte, tall and beautiful with her bright hair and shining green eyes, always cheerful with a song on her lips, was developing quickly into a woman, while not losing all of the clumsy playfulness of her childhood.

Murdoch had grown to be a serious young man with dark hair and swarthy features, thinner than most, but very quick and agile. He was very slow to anger, and put much thought into his words. Like Tamlyn, he had his father's deep brown eyes. Tamlyn, the youngest, was fair and freckled like his sister, clever with his hands, and curious about the workings and purposes of everything.

The return of Fearghal certainly was awkward, and now Ceana would have to explain the appearance of an uncle about whom the children knew nothing. It could wait, she decided, until Ronan returned. It would be more convenient, she thought, if he were to return alone. She had no reason to dislike Fearghal but was afraid that his sudden appearance—and his injury—meant trouble. The odds that her Ronan's stepbrother had merely decided after several years to be sociable was a poor bet.

-5-

Domnash ducked through the opening formed by the exposed roots of the giant chestnut tree. The hillside entrance glowed with diffused light, and rivulets of dirty water ran down the walls to pool on the hard clay floor. The air was thick with a sickly odour of sweat and urine.

The tall shape-changer held a lace handkerchief across his lower face and stepped forward. The chilling rain outside hadn't improved his foul mood, and he wished only to deliver his message quickly and collect his reward. A large rat scuttled past his foot followed by a broad approaching shadow. "Well, well, look who we have here." The voice belonged to Captain Madra, the outpost sentinel. He had almost stepped into Domnash in his haste.

The thin visitor caught a disgusting whiff of sour wine and straightened up, banging his head on the muddy ceiling. "Damn wormhole," he cursed.

Madra laughed and pulled a finger from his nose, wiping it on the dirty gray fabric of his belted shirt. "So you're late. What news then?"

"Tell your master the village numbers one hundred, it is not fortified, and they possess no equine advantage."

Madra grunted "Eck what?"

"They have no horses in number," Domnash replied slowly. "And I have not been paid."

"Hang on, you greasy bag of mucus," said Madra, reaching into his shirt. He flipped a gold coin towards the messenger and turned to leave.

"The agreement was for two coins," the shape-changer quickly reminded Madra.

"Not tonight," insisted the Englishman; "funds are low."

Domnash grabbed the captain by his neck and pushed him against the wall. Madra's milky eyes bulged in their red-rimmed sockets, and snot trembled on his upper lip. Unable to meet the messenger's gaze, the Teriz lowered his eyes.

Domnash could bear the stench no longer and bolted for the exit. "Filth!" he cried. "You shall pay double next time." A thick fog obscured the tops of the trees, and the shape-changer decided against flight, turning his collar up before making a quick departure.

Madra scuttled back down the passageway, having been told by his commander that any news must be relayed to him without delay. There was no time, he decided, to check the breeder's sinkholes. He would do so on the way back. The captain had no hesitation when it came to poaching from the breeders. They were Faustine's favourites, and he acted accordingly.

Madra's age and his twisted foot had kept him from joining their ranks. He had applied twice and was twice refused. A third attempt would only encourage further humiliation, so he took the post of reconnaissance captain and made his own fortune in the expansion outposts.

On the way to the command post, Madra passed two sinkholes, both guarded by sleeping sentries. The cylindrical holes were twice the height of a man and covered at the top with a deceptive weaving of plants and vines. Animals heavy enough to fall through the door were killed and eaten raw, but not before a new cover was quickly woven to replace the broken one.

The sinkholes were dug under darkness of night and located along well-worn forest paths, in an attempt to capture slaves as well as food. The narrow walls of the sinkholes were overgrown with slippery vegetation that offered no handhold. Once an unfortunate victim fell through the trap, there was no way out.

When Madra arrived at the command post, where the passageway opened onto a wide, dimly lit hall, the commander was seated behind one of three desks, laughing with a hissing sound at something that his partner had just said.

"Speaking of vermin," he said, under his breath, suddenly aware of Madra's approach, "'tis the esteemed Captain Madra, with important news."

The commander turned to the woman beside him. "I believe we need a runner after all." The runner, Molda, was dressed like a man, as was customary with most Teriz women. Only her long legs and facial features gave a clue to her gender.

Madra delivered his information quickly and stood silent while the commander scribbled a note on some parchment. He wrinkled his nose in distaste. By the smell, this fat pig had soiled himself.

At length the commander muttered, "Go," dismissing him without looking up. The captain was satisfied to be dispatched quickly and limped away with some haste, before the commander could call him back and bore him with another story about his imagined intimacies with the great Faustine.

-6-

"I will call together the councilmen, and you may put your proposal to them. Were it my decision alone, I would send all English back from whence they came. However, this matter will be put to a vote."

"I thank you, Portus. We could ask no fairer treatment," said Fearghal. "We are most grateful for your consideration."

Most of Lilyvine's tall narrow windows were broken, and much of the pink brickwork was covered with dead brown vines that snaked across its facade like a rusted veil.

Dafyd had argued that an empty building generated no income for a village and that he and Fearghal would supply the money and the manpower to transform the riverside structure into a much-needed center of strength. Councilmembers were informed of an impending danger, omitting any references to Teriz that might produce a general panic, and the small seed of fear quickly bloomed into a willingness to be protected from outside forces that the voting members knew very little about.

All but Portus voted in favour of allowing the strangers to proceed with their plans, and he grudgingly drew up the appropriate papers and inked his name in the bottom corner, secretly hoping that the cold air that whistled through the old building and the resident hordes of vermin would drive them out. Having signed his name to the document, the grocer put his misgivings temporarily aside, preferring a positive outlook to one of gloom. Perhaps, he thought, it was prudent to be prepared for all eventualities.

Journal entry:

Have not made a journal entry for a long time, but today is different. Tamlyn told me that the visiting Englishmen are here. This news did not please my father.

I have seen them myself. They are tall and dark with skin like the Romans. They met with the council this evening, and it appears they will be staying. I don't know if this will bode well for Dunradin. Father has asked that I keep a very close account of their whereabouts.

He is very suspicious of anyone from below the border of our River Sleath. I believe my father is overreacting. However I will do as he asks.

—Padraic

Padraic's father had insisted that his young son learn to write, and the boy was an apt pupil, who excelled at letters and had become an avid reader. His level of learning surprised some who assumed the youngster was nothing short of an idiot. It was Padraic who handled the store's accounts, while Portus saw to the lifting and transporting of stock. Padraic spoke to the customers with hand gestures and nods of the head, often responding to a comment with a broad smile or a wink.

While Portus was a large, barrel-chested man exceeding six feet in height, Padraic had inherited his mother's slight stature and fine features. The doctors were mystified at the fragile lad's inability to speak, as his hearing and comprehension were in perfect order. It was assumed that the area of his throat responsible for producing sound was underdeveloped. What the grocer's son lacked in speech had been returned to him in sight. The youngster's eyes, a bright blue that contrasted with his thick orange eyebrows, were sharp as an eagle's.

At two years of age Padraic lost his mother to pneumonia; he knew her only through his father's memory. The boy slept in a small, comfortable room above the store that looked out on the center square's cobbled street. The room contained a mattress, one chair, a writing desk, and an oil lamp.

Padraic's journal lay on the desk next to a pot of ink and a canvas packet of quills. On more than one occasion the youngster could be seen seated at his window burning the midnight oil. The large bedroom upstairs that had served as sleeping quarters for Portus and his young wife was now used for storage, and the widower slept in a pantry on the main floor towards the back of the building. Chowder, the wiry terrier, slept inside the shop's front door and was in charge of rat control.

Padraic understood that his father's hatred of the English dated back to Portus's boyhood. He knew nothing of the circumstances. Only the elderly Mcleary was aware that the boy's grandparents had been slaughtered by a marauding band of English soldiers while travelling to a market outside of Dunradin. It was rumoured that once Portus had grown tall and strong, he had taken care of retribution below the border. For many years after, the grocer hid his sorrow beneath a sea of whiskey.

His drinking days ended with the birth of his son, and he would no doubt have reentered those turbulent waters upon the passing of his wife, had it not been for the responsibilities of fatherhood.

Portus could toss a caber farther than any man but was also capable of shedding tears, despite the hard image that he projected. For this reason, the grocer was well loved and respected.

As Portus thought of the events of this day in the village, he could only shake his head. "Padraic, my son," he had once said, "if you are forced to barter with the English, keep one hand on your blade and the other on your purse, for as sure as the devil breathes fire, you'll have to buy or slice your way out of a bad bargain."

He wondered if he might be going soft in the head dealing with these snakes. For all he knew, this threat of invasion might well be a clever ruse to disguise some deeper intent, but he could not imagine why Fearghal and Dafyd would have any interest in the dusty old mill other than what they had stated.

Lately the big man had dreamed of endless corridors filled with windows of all sizes, some opening and welcoming while others closed rudely as he approached. He didn't know what to make of the recurring images and felt less inclined towards joviality than usual.

-7-

Earlier in the day, Charlotte had climbed the ridge ahead of her brothers, taking the lead along the narrow path that was bordered with tall switch grass and blue stem. The scent of wild rose replaced the warm, smoke-tinged air of the valley, and dragonflies cut across flower tops in wide-angled curves. "We can keep an eye on the road if we fish the second pond below the falls," she said, happy to have company and feeling a bit of an expert on the upper waterway.

In truth, her brothers were more familiar with the flatlands and moors west of the falls, which provided the family with eggs, meat, and grain. Murdoch in particular was very pleased when he could locate pheasant eggs, enjoying them more than the meat of the bird itself. The youngsters continued their hike, gradually climbing until the cozy valley was no longer visible behind them.

The upper falls fed a cold, turbulent lake, which in turn spilled into the smaller and much calmer pond below. Caster's Pond, as it was called, contained brown and rainbow trout, as well as golden perch. It was possible to swim across it, but nobody really did, because the waters of the tiny lake were said to be home to venomous snakes. The upper lake was a wiser choice for swimming despite the colder temperature.

The bigger body of water was split into two channels by a large rock formation called Horn Island, which appeared to grow from the very center. Access to it was only possible with the aid of an old rowboat which was lashed to a post on the other side of the lake. The boat was used to transport bones of the dead after they had spent their time under the ground.

The side of the lower pond closest to the trail which ran parallel to the road was edged with water lilies. A massive, extremely flat boulder offered the perfect point from which to drop a fishing line, as its edge overhung the water by a number of feet. Its sun-baked surface was carpeted with a soft growth of moss, and the rear underside of the rock was a good spot to dig for bait worms.

As the children climbed onto the rock, blue sky broke through the clouds, and a light sun shower dappled the surface of the pond. It lasted only long enough to urge the alyssum to release their sweet scent, then the sunshine came through in full force, followed by a sharp crack of thunder far to the north. Murdoch's dark dreams were all but forgotten in the warmth of a new morning's possibilities, and he felt much less ill at ease.

Charlotte helped Tamlyn bait his hook, and discussion turned to the matter before them. "If you want to catch a really large fish," she told her brothers, "you need a frog. They are best for casting. You put a hook through his leg and then throw your line out as far as it will go."

Tamlyn wondered aloud if this wasn't perhaps painful for the frog and decided he would stick with the regular method of dropping his hook over the side with a worm on board.

"You're a funny little imp," teased Charlotte. "You think nothing of snapping the neck of a quail."

"That's different!" said Tamlyn. "It's quick and painless."

"See," pointed out Charlotte, "he's perfectly happy to be of service." Charlotte's frog, as if to prove her point, sat staring at the young boy, seemingly oblivious to the hook that held him prisoner.

"Certainly," added Murdoch, "until he comes face to face with old One-Eye." Tamlyn laughed at the reference. Old One-Eye was a brown trout of mythical proportion, that had eluded many fishermen.

The children's easy laughter echoed across the pond, alerting a curious muskrat to their presence.

Before long, Tamlyn, who had less patience than his siblings, went in search of apples. A familiar tree not far from the rock yielded three shiny specimens that still adorned its branches late in the season.

Murdoch, who finished his apple first, threw the core into the center of the pond. "You realize, of course, what will happen now?" said Charlotte. "A fish will eat that, the seeds will sprout inside his belly, and before long there will be a tree growing on the far banks with bright red fish hanging from its branches, and we shall have only to harvest them as needed." Her buoyant mood was contagious, and her brothers laughed loudly at her imaginative musings.

As the shadows began to lengthen, the three children, who had a fine creel of trout, decided that they would return home with their catch, pleased at their pleasant day in the sunshine but somewhat disappointed at not managing to connect with the strangers. It was in fact Padraic who would get a first glimpse of the English as they came in search of his father later that evening.

Later Tamlyn sat outside enjoying the cool evening air. His eyes were growing heavy, and his head hung towards his knees. He became aware of the sweet smell of pipe tobacco somewhere close, below the ridge, and his eyes blinked with recognition.

Ronan climbed High Street at a casual pace, enjoying the rich tobacco that Portus had given him. The blacksmith's younger son, Tamlyn, was silhouetted in front of the house lamp, with an arm in the air. "Hello, Son," he called. "Have you been waiting for me?"

"Uh huh," replied the boy with a yawn. Ronan reached up and put out the lamp as his son took ahold of his other hand and led him into the cottage. "I'm the only one awake," claimed Tamlyn proudly. "Where are the English warriors?"

Ronan, laughing quietly, hung his coat and took a seat by the fireplace. "Well, Son, they are not warriors but are indeed Englishmen and are spending the night in town. I promise you that you shall meet them, as they may be here for some time."

Christoph James

"What are they like?" asked the curious youngster.

Ronan laughed again, pulling his son close. "You will see soon enough. Now it's time for night owls to retire; it's been a very long day."

"Good night," said Tamlyn, ready now to allow sleep to push him closer to morning.

34

-8-

Domnash gazed down at the Sleath from the high mill window. Moonlight danced across the water to the hill on the other side. A trio of bats dropped and spun at strange angles, blindly navigating below the limbs of a large chestnut tree. A light drizzle had begun, and the fine rain blew in through a broken window in gusts, playing a static tune against the dirty glass. The shape-changer could make out a church steeple across the river and recalled that the church was located in the back of the center square, quite close to the shops and narrow market alleys.

A pair of voices reached Domnash from below, and he took a step back into the shadows out of the moonlight that illuminated the small room. The sound of boots on the stone path receded, and he leaned out the window, sniffing at a low mist that had settled on the water. A young couple, huddled beneath an umbrella, was vanishing into the darkness on his right. Across the river, at the top of the rise, a light went out. Domnash glanced to the path below. A large rat, its coat slick with rain, sat on its haunches and lifted its head in the shape-changer's direction. Domnash met its beady-eyed gaze and sucked a bit of gristle from one of his teeth, spitting contemptuously at the rodent. The rat squealed in alarm as a bolt of foul phlegm covered its snout, wheeled, and vanished beneath a bush.

The dark stranger retreated to the rear of the room and bounded nimbly up the steps to the flat roof, where he leaped into the air and merged with the black night. He turned and flew over the village in a slow, descending circle, landing on the head of a gargoyle that scowled from a corner of the village church. Below the bird's perch was a square with entrances at the corners and open to the north and south. The wet cobblestones reflected an orange street lamp, and to his right a leaded window glowed faintly with the light of a small oil lamp. Beside the lamp on a narrow table beneath the window, a diminutive figure inked a quill, unaware that he was being observed between the rivulets of rain trailing down the uneven surface of glass.

Domnash remained at his roost until late morning observing the square as its inhabitants woke and went about their business. The rain stopped as the light of day arrived and the sun struggled to free itself from the cloud cover. It was two hours into daylight before the bird identified the grocer as he stepped from his shop. He was a bear of a man, with a thick red beard and ruddy complexion. His arms were large and well-muscled, as were his thick legs. He wore a leather grocer's apron, and carried a barrel of molasses under one arm.

As Portus continued down the street past the church, Domnash underwent his transformation and walked quickly towards the shop. He looked quickly in both directions before taking a small blade from his vest and scratching an indecipherable symbol into the surface of the door. Satisfied that he had located and marked the dwelling place of the "Beast of Dunradin," he turned and vanished quickly from the square.

Having delivered his goods, Portus returned to the square. He had exchanged molasses for two well-made pair of horseshoes that would fetch an equal price. The grocer passed Green's Guesthouse with a nod to Fergus Green, who sat on the stoop. "Morning, Fergus, your guests are sleeping late?"

"Ach no," replied the little man. "They were up and out to the river before dawn. Did nae stop for breakfast. None of my business though, long as I'm paid."

"Aye," replied Portus. "Well, watch your back. You know my views on the English."

Fergus shrugged and rubbed his forefinger and thumb together. Word had already spread among a number of villagers regarding the visitors, and it was said that an influx of workers with fat purses was imminent. Ronan, who was at work at the forge this morning, had told Portus to expect that a dozen men would occupy the mill.

Tamlyn, disappointed at having missed the Englishmen, was with his father. Ronan and Ceana had gathered the children and told them of their uncle, explaining that no one had believed him still living. The children in their amazement accepted the excuse and talked excitedly amongst themselves. Tamlyn, who was the most excited, had insisted on accompanying his father this morning.

His disappointment was tempered by the fact that he could tell Padraic his news, and the youngster was close on the heels of Portus, anxious to call on his small friend.

"Murdoch," called Charlotte, "hurry, I'm going down the village, and I'll leave without you." In reality she was a little frightened at the prospect of meeting her mysterious uncle, and was glad of her brother's company.

"I'm here," answered Murdoch, slipping on his boots.

Ceana called after them, "Don't forget the basket for your father." Charlotte carried the basket of bread and sausages for her father's lunch.

Ronan, pleased to see his children, wiped his hands and took his lunch to a small table. "Your brother has run off to find Padraic. You'll find that the young ones are probably hunting the English at this moment. They're bedded at Green's, but you'll likely not find them there until this afternoon."

Ronan gave each of them a penny and told them to go see Portus about some candied ginger for themselves. "Keep watch on that little brother of yours, see that he doesn't fall into the river."

Halfway back to the square the youngsters encountered the two Englishmen with Caymus and the young boys. Tamlyn's face beamed with pride. "Uncle Fearghal, this is my brother Murdoch and sister Charlotte."

Fearghal shook Murdoch's hand and bowed politely in Charlotte's direction. "It's an absolute pleasure to meet you. And this is my compatriot Dafyd."

Charlotte felt her cheeks flush as her eyes met those of the handsome stranger. She saw Murdoch turn to Caymus with a look of exasperation. She returned her attentions to Fearghal and addressed him courteously, "Father says you have been to the river. Did you find it to your liking?"

"Yes indeed, a very beautiful river. The walk brought back many pleasant childhood memories. We crossed to Lilyvine and had a good look about. Your father may have told you that our business will keep us here for some time."

As Charlotte and Fearghal spoke, Murdoch watched Dafyd. His eyes seemed flat and devoid of emotion, only appearing to brighten when he glanced at Charlotte. The young man took an instant dislike to the stranger. Charlotte decided that Fearghal looked pale and unwell. Perhaps his wound was a grievous one, and it would be best to let the gentlemen go about their business.

"It's been a pleasure, Uncle, but we mustn't detain you further." Excusing herself, the young woman directed the children towards the grocer's on the pretence of a forgotten errand.

"Why did you do that?" complained Tamlyn. "Uncle will think you're not fond of him."

"Well," replied Charlotte, "for one thing, I am not well enough acquainted with him to claim fondness, and did you not see the fever in his eyes? He was deathly pale. I'm surprised he could stand on his own."

"He didn't talk about his wound," said Tamlyn. "In fact, he was rather quiet. Uncle Caymus and Dafyd discussed the old mill, while Fearghal sat by the river bank. He looks much like father, don't you think?"

"Somewhat," interrupted Murdoch, "but Sister was busy looking at the strange one."

"I was only being polite," insisted Charlotte, blushing again. "In fact I find him just a little scary."

"He's not really an Englishman anyway," said Murdoch. "He's a Welshman, and I don't think I like him very much."

"Father said they were set upon by bandits on the journey here," confirmed Charlotte, "and that Fearghal has a wound in his side from a broadsword. He says that our mysterious uncle may have saved Dafyd's life." The youngsters continued talking as they made their way to the grocer's.

Murdoch, who was more curious and inquiring than his siblings, questioned the presence of Fearghal and Dafyd. "Why has he not returned before now?" the youngster asked. "And what is happening by the river?"

"Uncle Caymus says they are bringing business to the village," replied Tamlyn. "The mill building will be an armoury, in case we have to go to war."

"Who will we make war with?" inquired Charlotte in a sharp tone. "That's foolishness!"

"I don't know," her brother replied. "I'm just telling you what I've heard."

"Anyway," added Tamlyn bravely, "Padraic and I shall be soldiers if necessary."

Padraic winked in agreement and marched stiff-legged to the entrance of the shop. The other children followed him inside, laughing. If any of them noticed the small trident scratched into the door above its handle, they didn't mention it.

"Hello, Chowder," called Murdoch, as the small terrier ran to him barking loudly.

Portus appeared from the back room. "What are all you Maclearys about today? You've dropped in for some sweets, no doubt." The big man reached under the counter and tossed a packet of gingers to his son. "Here you go, lad, dole these out amongst yourselves. Do it outside in the fresh air, but don't be bothering those men at the smithy."

The children thanked Portus and took their leave as quickly as they had arrived.

-9-

"I agree with Fearghal," said Dafyd. "The building will suit our needs admirably, I will recruit workers and return with them within the week. Fearghal is not well enough to travel, of course."

Fearghal addressed Ronan and Caymus: "It will require a great deal of work just to make the building clean and inhabitable. The rats are worse than I could have imagined, and much of the roof leaks."

"Surely some of our villagers are employable?" suggested Caymus. "You might avoid an unnecessary journey."

"We have men comfortable with the nasty work of ferreting out vermin," replied Dafyd. "There is no need for your respected tradesmen to be bothered with the filthier work; their skills will be put to work soon enough."

"Agreed, then," said Caymus. "I don't enjoy working in the muck and shite, but if your men do, then so be it."

Dafyd smiled. "Whether or not they enjoy it is of no consequence. I shall employ Frenchmen who are anxious to remain on our green island and will do any sort of labour."

"You have a fine forge here, brother," commented Fearghal. "How is your skill at producing weaponry?" In answer Ronan reached into a section of low rafters and retrieved a narrow package wrapped in coarse jute sacking, laid it on the table, and unwrapped it.

Dafyd emitted a low whistle. "This is fine work. May I?"

"Yes," said Ronan with a nod.

The Welshman checked the impressive sword's balance, cutting an arc through the Scotsman's smoking forge. Fire from the bellows seemed to hang briefly on the edge of the blade. Fearghal, for the first time since returning to Dunradin, allowed himself a smile.

That evening Padraic was seated at his window with an open journal before him. Looking across the darkening village square, the young mute recognized the lone figure of Fearghal Mcleary. The Englishman walked across the square slowly with his hands clasped behind his back. He stopped at the edge of the fountain and took a seat. Wearily he leaned forward resting his head in his hands and remained that way for some time. When Padraic next looked Fearghal had produced a long-stemmed clay pipe from his coat and was firing some tobacco.

In the eave of Green's Guesthouse next door to the grocer, a tawny owl turned his head, pivoting it at an impossible angle toward a gently undulating ribbon of smoke from below. Padraic enjoyed this time of night the most, when the entire village was asleep. From his perch above the square the youngster was not unlike the owl.

When the lamplighter left the cobbled streets of the town, its center took on an orange glow. An occasional cat was seen hunting in the shadows, and once Paddy had even seen a shiny black snake slithering across the stones. He'd watched the snake, mesmerized by the strange movements, for several moments until it vanished around a corner. It was not uncommon to see a neighbour lurching past, deep in the drink and singing to himself.

Before long the grocer's son would tire of the solitude and crawl into bed. Tonight he recorded the day's events.

Journal entry:

I have made the acquaintance of F. Mcleary and his Welsh friend. Tamlyn and I encountered them at the Sleath and guided them across the bridge to Lilyvine.

The old mill building has not been used for many years, and the march of time has not been kind to it.

Structurally it is still very sound, but the odour of dead animals pervades the interior. In the lower entranceway we came upon the remains of a dog, whose hind legs had been chewed off. Its belly was swollen with maggots, and the eyes were no longer in the sockets.

Tamlyn and I decided to wait outside. Fearghal joined us at the river bank, appearing somewhat ill, his eyes seemed to sink into the greyness of his flesh, and his weak attempt at a smile, confirmed his lack of health.

I have promised Tamlyn that he and I shall keep these Southerners under close observation. We are too young to enlist as soldiers; however, if spies are required, we will join in that capacity. Murdoch does not trust them, especially the Welshman. Father, who of course trusts no one, suggests we mind our own business, but with eyes wide open.

—Padraic

-10-

The following morning Dafyd left Dunradin by horse. He journeyed for one full day before reaching the French. The next day, they would arrive in Dunradin with a tall wagon pulled by two huge Clydesdales. Rather than stay at the guest house in town, the twelve workers raised a broad tent on the slope behind Lilyvine and made camp.

The locals kept their distance, watching from the opposite bank of the river as the labourers began their work. Soon they saw that a deep fire pit had been dug out behind the building. The flame appeared to burn day and night, and a black pall soon hung over a section of the river, all the way from the bridge to the end of the cull. Old drying racks, loom beams, and fulling troughs crackled in the inferno along with hordes of rats and other unfortunate animals that had considered Lilyvine a home. The smell that floated across the river into town was indescribable, and those who complained were assured that it was only temporary but most necessary.

Before long the entire building had been scrubbed clean, leaving no refuge for even the tiniest spider. The Frenchmen were surprisingly thorough, going so far as to fill in the large fire pit before taking their leave. In fact no one saw the twelve leave, and it was almost as if they had never arrived.

The exterior of the mill remained much the same with the exception of a freshly painted sign above the front entrance that read DUNRADIN ARMOURY. Some of the broken windows had been repaired, but most were now boarded over. As promised, Dafyd and Fearghal began to recruit townsfolk for specific modifications to the building.

The first floor picking room was repainted, and a weapons rack spanned the back wall. To the left of the rack was a new door that opened on a small antechamber, whose use had not been discussed. The floor above, where the dyeing room had been, would become a barracks of sorts, and two of the huge dyeing vats had been retained to serve as baths.

Two flights of stairs rose through the ceiling and opened onto the third-floor drying room, which would contain barrels of dried foods and gunpowder. Roofers were hired to replace large sections to insure that everything would stay dry. Extra work meant that tradesmen had more coin in their pocket, which in turn found its way into the coffers of the grocer, the baker, and others. The inhabitants of Dunradin had been, for the most part, accepting of the strangers when it became apparent that the installation of an armoury meant more food on the table. They still questioned the need for a military center, but no harm had come of it, and no one had been inconvenienced in any way.

Some time after the French had departed; Fearghal paid a visit to his brother. Fearghal's appearance shocked Ronan, chiefly because his brother appeared to have made a miraculous recovery overnight. The color had returned to his face, and his eyes looked bright and alive. Fearghal's posture was improved, and the rich timbre of his voice had returned.

Ronan commented on his appearance, and Fearghal was quick to credit Dr. Mcleary. "Tyburn's skill with herbs has grown with the passage of time. I have much to be thankful for."

"Indeed," replied Ronan. "I have repaired your sword, brother. It was just a matter of regrinding the tip."

"Many thanks," said Fearghal, passing Ronan a cross of heavy silver the size of his palm.

The blacksmith shook his head. "There's no need to pay me, and in any event, this is far too much."

"Please keep it," replied Fearghal. "I have another favour to ask of you. If you would fashion me a dirk and inlay the blade with this fine metal, I would be happy to gift you with what silver remains."

"A generous offer," said Ronan. "Sketch me a design, and I will do my best."

-11-

Caymus had declined Fearghal's invitation to visit Ronan, choosing to travel to his father's instead. Tyburn had not been apprised of the changes in town, and Caymus wished to discuss matters with him.

Murdoch and Tamlyn also took advantage of the sunny weather, to leave the village. The boys had decided to hunt above the upper falls for pheasant. Charlotte managed to talk her mother into a walk along the river, and Padraic, as he did on occasion, was sleeping late.

By the time the boys reached the top of the upper falls, the sun was high in the sky, and they left the road, following a narrow trail into the High Woods. The outskirts of the Wood was where pheasant would be found, and they were best approached from the tree line. Murdoch would frighten them into an open area, where his younger brother would crouch with his sling. The boys were familiar with these woods and stepped noiselessly over large roots, avoiding fallen branches and badger holes.

Murdoch, who was ahead of Tamlyn, stopped suddenly. "What in the world?" Before him was an oversized mound of horse manure buzzing with flies. Both lads hopped carefully over the large deposit and moved on.

"Look" said Tamlyn, pointing to his left. Between two birch trees stood a large Clydesdale horse casually chewing at the tall grass. Behind the horse, obscured by brush and trees, a tall wagon rested on its side. Tamlyn recognized it as the Frenchmen's six-wheeler and raised a finger to his lips, with a signal to Murdoch to move forward carefully. But then he stepped on a fallen branch, snapping it with a loud crack.

"Who's there?" called a frightened voice. The two boys stepped to the side, coming within view of the wagon's interior. Inside was a wizened little man dressed in green clothing. In one hand he held a long jaw bone, complete with sharp teeth, and leaned with the other on a crooked cane. On his head was a leather skullcap that came down to his chin on the sides.

Neither boy had ever seen anyone with so many wrinkles. His brown skin was creased beyond belief, and long white whiskers protruded from his lower face, almost to his distended belly. "Ain't botherin nobody," he said in a cracked voice. "Move on, little boys." Some of the wagon's canvas covering had been cut and arranged like curtains, and a collection of wooden crates served as makeshift furniture. "Twas left here. Mine now," he added.

Murdoch realized that this was the strange little man's home and asked the obvious question. "Where are the Frenchmen?"

"Don't know nuthin' 'bout Frenchies. Only one man," he said. "You can have the horse; all he does is eat and shit. No good company. You got tabaccy? I don't spose. Go away then."

"You saw no Frenchmen?" asked Tamlyn, finding it hard to believe that they would abandon their wagon and fine horses.

"What I told ya," he spat. "You don't hear good. Was two Clydes, but one left. No Frenchies, not a one—now go bugger yerselve's!"

The boys thanked the little man unnecessarily and retraced their steps to the entrance of the glade.

"Well, that is most curious," exclaimed Murdoch. Tamlyn agreed with his brother's suggestion that they abandon the hunt and return to town at once.

"Don't forget the nag!" shrieked a voice in the woods behind them. The Clyde of course was too tall for either boy to mount, and to lead the beast from the woods would have meant risking a trampling.

"We should have asked that old fellow his name," said Tamlyn.

"I doubt he would have told us," replied Murdoch. "He seemed a miserable sort."

"Well, I think he spoke truthfully about the French, but what in blazes could have happened to them?"

A short while later Caymus came upon the boys traveling in the opposite direction. "Where are you lads back from in such a hurry?" he asked.

Murdoch described the strange encounter, noting the look of concern on his uncle's face. "We were on the way," he concluded, "to tell Father what we found."

"That's a very good idea," said Caymus. "I think I will question this little gnome that you speak of."

"He's not much of a gentleman," warned Tamlyn.

"He sounds harmless enough. Say hello to your father please, and let him know that I've gone to retrieve a draft horse, which Ill bring to him for stabling. If I can locate the other, there will be two."

-12-

"Are you sure it was the same wagon?" asked Ronan.

"I'm most certain," replied Tamlyn, "six wheels and black canvas, the very one."

"Yet only one Clyde," said Portus, who sat outside with the smithy, pondering the mystery. "We have an empty wagon, one draft horse, and twelve missing Frenchmen. They might have abandoned the wagon, having no further use for it, but to leave a valuable horse behind is inconceivable."

"Fearghal or Dafyd may be able to shed some light on this puzzle," surmised Ronan, "but I for one am baffled. If we were to imagine that they were set upon by bandits, there would be no wagon and no horse, but twelve slain Frenchmen, and that would indicate a large raiding party. There must be some other explanation."

"Well, twelve Frenchies don't just up and vanish," declared Portus. "They must have been taken prisoner or tricked into wandering off."

"Perhaps a trick of that heady wine they were fond of," added Ronan. "All pissed to the gills, stumbling about the woods drunk on the old dwarf's moonshine." The youngsters giggled at the comical image.

"I spoke with Fearghal this morning," said Ronan. "His health is much improved. I will step over to Green's with Caymus when he returns and inform our brother of the day's happenings. I don't believe this old recluse, as he is described, is of any concern in the matter."

Tamlyn said, "I don't think he'll be thrilled to see Uncle Caymus."

-13-

The recluse did not in fact see Caymus. Nor did he speak or answer any questions, for none were asked.

Following the boys' directions, Caymus entered the woods in the late afternoon, taking care not to alert anyone or anything to his presence. The big Clydesdale had wandered farther down the path into an open field looking for tender grasses.

As the wagon came into Caymus's view, he cleared his throat quietly, not wanting to frighten the old man into fleeing. What he found was a wizened corpse seated on a wooden box. The brown withered skin and white whiskers were as the boys had described. The unfortunate little man's throat had been opened cleanly with a sharp blade, and someone had reached in and pulled his tongue down and out through the wound so that it resembled a gruesome fleshy necktie. His hands were bound and the dead eyes stared blankly ahead. The symbolism of his death was easy to read. In someone's judgment, the little man had talked too much.

After looking about cautiously, Caymus returned to the glade where the horse was still feeding. He brushed a lazy wasp from the horse's lush mane and took hold of the bridle. "Come along, old man," he said. "Perhaps you'll talk to me. That little fellow was dead boring."

Leading the horse to the road, Caymus looked back over his shoulder with an uneasy feeling. Something told him it would be wise to not linger on the road, and he gripped the Clyde's mane and swung one of his long legs over the horse's broad back. A shorter man might have had trouble mounting a horse so large and with no saddle might have found it impossible.

"All right, then," said Caymus, "we had better give you a name." He looked up at the overhanging branch of a tree that was now very close to his face, half expecting a villain to drop from the dark foliage. "Your name," he said, "shall be Ghost," and with that the big horse began down the road. Caymus lurched backwards briefly and then corrected himself. With a fist wound into the horse's mane, he gripped with his thighs to keep from falling off the horse.

Eventually the bowman was comfortable enough to urge the horse into a trot while leaning forward, happy to put more distance between himself and the grisly scene in the woods. He shuddered to think what ill luck might have befallen his young nephews, had they not left the High Wood when they did. "Ghost," he said, patting the horse's neck, "if only you could speak."

The visit to Tyburn would be postponed until tomorrow, and there was certainly now much more to tell the old man. Caymus recalled Dafyd's description of the Teriz. Were they an enemy that would be fought amongst the trees? Was the little man too tough and wiry to be eaten? He would be glad to reach the village before nightfall.

Ronan cocked his head to the side, amused at the sight of his brother's approach. Fearghal, who was seated at the fountain, had a look of concern on his face and raised a hand in greeting. The look in Caymus's eyes told them both that the news was not good. The bowman swung a leg across the Clyde and slid to the ground. "Not an easy ride with no saddle," he said, flexing his tired legs.

"What did you learn from the dwarf?" asked Ronan.

Caymus dragged his forefinger across his throat slowly. "Someone got to him before I could." He went on to describe the scene, as they led Ghost to the blacksmith's stable. "Your boys were extremely fortunate to have returned when they did. I would not frighten them with the details, but I would caution them against tracking pheasant there again. There is something very nasty in the High Wood. I'm sure I felt eyes on me as I left."

Fearghal looked from one brother to the other. "Teriz," he whispered, glancing down. "The Frenchmen may have been taken underground. I was on my way to speak to Dafyd at the armoury; I will do so now."

-14-

"Well, I think he sounds dreadful," exclaimed Charlotte. "What a horrible little man. Mother and I had a glorious day at the river, collecting wildflowers, and we spoke with Dafyd. I should certainly like to see the horse, perhaps tomorrow."

"Father should be back soon," said Tamlyn. "I'm sure he'll tell us everything."

"I don't understand," said Ceana, "how our little village has suddenly become so mysterious. Strangers always mean trouble. I wonder if we have invited a nightmare into our midst."

"You don't mean Uncle?" asked Charlotte.

"No, I'm not suggesting that you mistrust Fearghal, but please keep your eyes open, and for goodness' sake stay out of the High Wood for the time being. Something has happened up there that we don't understand."

Charlotte didn't want to imagine her world as a dangerous place. She wanted it to be a place of fragrant flowers and romantic intrigue. The young woman had already made more than one excuse to stroll the far banks of the Sleuth, hoping to catch a glimpse of the handsome stranger.

Then today they had spoken. Dafyd offered to show the mother and daughter the interior of Lilyvine, but Ceana had declined the invitation, not wishing to encourage Charlotte's interest in the Welshman. Charlotte hid her disappointment with a smile and a small curtsy, not betraying her thoughts by complaining to her mother. Dafyd's glances had told her more than words could about his thoughts, and she found herself short of breath when his gaze brushed across her body.

For his part, Dafyd was not unaware of the young woman's attentions. Ceana's daughter was not of the age or inclination to wear corsets or bustles, as shown by the ankle-length dress that clearly allowed her to run with her brothers. Her woollen sweater, however, did not hide the fact that she was developing quickly. He was mildly flattered but preferred not to be distracted from his current task, and she was after all very young. *Perhaps later*, he thought, *when business here has concluded, there will be an opportunity for a bit of gaming.*

Ronan and Caymus agreed between themselves that the murder in the High Wood might well panic the villagers and that it would be wise to downplay the incident, while still suggesting caution.

The blacksmith returned home early in the evening and relayed what he could of Caymus's discovery to his concerned family. That night Tamlyn slept poorly. In his dreams of the brown-skinned stranger, the old man's leathery face twisted in a silent scream as the large draft horse stamped him repeatedly with heavy hooves.

-15-

The following morning was bright and clear. Caymus, who had found a suitable saddle for Ghost, cocked his crossbow and hung it over his back before starting for his father's home. The Last Market of Solstice was assembling in the square, and fine entertainment was anticipated. A wide cart laden with fresh corn was arriving as Caymus passed, and he waved at the farmer Thomas Smith.

Further along the road, going in the same direction, was Brendan Flood with a cartload of noisy chickens. Caymus intended to take the long road to Tyburn's, avoiding the woods entirely.

Ceana was happy to have a distraction for the children, who were clearly troubled by the previous evening's news. The last day of Solstice was always an event filled with color and music and dance that went far into the night, marking the season with costumes and magic acts.

Charlotte decided on a blue dress for the market, with a matching bag. It wasn't an occasion for fancy dress, but she wanted to look her best assuming that there would be a good number of young men in attendance. Tamlyn looked forward to watching the evening lights from the anonymity of Padraic's room, and Murdoch was always excited at the prospect of seeing jugglers. Edgar Twill's father was a sword swallower, and the older boy looked forward to seeing him, until Tamlyn reminded him that there had been an accident last year.

"Don't you remember? Now when he drinks beer it ends up all over his shirt."

Murdoch laughed, realizing he'd been had, and cuffed his brother lightly across the head.

-16-

The long road to Tyburn's wound around the base of the ridge and climbed at a gradual pace through farmlands and moors, approaching Tyburn's cottage from the other direction. The journey from Dunradin to the peak took Caymus ninety minutes on horseback.

As he passed over a small bridge midway to his father's, a hazy mist began to settle on the moors. To his right, a gentle rise wore a blanket of heather. Caymus noted several beehives adorning the crest of the hill. He felt safer here on the open road without the closeness of the woods. Caymus was not one who enjoyed crowds or large gatherings. Festivals and markets held no interest for him.

Companionship meant little to Caymus, and for this reason, he had never taken a wife. Ronan's brother was more than happy to occupy a small sleeping quarter above the stable. He spent much of his time visiting with his father, discussing plants and their various uses in the care of animals. Caymus was called upon if Mrs. Smith's cow stopped giving milk, or if Adam Lennox had a herding dog with distemper.

These back roads were more familiar to him than most, and he could sense when something was out of place. About a quarter of a league from his father's, he began to get an uneasy feeling in the pit of his stomach. The light breeze seemed to vanish, and everything became perfectly still. He halted, and sat motionless, listening. There was no sound whatsoever, not a bird, or cricket, no movement at all, just a complete and total silence.

Caymus could hear his heart pound, matching time with the breathing of his horse. After a long moment he began to hear the tiniest of sounds, further up the road, there was a buzzing of flies. Narrowing his eyes, he could make out a small white form in the distance.

He urged Ghost forward slowly. To the side of the road lay the lifeless body of a young lamb, its white coat streaked with red. A large raven crouched over the carcass, pecking at the eyes. As the rider approached, he opened his wings and took to the air. The horseman was astounded to see that the large bird had a band of gold, resembling a man's ring, around one of his legs.

As the beating of wings receded, the silence returned, filling Caymus's head with a numbing sense of dread. He stared at the animal's open belly, mesmerized by the writhing motion of the worms, unable to move. The bowman was unsure how much time had passed before Ghost impatiently stamped a hoof against the road, breaking the silence and the strange spell. It was as though cotton had been pulled from Caymus's ears. The sound of the breeze returned, leaves rustled, grasses whispered, and sparrows sang. Caymus dug his heels into the big horse's side, anxious now to arrive at Tyburn's cottage.

Soon he came to small trees along both sides of the road, thickening into woods as the horse and rider advanced. Soon tall trees threw long shadows across the narrowing entrance, and the stone cottage came into view. A small brook had been redirected with cleverly placed stones so that its course curved through a terraced herb garden that climbed to the back wall of Tyburn's home. The old man was slumped motionless in an ancient chair of twisted willow branches.

-17-

As the sun vanished behind the ridge, marketers put flame to torches, the lamplighter emerged to tend to the lamps, and small children lined up to have colourful candles lit. Tamlyn grinned at Padraic, who swung open the leaded windows, ushering in the sounds of festival eve. The music of twin mandolins and laughing villagers mixed with the odour of smoky meat and mulled wine. Directly below the window, Murdoch was seated in the store entrance chatting with a friend, and his sister Charlotte stood beside him scanning the crowd.

Padraic nudged Tamlyn and pointed below. Dafyd and Fearghal were approaching the children with broad smiles. Fearghal was leading a piglet at the end of a length of rope, which he passed to Charlotte with a gentlemanly bow. The boys could not make out the conversation below them, but it was apparent that the young woman was thrilled with her gift. She clapped her hands in delight and reached down for the tiny animal.

Murdoch's eyes lit up, reflecting a fiery baton that was tossed into the air from within a circle of revellers. He excused himself and strolled across the square to the crowd.

The entertainer spun the baton over his head creating a circle of light that traveled up and down the length of his lean body. Liam Twist was clad in black tights, with a scarf over his eyes. His chest was bare save for a patch of singed hair down the middle, and his strong shoulders shone with perspiration. A three-cornerer hat at his feet contained a bright red apple. Without missing a beat the young man reached into his hat and snatched the apple, beginning to eat the fruit while juggling with one hand. A quick flick of his foot sent the hat into the air, and Twist leaned forward allowing it to fall perfectly atop his head. He pulled off the scarf and winked at the crowd, who broke into applause.

Murdoch turned around to find his sister standing behind him and the piglet sniffing at his ankles. "What are you going to call him?" he asked.

Charlotte didn't answer her brother. She was watching the juggler as he doused his baton in the fountain.

"He's grown tall, our Liam has," continued Murdoch.

"Oh indeed" replied his sister, finally tearing her eyes away. The young woman looked flustered. "Well, I don't know any good animal names. You shall have to help me."

"How about Bacon?" offered Murdoch.

"Oh don't be cruel!" she said, picking up the piglet.

"Hello Charlotte Mcleary" said Twist, knocking the dust from his hat. "And where did you get such a fine little pig?"

"It was a gift" she replied, with a blush. "You've singed yourself Mr. Twist; you shouldn't play with fire."

Liam grinned. "Did you enjoy the show?"

"I'm afraid I missed it," answered Charlotte. "Tis a fine festival though." Murdoch had blended back into the crowd, leaving the two by themselves.

"Aye," replied Twist. "How's your family?"

"They are well; thank you, and your mother?"

"Fine indeed, I'll say you were asking after her."

Charlotte glanced over her shoulder but could not locate Murdoch. "Well, I'd best find what Tamlyn is up to. Nice to see you, Liam," she added with a smile.

The juggler returned her smile. "Don't be a stranger."

As Charlotte turned away, all thoughts of Dafyd evaporated. Twist had indeed grown to be an attractive young man, bearing little resemblance to the skinny lad who had teased her all through school.

Ceana enlisted Tamlyn and Murdoch to help carry her sacks of chosen vegetables to the top of High Street. Charlotte reluctantly accompanied them, carrying her new pet. The young woman was a little annoyed that she had been summoned loudly by her mother with the other children.

Tamlyn laughed as the piglet, which had leaned in his direction, wrinkled his nose at the scent of onions that came from his bag. Charlotte laughed also. "I think I shall name you Onion!"

"There we have it," added Murdoch: "you are Onion the pig."

Liam stood on the church steps scanning the crowd in hopes of spotting Charlotte. He tried to recall if he'd said anything foolish, for she seemed to have left abruptly. Young Twist had always been a little sweet on Murdoch's sister, but her appearance tonight had left him oddly tongue-tied.

Charlotte's father, Ronan, stood below the steps in conversation with two men of similar age that Liam did not recognize. The shorter of the two had a dark beard and a foreign look about him. Ronan waved farewell and headed towards High Street. The remaining gentlemen dropped into the shadows between the church steps and the adjacent building.

Twist watched curiously as the two men appeared to exchange harsh words. The taller of the two had his back to the wall and was waving his hands about. He angled his head back and out of range as the bearded gentleman leaned forward as if to whisper. Fearghal glanced up as if suddenly aware that he was being observed and shoved Dafyd aside before stepping out of the shadows.

Eventually Liam came to the conclusion that Ronan's family had left for home, and decided that he would depart as well. With the pennies that had been tossed into his hat, he purchased some hard treacle for his mother. The quickest route home was along the old trail by the river.

Liam's home was across the bridge past the old mill behind the cemetery. He paused on the bridge to admire the ripple of silver light that was cast by the low moon.

Young Twist continued along the upper road behind Lilyvine. A number of bobbing lanterns were visible across the river as the festival crowd made their way home. The Dunradin cemetery sloped towards the river and was contained on four sides by a low wall of stone. Liam leaped on to the top easily, and set one foot in front of the other along its length, using his baton as a balance. Then he dropped from the wall and crossed the grassy field behind the cemetery. As he reached a familiar footpath the ground beneath his feet suddenly gave way, and he vanished into a sinkhole too fast to cry out, but managed a sharp gasp of pain as he landed on the hard earth twisting his ankle.

It was apparent to Liam that he'd fallen into some sort of underground cavern, perhaps an old well or long-forgotten basement. Looking up a fist-sized circle of light from the moon told him he had fallen roughly twenty feet.

He wondered if the painful crack in his ankle would take any weight. He leaned forward in the darkness, and his hand came in contact with his baton. He used it to pull himself up. As he leaned against the wall, he heard what sounded like a muffled scream. "Hello" he yelled. The word seemed to die in the thin air, and his nostrils filled with the small of wet dirt.

He fished a tinderbox from his pocket and lit the end of his baton. Squinting through the smoke he saw a narrow passage to his left and a wider passage sloping gradually down to the right. Guessing that the right-hand side would lead down the hill and towards the river, he proceeded in that direction. The black smoke began to burn Liam's eyes so he doused the flame, deciding to feel his way along the wall in the darkness. Some instinct also told him not to call out again, and he limped along in silence.

-18-

The coach that rattled towards Dunradin had been designed to suit the needs of its occupants. Heavy curtains hung from the windows, letting in no light. The seats were padded comfortably and covered with rich leather.

A passenger dipped a long elegant finger into a silver snuffbox, filling his elongated nail with white powder, and raised it unsteadily to his nose. He inhaled sharply and coughed. He cleared his throat loudly and spat, spraying his travelling companion's white leggings with pink phlegm.

William Drake glanced down, unaffected by his companion's thoughtlessness, and crossed his legs. He reached forward, retrieved the small snuffbox, and tucked it inside his vest pocket.

Euther's throat clearing was constant as was the drumming of fingers against his leg. He was slightly stooped, and his thin hair was snow white. Dark circles under his eyes contrasted with the paleness of his skin, which appeared to be stretched too tightly across his prominent cheekbones. His steel grey eyes moved constantly taking everything in.

The old man stroked his chin, staring at his fellow rider with contempt. "Tell the driver to stop," he commanded. "I need a piss." Drake reached behind himself and yanked twice on an ornate braided cord that rang a bell beside the coachman's seat. As the coach drew to a halt, Euther's assistant leaned forward and using both hands slid open a panel in the floor, revealing the road below.

The assistant, without being reminded, turned in his seat to face the front of the coach while the old man relieved himself. Drake frowned into the dark oak at the odour that he knew would permeate the carriage for some time. He would be pleased when darkness fell, and they could continue with the curtains open. Leaning down again, he slid the slightly damp door back in place and gave the cord a single yank, and the coach lurched forward.

"Tell me something, William," said Euther, in a soft almost melodic voice, "what do you imagine will become of us? Not you and me, of course, but our type."

Drake, who understood that an answer was not required, shrugged. "You shall perish," he answered uncharacteristically.

Euther looked up in surprise and allowed a slow smile to transform his sallow face. "Were it only possible. I am so very, very tired. But one must go on, history beckons. Sometimes I wish I had your simple outlook, William, money in the bank."

Drake worked at a loose thread on his jacket and ignored his employer.

As the last of the day's light vanished into the hills the coachman spotted the dust of travellers on the horizon. They were moving quickly this way. He banged his fist rapidly against the wall of the coach at his back and reined in the horses. Not far up the road, a secondary trail was just wide enough to accommodate Euther's coach.

He remained there with his passengers until the horsemen had passed.

-19-

Tyburn Mcleary angled his head into the shaft of sunlight and stretched his legs out, letting his arms hang from the chair. Gardening had tired the doctor, and he soon dozed off, slipping into a frightening dream.

He dreamed of a black carriage with flaming wheels speeding across a field of grain, setting the crops ablaze as it advanced. The death wagon was driven by a child with lidless eyes. He had a blade between his teeth that cut into the corners of his maniacal grin. As the crops burned wildly, snakes slithered under the deadly wheels and were torn to pieces.

Tyburn screamed in horror, unaware whether he had screamed aloud or merely inside his head. The old man, who was not usually plagued by nightmares, thrashed about in an effort to wake himself.

"Tis no dream," said the voice; "you are here for the end of time." He felt hands on his neck. The cold traveled through his bones, numbing his entire body. Was this how it would be, he wondered—a painless fading … could it be that easy? Tyburn's flesh opened away from his bones in a bloodless ballet of death. "Dust to dust," whispered the voice. "Ashes to ashes." Tyburn was pulled from his body, watching his slumped form slide down in the chair. He fought against the force as his image receded.

Pain finally made its appearance, creeping in an arc from his lost flesh, enveloping the doctor's ghost. He knew that eventually the searing pain would be his daily existence, and anything other than its savage intensity would be unacceptable. When he embraced this pain and became one with it, there would be no reprieve, as it would vanish leaving him to suffer in emptiness. This was the nature of hell.

Pain became pleasure, briefly offering a taste of joy before mutating. It was a tiny reminder to temper the change with caution.

This was how Caymus found his father. The old man was bathed in sweat, and his arms trembled. His face twitched, as his lips mouthed silent unknown curses. Afraid that Tyburn might swallow his tongue, Caymus pried his father's mouth open. He jumped backwards, unprepared for the sight that met him. A large scarab like beetle rested inside his father's mouth, its six legs curled around the edges piercing the tender flesh.

Horror-struck, Caymus gripped the foul insect and tore it from his father's mouth with a sickening wet sound. He threw the beetle to the ground and crushed it with his heel, stamping the shiny black shell of a body into the dirt with disgust. Tyburn gasped, sucking in a huge mouthful of air. His eyes popped open at once, and he coughed, spitting out blood, his entire body shuddering from the effort.

He stared fearfully at his son, searching his face for some sign of familiarity. "Father," said the bowman, "it's me, Caymus." Gradually he understood that the stranger was not an enemy and allowed himself to lose consciousness. As Tyburn fell forward, Caymus caught him under the arms and lifted him against his body. Crouching forward, he hoisted him over his shoulder and made for the cottage entrance.

The moon had risen by the time Tyburn regained consciousness. Caymus had covered him with a blanket and placed a lantern by his bedside. "I can only imagine that I fell asleep with my mouth open," said Tyburn. "Some beetles carry a poison on their bellies, but they are not native to our island. I must have ingested some. I can't begin to tell you what horrifyingly vivid dreams I had."

"How are you feeling now?" his son asked.

"I feel very disconnected from my body, no pain, only weakness and confusion."

"Your skin is red in patches. Does it itch?"

"No but it feels very hot."

"Yes," added Caymus, "you look as though you have a fever."

"Tarragon," said the old man weakly, "in the garden, and nettle, in a tea."

Caymus left Tyburn, hoping he would be able to recognize the plants in the moonlight. He would make a tea according to his father's directions and hope that it had beneficial effects. When the bowman returned, he found his father's breathing had become laboured and quickly began to heat water for the brewing of tea.

Struggling to focus his eyes, Tyburn could make out the blurry profile of his son beside the fireplace. He tried to speak, but no sound would come from his tightening throat. His breath was soon coming in ragged gasps, and he waved his arms frantically. Caymus angled his father's head forward with one hand and poured the warm tea into his open mouth. Slowly, Tyburn's breathing became more relaxed, and soon the old man was sleeping soundly.

Caymus sat back in the chair by his father's bed and closed his eyes. Outside on the road, he heard the sound of horses approaching. They thundered past the small cottage without stopping. Caymus guessed that there had been three to four horsemen. The clatter of shoes on the road faded quickly into the night.

-20-

Fearghal looked in the mirror. The temporary cure had worked for several days, and there had been comments on his quick recovery and improved demeanour. Now the gray was returning beneath his eyes, and his skin, daily growing ashen and pale, was taking on a pouchy, tired look. His hands had begun to shake again, and the coughing would soon return. He knew what had to be done; they had told him that it was unavoidable. This second method afforded a much longer reprieve, but Fearghal had sworn that he would never walk that road under any circumstances.

As he took stock of the image in front of him, Fearghal began to be aware of another reflection nested behind the primary one. It was not a duplicate or a shadow, but a ghostlike companion. He gazed at it with curiosity and found that concentrating on the image brought it to the foreground The face bore no wounds or lines of concern, and radiated with wisdom.

The image faded as his concentration wavered, and Fearghal found that he needed to expend a huge amount of energy to hold the vision in place. Abruptly, dizziness overtook him and he collapsed in a chair close to his window. The argument with Dafyd had sent his mind in a tailspin and made him question the true purpose of his return to Dunradin.

Fearghal was now strongly inclined to avoid Dafyd, at least until both men put some thought into what had been said. He had asked the Welshman for certain assurances, but Dafyd insisted that an invasion was only days away, and favouritism had no place in the larger scheme of things. He ridiculed Fearghal for being sentimental and suggested that he deal with his weakness quickly.

The original time line was now unrealistic. Recent events, such as the discovery in the woods, had pointed out the need for haste, and the armoury was only partially functional. Despite his wish to stay out of Dafyd's way, Fearghal knew that it was essential that he take care of matters at Lilyvine in the morning. The hunger had returned, as he knew it would, and the beast within needed feeding again. Fearghal had managed to keep his habit under control for a time, but the skirmish on the trail to Dunradin, which had left him wounded, had made everything much more difficult.

-21-

Branan Stoke had arrived at Threstone in the evening and slept inside the twin-towered gatehouse, not wishing to stumble about the deserted castle in the darkness. Several days had passed since his confrontation with the enemy. The Teriz, it was believed, had been practically eliminated, and Branan was on the trail of the fleeing Faustine, who was said to have made his way north across the border. The tracker had lost one of his men in the previous skirmish and made arrangements to meet some recruits at the castle.

Threstone, to the southeast of Dunradin, was unique in its triangular shape. The castle's southern wall had been destroyed hundreds of years ago, and the turret at the left point had also been removed. The inner moat remained, surrounded by marshlands, and the turret on the right remained straight and tall.

The legend of Euther de Faustine had grown in the telling, to a ridiculous point of exaggeration. His followers dwelt underground, and hunted by darkness, it was true, but their numbers were highly exaggerated. Faustine commanded an army that Branan estimated had dwindled to perhaps fifty at the very most. In the last year a great number of so-called Teriz had been destroyed in their caves and burrows with gunpowder and bribery.

Now that the threat had been removed; it was imperative that Faustine be eliminated before he had an opportunity to rebuild. The myth of Euther's invincibility needed to be disproved, and Branan had been hired for this purpose. Faustine had been driven north and it was believed that even his most ardent followers had not been apprised of his destination.

The four recruits were Highlanders from the north who were skilled with sword and pistol. They arrived at Threstone with the first light of day, having been camped two leagues to the west.

Branan sat up at the sound of horses approaching. The riders were dressed in nondescript travelling attire that had gathered a considerable amount of road dust. All were bearded and heavyset.

They drew up, and Hugh Maclean introduced himself. "We came down the road above Dunradin, a small village below the ridge. There was nothing to see from Edinburgh down, at least not on the main roads. I gather we are to sweep north again from here?"

"We will do so at a careful pace," replied Branan, "mindful of any signs along the way, and what of this village of Dunradin? What are your feelings?"

Maclean blew a measure of road dust from his prominent nose. "I think perhaps if we find no signs to the north, we must return here, scouring every village on the way."

-22-

The pain in Liam's ankle slowed his progress through the passage, so much so that he decided to rest before going any further. He closed his eyes and breathed slowly, removing one of his shoes.

His ankle was swollen and painful to the touch. He came to the conclusion that he should attempt to sleep while keeping the weight off his ankle. With any luck, the approaching morning would allow some daylight to filter into the dark world in which he found himself.

Spending the night underground had not been a plan of young Twist's when he had set out for the festival the previous afternoon. He found that by keeping his leg perfectly still, he could concentrate on relaxing, and before long he managed to fall asleep.

After several hours of sleep, Liam awoke with a sore back and a throbbing ankle. A number of confused seconds passed before he recalled his situation. A reddish glow in the distance offered the hope of daylight.

He removed his belt and placed his baton along the length of his leg. Cinching it tightly below his ankle, he wound and tucked the remainder of the leather to form a makeshift splint. He found that he could grip the top of the baton close to his hip and make his way forward in this fashion. Thankfully the passageway was high enough that crouching was not required, and the young man started out towards the dim light.

He thought he could smell water and decided that he must have chosen the proper path towards the river. After what seemed like a very long time, he came to a division in the passageway. Twenty feet above the divide was the source of light. Sunshine filtered through the trap door of another sinkhole. If his sense of direction had not failed him, the path to the right would take him back to where he had begun.

He turned to his left and continued to shuffle along. He felt uneasy about the discovery of another sinkhole. They were clearly not an accident, probably some kind of trap, but for what animal? How long had the passage been here, and who had thought to dig it?

While Liam negotiated the underground trail, a similar passageway many leagues to the south was about to be destroyed.

Two trackers lowered a powder keg into the passage from the top of a sinkhole. The fuse had been lit, and the keg was lowered on its side, allowing it to roll. The trackers dropped the rope and fled into the woods.

Captain Madra snapped out of his stupor. The explosion had been very loud. Dirt and debris were still falling close to where he was seated. He scrambled to his feet and began to run towards the cavern entrance. The second explosion blew the legs off the fat reconnaissance captain before he could reach the other sinkhole and left him writhing in his newly sealed tomb.

The tracker dropped the coins into the informer's outstretched hand, noting the dark stranger's long fingers and pointed nails.

The blast had filled the cavern opening completely, and Domnash smiled, knowing that he would never enter the foul smelling tunnel again.

-23-

Fearghal Mcleary arrived at the old mill before Dafyd. If anyone who had observed him at the festival were to encounter Fearghal on his way to Lilyvine, they would be horrified at the change in his appearance and assume that he was close to death. All of his hair had greyed overnight, and his eyes had taken on the look of a desperate animal. He scurried towards the mill entrance, almost completely doubled over, placed a violently shaking hand on the door handle, and keyed it with the other.

He stumbled across the room, opened the small door to the left of the weapons rack, and vanished down the stairs.

Some time later, Dafyd arrived at Lilyvine. The Welshman found the door unlocked, entered cautiously, and quietly took a hand ax down from the weapons rack. The door to the basement was not completely closed, and a sliver of light escaped.

Just as Dafyd reached to ease the door open, Fearghal emerged, looking the picture of health. His eyes were clear, and his hair had darkened again. He appeared tanned and relaxed, as though he had just spent an afternoon in the sunshine.

"You should be more careful, my friend," said Dafyd. "Anyone might have walked in here and caught you at your game. I see you have taken care of health matters for the time being."

Fearghal glanced at the hatchet. "Hunting?" he asked.

"Just being cautious," replied Dafyd. "As I told you, they may have already arrived."

Fearghal took the weapon from the Welshman and placed it back in the rack. "There has been no indication. For all we know, their plans have changed, and some other unfortunate village has been chosen."

Dafyd shook his head slowly. "Listen to yourself. Denial will not change the inevitable; you of all people should understand the nature of fate. It is not as if we ever had a choice to do anything other than survive. Accept what you cannot change. You found us, we did not seek you out. We shared our knowledge with you. We have united to defeat those who condemn us. I personally tutored you and provided for you as your illness grew."

"You!" screamed Fearghal. "Were it not for you, I would not be imprisoned in this double life. You brought this affliction about! I damn you for all time."

Dafyd stepped forward and wrapped his arms around the other man. He brought his mouth close to Fearghal's neck, whispered, "Trust me," and softly kissed him.

Fearghal broke away from Dafyd and calmly walked to the door as though having decided to break from his misery. He turned before leaving, "never again" he said "not your way."

The Welshman stood in silence for several seconds, staring at the floor, and then retrieved the hatchet and stepped through the door to the basement. Fearghal had knocked over a case of wine in his haste, and Dafyd sidestepped the broken bottles and walked across the clay floor to the back of the small wine cellar where a narrow curtain hung between two tabled casks. He swept the curtain aside and stepped onto the landing of another set of stairs.

Fearghal set out along the river path in the direction of the town center, striding with purpose and determination. It had been a mistake to leave the guesthouse. He knew that he should have boarded himself in and ridden out the horror of withdrawal. This time, he told himself, would be different.

-24-

As Liam negotiated the channel on the left, he began to sense a change in the air. The smell of human waste wafted through the tunnel, increasing with every step. Another, more horrible smell assaulted him as he continued. It was like nothing he'd encountered before and froze him with fear. He considered turning around but slowly crept ahead, one hand over his face.

Eventually he noticed that the passage was becoming lighter. Before long the path ended at the opening of a large chamber. Liam approached the flickering light of the opening cautiously. A wet grinding sound made him want to retreat at once, but curiosity pushed him forward.

Nothing could have prepared the youngster for the sight that met his eyes. The underground chamber was dominated by an open fire pit in the centre. Several bodies were chained to a stone wall on one side of the room, bearing all manner of wounds, from small punctures to hacked and missing limbs.

Liam understood at once that the smell that has previously puzzled him was the odour of death. Almost directly below the opening, a dark-haired man stood leaning against a short ladder. He was energetically feeding on what appeared to be a human forearm.

Liam fell back against the passage wall, covering his mouth with both hands to stifle a scream that was trying to burst from his throat. His heart beat wildly, and his head spun as he fought to avoid vomiting. It occurred to him that he might possibly have died in the fall and gone to hell.

Twist lay there paralysed with fear, praying that the flesh-eating monster below would not turn in his direction. As luck would have it, he had not been observed, and when he found the strength to turn his head again in the direction of the hellish scene, a brief glimpse of lantern light appeared as the stranger vanished through a heavy curtain at the top of a flight of stairs across from where Liam sat.

The juggler's instincts told him that, if he wanted to see the light of day again, he would have to cross the floor and climb the same stairs. Before that, he would have to manage the ladder below. He imagined himself waiting in the shadow at the top of the stairs. If the stranger returned, he would trip him up and bolt past.

His thoughts were interrupted by a low moan. One prisoner was missing an arm from the elbow down, and there was a tight tourniquet just above the ragged stump. He seemed to be motioning towards the fire pit with his other arm. Liam glanced down and saw where the monster had discarded his meal. The remaining bones and curling fingers were blackening in the coals. Liam slid down the ladder, being careful to avoid landing on his injured foot.

"Je suis malade," cried a tortured voice in a language that Twist was not familiar with. *"Attendez,"* called another, as he struggled up the stairs. Liam could not bear to look at the poor souls chained to the wall and backed into the shadows by the curtain. The effort of crossing to the stairs had set his ankle throbbing painfully again. He closed his eyes and concentrated on stilling his thoughts.

-25-

Caymus woke to the sound of hooves rattling along the road. This time they traveled in the opposite direction.

Tyburn was already awake and brewing tea. "Good morning," he said. "There seems to be something afoot out there," he added, pointing towards the road. The old man carried a cup of strong tea to his son.

"You are well?" asked Caymus rubbing the sleep from his eyes.

"Yes, thank you, much better. In fact, after a night of some very revealing dreams, I am perhaps a little wiser or more confused for it. That very special insect that attached itself to my tongue did not do so by accident. Had you not removed that beetle from my mouth, I would have ingested all of its poison and surely perished.

"I had two visions last night. One involved a shape-changer that loomed above me as I slept in the garden, a black-feathered fellow with greedy eyes. I also dreamed of a death wagon or hearse that was pursued by five horsemen. Enemies are in our midst. I believe Fearghal's warning may have come too late."

Caymus told his father what had transpired in the High Wood and said he was sure he had been watched from the trees.

"That may have been our little dark friend," suggested Tyburn; "you were wise to leave the woods quickly. I think we had best join Ronan and Fearghal without delay."

"I agree," said Caymus. "If you feel you are strong enough, we should probably leave at once."

Tyburn's horsemanship was not diminished by his limited use of one hand, and his mount, despite being smaller than the Clyde, was swift enough to keep pace with the larger horse.

It was decided that, for the sake of expediency, they would take the shorter route down past the falls.

-26-

Fearghal strode into the smithy with a smile and greeted Ronan. "It's imperative that I leave Dunradin for a day or so," he said, "and I wished to let you know."

Ronan returned his smile. "I have something for you," he replied, reaching under his bench for a package. The knife was a work of art. Ronan had fashioned the handle from a stag horn, and the blade shone brightly in the fiery lighting of the blacksmith's shop. An intricate snake of inlaid silver twisted down the center almost to the dagger's point.

"You are a true artisan," said Fearghal, handling the blade carefully. "I am much in your debt."

Ronan had designed a simple leather sheath for the knife, which he also handed to Fearghal. The brothers talked for a short time until Fearghal excused himself with a promise to seek out Ronan and Caymus upon his return. As he returned to Green's Guesthouse, he pondered whether he might have seen his brother for the last time. If he was unable to defeat his craving this time, he vowed he would end things with his blade. He climbed the stairs to his room and began to prepare for the ordeal.

To begin, he dragged a heavy chest across the room and pushed it against the locked door. Then he situated the dresser in front of it, with the mirror facing the trunk. He placed the silver dagger on the bedside table and removed his boots. He loosened his clothing, aware that he would alternate between fever and chills, and then decided to completely disrobe and lie beneath the blankets. First he remembered to draw the curtains and place the empty washbowl beside the bed.

He crossed his arms over his chest and tried to recall the ghostly image he had seen in the mirror previously, the vision that had offered him some peace. Suddenly a thought occurred to him and he threw the covers aside. He dragged the dresser to the foot of his bed and pivoted the mirror on its hinges until it reflected the pillow where his head would rest. Resuming his position in the bed, he looked into the mirror at his reflection. A pale, shimmering aura appeared almost at once.

He concentrated on the aura while attempting to avoid looking into his own eyes. He found it an easy matter to relax his focus while slowing his breathing, and before long his peripheral vision narrowed to the point that everything outside of the dresser melted into darkness.

His sense of time drifted, until he no longer knew whether it was day or night. As he attempted to avoid his face in the mirror, it changed slowly from his own to that of a mocking beast. The ape bared his teeth and laughed silently as though he were daring Fearghal to challenge him. He reached up and touched his face with both hands, and the simian mask dissolved until nothing remained where there had once been features from brow to chin.

He pushed against the flesh in a panic leaving red lines where his hands touched. With his forefinger he drew a red circle of blood where a mouth should be and a vertical stroke above that to signify a nose.

He dug both thumbs deeply into the flesh where the eyes had been, and formed two deep sockets. "Not real," he said aloud, repeating the two words several times, with eyes closed until his heartbeat slowed to a manageable pace. He looked in the mirror once more and saw that his face had transformed into a brittle hornet's nest.

Insects crawled from his nostrils, into his ears, and between his lips. He clawed at his face in a panic, breaking away the fragile paper like form of the hive, revealing his reddened flesh marked and swollen with venomous stings. Finally he lost consciousness and began to pass in and out of a comatose state.

-27-

Padraic was on the roof of the grocer's feeding his pigeons when he saw Tamlyn arriving from High Street. The youngster was approached by an elderly woman Padraic recognized as Mrs. Twist, the mother of Liam. She seemed upset and Padraic decided he would join the pair downstairs.

When he arrived at the door, Twist's mother was gone, and Tamlyn was brushing at the door with a puzzled look. "What's this then?" he asked his young friend, pointing at the trident design above the door handle. Padraic examined the strange symbol closely and shrugged.

The two thought nothing more of the matter, as Tamlyn quickly changed the subject. "Liam Twist has vanished," he said excitedly. "His mother was just here asking folks if they had seen him. I told her we'd all have a look about. She certainly is worried."

Tamlyn smiled at his friend "Ha, you've been with your pigeons," he said. He laughed at Padraic's puzzled look as he removed a small feather from the boy's tuft of unruly red hair. Padraic pointed up High Street. "Yes," replied Tamlyn, "we'll go and get the others; four is better than two."

"I don't understand," said Charlotte. "Where could Liam have gone? What could have happened?" The young woman was on the verge of tears.

"You children look down by the river," said Ceana, "but please stay together, and be very careful." She was more alarmed at the news than she cared to admit, having been told by Ronan of the murder in the woods. "Don't wander anywhere near the High Wood," she added, "and tell your father where you're going."

The children agreed to go directly to the stables and started down the hill. "We'll go upstream along the close bank first," Murdoch told Ronan, "then loop through the quarry and back over the bridge to the other side."

"Aye, very well," said Ronan, handing Murdoch a coil of rope. "Take this with you. If he's fallen at the quarry, you may need it, and keep a sharp eye out for anything out of the ordinary." As they prepared to go on to the river, Portus stepped from the shop and greeted them. After hearing their news, he promised to scour the village for any sign of the lad. He had told Liam's mother earlier that he would keep his eyes open but, after witnessing the children's desperation, decided to mount a search of his own.

Tamlyn led the search party with the others following in line. They took a shortcut to the river, traversing the marshy area by stepping single file along a narrow path. The reeds and cattails reached above their shoulders, even at times towering over them, until gradually the ground rose to the open area beside the river bank.

The children knew the old stone quarry better than anyone else, having spent countless hours at play in the horseshoe-shaped cleft that had supplied stonemasons for many years. Generations of youth had fought mock battles in the deep gorge, and scores of lovers had found privacy in its cool evening shadows. The Macneil brothers fell in line for the search along the way, and, as the strange assortment of children passed more homes, the word spread until a small army of youngsters had fanned out in the direction of the quarry.

-28-

Branan Stoke raised his hand, bringing the highlanders to a halt. The wagon tracks that they had been following suddenly veered off the road to the right through a cut in the trees. "See here," he said to Hugh Maclean, pointing at the markings. "A carriage entered here and was unable to turn around or back up. Judging by these hoof marks, the driver released the horses and hitched them at the back of the carriage to pull it out to the road."

"Of course," replied Hugh, "then he brought them to the front again and continued on. They must have seen our approach and blended into the woods while we thundered past."

"Yes," agreed Branan, "this side stop is not visible to southbound travellers, and they would have doused their lanterns as well. At any rate we now know we are headed in the right direction."

Stoke stood up in the stirrups and surveyed the horizon. He patted at his cloak, withdrew a small box, and extracted a twist of tobacco. After tucking the tobacco beside his gum, he returned the box to his coat, momentarily running his fingertips across the small Bible that shared refuge in the pocket. "Gentlemen, if we wish to catch this devil, we must ride hard. He may be several hours ahead of us, or he may be laid up at another road stop, so proceed swiftly, but observe everything."

"The entrance to Dunradin is a half hour from here," said Maclean. "I suggest we stop there briefly and scour the road for signs."

"Agreed" said Stoke, spurring his horse forward. At the Dunradin gate, the riders came to a halt. Hugh Maclean dismounted and motioned to the wheel rut in the mud. It appeared that a carriage had at some point sunken a wheel into the soft earth.

"Over there," called one of the highlanders. Just visible farther down the road through the trees was a black carriage. Hugh motioned his man for silence, holding a finger to his lip.

"They make for Dunradin," said Branan quietly. "Secure the horses, and have your men draw their weapons."

The wooded area where Euther's carriage had come to a halt was deathly silent. The highlanders advanced, taking all precautions to do so soundlessly. As they reached the carriage, it was apparent that the horses had not remained with it, and Branan guessed that the passengers were gone also. He drew the curtain aside, and his thoughts were confirmed. The coach was abuzz with flies that circled a congealed pool of blood on the seat and floor. Through the open door on the far side he saw the prone body of the driver.

He circled the carriage with Hugh and examined the body. The driver's throat was torn out to the extent that his head was attached by only a thin string of flesh. The tracker crossed himself and turned to Maclean. "Two horses missing may signify two passengers, unless we stumble across more bodies. It appears that our villain decided to abandon his coach, but not before having a bite to eat."

Hugh looked horrified. "You're not suggesting that this Faustine is—a flesh eater?"

"I'm not suggesting anything; it's a fact. Euther de Faustine is a Wraith. His health is maintained by the drinking of blood. In order to avoid having to drink blood every three days or so, he resorts to cannibalism. Ingesting the flesh with the blood will maintain his strength and well-being for up to a month. He is not traveling with any number of his kind, so I suggest that he has a rendezvous in the works.

"I doubt very much that he has any idea how many of his followers we have done away with recently. When they are buried alive in their tunnels, they are no longer of any concern. They expend all their strength trying to dig themselves free and eventually die.

When they are above ground, it is a different matter. Staking them through the heart as they sleep is a fool's myth. It is dangerous and unproductive. The only way to kill them is to introduce pure silver into the bloodstream."

Branan took a leather pouch from his belt and showed Hugh the contents. "This is lead shot mixed with silver," he said, opening his hand. "I have enough to supply a few pistols, and I would suggest that your men discard their ammunition for mine."

"Tell me something," said Maclean. "How does this differ from the Teriz that we track?"

Branan reached for another twist of tobacco before offering an explanation. "I have followed this Faustine for many months," he replied. "At one time he had hundreds of children, whom he referred to as Teriz, in order to create fear and to form a sense of community within their ranks. They are victims who have been cursed with his hunger and his immortality. If he were to infect you with his blood, you would develop the hunger, and the need to feed on others."

"And what if I refused to participate in these foul practices, what would become of me?"

"You would wither and rot much like a leper, but remain alive, a tortured soul who could not bear the light of day. Your only release would be to end your life in the manner that I have described with the use of silver. Those who have been destroyed in the manner of this unfortunate driver are spared the horror of immortality.

"There is one exception to the rule. When a Wraith lies with a mortal woman, the resulting child has a much stronger ability to withstand the degeneration that results in the refusal to partake of blood or flesh, although the immunity is thought to be temporary. It is believed that Faustine was fathered hundreds of years ago by a Wraith who had fallen in love with a mortal, which would explain his ability to have survived all these years. It's not known if Euther has fathered any children in this manner, but of course the possibility exists."

-29-

Liam drew the curtain aside, enough to get a glimpse of what was beyond it. What he saw was a dimly lit wine cellar and another short set of stairs with a wooden door at the top. As he stepped awkwardly between two large wine barrels, he heard a commotion from the room of horrors that he had just exited. Peeking back through the curtains, he saw three emaciated men leap to the floor of the dungeon from the mouth of the tunnel. There was no turning back now, and the youngster retreated, not wishing to witness anything like the disgusting feeding that he had seen earlier.

He crossed the room as quickly as he could and managed the stairs. Then he paused at the door. What if it was locked? Realizing that he'd run out of options, he tried the handle carefully. It clicked open with a sound that made him cringe, and he peered cautiously into the room. Twist knew at once that he was in the front room of the old mill. The River Sleath was visible from the window. He looked about the room astounded that such a nightmare as existed behind him was possible right here in Dunradin. Liam heard a man cough and then spit on the stones outside the door.

With trembling hands he turned to the weapons rack and grabbed a rapier. The youngster backed towards the side wall and limped into the stairwell that led up to the next floor. Praying that he would not encounter anyone, he decided to make his way to the roof. Using the sword and scabbard as a cane, he struggled up the stairs, cautiously peering about until he finally reached the roof.

He collapsed on his back pulling in deep draughts of clean fresh air, hugely relieved to be far from the heat and stench of the tunnel. Lilyvine's flat roof was enclosed by a four-foot stonework, tall enough to crouch behind, yet easy enough to see over. At the four corners and the midpoints, stepping stones rested below ornate gargoyles.

Liam leaned against the wall. His ankle hurt, and his stomach was a twisted knot. He was thirsty and hungry. Suddenly he remembered the treacle candy he had bought the day before and retrieved the waxed package from his vest pocket. He pushed a piece of candy into his mouth hungrily and savoured its sweet flavour.

Then he returned to his thoughts. How in the world could such evil have found its way to his quiet little village? There had been something familiar about the dark stranger in the dungeon. He recalled the black beard matted with blood and remembered the two gentlemen he had seen arguing in the shadow of the church steps. How the devil was Charlotte's father connected to this vile business?

He stepped onto one of the stones at the centre of the wall and peered below. There was no sign of anyone at the entrance. As his eyes scanned the river, he became aware of a large number of children scattered amongst the trees on the other side. They were all moving downstream towards the quarry, looking for all the world like a search party. "By God," he said aloud. It had taken Twist a full moment to realize that they were looking for the missing person that he'd become. His first instinct was to call out across the water, but he realized his voice would only carry far enough to alert whoever might remain in the old building.

-30-

Because Euther had torn out and consumed the driver's throat, he was much less susceptible to the effects of daylight; nevertheless he wore a pair of darkened spectacles. The circles of glass were black and gave the woodland trail a strange shadowy appearance.

He and Drake had arrived at the upper falls and dismounted. The trail to the village forked above the falls, and the road to the right descended past the lower falls into the village. Euther instructed Drake to ride a short distance to the right then double back and join him on the trail to the left. If anyone was following their tracks this would confuse them, and perhaps the pursuers would become the pursued. To the left they soon emerged from the trees and crossed onto the Glencairn Bridge. Stopping in the center, they could see beyond where the river dropped suddenly to form the upper falls.

Across the bridge, the narrow road wound to the right and ran along the far shore, passing the lower falls and eventually joining the direct route into Dunradin.

Although he was unaware of this fact, Faustine had chosen the longer but more obscure route to the village. He was not unfamiliar with the roads in this area, but many years had passed since he had travelled the river above the town. He presented a sinister image as he slipped from his horse and led the beast through the trees. He walked with a stoop, taking very long strides through the greenery, looking to the left and right. His long jacket swished through the grasses, and his tall boots shone with moisture from the forest floor. His thin lips moved constantly as he mumbled aloud to himself.

William Drake followed his employer silently. Drake was capable of turning a blind eye to anything, as long as the price was right, and it seemed he was no longer shocked or disgusted by anything.

-31-

The pair of riders made a somewhat comical sight. Caymus the bowman, on his Clydesdale, towered above Tyburn on his swift but much smaller pony. The old man's cottage was not far from the road, and before long they were travelling the same route that Branan and the highlanders had taken. The abandoned coach did not shock Tyburn and his son to the same degree, as the highlanders had dragged the driver's mutilated body into the brush where it was not visible.

Caymus briefly considered hitching Ghost to the carriage until he looked into the coach's interior. The darkening blood had a nasty smell to it, and the bowman pointed out to his father that apparently another murder had taken place in the woods.

The trail was muddied with a variety of markings that were difficult to interpret. One scenario told the story of a coach being waylaid in the woods by several riders who continued on their way with the extra horses. There were no bodies about, which suggested abduction. The more likely scenario involved a coach left by the road in favour of horses, with another group of horsemen passing the scene at a later time, yet there remained the blood in the carriage to explain.

Before long Caymus and Tyburn came within sight of Branan Stoke and the trackers who had stalled at the crossroads while attempting to decipher some confusing tracks. They slowed their approach, being clearly outnumbered, and prepared to make a run in the event that an attack was forthcoming.

Maclean's men turned and looked for instructions to Hugh, who stepped towards Branan. "They appear to be locals," said Stoke.

One of the highlanders spoke up. "I know this man," he said, pointing towards Caymus. "He is cousin to my wife."

The trackers lowered their weapons and raised their hands in greeting. "This is young Woodruff, Teala's son," said Caymus to his father.

"No longer so young," replied Tyburn, relaxing the hold on his weapon. The men exchanged greetings, and Caymus questioned Branan regarding the abandoned carriage. In this manner Tyburn and his son learned that Faustine was a monster soon to appear within their midst.

It was indeed a revelation to discover that Euther was a powerful Wraith. Tyburn had heard of blood-drinkers as a child, but put no stock in exaggerated tales of gruesome night stalkers. Now the old man had come close to being witness to a bloodletting.

"These so called Teriz are no longer many in number," explained Branan. "I now believe that Faustine has chosen your village as an obscure outpost, where he can create a wormhole from which he may feed while replenishing his numbers."

Caymus, alarmed at the degree of danger that Branan revealed, spoke up. "We were warned of a Teriz incursion the week past and have made preparations." He went on to explain the formation of an armoury and named those who had instigated the preparations.

Branan was puzzled. He was not aware that anyone other than himself had been delegated to quell the advance of Faustine. "No one is to be trusted. I am here on the authority of the Queen. I'm not familiar with this Welshman Dafyd, and I fear he does not have your best interests in mind. In fact I believe it to be possible that he is in league with Faustine."

Tyburn and Caymus both looked deeply concerned. "Then we have no time to waste" said the old man.

"Indeed," said Branan. "I suggest we divide at this point and reunite at the village. Woodruff will join you on the narrow road, and I will continue with the others to the right. If you can get a shot away, highlander, do so without hesitation. Do not be soothed by Faustine's mellow tones. He is a very charming and convincing actor. In short, kill him on sight." He pointed to Caymus's bow. "Your bolts may slow Faustine but will not kill him; be warned."

They started out at once with three men apiece to cover both tracks.

-32-

Liam turned his attention from the river. He had heard the sound of voices from the floor below his feet. To his far left was a small skylight. He crept over to it and peered into the room. He counted nine men, if indeed that's what they were. The windows of the room were heavily blanketed, and the only light came from the stairwell door to the roof.

"Within the day, I am told," said an oily voice.

"You may trust the Welshman," replied another, "but there are some of us as wants to see the proof. Word has it that the master has moved on."

A deeper voice joined the conversation. "You filth would do to stop your whinging. Have you not been fed like kings of late? You didn't die in a rat hole like the others. Look at that meat market out there, and stop your puking and pissing."

Liam had heard enough and crept away from the window, wondering if there was any way to lower himself from the side of the building. He tried to remember the layout of Lilyvine and seemed to recall a ladder that ran the height of the building somewhere to the rear. He cursed his painful leg as he padded to the rear of the building. The outside of the back wall was thick with vines that covered anything that might resemble a ladder and grew over the top edge onto the roof.

He reached through the twisted growth, feeling for a telltale iron stanchion that would lead him to the ladder. Moving along the wall was slow work for Twist. He would have felt more comfortable if the door to the roof had not been left open. Closing it now was out of the question, with the Teriz just below.

Before long a light rain swept across the river and approached the mill. Liam watched the skylight go from muddy to clear as the raindrops began to increase in size. He cautiously approached the roof entrance, hoping to shelter under its eaves, when a loud bang dropped him to his knees in fear. Someone from inside had slammed the door closed.

Liam's pulse raced, and water from his hair ran down the back of his neck into his collar. If he could only locate the ladder and find some shelter, he might have a chance to warn the town's children of the horror in their midst. Something had gone very wrong in Dunradin. Evil had been birthed and was developing rapidly. Surely someone else must be aware of the madness breeding below.

-33-

Most of the children go to the quarry at about the same time. Some of the older ones were already there before Charlotte and her brothers, milling about with no particular sense of purpose. Word had spread that the quarry was being searched, and by noon, half the youngsters in Dunradin were in one place. A good number of the children seemed to have no idea what they were looking for, and before long the outing began to resemble an Easter egg hunt.

When it became apparent that Liam was not at the quarry, Tamlyn drew his brother and sister aside and suggested they cross the river to the cemetery and continue along the far bank. "Yes, I agree," said Charlotte. "These clouds look close to breaking." A peal of thunder in the distance confirmed her prediction.

They crossed over to the graveyard and followed the edge of its rear wall through the grassy field. One of the Macneil brothers stumbled and called out. "Look here, I near fell in this well, or whatever it is. Perhaps our Liam done that very thing."

Murdoch lay on his stomach and edged forward, until his face was over the opening. "I can't see a thing down there," he said, getting to his knees.

"Here, tie this to your rope," said Tamlyn, passing his brother a stout piece of wood. "Lower it in and measure the depth." The log met the bottom with a soft thump, and Murdoch hauled it up a foot at a time, with his brother counting aloud.

"Nigh on twenty foot," said a Macneil. "It's a long ways to fall."

Murdoch returned to a prone position and called down the shaft. "Liam! Hello, Liam!" His voice echoed with no response.

Just then the clouds broke and the rain began. "Sounds like that hole opens on a tunnel," said Tamlyn as they ran for cover.

-34-

"Keep your eyes peeled, Drake. There are some nasty types about."

Drake could see the sneer without turning around. He was tired and didn't feel the need to respond. Euther had his little box of powders for when his energy flagged, but Drake didn't indulge in any of Faustine's destructive habits.

William Drake was a strong, healthy individual, who lived cleanly and took good care of himself. He was intelligent and well spoken, and might have been considered a complete gentleman, had it not been for the fact that he was absolutely devoid of morals. He neither worshipped nor hated Faustine and made no effort to understand him. He simply mapped his way through life from one event to the next.

Drake was only concerned with becoming wealthy. What he would one day do with his wealth was not his concern. He stayed alert by being in touch with his surroundings, watching every movement of the wind and responding to it.

The pair moved along the trail with no urgency, appearing to float, as a gloom began rising from the ferns to meet the rainfall. "I believe we have lost many of our numbers, William. It is a shame, yet in some terms it may be fortune smiling on us. Fewer mouths to feed, you know. It's not that I don't love all my children, but—" He hesitated and readjusted his spectacles. "You know, William, you must always regard your mortality as a blessing."

They had dismounted and were now walking the horses. Euther dropped his horse's lead and continued to walk. This was his silent way of informing Drake that the horses were no longer needed. Drake patted his mare's neck and released the animal. For a long while they walked in the rain without speaking.

"Did I ever tell you about the time they hanged me?"

"Yes," replied Drake, knowing the story well.

"It was the damnedest thing," continued Euther. "If only you had seen the look on their faces. I still maintain that a number of onlookers soiled themselves on the spot. But I was younger then and could withstand the rigors of man's justice." He began to sing quietly.

"Twist the rope and stretch his throat
Drown him just to see him float,
Break his neck and hang him high,
But the monster will not die."

"Hundreds of years' worth of memories … you know it can sometimes be a burden. Oh dear, I'm rambling on. I believe sleep is required, William."

Drake was weary as well and pointed towards a grouping of large trees, where the lower limbs of two massive evergreens branched across each other. The ground beneath was dry and covered in pine needles. Euther lay on his back with his long hands tucked into the pockets of his cloak. William Drake sat against the trunk of one tree and let his head hang to his chest.

-35-

Fearghal did not sleep so easily. His chin was on his knees, and his arms were wrapped about his legs, holding himself together as his body shook with tremors and spasms. He had vomited a foul bloody stew into his sheets and pushed them from his bed.

The short path to salvation was always a temptation, but Fearghal understood that once he had eaten flesh, he would be lost for an eternity. Dafyd mocked his reluctance, but Fearghal was firm in his resolve. He'd been seduced by Dafyd into the ritual drinking of blood, after observing its restorative power. It began with a fall from his horse. The Welshman used a syringe of glass to transfuse Mcleary with some of his own tainted blood. Fearghal had watched with fascination as Dafyd withdrew the blood then offered it to him as a token of brotherhood. From the moment that Dafyd slowly pushed the plunger down, sending a measure of rejuvenating liquid into Fearghal's arm, he had decided that this was his new religion. In the beginning he was horrified at the prospect of drinking blood from the living, but became desperate when Dafyd refused to inject him, and the first phase of degeneration had begun.

Fearghal's body was covered in a cold sweat, and every pore called out to be fed. He suddenly jerked into a rigid position, gripping the sides of his bed with arms and legs as it rocked and spun wildly. In reality the bed was motionless, but in his mind it was intent on tossing him to the floor.

The mattress slowed its spinning and began to come alive with an army of spiders that grew from its ticking and crawled into his pubis. Fearghal clawed and scratched at himself, as the army of insects traveled up his belly towards his face. Fully conscious now, he jumped naked from the bed and stared into the mirror.

His bed was reflected, and the room behind it. He waved his arms about and saw nothing. He looked down at his feet; he was here but did not exist in the mirror. He ran his hands across the glass surface and saw no change.

It appeared that the fever had passed, and the hunger was diminishing. Fearghal stepped into his clothing carefully, and ran his hands down the length of his face. Suddenly his stomach convulsed, and he vomited forcefully across the bed, staining the mattress with a red stickiness. Rather than weakening him, the expulsion seemed to make him feel stronger and less drugged. His clothing hung loosely on his diminished frame, and his hair had turned snow white.

He walked to the window and looked outside, briefly catching his image in the pane of glass. He turned and looked again into the mirror. His body appeared as a semitransparent form that he could observe now, but the window and desk behind him were visible through his reflection, and he looked for all the world like a ghost, or what he had always imagined a ghost would look like.

As he stood there, his form began to fill in slowly. He was amazed at the change in his mien. His hair had taken on the appearance of a powdered wig, and even his whiskers had turned white. The thinning flesh of his face made his cheekbones more prominent, and his eyes had lost the sunken haunted look.

He was surprised to see that the shining aura had returned and appeared to be permanent. Most important, he seemed to have lost the dreadful craving that had plagued him for so long. A sudden weariness weakened him then, and he collapsed in the chair with his eyes closed.

Fearghal's recent past, which had been obscured by hunger and obsession now stood out clearly like an open wound. He had not killed for blood but bore the same weight of guilt, having sucked the blood from others' victims, caring not who they were or were becoming.

How many had he used to slake his thirst? Though the number was probably unimportant, he couldn't help but think that the few he might have infected must have carried on to amass a number of their own victims. Now, resting here with closed eyes as he came to understand that it was over, Fearghal tried to imagine what life would be like without the wonderful sensation of fresh hot blood running down his throat, filling his entire body with that orgasmic rush of controlled power. That maddeningly perfect brush with rejuvenation and immortality. He would recall the sensation from minute to minute and month to month, and then one day far in the future, he might be allowed to think of something else. It was so easy to recall the beauty of the blood and to forget the horrors of the hunger.

-36-

"No, no, no, don't be so foolish," cried Charlotte. "It's bad enough that Liam may have fallen in there, but you are not going down!"

"All right, then, what do you suggest?" asked Murdoch impatiently. "We have to place something over the opening so that nobody falls in."

"You Macneils, drag that large branch over here. We'll lay it across the opening and tie the rope to it. That way, if anyone is down there, they can climb out. We can't just stand here in the rain. We'll head for the Old Mill."

The other children saw her logic and made the preparations. Soon the small group continued across the field and made their way down onto the river road that led to Lilyvine, hurrying to reach an underpass where they could shelter from the rain. The youngsters huddled together, wringing the water from their hair. The summer rainstorm was increasing in intensity, and the sky became darker. The larger group of children across the river had broken up and scattered towards their homes to shelter from the weather.

"The way I see it" said Tamlyn, "we can either go to the new armoury until the rain stops or just go back to the square with Padraic. Portus will let us dry off in the shop, and then we can determine if anything has turned up there."

Charlotte wrapped her arms around herself and shivered in her damp dress. "All I know is I'm very cold, and I don't want to spend the rest of the afternoon here," she said through chattering teeth.

"I'm for the armoury," said a Macneil.

"Aye, me as well," agreed the other. "I hear there's a whole rack o' weapons in there."

"That's what an armoury is, you dunce," replied his brother. Caleb and Cardiff were twins who were identical in appearance, except that Cardiff was somewhat larger and slower.

"Bugger you!" said the larger twin, swinging a fist in his brother's direction. Caleb sidestepped it easily and laughed at the miss.

"Stop that, you two," said Charlotte. "There's absolutely no need for that."

"I agree indeed," said Caleb. "None whatever, you've made a real sample of yerself, Cardiff."

"Example?" corrected Charlotte.

"For certainly," he replied.

"I'm hungry," said Tamlyn. "Let's make for town." Murdoch agreed and the three bade the twins good-bye.

The Macneils headed in the other direction, anxious to have a look at the new armoury's collection. "Why are you always slaggin me then?" whined Cardiff.

"Because I love you so, and it'll make a man of you. Now stop stepping on my heels."

The boys approached the armoury and ran up the steps. They swung open the outer door and entered the common area in front of the main door. Caleb wiped rain water from his brow. "Go ahead; I don't think we need to knock."

"Why do I have to go first?" asked Cardiff.

"Because yer standin' in front of me, so it makes sense," replied Caleb.

"Funny though, isn't it?" said Cardiff. "Whenever there's food to be had, it's you standing at front o' me."

"Oh aye," said Caleb quickly, "and if ever our food is poisoned, you know who'll croak first, just you remember that."

Cardiff pulled the door open and nearly jumped out of his skin. A stern-looking bearded gentleman stood directly in front of him, staring down at the youngster. He had been at the door on his way out when he heard the boy's voices and paused to listen. Cardiff stood there tongue-tied.

"Well," said Dafyd, "what have we here? Am I seeing double?"

"We thought we might have a look, sir," offered Caleb.

"Well then, by all means," said the amused Welshman, stepping aside to allow them in. Caleb pushed his brother in the small of the back, and he stumbled forward.

"Rather inclement weather to be out touring, is it not? unless of course you're a pair of spies."

"Oh n-n-no, sir," stammered Cardiff.

"Please, come in and look around. I'm just having a little fun at your expense. Only," he continued, "the upper floors are off limits, full of all sorts of villainous characters, I'm afraid." He winked slyly at the twins and busied himself behind a large desk.

"Look at that." Caleb pointed admiringly at a full suite of armour in the corner. His brother was running his finger along the length of a massive claymore. The impressive sword stood taller than he was.

A good many of the weapons were from a bygone age. They had come from retired soldiers and old farmers. Nevertheless there was a collection of firearms in a cabinet behind Dafyd. The Welshman quietly polished a pearl-handled duelling pistol while the Macneils continued to look about.

The shining flintlock caught Caleb's eye, and he edged closer to the desk. "Here," said Dafyd, offering Caleb the pistol. The inquisitive youngster took it carefully by the handle. "It's beautiful, isn't it?"

"It's heavy," said the boy.

"Hold your arm straight out," Dafyd instructed, "and fold your other arm behind your back. Now place one foot in front of the other, and keep your chin up." He began to laugh. "There you go, little spy, now you are ready to kill a man. Go ahead, squeeze the trigger." He continued laughing until Caleb became unnerved and handed the weapon back.

"Seen enough?" he asked quietly, motioning towards the door with his head. The boys backed that way and left quickly without a word.

"That fellow's not right in the heid," said Cardiff as they hurried down the road.

"Ya don't say," replied his brother.

Liam watched from the edge of the roof as the boys vanished into the evening. He wanted to wave frantically and call out but then realized he would be endangering their lives as well as his own. What had happened below? Had they seen anything, and how were they allowed to leave?

He returned to the other side of the roof and resumed his search for the ladder. He felt a growing desperation now as night approached. He was sure there was a ladder—there had to be one. His hands were cold, and he was feeling the lack of food and water. *You can do this,* he kept telling himself.

Suddenly his hand came in contact with the top of a ladder, and hope returned as he realized that he was no longer trapped. He managed on the second attempt to get both legs across the wall to the top edge. The ladder was not visible beneath the tangled growth of ivy, and the rock edging was slick with rain, making any movement treacherous. "Don't look down, Liam," he whispered, gripping the iron ladder.

Young Twist had exceptionally strong hands and would need every ounce of strength in them to negotiate the descent. He swung across, hanging by his hands, and struggled with his good foot to find a rung beneath the vines, still unable to support himself with the other leg.

The rain ran into his eyes as he worked his foot through the growth and gained a toehold. He thought of his mother. She would be worried and had no doubt asked about him in town, prompting his friends to organize a search. If he was to slip to his death, how would his mother get by?—besides which, someone would have to get into town and raise the alarm. The rear of the building was a dark green tangle of shadows.

Liam moved slowly and with purpose, telling himself that there was no pain in his leg. The rain and the lack of light were advantageous in that he wouldn't be heard or seen, but nevertheless he proceeded with caution. If he was discovered now, there would be little he could do, and he didn't fancy becoming a meal in the dungeon. Flesh-eaters in Dunradin! Who would believe him? It was too outrageous.

Three quarters of the way down the ladder, Liam reached a window that was barely visible beneath the foliage. Pulling the vines aside, he risked a glance inside. A gold light shone through the murky glass.

Suddenly a face appeared in the window like a ghastly reflection. One of the Teriz had decided to check the weather at the precise moment that Liam had drawn back the vines. The spectre's milky eyes widened with shock, and he leaped back in surprise. Liam gasped aloud and lost his grip, slid the remainder of the way down, and fell heavily on his back. He landed with a thud on a pile of refuse that had recently been thrown from the building, and lost his wind. Liam struggled to catch his breath before the stranger inside could rouse the others.

The Macneils, who had circled back along the upper road towards their home, were hurrying across the area behind and above the old mill, when they saw a figure slide from the wall. Caleb recognized Liam in the dim light, but neither boy was familiar with the three individuals racing around the corner of the building.

Cardiff reacted quickly, picking up a sharp rock. He took careful aim and threw the projectile forcefully. It smashed into the face of the first Teriz with a wet tearing sound, forcing his eye from the badly broken socket.

"Good one," yelled his brother, throwing a rock of his own, as the remaining Teriz glared up at the hill. "Liam!" he called. "Up here."

The one-eyed creature was still howling in pain.

Liam, who had recovered, looked up in disbelief. "I can't" he called "My leg."

Cardiff launched a second rock, narrowly missing the other Teriz who, turning to retreat fell over the third. The brothers scrambled down the hill towards Liam as the injured howler joined the retreat.

"Who or what the bloody hell were them?" asked Caleb, helping his brother raise Liam to his feet.

"Oh, good Lord you wouldn't believe it." replied Twist, "Let's get away from here quickly; there's more of them inside." Caleb and Cardiff hauled their friend up the hill as he hopped on one foot.

"Are they all as ugly as that first bastard?" asked Cardiff.

"I didn't really get much of a look," Liam replied, "but I'll tell you this much, they're not from here, and they're big trouble."

The three turned towards Liam's home. "We were in the armoury ourselves," said Caleb.

"I know; I saw you leaving, why did he let you go?" asked Liam.

"Who, the bearded fellow?" "He seemed a little off to me," said Caleb.

"You don't know the half of it, they have prisoners below, I think they might be French." Liam winced at the image that came into his head. "We have to tell someone," he added, his voice suddenly desperate. As they approached his home, he explained how he had come to be on the roof of the armoury and what he had seen inside. "Not a word of this to my mother, at least not yet. I don't want to frighten her, and I don't want her left alone with those creatures about. I'll stay here, but you two must get word to Portus and Ronan. Pass on exactly what I have told you."

-37-

Padraic could find his father nowhere. Charlotte and her brothers had gone off towards the stables to find their father, and the mute was alone in the grocer's, surrounded by silence. There was a bad smell on the main floor, and Padraic opened the front door to let the night air in.

The rain had slowed to a drizzle, and he watched the water flow between the cobblestones towards Green's Guesthouse next door. There was a single light burning on the upper floor. Padraic remembered that the one place he had not looked was the cellar. He doubted that Portus would be there at this hour. There was not much down there aside from a crate or two of wine, and some root vegetables.

As Padraic passed the entrance to the cellar, he noticed that the door was ajar, and his nose told him that this was definitely the source of the bad odour. He approached the door but recoiled as his nostrils filled with a scent of rotting vegetables.

He made for the kitchen and retrieved an oil lamp which he carefully lit. Holding a handkerchief over his face, he opened the door with one foot. An animal must have crawled down there and died. Padraic held the lamp above his head and stepped forward, wondering where his dog Chowder had gotten to.

The shock of what he saw nearly made him lose his footing. He opened his mouth in a silent scream. The hand in which he held the lamp began to shake. He dropped the handkerchief and held the light with both hands as he fled from the doorway. There was no doubt that the body in the cellar was Portus—or what was left of him. He had not fallen and injured himself, but he was most certainly dead. Padraic knew this as clearly as he knew day from night.

As he rushed across the floor in panic, the assassins descended the back room steps, first two of the creepers, then four more. Padraic leaped out the shop door and rolled across the cobblestones, dropping the lamp. Getting to his feet, he continued down the alley, not daring to look back.

"Let the mute go," commanded Dafyd, holding the severed head aloft. "We have a delivery to make." Euther's underlings had exacted his revenge on the "Beast of Dunradin," and Portus's past had caught up with him. The big man had been indiscriminate while avenging the death of his parents, and several victims had been killed merely because they were English, and in the wrong place during the night of madness. Euther's wife, Morgana, was one of the victims.

"Here, wrap this up to go," said Dafyd, tossing the head to a smaller man. "Faustine will be here tomorrow for an inspection, wanting his trophy. Let's move, and close the door behind you."

The five Teriz left quickly, keeping to the shadows. Dafyd held back for a minute and stood in front of the guesthouse door, contemplating the situation with Fearghal. He didn't appear to have the fortitude required, and it would be up to Euther to decide his fate. Dafyd knew Faustine's mind. Fearghal would be told the full truth this time.

The Welshman had always been aware that Euther's full name was Dorian Euther de Faustine. He was Fearghal's real father, who had not in fact perished in a fight years ago.

Fearghal would be given the opportunity to prove his loyalty by killing Tyburn, and Dafyd would deal with Ronan, Caymus, and the other Maclearys. *Perhaps,* he thought, *the girl Charlotte will be spared for his amusement.* He decided to speak with Fearghal in the morning. The entire tale would be common knowledge. There was no longer a need for secrecy.

Faustine and his clan had been driven north, and Dunradin suited his needs on several levels—his wife's murder avenged, and before long, a population imprisoned. One way or another Tyburn would be done away with, and his little village would become Euther's private slaughterhouse. The elders would be fed upon, and the youth would serve as breeders. He would restock his half-blood army and fortify the village against intruders. Dafyd filled his lungs with cool night air and disappeared into the shadows.

From the window above, Fearghal watched his passage, pleased that the Welshman had not chosen to come up. He had watched the five Teriz slip down the same alley minutes earlier. *So it has begun.* The plan that had been set in motion so long ago was actually coming to fruition. The Teriz, or at least a number of them, had arrived, and no doubt Euther himself was close by. He had told himself for months that Tyburn and the others would be unharmed, but now that his lust for blood had abated, Fearghal saw things for what they were.

No one would be spared a role in this horrendous theatre of madness, and he had helped to provide a stage for Faustine and his followers. Fearghal had little idea of the monster he had become, but a keen awareness was beginning to creep into the back of his mind. As the truth began to come into view he had yet to realize the true cost of his recent battle with the demons in his blood.

For the most part, he felt strong and revitalized, but he knew it was not immediately apparent what he had lost. Because he had forsaken the treachery of his blood, he now lived, if that was the right word, without his previously vital body fluid. Every part of his body that had been fed with blood was in the process of changing. He felt an exhilarating lightness of being that confused him.

He waited for the heavy cloak of guilt and remorse that should be weighing him down, but he felt no such weight. Raising his hands to his cheeks, he observed that they had become extremely white and almost translucent. He watched in amazement as the lines of his palms seemed to shimmer and pulsate.

He stepped to the mirror and gazed with fascination at what he saw there. His lashes and eyebrows now matched the whiteness of his hair, and even his eyes had faded to a light gray. Blinking with disbelief, he lifted his shirt and discovered that his torso was the color of milk. He had the distinct feeling that he was fading, and suddenly wondered if it was possible that he might disappear altogether.

Eventually the obvious occurred to him: he no longer contained blood. *How is it that I am still living?* He gradually grew obsessed with the thought. *Perhaps I am no longer amongst the living. Did I perish in my attempt to break free of the craving?* He finished dressing, determined to discover the nature of his fate.

-38-

The sharp-eyed youngster Woodruff pointed to the grazing horses. "We no longer track horsemen" he said.

Caymus and Tyburn dismounted and searched the immediate area for signs of Faustine. "Nothing," said Tyburn. "I suggest we stable this pair with Ronan, and in the meantime lead them on foot with the other horses. Faustine could be anywhere in these woods."

Woodruff secured a length of rope through the bridles and joined the pair to the big Clyde. As the daylight began to dwindle, the party increased their pace, and before long they reached the smaller falls. Branan, Hugh, and the highlanders were seated on the very rock from which the children had earlier fished.

"He appears to have eluded you as well," said Brannan to Caymus.

"Aye," came the reply. "We have inherited two horses, so I assume that we are tracking a pair of villains."

"Unless of course," suggested Tyburn, "they are now tracking us. I feel we should now make for Ronan's stable in the village without delay."

"Agreed," said Branan. "Will we arrive before nightfall?"

"Certainly, if we leave at once," confirmed Caymus.

Ronan was somewhat startled to see the entourage of seven horsemen arriving at his stable all at once. Introductions were made, and all nine of the horses were stabled.

The children had previously returned to the top of high street with instructions to stay with their mother. Ronan had suggested they inform her of their strange day but without worrying her. He told them he would join them at home for supper shortly.

Caymus suggested that someone step over to the grocer's and call on Portus before they discussed very much and then volunteered to do it himself. "The grocer's is but a few minutes away, we will return very soon."

Seconds earlier Fearghal had decided that he should investigate the situation next door. It was quite obvious that something had gone amiss. Dafyd hadn't looked panicked when he left, but Fearghal wondered what business had taken place in the shop. If Portus was in when the strange occurrence took place, he would have seen Dafyd's Teriz companions, and that would not have been a favourable meeting.

He slipped down the stairs and entered the grocer's quietly. The smell hit him at once, and he made for the source. The main door opened as he was about to enter the cellar, and he closed the cellar latch silently, without entering, and stepped into a corner.

"Hello, Portus," called a voice. It was Caymus, the bowman. "Hello, big man. Are you about?" Caymus squinted in the darkness and stepped down the hall in Fearghal's direction. He glanced in the corner where Fearghal had just been before stepping out of the light to conceal himself.

Something made Caymus halt his retreat. He seemed to be looking directly through him, seeing nothing but the expanse of hallway beyond.

Fearghal closed his mouth and took a step forward into Caymus's path. The bowman suddenly stepped forward also and strode directly through the stunned Fearghal, stopping behind him. "No one home?" he called.

Fearghal reeled and caught himself against the wall. The sensation of another being stepping through his body had been intense. In that brief moment, he had connected with Caymus's emotions, feeling the fear and curiosity that occupied his stepbrother's thoughts.

An image of several horses flashed across his eyes. In that second he realized that if they stood together on the same spot, no secrets would be denied him. This amazing knowledge animated him, but he fell to his knees, stunned by the awareness that he had become some sort of ghost, unlikely to ever walk beside his fellow man again.

This was the price, then. The cost of his freedom was death, or more precisely, the narrow road between life and death, for surely this was not finality? He wondered if it was the memory of his body that appeared to contain him. Would it fade altogether to nothing? If this was his invisible spirit, then where was his actual body, the vessel of flesh and bone that he had inhabited for so many years?

Caymus closed the door and stepped into the street with a look of distaste on his face. It occurred to Fearghal that he should return to his room in the guesthouse and think things through. He walked to the door and reached for the handle, half expecting to reach right through the wood, but to his surprise this was not a problem.

Padraic, high above the street, saw the door open and close again of its own accord. The youngster rubbed his eyes, still wet with tears. He needed to retrieve ink and paper from the bedroom below. Lowering himself at the right-hand side of the roof, he clung to a drainpipe that passed the small side window of his room. An adult could not pass through the tiny leaded window, but Padraic could. He found his journal, some ink, and a pocketknife. Climbing up the pipe proved to be more difficult, but the youngster managed to return.

Settling into the dry warmth of his pigeon coop, the mute began to compose a message: *Portus dead in cellar I'm on roof beware Welsh – Pad.* He tore out the page and ripped off the excess paper, folding the note until it was the size of his thumbnail.

Padraic opened his knife and cut a small strip of fabric from the bottom of his shirt. *Arrow, you will do nicely,* he thought as he picked up a favourite pigeon. He held the note against Arrow's leg and wrapped the fabric around the message twice before knotting it. He lifted the bird in the air and flung it skyward. The carrier pigeon's release was witnessed by no one, with the exception of the large black bird roosting atop the church.

Padraic sat against the wall and put his head on his knees. Arrow would land on the sill of Tamlyn's window as it had been trained, and soon Ronan and the other adults would be aware of Portus's fate.

Padraic wrapped the blanket that he'd retrieved around himself and curled into a corner of the coop hidden behind a bale of straw, too stunned and racked with grief to consider any other options.

-39-

"What do you make of these tracks, William?"

"We appear to have been overlooked," replied Drake. "I don't believe we will have any difficulty reaching Dafyd before daybreak." The rain had stopped, and moonlight illuminated the narrow woodland path.

"Beautiful country, isn't it, William? I must say it will be very pleasant to reside in the valley."

The pair moved forward at a steady pace.

"I quite enjoyed my army days here. A pleasant people, these Scots, but you'll find they're a little on the excitable side. I do like a good challenge, though. Would that be the lights then?"

"Yes indeed," replied Drake. The village square lamps were visible in the distance. "If everything is in order, we shall have no resistance from Treacher." He was referring to Portus, who in Faustine's opinion was overdue, a reckoning, by a number of years.

"He probably thought he was going to live forever, the fat villain. He had more years than he deserved. I could never figure a man who would take up the practice of murder without the understanding of balance. You and I will suffer a small eternity of misery for our sins. Bit of a shame, really, but when it comes to sin, I simply cannot help indulging. Seriously, can you imagine anything worse than the drudgery of sainthood?" Euther rambled on in this fashion for some time until they reached the edge of town and he fell silent.

Meanwhile, at the smithy, several men were involved in a lively conversation. Ronan had assured the visitors that they were welcome to bed down in the stables, and Caymus was describing the morbid discovery in the High Wood to Branan Stoke and Hugh Maclean. The brothers of Fearghal would have preferred to have him present, but after being told of the abandoned carriage, they understood the urgency of the situation.

Caymus addressed Branan: "So you are telling us that the Welshman may be in league with this Faustine?"

"All I can tell you is that I don't know who he is, and I do know that he is not an agent of Her Majesty."

"Then why," interrupted Ronan, "would he warn us of an invasion, if he were part of that plan?"

"It's possible he needed to gain a foothold here and did so in a very clever manner," answered Branan.

"And what of Fearghal?" asked Tyburn. "What does his association with Dafyd imply?"

Branan glanced at Tyburn and then back to Ronan. "I'm afraid it appears that all three of them are Wraiths. I'm also concerned that their formation of an armoury here may indicate that a larger number of Teriz have avoided our traps than we first believed."

"Perhaps," suggested Hugh Maclean, "the villagers living closest to the armoury should be evacuated."

"We will have daylight on our side soon," said Branan. "I think Hugh makes a good point, and we should do that very thing. Fearghal and Dafyd's whereabouts must be confirmed without delay. If we can confine the enemy to the mill side of the river, it may be possible to organize and protect the population."

Tyburn merely stared at his sons in disbelief, and the brothers mirrored his shocked expression.

-40-

Liam Twist needed no encouragement to cross the river into town with his mother. He already felt uncomfortably close to the armoury and decided to take the pony his uncle had left, hitch it up to the hay cart, and ride across the far bridge to the other side of the river at first light.

The Macneil brothers were, as usual, in disagreement over which course of action would be the most practical. Cardiff shook his head. "I say we find one of them Maclearys and tell 'em what we seen, then go back home."

"Well, that's just plain stupid," said Caleb. "I don't like the idea of walking by the marsh in the middle of the night, then turning around and doing it again. I say we stay in town until morning, and then we head back."

"Aye and what if a group of those squinty-eyed bastards decides to go a-lookin' for our house?"

"Fine then, you go home and talk to the old folks, and don't answer the door. I'll go into town; there must be someone else knows something about this. And don't go falling in any holes."

"That's nae gonna happen," said Cardiff, turning and starting for home.

Caleb knew their plan made sense but still felt anxious about heading to town center in the dark, the more so now that he didn't have the company of Cardiff. His brother could by no means be described as clever, but his physical strength had come in handy more than once. The truth was, Caleb enjoyed the company of his brother. The lads' mother and father were very old and not terribly big on conversation. Gussie and Corb Macneil raised chickens, and kept to themselves for the most part.

The marshy area across the bridge was spanned by a narrow sandy path. In the wetter sections planking had been laid down, but it was rotting and slippery. The marsh path repair was long overdue. The cart road up towards the cemetery was used for horse and carriage, and took three times as long by foot.

The youngsters of Dunradin all knew the story of the Dead Man of the Marsh. Billy Bottlefly, many years ago the town undertaker, had met an untimely death crossing the street. A spooked horse kicked Billy in the head, and he died instantly. According to the story, an inexperienced assistant tried to transport Billy's coffin along the edge of the marsh without securing the box properly. When the death wagon hit a rock, poor Billy was tipped into the marsh and sucked beneath the mud, never to be retrieved.

Caleb sang nervously to himself as he negotiated the path. "Poor Billy Bottlefly crossed the road just to die, caused his widow untold grief, as he sank beside the Sleath." The youngster stopped singing and froze in his tracks. Not thirty meters away three approaching figures were silhouetted against an eerie light that had begun to form on the swampy lowland. Caleb could not retreat without drawing attention to himself. Not far to his right were the remains of a dead tree that had been sheared in half during a lightning storm years ago. It marked the halfway point of the trail.

As reluctant as he was to enter the swamp, Calebrealized this was his only option and quickly made for the dead tree, which was barely taller than himself. Fortunately the stump was wide enough to conceal the frightened youngster. Caleb quickly waded into the mud, making as little noise as he could. Crouching behind the trunk he held on to its side as mud and water oozed into his trousers. His knees began to sink into the slime and within seconds he was chest high in the bog gripping the tree roots in panic to keep from sinking further.

As they approached, Caleb recognized the bearded stranger. He narrowed his eyes lest they reflect the moonlight and give him away. He suppressed a shiver as the three stopped briefly opposite the tree. "Is it much farther" asked a whining voice, unfamiliar to him.

"Just across the way here," replied the bearded one.

"Well, let us carry on," continued the first voice. "I'm absolutely starving."

"I believe you'll find preparations to your liking" came the reply.

"Well, I would feel happier if your brother Fearghal had come to greet us as well."

The voices faded as they departed for the armoury. Caleb did not wait long before attempting to free himself from the mud. His foot found something solid close to the tree. *I'm standing on Billy Bottlefly's head*, he thought. *Don't be daft*, he argued with himself, half expecting a bony hand to pull him in.

The bog gave way with a moist sound as it released him to the path. He got to his feet quickly. Dripping with slime, and teeth chattering, he made his way up the remainder of the trail. It was slow going as his clothing was heavy with marsh mud, and his shoes in particular felt like heavy weights. The bog would have kept them, had they not been tied on so securely.

He had urinated in his trousers as he clung to the tree, realizing that it would make little difference. *Take that, Bottlefly.*
He recalled that his father had once told him about taking a tin of urine to the mill when he was young. It was good for cleansing the wool and profitable for the boys who made penny a piss.

Caleb soon reached the square and made for the smithy stables. The youngster was of course unaware of the gathering that was still taking place in the shop. The men were equally surprised to see a swamp-soaked youngster wander into the smithy at this hour.

"Young Macneil!" exclaimed Ronan. "Is it Cardiff then?"

"It's Caleb, sir."

"You're a hell of a sight, lad. What's happened?" Caleb recounted all that Liam had told him and included his armoury visit with

Dafyd and the rescue of Liam. He described what he had seen of the other two men.

Branan was particularly interested in the sinkhole that the youngster had described. "And there's the mystery of our missing Frenchies solved," he declared. "Eaten alive, I'll warrant."

"Ronan, if you possess more silver, I would appreciate the use of it," said Branan. "Faustine is no doubt settling happily into his new home. We must manufacture a little surprise for him. Young Caleb, get out of those wet clothes, and take what rest you can. Then I will require you to gather some trusted friends across the river to organize a retreat. You should all carry a staff across your shoulders, in case you fall into one of those damn holes."

Tyburn spoke up: "It was some brave of you to come through the marsh at night, lad; you may have already saved several lives."

Ronan winked at Caleb. "I'll bring some of Tamlyn's clothes. You're about his size." He slipped from the room and reappeared moments later.

Caymus had a question for Branan. "Tell me, why is it the Welshman walks amongst us, yet the others cower from the light of day? Even Fearghal does not fear the light."

Branan smiled. "The answer is not all that complicated. If the Welshman walks in light, it is because he consumes the flesh of others. If he were merely a blood-drinker, he could only tolerate the light briefly."

Ronan looked alarmed "Do you mean to imply that Fearghal is also a flesh-eater?"

"The Welshman was observed in his lair consuming man's flesh," said Branan. "Fearghal, by your claim, was born of a gentlewoman. Therefore, if we imagine that he is related to Dafyd as I have been informed, his natural father may have been a Wraith, which makes him half-caste and able to bear the light."

"I slew the man that fathered Fearghal myself!" exclaimed Tyburn. "He could not have been one of these creatures."

"Unless," interrupted Branan, "he feigned death. A wounded Wraith can take on the appearance of a corpse for several hours."

"No, it could not be," said Tyburn. "Dorian could not have been alive all these years, it would be too unfair."

Branan's eyes opened wide. "This name is known by few," he said quietly. "Dorian Euther de Faustine is the beast's full name. He forbade his followers to utter the name Dorian. I would hazard a guess that Fearghal and Dafyd are not cousins but half-brothers."

"I wish I knew where Fearghal has gotten to," said Caymus. "I would burn him in the square." Tyburn sat in stunned silence. At length he announced, "I will try to sleep a little now." The old man suddenly looked very tired. Caymus took him to his bed and fetched an extra blanket for himself.

-41-

Fearghal looked down at the cold body on the bed. It was himself he saw, pale and dead. The sheets beneath his body were red with blood. He wondered briefly whether he wasn't better off here in the spirit world, ageless and endless. He was out of harm's way, but here was no sleep and no death. He feared he would go mad and considered that madness might be the ultimate escape. Unfortunately, Euther would kill them all, and he would have no choice but to witness the carnage.

He couldn't allow this. It would not be long before Dafyd would grow curious and wish to speak with him. They would come to the guesthouse and discover his body, and it would be buried, or worse yet taken to the armoury and devoured. Considering that his corpse appeared to be devoid of blood, he thought that the last option was unlikely, but he realized that his body had to be removed and hidden.

An image of the bell tower across the square came to mind. He didn't have a lot of time before the sun would rise. He sat the body up and wrapped the arms around his neck from behind. He leaned forward, tightly gripping the wrists, and walked forward dragging the almost weightless body from the room.

If anyone had been in the town square, they would have witnessed a bizarre and frightening sight, a naked stranger, pale and white-haired, appeared to lurch forward towards the church, gliding across the stones on his toes. His arms were joined together in his front like a ghostly diver, with his head hanging askew to the side.

Fearghal climbed through the bell tower's trapdoor and pulled the body inside. After hiding it in a musty corner, he left, closing the door above him, and slipped out of the church to recross the square.

-42-

Caleb had discarded his wet clothing and lay by the smithy fire wrapped tightly in a clean blanket. Unsettling visions of the three pale creepers plagued his dreams that night, and the youngster tossed and turned as he slept.

In his dreams, Caleb encountered a ghostly and pathetic character that sat in the square begging. The ghost was naked to the waist and his emaciated chest was covered in deep scars. Wooden nails had been pounded through his outstretched palms, but the wounds refused to bleed. "Pull them out," implored the ghost in a mournful voice. "Please, the pain. Please, let me bleed!"

Caleb reached across and gripped the nails, one in each fist, and pulled them easily from the spectre's hands. Another pair of nails replaced the first immediately. "Let me bleed," begged the ghost again. Caleb reached down and pulled out the nails again and again, over and over, tossing them onto the cobblestones with a clatter until the square was filled with nails.

The central fountain and square began to revolve in a great spinning circle, with Caleb and the ghost at its centre. Around the circle's centre appeared frozen-eyed ponies, attached to carousel poles. Upon one of the sad animals rode his father.

Corb Macneil held tightly to the pole while his head nestled in the crook of his other arm. Corb's mouth was contorted in a ghastly grin, and the tail of a blood red snake protruded from his nostril while its head hung from between his clenched teeth. His father spun quickly past, replaced by another horse on which his mother's ruined body rode. Her arms had been shorn off at the shoulders, and she swayed precariously while blood leaked from her wounds like dark syrup. Flies covered the lower half of her face like a beard of hungry insects. The following pony was ridden by a bone thin stranger. He sat in the saddle backwards and swung a huge white phallus in the foetid air, slapping it against the hind quarters of the animal beneath him.

Caleb gnashed his teeth and groaned, mercifully waking himself up long enough to pass from the nightmare into a gentler dream in which the dead had no part to play.

-43-

As he crossed the square again, it occurred to Fearghal that he could no longer discern any details of himself. His limbs were not visible, and he felt as though he were passing through the air like a breeze. He could no longer reach out and open a door but instead could pass through it easily. If he had not hidden his body when he did, it would have remained in the guesthouse, for he no longer had the ability to move solid objects.

The various details of the village were beginning to fade. Glancing towards the grocer's, he could now see into the rooms of the lower floor. He approached the building and could see into the cellar from the outside. He recognized Portus at once, despite the fact that the big man's head was no longer there. This was the work of Dafyd, he was certain.

Tyburn, he decided, must be made aware of his oldest friend's killing. Looking about, Fearghal could see no sign of the youngster Padraic. He turned towards Ronan's shop, hoping that Caymus would be bedded there as usual. Even better: upon his arrival, there was Tyburn himself. Fearghal looked down at his stepfather, the man that he owed much to. "Portus is dead in his cellar," he said, leaning close.

He had spoken aloud and was surprised at the hollow echo of his voice. "Portus lies dead in his cellar," he repeated with more volume. Tyburn stirred, his lips moving wordlessly. The old man's eyes fluttered. "Portus?" he mumbled, then turning on his side he began to snore.

Fearghal looked about the smithy workshop and then the stables. Several men were bedded there, and he recognized Caymus amongst them but did not see Ronan. He paused, undecided as to where he would go next. Then it came to him. He had no option other than to cross the river to the armoury, where he would see to unfinished business.

Before long, Ronan returned to his shop with Tamlyn and Murdoch. The sun had risen, but was hidden behind heavy clouds. Charlotte remained at home, extremely displeased with her father. "I don't want your mother left alone just now," he had explained.

"Then leave Tamlyn at home," she replied angrily.

"I need your help with sewing," said Ceana, "and Tamlyn is useless with a needle and thread." The old woman knew how anxious her daughter was to see young Liam but insisted that she stay. The story that Ronan had relayed to her was horrifying, and she was frightened enough for her sons but understood from all that she had heard that the daylight hours were not dangerous. There were after all only six families to be evacuated from across the river and with any luck they would all be safely in town before noon. She was not aware that Liam and his mother were already on the river road, and word had spread amongst the other families that they were to leave as soon as possible.

-44-

Faustine's arrival at the armoury the previous night coincided closely with the arrival of Dafyd, who had managed to enter the village for the purpose of murder and return to Lilyvine with alarming speed.

The Welshman, still robed in blood and sweat, greeted Euther with a wet handshake. "On a platter, as it were," he said gesturing towards the grisly trophy behind him.

Portus's head sat on a pewter serving dish, and a shiny green apple had been pushed into his mouth. "Oh my dear, aren't you special?" said Faustine, winking at Dafyd. "I am feeling somewhat peckish"—he approached the head carefully—"and you saved me the eyes, how thoughtful."

Drake, who had no desire to witness the ritual further, decided to take his leave and bowed graciously. "Gentlemen," he said, "bon appetit." He paused, "if I may retire?"

"Up those stairs to your right, Mr. Drake," replied Dafyd. William Drake, who was accustomed to his benefactor's strange hours, had decided to sleep while he could. Morning was drawing close, and he wanted a short rest before exploring the river by daylight. He turned on his heel and quickly departed.

"We will take our repose below" said Dafyd, anxious to impress Euther with his accomplishments. Amongst other matters, the situation with Fearghal required attention. Drake had the choice of a large armchair or a low cot which was covered in a single blanket. He could smell the blanket from where he stood and opted for the chair. Dunradin seemed a cold damp place and the chill rested in his bones. He was hungry himself, but nothing had been offered, and soon after deciding that he was getting to old for this nonsense, he fell asleep.

-45-

Domnash spotted the pigeon in flight below him and began to dive. As his speed increased, he flexed his talons. When his streaming form arrived swiftly over the pigeon's body, the sharp talons ripped through feathers and skin into muscle.

Domnash landed with the bird's neck in his beak. The shape-changer took his alternate form quickly and picked up the pigeon by its feet in order to remove the cloth wrapped around its leg. A folded note fell to the ground, and Domnash reached down and retrieved it. After reading Padraic's message, he tucked it into his vest and tossed the bird aside.

Minutes later he was circling in the brightening sky above Lilyvine, a dark silhouette visible against the white and gray morning clouds. To the roof sentinel he grew in size with each descending circle, like a charcoal drawing come to life. The messenger was not unexpected. Bergil had drawn the short straw for daylight duty, and it pained him to scan the skyline even with the dark glass spectacles of the watch. If those selfish bastards below would have allowed him some man food, his head would not be aching just now.

The raven fell to the roof like large dust particles that swirled hypnotically into the form of a lean, menacing stranger. He glanced briefly at the guard and stepped past him into the stairwell with no acknowledgment.

-46-

After a short sleep, Drake rose, anxious to take in some fresh air. The armoury carried a subtle stink of dying Frenchmen that wafted up through the heavy floorboards like a whispered insult. None of the night dwellers appeared to be about as Drake buttoned his greatcoat and slipped out the front door.

A thought recurred in his mind as he made his way toward the river: *What if I kept walking; walked straight into town and spoke with the trackers? What if I purchased a horse and rode across the border, and all the way home to London?* Before many days passed, Dafyd's wife Colette would arrive. Dealing with the Welshman's shifting mood was one thing, but dealing with that shrew Colette was an entirely different matter.

Drake found himself strolling along the Sleath as he pondered his next move. The fact was, he had grown bored with Wraiths and sensed that their luck was running out. He was no longer a young man and had amassed a tidy fortune that would allow him to retire comfortably and perhaps write an account of his adventures.

Faustine was a creature who feared his own death deeply, yet craved it more than anything else. There was a time when Euther's only desire was to rid the earth of blood-drinkers by breeding the disease out of their systems. Creating new breeds was an idealistic experiment that backfired: he quickly lost interest in it, and before long he was saddled with a growing army of underlings. When the cannibalism started, Drake realized that Euther's "in the name of science" credo no longer held water, and it would only be a matter of time before the situation deteriorated completely.

William clasped his hands behind his back and made for the bridge just as a horse and cart came into view, followed by a second and third. He smiled and resisted the urge to wave them on. It appeared these Scots were on to Faustine's game. The small cavalcade was preceded by Cardiff, Tamlyn, and Murdoch carrying wooden staves The youngsters jousted playfully as they closed the distance between the quarry and the bridge. A small number of younger children tagged along behind them.

Nelly Maguire skipped along happily, pleased to be out for a morning's adventure with the larger children. Drake watched the youngster, wondering if it was possible that he had once been that young and carefree. Little Nelly spotted a gaily dressed doll that lay two feet off the road on a small path and raced towards it with a squeal of delight. Megan, the youngster's mother, ran after Nelly, unaware what had caught her youngster's attention.

The young woman gave a cry as Nelly vanished before her eyes. "Nooo," she screamed, falling to her knees. William Drake knew at once that a sinkhole must have been strategically placed on the narrow path and raced to the spot with no hesitation. "Quickly, your staves" he demanded, removing his belt.

Murdoch and Tamlyn passed the stranger their jousting sticks quickly and watched as he fastened them together and lowered the long pole into the opening. The tall stranger then lowered himself into the darkness. The child's dress had caught on a severed tree root, and she was suspended a mere three feet from the hard clay floor of the damp tunnel. Tears ran down Nelly's face as she reached for William and wrapped her little arms around his neck, sobbing convulsively.

Drake could not recall when, if ever, he had held a small child. Looking up, he saw the three boys peering at him from above. Cardiff and another lad took hold of Tamlyn's ankles and lowered him headfirst.

"Hold tight," he squeaked; "don't drop me."

Drake raised Nelly above his head, and Tamlyn was able to grab her tiny wrists. "Pull now," he called, and soon little Nelly was in her mother's arms.

Drake, gripping the pole and digging his heels into the wall of the sinkhole, soon returned to solid ground. "Thank you so much," cried the child's mother, embracing Drake.

"This must be filled in," said William, carefully releasing himself from the woman's arms. "As soon as possible, but you must move along quickly; leave it to me."

"Hurry now, there's nothing to be gained from all this sentiment." Drake brushed the dirt from his breeches and turned back towards the bridge. As he moved along, a shudder seized him at the thought of what might have been, had he not removed the youngster from the sinkhole. Murdoch seemed to sense the stranger's unease and urged the group of travelers to continue on their way more rapidly.

William made his way to the river's edge at the base of the bridge and washed the mud from his hands. The face he saw reflected in the water was shockingly unfamiliar. Tears had run from his dark eyes, leaving curious damp trails across his craggy face.

He lifted his head and stared at the armoury and then glanced about at his surroundings. The quiet little village of Dunradin appeared to grey and wither before his eyes as he considered what Dorian had planned. It came to him like a sharp needle to the heart: His entire life had been a complete and utter failure.

He removed his coat and used the collar to wipe the tears from his eyes. He looked around and quickly found a heavy boulder which he placed in his open jacket. No one would miss him, no small child would cry for him. Drake was completely destroyed by the sudden onslaught of emotions that were so foreign to him.

He slung the heavy stone across his shoulder and made his way laboriously to the center of the bridge. Then he lifted the weight with a massive effort to the wall of the bridge. Leaning forward, he wrapped the sleeves around his neck and tightly tied the knot. With no hesitation William Drake threw his long legs over the side. Then, gripping the weight, he dropped to the water below.

As they approached the town center, Tamlyn imagined that he heard a splash back in the direction of the river, and glanced behind him briefly. "Do you know something?" he said to his brother. "That gentleman didn't tell us his name, but it's certainly fortunate for us that he came along when he did."

-47-

Padraic rubbed his eyes and yawned. He had slept late into the morning and was dreaming of breakfast, until the terrible reality of the previous evening returned. Portus was slain, and he was trapped on the rooftop, afraid to leave the safety of his pigeon coop.

Where was Arrow? He should have returned by now. The youngster stumbled to the front of the roof and peered cautiously over the edge. Below lay the body of his father. His upper extremities were covered with a blanket and one of his large boots was missing. It had taken six men to lift the body onto the undertaker's cart.

Padraic began to tremble, and his eyes filled with tears again. He was puzzled. Tamlyn should have arrived by now if his message had been delivered.

The distraught youngster sensed a movement behind him and turned quickly. Here was a lean-looking villain dressed in black, his arm a blur as he released the knife that flew through the air, grazing the boy's shoulder as he dove for cover. The blade sunk into the wood behind him with a thud. Padraic yanked the homemade whistle from his shirt and blew into it as hard as he could, producing a loud shrill note. It was a full two seconds before the whistle's call was matched from below.

The dark stranger glared at the lad, then rose into the air and took the shape of a raven. Padraic got to his feet and watched in amazement as the creature flew off in the direction of the river.

"Padraic, down here," called Tamlyn. The mute leaned over the wall again and waved at his young friend, indicating that he was on the way down. He pulled the heavy-bladed dagger from the wood and recognized the note that was bound to the handle with sinew. The youngster's face flushed with anger as he understood the fate of his prize pigeon.

He tucked the blade into his belt and swore a silent oath, promising to return the knife to its owner. Grief had, in a very short time, hardened the young man with a bitter dose of reality. Grim determination remained on his face as he was greeted with sympathy by his friends below.

Tamlyn was quick to assure Padraic that he was not alone, and they would all stand together. The mute took in the collection of faces that had gathered in the store and nodded slowly. Several of the strangers returned his gaze with curiosity.

Ronan broke the silence. "With your anticipated blessing, Master Padraic, we have formed emergency council here in your father's shop, as we arrange the details of his, er, finalities." He placed a hand on the boy's shoulder. "With our deepest sympathies," he added quietly.

Padraic wiped his eyes and indicated to the gentlemen that they should continue their business with haste. Still numb with grief and fear, he sat with Tamlyn, content to observe the meeting.

"I propose," continued Ronan, "that we take Portus to the burial rock as soon as possible." Everyone nodded in solemn agreement. "Fergus Green has kindly agreed to put up families at no cost, and the homes this side of the Sleath are now being evacuated. Word has spread quickly regarding the enemy in our midst. There are perhaps thirty able-bodied men here now and another twenty arriving from river's edge, and I assure you that all of us, man woman and child, are now regarded by our former guests as—food."

"Indeed," added Branan, "the consumption of human flesh strengthens these Teriz to the point that they are no longer afraid of daylight. If you avoid being, shall we say, consumed, the horde will be driven into darkness. We have already discussed the danger of sinkholes, and I urge those of you who are aware of them to pass on the information to others. Once located, they will be blown up."

Fergus Green raised his hand. "Being as we can see the river from here, I'm for placing a chap up on the roof as a spy-type feller."

"Excellent idea," agreed Ronan, "highest point this side of the village."

Branan said, "I would suggest a series of watchers be placed above High Street to guard against entry from the forest as well."

"Certainly," Ronan replied, "and I think possibly the young ones would be willing to take care of that." He glanced in the direction of his son. "Many eyes will be needed, and the sharper the better, perhaps something along the lines of a civil defense league."

For some time the decisions were discussed and reaffirmed, as more and more Dunradians arrived at the store. The remains of Portus had been quietly removed from the square as to not cause a panic amongst the townspeople. Caymus offered to help make crossbows. The bolts would have points forged with a large percentage of silver from Ronan's shop. A few of the townsfolk were leery of the trackers, not trusting their intentions. Soon, however, it was understood that they were not responsible for the Teriz occupation and were in fact invaluable due to their knowledge of the beasts' habits.

"Let it be clear," repeated Branan: "these Teriz are here for one reason, to feed on you and your children. Furthermore, they had planned to breed you as a source of food for generations to come. Be assured that, as painful as it is to realize, any livestock or pets you have left behind will not survive."

Branan cleared his throat. "I ask you to pardon my bluntness, but this is no time to mince words, and I want everyone to understand how close your village came to annihilation. We are all very fortunate that young Twist and his companions stumbled across Faustine's lair when they did."

"I think the younger children should be housed in the church with their mothers," offered Ian Finch. The group was in general agreement, and Charlotte was asked to organize the task of seeing to the little ones. She was pleased to be considered mature enough for the job and left at once to see to the details.

Padraic passed a note to Ronan. "Please regard the room you are in as a war room," he read aloud. "Portus would have had it no other way." The youngster had established his ownership of the building and displayed his intelligence and generosity without missing a beat.

-48-

The raven Domnash was not anxious to report back to Faustine, having failed in his attempt to kill the boy. He paused at the top of the armoury to mull over the situation. The shape-changer's thin legs carried him across the roof in a nervous pacing of sorts. He muttered, "Options, options are what I have, no worries … just think, think."

Suddenly he stood perfectly still and stared blankly at the entrance to the stairwell for a full minute. "Flight," he said aloud and took to the air.

The raven caught an air current and levelled off high above the river. The town center below was crawling with people. He dropped his right shoulder and began a descent towards the spire of Dunradin's church.

Caleb Macneil grabbed his brother by the shoulder and pointed skyward "Look at the size of that bleedin bird," he exclaimed.

Cardiff angled his head in Domnash's direction just as the shape-changer passed above and released the contents of his bowels. "Shite!" he bellowed. Caleb and Murdoch broke into peals of laughter.

Cardiff cuffed his brother across the ear and hurried to the fountain, anxious to clean the muck from his forehead. Caleb laughed all the harder when his brother entered the fountain and ducked beneath the water. He remerged sending broad handfuls of water in the direction of his comrades.

Soon a full water fight was under way, and the village square rang with the catcalls and challenges of young boys. Their gaiety provided a respite from the dark business at hand for several minutes, until the morning air was shattered with a panicked scream from the direction of the church. Several heads turned sharply toward the steps where a woman stood holding her shaking hands to her mouth. She leaned against the doorway looking pale. It turned out that one of the curious children had found a body in the bell tower.

Presently Ronan appeared at the foot of the church steps, his mouth set in a grim frown. He confirmed in a tone of disbelief that the body was in all likelihood that of Fearghal. Poor little Winston Green was visibly traumatized, having discovered the remains of Fearghal in a less than attractive state of decay. He could not keep his bulging eyes from staring blindly at the entrance to the tower.

Caymus seemed less shaken by the news than the others and suggested that perhaps now they would never know the full extent to which Fearghal was involved with the plot. The bowman had arrived to find that rats had very recently chewed through one of the cheeks of the deceased, and his exposed teeth formed a ghastly, mocking grin. After covering the corpse with a blanket, he arranged with the trackers to have the body moved to the same location as Portus.

-49-

In the meantime, the young people, who had been swiftly returned to the reality of their situation, held a meeting and decided that the proposed Defense League should be headed by one of their own, elected by vote. It was also decided that thirteen would be the age limit for inclusion in the league.

Liam Twist was the unanimous choice, and that evening Ronan offered the use of his stables as league headquarters. Liam, whose leg was much improved, nodded in agreement as Branan Stoke repeated his warnings. "Please understand, you are to take no risks. I can't stress this enough. Your observations may well be the key component of our survival. Keep your eyes open, and communicate with each other at all times. Assign yourself a captain, Mr. Twist, and see that you all arm yourselves in your preferred fashion."

The discovery of Fearghal's body had put everyone in a sombre mood, following closely as it did the brutal death of Portus. The fact that there was no apparent cause of death and no visible sign of any type of confrontation, only added to the fear enveloping the citizens of Dunradin.

Outside of the circle of trackers, the fact that Fearghal's body was devoid of blood was not discussed. This detail was intentionally downplayed in the hopes of keeping everyone's spirits elevated. Murdoch was pleased to serve as Liam's captain and spoke to his uncle Caymus about weaponry.

"Your designation is that of guardian and observer. Therefore, I would suggest, as your role involves defence, that you all carry something small and sharp, but as you will find, your voice will be your best weapon against the Teriz.

"I suggest you each wear one of Padraic's clever whistles around your neck.

"Raising the alarm is really all you can do. You may slow the enemy briefly, but you cannot kill them.

"Remember," he warned, "the Teriz are the lower caste of these creatures but are just as crafty and dangerous as the Wraiths themselves—or so we are told. I would like to put that theory to the test myself."

"What about silver?" asked Murdoch.

"I am told that silver mixed with lead shot will be effective," replied Caymus. "Your father is at his forge now, crafting a variety of projectiles Ask Ronan to forge you each a hand knife with silver at the point, then pray that you won't have to use it."

Branan, who had not spoken to this point, stepped forward and urged the group of youngsters to come closer. He spoke in a hushed tone. "If by some great stroke of misfortune you are captured by one of these creatures, I would strongly urge you to consider using the blade in this fashion." He plunged an imaginary knife into his chest. "Better you should die then become like them."

Caymus glared sharply at Brannan. "You will scare these lads witless!" he exclaimed.

"Better they should know the truth, than be saucing about like boy soldiers," the other retorted. "Knowledge is often the best weapon." Murdoch and even Liam had indeed grown somewhat pale, and Tamlyn's eyes were like saucers. "At any rate," said Branan, putting a hand on Tamlyn's shoulder, "although the defense of Dunradin does not rest on you, we will rely greatly on your assistance. Leave what is beyond the river to us, and keep an eye turned inward to the streets of your village. Be vigilant and trust no one."

As they left the blacksmith's, Stoke grinned at Caymus. "Those lads are made of stern stuff. Still, I am sending Woodruff north today to rally some highlanders to our cause. Your men are hardy enough, but they are farmers and more used to pitchforks than pistols."

"Well then," replied Caymus, sounding peeved, "silver their forks, and watch how handily they might harvest this crop of Teriz."

"I count on it" said Branan. "And I'm sure you will impress me with your bowmanship."

-50-

"Poor wee lad!" exclaimed Ceana. "Having to see that frightful sight, and right here in the blessed kirk, of all places."

"Don't you think that sleeve is long enough, Mother?" asked Charlotte.

"Oh my goodness, look at that, I've been so distracted that I've knit myself half way into next week." She yanked on the wool, unraveling much of what she had done in the last hour, and shook her head. "Why has this horror come to our little village?"

"I'll make us some tea, Mother," said Charlotte.

"That's exactly what I need, thank you. I know you'd prefer to be with the boys, especially Liam, but I really need your help here, and Mrs. Green is quite useless at the moment." Makeshift beds had been prepared for the children, and a thorough search of the building had been mounted to reassure the women that no intruders were hidden upstairs or down. Although nothing had been found, they still felt uneasy, so a guard was posted at the front entrance, and Hugh Maclean promised the ladies that he himself would walk past every hour.

Ceana confided to Charlotte that she had not slept well from the first day that Fearghal had returned to Dunradin. She wondered why he had not come sooner and whether he'd perhaps known more than he had let on. There were too many unanswered questions for her liking, and it was the variety of possible answers that kept her awake at night. Ronan's wife was a woman who preferred a predictable and balanced life, and she was already fussing about her house at the top of the street being unprotected from whatever menace that was lurking out there.

After tea had been brewed, she suggested to Charlotte to take a quick jaunt over to the grocer's to pick up some blankets and see what news there was. If anything of importance had happened, she wanted to know, and the errand would give her daughter a chance to check on the welfare of her younger brothers.

Ceana was always thinking ahead and realized that if they were to be bunked at the church for a length of time, the weather would soon be cooler as autumn was on the way down from the mountains. The young woman was thankful for the break from the children, as they were quite tiresome. Most of them were oblivious to the situation and buzzed about full of energy, feeling that a prolonged outing in town was as natural as a summer fortnight camping in the hills.

Nelly Maguire, who had recovered completely from her fall, expressed the wish that she should never have to go back home from this perfectly wonderful holiday. The young girl was of course unaware that it would be a matter of some time indeed before anyone would be allowed to occupy the homes along the banks of the Sleath. Some of the citizens were already questioning the abrupt exodus that had left the north bank empty. They had yet to see any personal danger and had abandoned their homes quickly in the general panic that had spread through the lower village.

Quite a number of the men and a few of the women were gathered outside the grocer's when Charlotte arrived from across the square. The young woman looked up and saw her brother on the roof. Padraic and Tamlyn had noted her approach and motioned for her to enter the building through the seldom-used side door. She bounded up the stairs to the roof, more than a little disappointed to see that Liam was not with them.

"Look there," said Tamlyn, pointing to a wisp of smoke in the eastern sky. "That's a river home burning this side."

Charlotte squinted into the fading light of the early evening. "You can see miles from here," she said with surprise. "Where's Murdoch?"

"He and Liam have gone down through the woods toward the river to see what they can. Don't worry" he added, seeing the alarm register on her face. "They won't go too close, and we'll see them returning from here."

-51-

Only after Jubilant Smith stumbled into town with half of his scalp missing did the crowd settle down and begin to realize that they were better off here on the high ground.

Smith had sworn that he would never give up his cottage and his chickens to a bunch of smoked-out Frenchies and refused to leave with the others. He collapsed in the middle of the square, mumbling incoherently as his blood stained the grout between the cobblestones. "Filthy sons o' whores," he managed to gurgle, before someone turned him on his side to keep him from choking.

A note was sewn to the shoulder of the old man's soiled jacket. It contained two symbols in red, the Roman numeral II and a three-pronged fork. Seth Willitt, who had turned the man over, crossed himself quickly and leaned in closer to see if Smith was still breathing. A final sharp intake of breath signalled the old farmer's demise. His legs shot out straight and his head snapped back with a moist cracking finish.

"Damn it, Jube, you stubborn fool," said Raine Waters, who had joined the small crowd that gathered around the body.

"Looks like someone parted his hair with a claw hammer," added Willitt. I'm surprised he made it this far."

Tyburn Macleary, who had been called to the scene, tore the note from Smith's jacket. "I think he was allowed to come this far," said the old doctor. "This is a warning."

When Ronan arrived, Tyburn drew him aside and passed the note to him. "Unless I'm mistaken, the Teriz are not aware of Fearghal's misfortune. My guess would be that they are referring to this victim as number two after Portus."

"I think you're probably right," agreed Ronan, "which makes Fearghal's death all the more confusing. I had better speak with Branan."

Willis and Waters carried the old man's body away, and Fergus Green brought a bucket to wash the blood from the street.

-52-

Liam and Murdoch peered over the hedge towards the spiral of smoke that was beginning to darken the sky above their heads. "They're going to burn all the homes," whispered Liam.

"Let's go back," urged Murdoch. "They will have seen the smoke back in town by now anyway."

The two boys had dressed in the colours of the forest and rubbed wood ash on their faces. They were close to invisible as they made their way back to the village through the trees. Murdoch came to a sudden stop and pointed wordlessly at the ground in front of him while he sidestepped a sinkhole. Liam nodded and took a length of white ribbon from his pocket and fastened it to a branch that curved conveniently across the trap. They hurried on, anxious to be back in the town center before the light of day completely vanished.

"There they are" called Tamlyn. Charlotte, who had gone down the stairs to find blankets, didn't hear her brother and went about the business of completing her errand. She had stayed on the roof longer than necessary and felt that she should get back to the church before the little ones had turned in.

Padraic peered over the edge of the roof at the two figures that were scrambling across grassy verge that stretched from the foundation of the grocer's building along a gentle slope to the edge of the trees.

-53-

"Damn you, Drake!" the shrill voice called. "Where is that slinking bag of vermin?'

Euther had consumed far too much wine, and he was in the mood for some powders. His shirt was stained deep red with food and drink. What remained of Portus Treacher's head lay on its side in the corner. Most of the skin had been gnawed off, and it glistened in the candlelight, empty mocking sockets black against the pumpkin-coloured flesh.

Faustine stared back at the trophy and whimpered in a childlike voice, "William dear, where are you, naughty William?"

The knot in Drake's jacket had come loose, and he'd floated to the surface and drifted into a tangle of tree roots that held him to the shore. Dafyd poked absently at the bloated body with a long stick while scanning the outline of the village which was emerging through an early mist. *What in the name of hell has happened here?* he wondered. There was no love lost between him and Drake, and the death was going to be nothing more than a huge inconvenience. Faustine was too used to having a servile monkey at his side, and Dafyd had no intention of filling the void. *Damn you, Drake,* he thought, *and damn Fearghal for vanishing when he did.*

The Welshman's eyes hurt. He turned and made his way back to Lilyvine. High above on a branch of the tree, Domnash looked about. The sun was slowly breaking through a mixture of mist and smoke colouring the Sleath an unhealthy pink. He cocked his head to one side wondering if there was anything of value in Drake's pockets.

Tanner Smead sat on the armoury steps and concentrated on cleaning out his nose with one long twisting finger. "Job done," he said as Dafyd approached. "Payment expected."

"When you have completed the task," the Welshman replied. "The agreement is one house per night until they are all destroyed." Dafyd moved his boot closer to the servant's leg, ready to direct a kick to his ribs if necessary.

Then he looked down his nose towards Smead, suddenly revaluating the young man. "Tanner, how would you like to deliver a message for me to the chief?"

Smead was puzzled by the kindly tone. "Big Chief?" he asked.

Smead lived behind the hill that rose up at the rear of Lilyvine. His home was a small shed on the outskirts of the village. The general opinion in town was that Tanner, a man of twenty-seven or so years, had the capabilities of a five-year-old child. He was rarely seen and mostly forgotten.

"You go inside and tell Big Chief that William has drowned in the river."

A worried look colored the youngster's face. Smead was in awe of Faustine, who he had met on two previous occasions. "It's okay?" he asked.

"Yes it's fine. You go on in and tell him what I told you. Then do just as he asks, and you'll be paid a very large reward." He feigned a smile and nudged Tanner towards the door.

Dafyd knew that Euther had been drinking all night and was on the verge of passing out. He would wait until Smead had located Faustine before entering the armoury himself for some much-needed rest. Soon he heard the scream from outside the large door and waited another full minute before slipping quietly into the building.

-54-

Despite the increase in occupants, Green's Guesthouse was very quiet, and Dunradin's city centre appeared to have survived its first overpopulated night without incident. Women and children had bedded down in the church, and Green's housed husbands and fathers who had seldom spent a night away from their spouses.

For a time, in the early hours of the morning, the guesthouse walls vibrated with the sound of snoring farmers, which was eventually replaced by the much more melodic tunes of songbirds. Next door on the roof of the grocer's, pigeons cooed, and down on the street a horse tethered by the fountain whinnied and stamped a heavily shod hoof. The sun rose in a clear sky, and there was only a hint of smoke in the air from the previous evening's fire. Up on the roof, Murdoch, Liam, and Tamlyn had burrowed into the straw-laden coop and were huddled in one corner still asleep while Padraic took advantage of the early light to write in his journal.

Journal entry:

Much has happened since my last journal entry. It's hard to know where to begin. My father, rest his soul, was right to be suspicious of the visitors from the south. They have killed the dear man in a most brutal and violent manner, leaving me with a broken heart and a bleak outlook for the future.

We are, as I write, on the brink of war, here in our little village, beset by spectres who seek to control our very existence. The only thing standing between ourselves and the creatures is the river Sleath.

Liam has described a horrible scene of carnage in the basement of the old mill that is the stuff of nightmares. He is the leader, along with Murdoch, of what we are calling the Home Defence League. It's generally believed that Ronan's half-brother Fearghal took his own life. That brings the count to five dead in a very short span of time, if you count the dwarf in the woods, and I didn't really know either of them.

Until last week nobody in my lifetime had died by anything other than natural causes. I pray that the killing has ended but I fear that this may only be the beginning.

—Padraic

Padraic looked up from his journal. Tamlyn was brushing straw from his jacket and grinning at his older brother. Murdoch had sat up suddenly, not remembering where he was. Straw stuck out of his hair at all angles, and the wood ash from last night was still covering his face.

He stared back blankly at Tamlyn and then shook his head. He stretched out a leg and kicked Liam in the arm. "Rise and shine boss, we're under siege!"

Liam sat upright in a panic. "Well, not quite yet, old son," said Murdoch.

"You're a wanker," said Twist. "I'll have my breakfast and yours for that trick."

"I don't know that any of you should have breakfast until you've been in the fountain," exclaimed Charlotte. "What a sight, have you seen yourselves? I have a little pig at home that's cleaner."

The young woman placed a tray with boiled eggs, bread. and a pitcher of milk at their feet.

Liam took note of the white flower that Charlotte had placed in her hair before climbing the side stairs. "And you, Mr. Twist, should you be up and down hills on that bad ankle?"

"It's much better now, thank you," replied Liam, enjoying the attention. "How are doings at the church?" he asked as Charlotte turned to leave, hoping to prolong the young woman's visit.

"Very well, I should say, but those youngsters aren't half noisy at bedtime. I've never heard such a racket. Anyway, I like them. I think I might wish to become a schoolteacher," she said, blushing slightly on her way out.

Across the square Ceana spoke with Ronan. "Please, for goodness' sake, watch that those boys don't come to any harm."

"Good Lord," Ronan replied, "it's all I can do to keep our daughter from picking up a weapon and joining her brothers. Don't fret, they won't be allowed anywhere near the river."

"This is just too horrible," she cried, tears suddenly welling up in her eyes.

Ronan touched his wife's cheek gently. "I give you my word, they'll be fine. I'm more concerned with the approach from the north, through the High Wood. We're going to build a barricade today, and no one will be allowed beyond it. Tyburn is not pleased, as his cottage will be left unguarded, but I've told him there is no other way to guarantee his safety, and quite likely we will require a doctor in closer proximity, given the situation."

By the time Ronan finished eating; construction of the barricade was well under way. Every able-bodied citizen, man and woman alike, was clearing the saplings that covered the northern edge of Dunradin and were fashioning them into a deadly fence of long, spear like pickets that pointed at a forty-degree angle towards the woods. The young trees were being felled a foot from the ground with wood saws and the remaining stumps would be sharpened laboriously, leaving the twenty feet or so between the fence and the tree line impossible to navigate.

Caymus surveyed the progress from the large horse that he'd named Ghost. He stood up in the stirrups and gazed high above the village. Soon he would ride up with Tyburn soon and help him gather some herbs and medicinals, before closing his house. The bowman didn't fancy returning from his father's farm in darkness.

A small crowd of the very oldest townsfolk stood and watched the busy construction. Squire Stubbins patted his young granddaughter on the head. "That there fence is so's you don't wander off," he said with a chuckle, spitting a plug of tobacco out of the side of his mouth. Watching all this exertion was thirsty work, and the old man wondered if the Ale House was offering free beer today. Sure as hell would be a sensible idea, he thought.

-55-

"So Drake has taken his leave, the ungrateful little shit, and I'm left with this simpleton!" Euther was in a rage. "I don't suppose he had the decency to leave his medicine bag behind?"

Dafyd dropped the satchel at his feet. Faustine sprang up with surprising agility and grabbed the Welshman by the throat, pinning him against the wall. Smead let out a panicked cry, and Euther let go of Dafyd. "Well now," he said, brushing some imagined dust from the shoulder of his assistant's jacket, "suppose we get a hold of our emotions and discuss matters." "Tanner dear, a glass of water if you please."

Smead stared at Dafyd who quickly pulled him aside. "Tanner, when Big Chief tells you to do something, don't look at me, just do it, or he will eat you." To drive the point home, he mimed the act of cannibalism by placing his arm in his mouth and baring his teeth. Tanner needed no more encouragement and ran from the room quickly.

"William didn't strike me as the type that would take his own life. Did you examine the body?"

Dafyd lied, "Yes, he'd been run through with a sabre and drowned."

"Hmm," Faustine grunted, "and still no sign of Fearghal?" The Welshman shook his head. "It seems a simple matter of mathematics then," concluded Euther. "One minus one leaves nothing."

"Poor William ... well, no matter, he was overpaid anyway. Call Bergil and his boys. Tell them there's a meal to be had by the river." Euther retrieved Drake's satchel and retreated to a dark corner. "I'm not to be disturbed."

-56-

"Hand me your glass."

Padraic passed his telescoping spyglass to Liam and turned to see what he was concerned with. A plume of thickening smoke was visible across the river in the dwindling light.

"It's another burning." He focused the instrument. "Oh Mercy," he cried. "They're burning our cottage." He handed the glass back and sat against the wall with his head between his knees. "Mum will be heartbroken." He sniffed "I'll have to tell her in the morning." His companions had no idea how to console their friend, and they sat in silence for some minutes.

Eventually Murdoch spoke "They want to work on our heads. I'll wager that they've decided to burn one a night, the scum!"

Across the river, Smead was seated on the ridge a safe distance from the burning. As he rocked back and forth, the firelight painted a wide grin across his face. "Fire for Chief," he said, digging his knuckles into the ground.

Fearghal, or what was left of his spirit, also noticed the flames. He had crossed the bridge with some difficulty but found that he could slowly move forward by crouching close to the ground. He made his way carefully along the riverbank, avoiding the wind, which made it difficult to navigate.

Before long he came upon a scene of horror. William Drake's body lay on the river's edge, open from throat to groin. Six Teriz, three to a side, leaned into the cavity as they fed intently on the various organs. One of the creatures was pulling yards of intestine from the body, coiling it from thumb to elbow like a long grisly length of sausage.

Fearghal brought his hands to his mouth to stifle a gasp. He rose to his feet in a reflex to flee and was carried across a wide expanse of lawn by a stiff breeze. *What am I to do? I am a slave to the winds. I can affect this conflict in no way.*

He found himself against the lower wall of Lilyvine and thrust his head forward. As he passed through the stonework, a musty scent of decay filled his senses, followed by an overpowering smell of rotting meat that seemed to saturate his being. He was in a narrow storage room that, by his reckoning, lay directly in front of the dungeon.

He reached instinctively for the door handle, before recalling that it was not necessary. Beyond the sway of the winds, he found himself able to steer around corners with the movement of his shoulders. "Truly then, I am naught but a ghost," he said aloud. His voice refused to resonate in the narrow stairwell. "One of the undead," he whispered.

He halted briefly on the stairs, considering the situation. "Am I doomed to roam the world in this manner? Is this my punishment? Were it not for the horrors around me, this lighter-than-air existence might be agreeable. But this is madness: one world ends where the other begins. I wouldn't be surprised to find that I've taken complete leave of my senses." He rushed up the stairs with no plan other than to escape the stench from below.

Fearghal had the advantage of going about Lilyvine unseen, and it occurred to him that he might exist in this fashion at the armoury indefinitely. In fact, he concluded, there really was no other choice. He began to understand how ghosts came to haunt dwellings—not by choice but by history. Could anything be more unbearable than immortality? Surely the only respite lay in embracing madness.

He moaned loudly, startling a number of creatures who lay within earshot. He let out a moan, longer this time than the first, enjoying the release of emotions. This time two of the Teriz leaped up in a panic and rushed right into each other, cracking their heads. A fight soon ensued involving several others in the room who were extremely vexed at the interruption to their sleep.

-57-

Caymus followed his father's directions, choosing the herbs that were in season and wrapping them in bundles of parchment. Tyburn was inside gathering his instruments and potions, reluctant to leave but anxious to be on the road before the long shadows of evening.

"It pains me sorely to leave this garden," he said, emerging from the house. "I suppose we had better close up and move along."

Caymus took a number of bottles from his father and packed them carefully in his saddlebags. "Hopefully it won't be for long, Father. Stoke sent Woodruff north today to recruit more highlanders. These demons are less effective in daylight; I'm for storming the armoury in full sunlight and slaughtering the lot of them."

"They would flee down those wretched passages and return by night," replied Tyburn, mounting his pony. "We have no idea how far the sinkholes reach now. There may be a vast network of tunnels under the entire area. It's a situation that requires a level head and much planning. We must think of the river valley as a large cheese filled with rats." He cast a final glance back at the cottage. Then they started for town, anxious to avoid darkness.

It had been decided that the shorter route through the woods was not worth the risk. The remains of Portus, Fearghal, and Jubilant Smith had been taken to Horn Island, and now the area was off limits. It was not known when their burials would take place, as the cemetery was situated on the other side of the river.

Soon they reached the high road above Dunradin, and from their vantage point a thin veil of smoke was visible. "More burning," called Caymus to his father, who urged his pony forward. The bowman had chosen a horse similar in size to his father's mount. Brandy was named for his colour, and Caymus spurred him forward to match his father's pace. A full moon was rising, which was fortunate, as travelling on horseback in total darkness was a dangerous and foolish practice.

Ronan Macleary grew anxious as the day's light faded and decided to walk over to the western approach in hopes of greeting his brother and father. Every unused cart and crate in town was stacked across the road, which wound into town from the outlying farms.

Virgil Mason and his cousins, who lived on the farm closest to town, manned the barricade. Mason, drawing on a long-stemmed pipe, raised a hand in greeting. "Nothing yet, Mr. Macleary," he said in his slow drawl. "Don't spose they'll be long," he added.

The Masons were hardworking dairymen who spent as much time in the Ale House as they did with their cows. Mason's pasture was visible from the road and visible also to Tyburn and Caymus as they moved quickly towards the familiar landmark. Ronan was also anxious to know if there had been any sign of Teriz north of town. "I heard tell another home were burned riverside," said Virgil, as if reading Ronan's thoughts.

"Yes, young Liam Twist and his mother this time," replied Macleary.

"There they be," interrupted a cousin, pointing towards a spot in the distance where rapid hooves were kicking up a cloud of dirt.

-58-

The following fortnight proceeded uneventfully, due mainly to a prolonged change in the weather: heavy rains soaked the valley without letup the entire time. The storms were considered by the most rational of citizens as a blessing, given that they put an end to the fires.

Not everyone was pleased with the weather, though, and the Ale House was filled daily with grumblers and complainers who had quickly grown bored with their enforced holiday in town. Some had even spoken of returning to their homes. The most vocal of these dissidents was Seth Willitt, who, being markedly fond of the drink, spent most of his time in the Ale house behind a tankard.

The publican, Ezekiel Bardwyck, cast a stern eye in Willitt's direction. Old Zeke had been unable to send his son out of town to arrange a barrel pickup for some time, and the supply of beer was dwindling. Some of the river folk had taken advantage of the free drink, which was not a problem, but this Seth Willitt character had proven to be a first-class freeloader, who liked to stir things up.

"I'll warrant all this water has washed those so-called Teriz out of their tunnels. I'm not frightened," he boasted. "I'm for going back tomorrow."

"Easy for you, Willitt," chimed in old man Stubbins. "You've no family to be concerned about. Have you forgotten what Jube looked like with his scalp hangin' over his eyes?"

"They don't scare me. Zekey, give us another ale."

"Sounds like liquid courage to me," said Stubbins.

Willitt ignored the remark. "C'mon, barkeep, another round," he bellowed.

"You've had your share, and more," answered Bardwyck. "Sleep it off at Green's, and come back next week," he added, knowing that by this time next week there would be no drink.

"Bugger that," said Willitt, knocking his chair over as he left.

Liam Twist said good night to Charlotte and turned up his collar against the rain. Water dripped from the brim of his hat as he descended the church steps. When the storms had showed no signs of slackening, the youngster volunteered to help Charlotte with the children. They had spent a great deal of time in each other's company during the last week and grown even more fond of each other.

Dunradin was now effectively cut off from the rest of the country, and if this week was any indication, it would not be long before food supplies would begin to dwindle. Charlotte had kindly baked some biscuits for Mrs. Twist, and Liam would stop at his mother's lodgings and share a meal with her before standing his watch at the grocer's.

The old woman had lost a husband three years earlier and now her house but remained miraculously optimistic. As a small child Liam had learned an array of survival skills from his father. William Twist had also been thoughtful enough to temper his lessons with some joyful pursuits, such as juggling and fiddle playing.

Liam crossed the square quickly, reaching the foot of High Street just as Seth Willitt turned the corner and staggered down the footpath towards the river. *What's that all about?* wondered Twist, continuing on to his mother's.

I think that qualifies as suspicious behaviour. He made a mental note to speak to Ronan as soon as possible.

Not far away at the grocer's, Caymus and Stoke were taking an inventory of the remaining food supplies. The week's consumption had been increased due to the arrival of severe storms. It appeared that when Dunradians were limited in their outdoor activities, more meals were eaten.

"Fourteen bags of flour remaining," said Caymus. Branan made a notation in his book. "How long do you think, before we are without food?" asked Caymus.

"It's hard to say," replied Stoke. "I think it would be wise to start rationing, though. Are you in favour of a voucher system?"

"I am," answered Caymus.

"At the risk of inciting anarchy, I would suggest that everyone with a cold cellar bring their vegetables and such here, to be distributed equally."

"I don't think that would be a very popular suggestion," said Caymus.

"It may prove to be the first of many unpopular suggestions," replied Stoke.

"How is it," asked Caymus, changing the subject, "that you come to know so much about these Wraiths?|"

"It's my job," responded Stoke. After a pause he added, "On top of that, I had a brother who met his end due to dealings with Faustine's type."

"You are on a mission of revenge?"

"I try my best to not bring sentiment into my work," answered Branan. "His name was Leeman" said Stoke, momentarily lost in thought. "My brother became one of them and eventually had to be destroyed. It's a long time since I've spoken of it, and yes, his death drives me to do what I do."

Caymus said, "If we could eradicate their kind completely—"

"Or find a cure," Stoke interjected. "What we speak of is a disease of the blood, which is transferred through fluid exchange. The majority of these creatures are victims."

"Would you have them segregated in colonies like lepers?"

Branan nodded. "Yes, I would. You may be surprised to learn that leprosy is not contagious, whereas this form of cannibalism is in a fashion infectious as well as being an addiction."

"Well," replied Caymus, "I think I know what you're saying. I'm sure Tyburn would be more familiar with your manner of speaking however."

Branan smiled. "Forgive me, my brother and I were both doctors in Inverness. "I would be most interested to speak further with your father, I sense there is more to him than meets the eye."

Caymus knew what the highlander meant. He was as close with his father as any son, but there was always something of Tyburn's true nature that remained hidden. It was as though the old man harboured a secret. Widowers left to their own devices who didn't remarry were often thought of as mysterious, and the elder Macleary was no exception.

Liam excused himself after a quick meal and entered the grocer's in search of Ronan. Finding that Ronan was absent, he passed on his observations to Caymus and the highlander.

"Ah, Willitt, the damn fool!" replied Branan. "What is he thinking? Well, I'll not waste men rescuing him. That'll be the last we've seen of him" he concluded. "Has he family to be notified?"

"No," answered Caymus. Stoke addressed the youngster. "Thank you, Twist. How are things above?" he asked, referring to the rooftop watch.

"Very damp and uneventful, sir," he replied. "Well, let the other lads know, and keep an eye peeled for that half-wit Willis. He may wander back if the gods are with him." The tracker didn't sound very optimistic.

In the meantime, Seth Willitt negotiated the narrow trail to the river unsteadily. More than once he'd travelled this route home from Bardwyck's Ale house, and often more inebriated than he was tonight. His small stone cottage lay on the banks of the Sleath just below the quarry. Tonight, however, Willitt would not make it that far.

-59-

Colette Kendrick peered up at the roof of the tunnel, unimpressed with her surroundings. "We must be close now," she said to Godwyn.

The final leg of their journey carried them underground, where the tunnels were slippery; in some places the foul-smelling water was a foot deep. In one area the corner of a shroud was visible, and bones protruded occasionally from the walls. Diggers had inadvertently tunnelled below the cemetery exposing the remains of Dunradin's dead. What lay at this level was the old graveyard which had eventually been covered by the new cemetery. The skull of Fergus Green's great-great grandmother stared blindly from the clay above Colette's head as she passed.

Many years ago the dead had been placed in simple graves dug into a vast bed of clay beside the river. Coffins were not in use until the cemetery became overcrowded and it was necessary to transport hundreds of yards of soil to cover the graves which were no longer recognized. The newest bodies were exhumed and reburied above the old. Currently the practice was to leave the newly deceased at Horn Island until nothing remained but bones, which would be gathered with much ceremony and taken to the new yard for burial.

Godwyn was a large very thirsty employee of Faustine. He was not pleased with this leg of the journey. It was too hot and close for him in the tunnel, and he plowed ahead, ignoring the woman's remark. If the crone were anyone but Dafyd's wife, he would have abandoned her days ago.

Behind them, for close to a quarter of a mile was a single file of Teriz numbering 140. These were supposedly the last and the hardiest of the survivors. They had entered the tunnel at the edge of town beyond the burial grounds. Of the 140 men travelling through the tunnel, twenty were considered to be blood for the others. They were chained together in the middle of the pack and urged forward with short whips.

The third floor of Lilyvine was littered with mattresses, some of them still smelling damp. They had been taken from the river homes along with as much furniture as could be carried. Under the cover of rain and darkness Euther's Teriz had looted the river homes, taking whatever proved edible or useful and brought their spoils to the armoury.

Fearghal's antics kept the creatures confused and anxious. Many fights erupted daily, much to the dismay of Bergil and his assistants, who attributed the unruliness to a lack of activity brought about by the autumn storms.

"Get your men in order!" the Welshman had screamed. Even Dafyd, the most level-headed of them all, was on edge. He had been awakened by strange voices repeatedly in the last week and had not slept well for many days. Godwyn's men would be here soon, and the food supply was a concern.

Thus Godwyn and Colette found their hosts in a less than appreciative frame of mind when they arrived. Bergil's men eyed the slaves hungrily as they attached them to the dungeon walls which had formerly been host to the French.

"Well then, my plump little beauties, welcome to Lilyvine." Dafyd had dark rings under his eyes and appeared to be using the door frame for support. "That thin one there," he said, pointing.

"Take him with you for your men, Bergil." Dafyd stepped back to allow the men to leave with their struggling prize.

"Hold a minute," he said as they passed. The Welshman looked the trembling man up and down and then reached for some wine, passing Bergil two bottles. He smiled at the victim. "Yes, definitely red wine."

Fearghal hung in the air like a pall of smoke, drifting softly across the ceiling. He had few needs. Food and drink were of no use, and sleep was not possible.

It occurred to him that he was not entirely unhappy with the situation. His lack of ability to grasp solid objects was only a slight hindrance, and with time he came to understand that it was really not a necessity. His voice, although a shadow of what it had been, was still audible and proved quite useful.

Faustine was seated at a large oak desk directly below him, talking to himself while rummaging through a medical bag. "Yes, yes, William, mince pies with powdered sugar, please." He turned the satchel over and emptied the contents onto the table with a clatter. The first tin contained what he was looking for. "Here we are, my sweets," he said, twisting off the top. The white powder reflected in his greedy eyes.

"That's a filthy habit, Dorian," he whispered, with a chuckle. Fearghal was tempted to verbalize his agreement but decided to investigate the noise that had broken out below.

A large contingent of Teriz was marshalling in the lower concourse, which was awash with mud. A taller than average woman was commanding their attention. She might have been considered attractive, were it not for the fact that her dark hair was shorn very close to the skull and a white scar ran from the corner of her mouth to the back of her neck.

From the moment she arrived it was clear that Colette called the shots. Dafyd for the most part didn't interfere with her handling of the men. Godwyn was an adventuresome lout with no desire to take part in the blood-drinking, and Dafyd grudgingly admired the way she had him wrapped around her finger. Because Godwyn was in no position to do anything other than serve Colette, he was ruthless with his men to the point of obsession. They were constantly reminded how close they were to being on the menu.

Dafyd despised Godwyn's lack of will and refused to speak to him. For his part the Welshman wished only to please and even to some extent control Euther.

Fearghal, having now witnessed the Wraiths in less candid moments, began to feel something akin to pity. Euther was fast becoming addicted to the medicine bag. Laudanum or perhaps an extract of coca leaves was gaining a hold on Faustine, and his ability to make effective decisions was in jeopardy.

William Drake had been careful to track Euther's consumption, cautiously insuring that a problem did not arise. *After all one did not kill the goose that laid the golden egg.* In Fearghal's opinion Dafyd was the true villain. Once upon a time, Euther had possessed a pinch of morals, whereas the Welshman had descended to a level nothing less than demonic.

-60-

"The old tosspot," said Murdoch. "What was he thinking? He'll be at the bottom of one of those holes quicker then Nelly!"

Liam frowned. "You're probably right. In any event we're to keep an eye open for him. Ronan won't send anyone after him, that's for certain."

"Neither would I," said Murdoch, who often recalled a day one summer when Willitt had set his dog after him for stealing an apple from his market cart.

Tamlyn smiled at the memory. Summer market seemed a long time ago in this gloomy rain.

Suddenly he recalled a treat in their provision bag. "Look here," he said; digging it out, "Padraic brought some licorice up from downstairs!" He offered it to the other boys, who chewed on the sticks without speaking.

"It's never gonna stop raining," said Caleb Macneil eventually. "That's it, forty days and forty nights, may as well start swimmin' now."

"You're daft!" said Cardiff.

His brother grinned. "Yes, I know. What I really am is tired of standing up here all night looking at nothing. I wish something would happen."

"A few of those creepers come up the hill here, and you'll change your tune," insisted Liam.

"Hey, who rescued who?" asked Caleb. "You were hopping around like an old hen on one leg while we were crackin' haids "

"Aye, that's true," laughed Liam. "You were brilliant." He paused. "I noticed you had to change your pants later, though."

The young men's laughter echoed in the narrow alley between the grocer's and the guesthouse. The rain had slowed, and high above in the branches of a tall tree, the shape-changer shook the water from his feathers. He peered at the three pale figures inching silently up the side of the building below. One of the creatures wore a soiled bandage over his left eye, and all three carried blades between their teeth.

Domnash, who had weaselled his way back into Euther's good graces, was paid well for his information. "It's rare that they cast an eye to the alley," he'd said; "this is the best approach."

Feodor, the Teriz who had lost an eye due to Cardiff's fine throwing arm, was the first to volunteer for the night's adventure. Faustine wanted the boys taken alive. He didn't specify any condition other than insisting that they were still able to speak.

"We doesn't need our eyes to speak wif, does we?" said Feodor. It was less a question than a statement. Bergil, Feodor, and Margus climbed at the same speed, three abreast clinging to the rungs of their narrow unsteady ladders.

"Perhaps an old fashioned catapult device," suggested Caymus. He and Stoke, after leaving the grocer's, were comfortably seated in the smithy talking with Ronan and his father.

"Perhaps, but I do feel we should strike first, whether it be from a distance or not." Ronan paused to relight his pipe. "Two sides attempting to starve each other out is foolishness. We have the advantage of daylight, and they will attack at night. We are too few to divide our strength between defence and attack, so let's discuss one or the other."

"How many are we, until Woodruff returns?" asked Branan. "It's been close to a fortnight, and I expect him soon."

"Three score or less, by my reckoning," said Hugh Maclean, "all untrained save us highlanders."

Branan Stoke looked at Caymus and narrowed his eyes. "Your crossbow there, how difficult would it be to fashion a similar one at, say, six or seven times the size?"

Caymus met his gaze silently. Eventually he smiled. "I see what you're thinking. It would need to be anchored for accuracy." He motioned to Ronan. "Paper, please, if you have it."

Stoke said, "I wonder what the distance is from the lower marsh to Lilyvine. Is there gunpowder to be had, Hugh?"

"Aye, one barrel at least," he replied.

The scream began as a loud croaking call like that of a raven and rose in pitch, ending as the wail of a dying man. Domnash saw the wolf at the last second, and even then only as a shadow. The beast had crept up behind him as he stepped through the alley and pounced before his victim could take to the air. Feodor stared down from the height of his ladder, transfixed at the sight. The huge wolf shook his head as his fangs ripped into the chest of his victim.

Murdoch leaned over the wall just as the wolf tore out his prey's heart, almost failing to notice the Teriz who were cringing close to the brickwork. He grabbed the top of the ladder and pushed as hard as he could, sending Feodor towards the other wall. Liam and Padraic were struggling to keep the other two creatures from gaining purchase on the roof.

The sound of struggle was punctuated by a shattering of glass as Feodor plunged through the skylight atop the lower guesthouse opposite the grocer's. Caleb and Cardiff leaped towards Padraic and pulled Bergil off him. Margus, using the wall as leverage, sprang over the head of Liam, somersaulted towards the stairwell, and disappeared through the opening.

Suddenly Bergil went limp and dropped to the floor. As Cardiff drew his leg back to deliver a kick, the clever creature rolled quickly behind him and slammed his fist into the back of the youngster's knee. Cardiff tumbled forward and knocked his brother over.

The creature was on him in a flash, holding a knife to his throat. "We'll meet again," Bergil said, running his tongue up the back of Cardiff's neck next to the handle of his knife. Cardiff spun, meaning to elbow his foe in the head. He missed as the Teriz leaped for the stairwell and descended close behind Margus. Cardiff wiped at his neck, disgusted.

Caymus approached the grocer's at a run. When Bergil flew through the doorway, he dropped to one knee and aimed. The bolt pierced the creature's skull just above the right eye and drove him backwards into the store.

Seconds later Stoke arrived and pulled a silver-edged dirk from his belt. "Nice shot," he said admiringly. Using the short arrow as a handle, he pulled the head forward and sliced deftly through the flesh of Bergil's throat, releasing a stream of blood that covered Caymus's boots. "Sorry, it was necessary. I should have told you to step back."

"In the alley," called Liam, pointing towards Green's. Caymus and Branan gripped their weapons and made for the alleyway. They returned to the front a minute later, as Maclean and the others arrived.

"Nowt there but some ladders and a wide trail of blood into the bush," said Stoke.

"A wolf!" said an excited Murdoch. "And a bloody big one it was!"

Ronan was concerned. "Well, it's gone now. Anyone hurt?"

"Just Cardiff," said his brother Caleb. "I think he may have been impregnated."

The group's nervous laughter was cut short when Squire Stubbins emerged from the doorway next door in an obvious state of bewilderment. "Some chap's dropped through the top window," he cried. "I think he's daid Ended up wi' some a my silverware stuck in him."

"One-eyed fellow?" asked Murdoch. He felt a little sick to his stomach realizing that he had perhaps just killed someone.

"I think there were three," said Liam. "One of them got away." He stared wide-eyed at the body on the steps.

Cardiff wiped at the back of his neck again. "Yech."

"You're certain it was a wolf and not just a large hound?" asked Branan. "To my knowledge the last wolf in the Highlands was shot some years ago."

"Well, one thing is certain," said Murdoch: "I would not like to meet a creature like that on the ground. Padraic says whatever he dragged off was the thing that he saw on the roof two weeks back."

"I suppose the animal has done us a favour then," suggested Tamlyn, who had not said much to this point. Murdoch was relieved; he had worried that this might have all been a bit much for his little brother.

Maclean and another tracker emerged from the guesthouse with the body of Feodor. "Take them down the hill and drop them in one of those sinkholes," said Stoke, passing his dirk to Maclean. "And watch for that deerhound or whatever it is."

Secretly Stoke knew just what it was. He'd seen the shape-changer late at night on the crest of a hill, just before the weather had changed. The big wolf was stalking something, and the highlander decided to keep this fact to himself. He wasn't sure why but told himself that there was no need to panic everyone into a hunt.

"You learned nothing from your captive?" asked Euther.

"Nothing of use," said Colette.

"Well, keep pouring wine into him, and squeeze him a little more. I don't imagine he's made of very stern stuff."

"He's a slobbering drunkard. If he knew anything, he'd have spewed it out by now. We might keep him for bait."

"Yes, we might," agreed Faustine. "Keep him marinated. If this weather breaks, we'll have a little cookout down by the bridge."

Margus tried to keep from stuttering in front of the commander. "He—uh, th-they are both dead," he said in a small voice.

"Killed by little boys, presumably?" asked Godwyn, leaning into his face. "And how did you survive? by telling stories?"

"No sir. Th-there was a wolf."

Godwyn's gaze rose to the top of the creature's spotty forehead.

"And highlanders," he added quickly, trying not to squirm.

The commander's demeanour changed at once. "How many?" he asked. He grabbed Margus by the ear before he could answer and dragged him towards the makeshift dungeon, kicked the door open, and pushed him inside. "Tell her what you just told me."

"Highlanders," croaked Margus.

Colette looked up from the pit and then back to the table where she had Seth Willitt strapped down. "You'll burn for this," she hissed at the apple pedlar who was too drunk to understand. She had to give the pig credit; he hadn't spilled that little piece of news. He had some balls after all. Well, for the time being, at any rate.

Euther sat back in the chair picking powder from under his nails. "Half a dozen trackers?. Are you getting soft, Dafyd? You're not telling me a handful of highlanders are a concern. Are you?"

"Where there's six, there will be more, I'm just saying we might exercise a little caution."

Euther smirked. "I understand the goose is cooked," he said, referring to Domnash. "Maybe it's time you had a look yourself, hmm?"

Faustine had seen that the armoury's second floor was clean and sparsely furnished. An old dyeing vat in a room to one side served as his bath, and other than a desk and chair, the centre room contained no furniture. He preferred to sleep either in the chair or on a thin mattress.

No one entered the second floor unless invited to do so. The front stairwell offered floor access at all four levels and also served as an exit. The only way to exit any of the floors was to turn around and go back out the wide doorway to the stairs. The main floor was different in that the foyer, or rotunda as it was called, spanned the three front sides of the building. The room at the centre of the ground floor was the largest, and two smaller rooms lay to the right and left with doors opening onto the rotunda.

The centre rooms on all four levels were the largest, having been the work rooms of the old mill. The third and fourth floors now housed the Teriz in a dimly lit world of damp mattresses and foul smells. Below the main floor lay the pit, which served as a dungeon. It had been dug from the clay bed below the building by the French labourers who ended up chained to its walls. The last of the Frenchmen's remains had been eaten, and now Seth Willitt was the dungeon's only guest. One arm and leg were shackled to the low wooden table where he lay on his side moaning.

Dafyd entered the dungeon and leaned against the table beside Seth. "Good morning," he said cheerfully.

Willitt groaned and opened one eye. The other was swollen shut.

"I have a question for you, if it's not too much trouble," said the Welshman with mock politeness. Willit said nothing. "Where are the highlanders housed? Where do they sleep?"

The prisoner's one good eye took in his guest with curiosity. He didn't recognize the heavily bearded inquisitor. "Blacksmith," he said through cracked lips.

"Good chap," said Dafyd getting to his feet. "You take care now." He stepped up the short staircase that exited the pit and entered the small wine room that was situated between the dungeon and the front foyer, choosing a red wine to carry to his room. "Colette!" he called out. She must be occupied elsewhere; he would have to do this himself. The Welshman seated himself by the wash basin and propped a hand mirror behind it. After opening the bottle of wine and pouring himself a glass, he opened the straight razor and began.

-61-

Charlotte threw open the church doors and smiled. The storms had finally ended, and the sun was shining bright and clear in a cloudless sky. Liam waved from across the square, walking slowly towards the young woman with a large bunch of daffodils held behind his back. He climbed the steps and then bowed with a flourish, offering them to Charlotte. She blushed fetchingly and turned a cheek in his direction to receive a clumsy and somewhat hasty kiss.

"Come in," she said softly. "You can help me serve breakfast."

"Your brothers have taken to calling me Uncle, the cheeky scamps."

Charlotte laughed. "How are they? I worry about Tamlyn, after that horrible business the other night."

"They are well. Don't worry; we have a tracker staying on the roof with us now. He's a very large fellow named Duncan, and he carries the biggest claymore you can imagine, as well as a brace of pistols."

"Okay," Charlotte replied.

Liam heard a tiny voice say, "Miss Charlotte, do we have to have porridge again? We want eggs."

"Oh, Harold, you silly lad, porridge is good for you. Don't you want to grow up big and strong like Liam here?" Twist puffed out his chest and smiled at the small boy.

"Hmm," said Harold, sizing up Liam. "Not so big. My mom is bigger than that."

"You rascal," said Liam, tousling the youngster's hair.

"I'm going to march them all around the square this morning," said Charlotte. "They've been inside far too long; even their moms are driving me crazy."

Ceana smiled at Liam. "Oh, look at those beautiful flowers. What a lovely autumn day ... you brought the sunshine with you, Master Twist."

"I hope it's a sign of good things to come," he replied.

Virgil Mason and his cousins might have been more pleased than anyone at the change of weather. Manning the barricade had been a dreary task indeed.

When Virgil caught sight of someone approaching, he stood up and addressed his cousin. "Who's this, then?"

An odd looking fellow with a battered top hat was drawing near on a tired-looking donkey. He had apple red cheeks and a receding chin that gave him a comical appearance. "Nice day," said the stranger.

"Oh aye, and about time," replied Mason. "I thought I were gonna have to learn yon cows how to swim."

"What's this all about?" asked the stranger, referring to the barricade.

"I don't believe I know you, mister," said Mason, ignoring the question. The stranger looked amused. "Keelin Tyndall" he said, "purveyor of fine wares, at your service."

"A tinker then are you? There's nae much call for your type here."

"In any event," the tinker continued, "I have a cart a ways back on the main road, and I'm only stopping to enquire where I might purchase a horse, as my nag has dropped dead all of a sudden like."

"Well, I guess you could ask at Macleary's down the way. You'll have to leave your ass here though." Virgil's cousins erupted with laughter at the double meaning.

"Very well," said Tyndall, hopping off the animal. "His name is Beelzebub, and he's partial to turnips." He took his hat off and bowed before starting down the road.

"Some has no sense of humour," quipped Virgil dismissively.

The stranger decided that a quick detour into the Ale House might be beneficial and ducked into the drinking establishment. "Good day, sir" he said, greeting Ezekiel Bardwyck affably.

"It is a good day," answered the barkeep. "We've only ale left and not much of that, no bitters and no stout," he said, towelling the top of the counter with gusto.

"Ale it is then," said Tyndall.

"New to these parts?" asked Ezekiel, pulling a pint for the early customer.

"More or less," he replied. "I've an old friend who settled here some years back. You might know him—he's the apple farmer, Seth Willitt?"

"Aye," said Zeke frowning. "Truth is, he's not been in recently. I had to cut him off for a spell."

Tyndall chuckled. "That sounds like Seth, all right."

Just then two highlanders entered, and the tinker took his ale to a corner table.

"Who's that?" asked Hugh Maclean in a low voice, gesturing with his eyes towards the table where Tyndall sat.

Branan eyed the man briefly. *Another drunk*, he decided. Branan Stoke and Hugh Maclean had not come into the Ale House for drink but rather for a quiet place to mull over Caymus's drawings.

Maclean unrolled the sketch and spread it out across the table. Stoke pointed: "Here is the triggering mechanism, and here the restraint. Caymus tells me that cocking the device might prove to be difficult but not impossible."

"Yes, I begin to see," replied Hugh, then abruptly turned and looked up. Neither man knew how long the stranger had been standing behind them.

"Please pardon the intrusion, sirs. I'm of a mind to purchase a horse, and I wonder if you could direct me to a stable."

Stoke stepped towards the door, looking impatient. "Down that street to the left," he said, pointing through the door.

"Much obliged," said the stranger, with a bow.

The tinker glanced from left to right as he ambled up the street towards the blacksmith's. His eyes drank in every detail: the barricade of sharpened saplings, the swarm of children outside the church, the guard at the door of the grocer's, and even the small dog in the dressmaker's window.

He circled up behind Macleary's and approached the smithy, taking care not to be seen. As he turned the corner, leaving the shadows of the stable, the glare of the sun filled his head with a searing pain. He stumbled backwards to the shadows and covered his eyes, waiting for the ache to recede.

The sound of hooves soon filled the street. Tyndall, shaking off a wave of dizziness, got to his feet and crossed to the rear of an adjacent building. He counted twenty nine highlanders on horseback as they passed and swore under his breath.

"That will be Woodruff returned," said Stoke excitedly, hearing the clatter of horsemen outside. He rolled up the sketch and rose from his chair.

"Has that gentleman been in your establishment before?" Maclean asked Ezekiel.

"First time I recall seeing him," said the publican, "but he seemed to know Willitt well enough and there was something familiar about his look."

"Thanks for your time, Ezekiel. If he comes back, please let me know." The trackers headed across the square, anxious to greet the recruits.

The children, who had been gathered by the fountain along with Charlotte and the children's mothers, were running up the street towards the smithy, with the women close on their heels. The entry into town of more than twenty mounted men was an event that had not been witnessed in Dunradin for more years than anyone could recall. Previous to today, the last show of such a force was an invasion by the English almost two hundred years ago.

Stoke greeted Woodruff with a clap on the shoulder. "Well done, lad! Twice the number I had hoped for." He recognized more than one face in the bunch. "Macintosh!" he called.

The twins Donald and John turned and smiled. "Hello, Branan," said John. "Our father sends his best wishes. He would be here but for a nasty spell of the gout."

Donald nodded. He was the quiet one. Telling the twins apart was close to impossible until one of them spoke.

"I know he would," agreed Branan happily. After some discussion it was decided that more than half the horses would be brought to Mason's cow pasture, as the stables simply could not house that many. In turn, the schoolhouse would be used to lodge the recruits. As good fortune would have it, each of the highlanders had stocked his saddlebags with biscuits and jerky.

Padraic watched the excitement from his roof, in no mood to join his neighbours. He had waved off the others and chose to remain on guard. The youngster stared ahead, taking in the action unemotionally.

The reality of his father's violent death was finally sinking in, and Padraic found himself smothered by a cloud of gloom. His dismal outlook was at once reversed with the arrival of Duncan, the largest of the Highlanders. The mute heard Chowder's excited bark and spun around in disbelief.

"Someone here to see you," said the big man, laughing loudly as the terrier leaped from his arms. The small dog's entire hind end waved back and forth as he his short tail wagged wildly. Padraic was overcome with joy as Chowder climbed into his arms and licked his face frantically. He had assumed that his pet had been killed and carried off by the same beasts that had murdered his father, and Chowder's return was just what he needed to shake off his gloom.

The little dog looked thinner and much in need of a bath. He'd only just made his way back to the grocer's when Duncan scooped him up and brought him to the roof. "I think your friend is hungry," said Duncan. "Why don't you take him downstairs and feed him, while I stay up here?"

The big man grinned. It was nice to see the youngster's reaction as he scampered downstairs without a backwards glance.

Duncan leaned across the rear wall and scanned the river valley below. A movement caught his eye beyond the river. A figure was seeking out a path through the trees, moving quickly away from the town. He carried a battered top hat in one hand and appeared to be shading his eyes with the other. Duncan watched the man as he wove through the landscape, shrinking into the distance, then dropping from sight altogether.

This was the first time the highlander had seen movement in the valley, aside from an occasional torch flickering in the distance.

"By the way" asked Branan "Was a ruddy-cheeked fellow here looking to buy a horse today?"

"No" replied Ronan, "and in any case, I would not have had an animal to sell. Why do you ask?"

"It's possible we may have a spy in our midst." He went on to describe Tyndall and warned Ronan to be wary of the man if he showed up. "I'm afraid your little village is becoming quite crowded" he added.

"These are good men that Woodruff has brought to us. I know several of them. I'll send the Macneil twins to the barricade to relieve Mason and his men. No one else will get through. Virgil can tend to the horses."

"How is your father?"

"Improving," replied Ronan. The doctor had developed a mild ailment of the lungs and was resting in the guesthouse. "I am on my way shortly to see him."

"Very good," said Stoke. "Please advise him not to take in too much night air, and assure him that I would be happy to assist in my limited capabilities with any of his patients. I tie a very handsome tourniquet should the need arise."

Ronan thanked Stoke and headed at once to the guesthouse.

The lobby of Green's Guesthouse was a very comfortable and inviting room. The wallpaper was a lively pattern of ivy, and the furniture was upholstered with a rich green fabric.

Tyburn was sharing a pot of tea with Fergus and thanking him for the use of his lobby. He knew that Green had not done very well after the mill closed and wanted the old man to know that his generosity was appreciated.

"Tis nae problem," said Green. "Them that can has slipped me a coin here and there and your wee Murdoch has offered to help replace the window on the roof."

"I may just board it up to keep those creepers out."

"Ach, there's yer boy, here for a look."

Murdoch greeted Fergus and his father. "Is Ronan boring you with tales of medical horror then?" He gave the gentlemen a second-hand description of Keelin Tyndall, referring to him as a suspicious character, and praised Woodruff's recruitment skills.

Dafyd rubbed the rouge from his cheeks and loosened the tight knot in his hair. The face reflected in the mirror became recognizable. Except for the lack of beard, he looked much like himself again.

"I'm not sure I like your new look," said Colette.

"No harm done" replied the Welshman. His dark beard would grow back in a week at the most.

"What did you discover?"

He turned from the mirror and faced his wife. "What I learned, my dear, is that Dunradin is now home to more than a score of stout, well-armed soldiers from the highlands of Scotland, all mounted on dark fiery-eyed steeds."

"Really," she replied in a lilting tone. "I'm almost tempted to prostrate myself at their overly large feet."

He continued, unamused, "What I did not learn was the whereabouts of our sickly friend Fearghal. I found no signs of him anywhere. He had no stomach for a fight and has doubtless slithered off into the woods."

"Well, you tell Big Chief the news," she replied, mocking Smead. "I have to arrange a cookout."

Dafyd watched in the mirror as she left, mumbling under his breath, "Whore."

"You might try hot needles under the toenails; very efficient. I shouldn't have to be telling you this, Godwyn; you should have learned these techniques by now.

"You know, being a villain is not an easy job. Most people think it's merely a matter of doing a few evil things and sauntering about in dark clothing. One doesn't just run about knocking folks' heads off either; there's a lot of thought goes into it.

"To be a good villain, you have to make people suffer a great deal, and that's not always a walk in the park, mark my words. Of course any decent villain worth his salt has other people do the really nasty stuff for him. I learned this a very long time ago.

"Now I want you to go down there and strip the flesh from this man until he tells us what we want to know. "

Faustine looked up as Dafyd approached "Ah , what news of Fearghal?"

Godwyn exited quickly, relieved to be excused.

"Fearghal is gone," Dafyd lied; "no one knows where." He waited for a response, and when none came, he continued, "The northern approach through the woods is well fortified, and the road is barricaded at the western entrance. It's manned by half-wit farmers, who gave me leave to enter. As far as I can discern, the highlanders are fashioning a projectile weapon of some sort, which to my mind indicates a distance attack or defence. Their number has been bolstered by approximately thirty of the northerners on horse. I heard nothing to suggest that more were on the way."

Euther turned his palms up and stared at the lines for almost a minute. "Well, very useful information. I'll be frank with you: I had hoped that Fearghal would provide some insight into Drake's source of medicines. It's a pity. Nevertheless, I must proceed without it. It tends to thin the blood anyway.

"Tell Smead to burn another home, please."

Secretly, Faustine had already sent Margus to the docks of London on a mission of redemption. "Travel alone, speak to no one. Bring the opium back here by the end of the month, and you will have Godwyn's head and his position."

Godwyn had been outspoken about Margus's failure to produce a hostage, and among the Teriz it was assumed that he had been quietly done away with. Margus was no fool and jumped at the chance to redeem himself or to make good his escape. Either way, he would gain a new lease on life. Only time would tell which way the wind blew.

-62-

For two days the sun shone high in the sky, but on the morning of the third day clouds returned, and temperatures dropped suddenly, ushering in the first signs of winter. In the valley a fine frost covered the marsh, and geese were heard high in the sky winging south.

Ceana had finished knitting a sweater for Tamlyn and begun another that she intended to give to young Padraic. The youngster was in much better spirits since the return of his dog, and Chowder refused to stray more than a few feet from the boy, unless it was to accept a treat from Duncan, whom he had grown quite fond of. The big highlander, for his part, was impressed with Padraic's fortitude and enjoyed spending time with him on the roof.

Woodruff's recruits were gathered on the lower lawns that looked out across the river valley from below the grocer's. Murdoch and Tamlyn watched them from the corner of the roof as they sat or strolled about cleaning their pistols and shouldering broad-bladed swords. Some of them were in conversation with villagers, while a few sat quietly smoking while staring at the large building across the river. They seemed restless, and Murdoch wondered who would make the first move.

A low rumble followed by a muffled explosion shook the ground as if on cue, and every head within earshot turned towards the river. The trees emptied of birds all at once. and the stone bridge, which had spanned the Sleath for as long as anyone living could recall, crumbled into grey-brown turbulence in the water. A frontal attack on the armoury by horsemen was now out of the question. Murdoch fancied that he could hear cheering from the windows of Lilyvine.

Minutes later several fingers of smoke and flame burst through the roof of another riverside cottage, pointing to the low bank of cloud that had drifted closer to the village. The residents of Dunradin who had witnessed the explosion stood in stunned silence, not sure what to say. Clearly the gauntlet had been thrown down.

"There is a footbridge further down the river by the quarry," said Ronan, grimly addressing Stoke. "It will support a crossing of many men, without horses. They won't cross by daylight."

Branan frowned. "And no other bridges then?"

"The Glencairn Bridge crosses the upper Sleath to the north, but given the distance, the village would be unguarded for a dangerously long time."

"Well done, Keita!" yelled Godwyn amidst the cheering. To be certain, the Asian was skilled with explosives, and the bridge had fallen in one stroke, as requested. Running his finger down the specially constructed shutters, he stepped back from the window and placed a large hand on the little man's shoulder. "Euther will be very pleased."

Faustine had insisted that the bridge be destroyed in dramatic fashion. If those damned highlanders were going to stand up on the hill all day staring into the valley, he would give them something to look at. Lines would be drawn and challenges sent. He'd had enough pissing about in the rain and was anxious to begin the game.

Godwyn Blunt knew better than to disturb Euther now. It would only look like a pathetic call for approval on his part. The old man would be pleased well enough with the way he'd handled things. He wasn't like that whimpering fool Margus, who'd run off with his tail between his legs. Yes, he'd handled things just fine.

Fearghal lingered in Euther's chamber considering how he might deflate the Wraith's buoyant mood. Dafyd had just left after calmly informing Faustine that he had taken care of the bridge in the manner requested. He had opened a bottle of wine for him and departed.

After finishing the bottle, Euther felt his eyes grow heavy, and his chin was soon on his chest. Fearghal drifted close and leaned close to Euther's ear. "I have betrayed you," he said in a soft voice. Euther's eyelids moved ever so slightly. "I have betrayed you, Faustine." The two lines between the chief's eyes deepened, but his eyes remained closed. "I live in the forest above the village plotting your demise."

Euther swung wildly in the direction of the voice, knocking over the empty wine bottle. He stood up quickly, grasping at the empty air. "Smead!" he called out.

"He's out burning homes," said the voice, as it passed in front of the desk on its way from the chamber. Euther sank back down and closed his eyes, which seemed to pulse with each beat of his heart. *Calm down,* he said to himself. *It's just a trick of the mind, a reaction brought on by the lack of opiates.* It had been Fearghal's voice, though. He could have sworn the Macleary bastard was right there in the room, inches away.

"Leonardo da Vinci developed a giant crossbow," said Caymus. "I believe it was meant to fire large stones or even flaming bombs. He used a crank like this." The bowman drew an illustration for the others. "Right here, you spin this crank to pull the bow back and achieve tension. There is a holding pin here, and once the ammunition is loaded, a second person knocks the pin out with a mallet to launch the projectile. Leonardo's bow was massive, much larger than we would require, and I'm not sure if it was ever built, but I would like to try."

"As long as it would have the range we desire, my suggestion would be that you attempt to build one at once," urged Branan.

"With regards to the ammunition," said Hugh Maclean, "an incendiary devise peppered with silver shot might prove effective."

"Aye," said Stoke. "The silver shot is a wee bit soft, but a very small wound will introduce it into the bloodstream handily. The problem is that serpentine, our black powder, does not detonate. We cannot deliver a projectile that explodes on contact."

"Unless it had a wick like a candle which was lit first?" asked Ronan.

Stoke shook his head. "There's no guarantee it would stay lit. You might as well walk over and hand the bomb to Faustine yourself and ask him to light it. Make one if you like, but don't waste any silver shot on it."

-63-

As night drew on and the skies began to darken, small fires appeared along the length of the riverbank at ten-foot intervals. "Well, will you look at that?" said Stoke with a laugh. "Mr. Macleary," he called, "I believe you have been supplied with an ignition device for your bombs, provided you can land one on target."

Ronan looked across the valley at the line of fires and grinned. Turning, he strode quickly across the square and up the street. Macleary wasted no time in firing up the forge and quickly turned to the task of seeking out an appropriate mould for the bombs.

Tamlyn gazed across the river at the lights. "They almost look pretty," he said to Padraic. "Were it not for the fact that those fires lie between us and the creepers, I might enjoy them."

"I wonder," said Liam, "if they are a distraction, placed there to keep our eyes from looking elsewhere."

Charlotte turned and saw herself reflected in Liam's eyes. "I find them a little frightening, as if they light the way to death."

"Something is happening on this side of the river," said Murdoch. "I saw movement down by those trees."

Duncan peered into the darkness where the youngster had pointed. Looking over to the lawns, he saw that some of the highlanders had noticed the movement as well. Several figures were visible in the dark area between the marsh and the upper lawns. They appeared to be constructing a pyre.

"What the devil are they doing?" asked Maclean "Do they presume to threaten us with fire on this side of the river now?"

One of the Teriz, larger than most, appeared suddenly as a torch caught. He thrust it into the wooden pyre and vanished quickly. Every head turned as the scream burst from Seth Willitt's throat. He was bound tightly to a stake at the centre of the blaze and had begun to taste the flame.

The spectators stared in mute disbelief, and up on the roof, Liam pulled Charlotte close, turning her away from the horror. As Willitt's screams rose in pitch, Caymus raised his crossbow and took careful aim. The deadly bolt whistled through the air and pierced his heart. The screams of agony ceased. Macleary lowered his weapon. "I had no love for the man, but no one deserves such a death."

"That will give them something to think about," said Euther. He was leaning against the armoury roof watching the burning. The apple farmer was either a very brave man or simply knew nothing of the trackers' plans. He was quite certain that bravery had not been one of Willitt's more prominent traits.

It might have been useful to send the farmer back to the village as a spy, but Colette had removed far too much of his skin to make it convincing. The old fool would have bled to death soon enough. So, not one to waste a good corpse, Euther had decided to send a direct message to the Dunradians: *Enter the valley at your peril.*

Caymus joined Ronan at his forge, and the brothers toiled through most of the night.

Ronan pondered the possibility of making a brand-new mould that would house a charge of black powder and silver pellets. "This is pointless," he said to Caymus, who was finishing the fittings on his large crossbow.

"Wait," he said, snapping his fingers. "Cay, design it to launch an arrow this size." He spread his arms to show him. "Speed is no factor. Distance is the only concern, and accuracy."

"As you wish," replied Caymus, unimpressed. "I only have to redesign half of the bloody track."

"It'll be worth it," said Ronan as he rushed off in search of something.

-64-

"It came to me last night. I have dozens of these tins that horse nails are packaged in. They're just the size and shape to attach to an arrow or large bolt. If we carve a recess in the bolt, no more than one third deep the tin's cylindrical shape will adhere to it nicely with a leather thong that can be gummed into place."

Branan and the others watched as Ronan made the mixture. "Saltpeter, sulphur, and carbon," He said, "commonly known as black powder." He poured a small handful of silver shot into the wooden bowl and stirred it gently. "A little silver and some horse nails, and we're in business."

Caymus spooned some of the mix into a tin and pushed a wooden plug into the end. "Next," he said, "we seal the plug in with beeswax and strap the tin to the bolt. Our best marksman aims the crossbow, and the bolt, providing it reaches the river, lands in one of their fires, explodes, and drives the silver shot into the flesh of anyone within twenty-five to thirty feet."

"It seems plausible" said Branan, trying to hide his excitement.

Padraic watched from above as the highlanders approached what remained of Willitt's pyre. The entire valley was covered with a beautiful hoarfrost so that the woods looked as though they were carved from crystal.

Wisps of smoke feathered through the air above the delicate pyramid of woven branches that held Willitt's remains. Pink and grey mingled with a red sinewy twist of muscle along the blackened frame of his broken body. The legs were a tortured mess of congealed blood and bone that still bubbled in the coals.

Woodruff pulled the end of the rope and stepped back as the monument crumbled into a smoking heap.

Duncan watched Padraic as he retreated to a corner of the roof and took a worn leather-covered journal from his vest. It hadn't occurred to him that young Treacher was a man of letters, so to speak. The big highlander was mildly envious, as he had never been afforded the opportunity for scholarly pursuits. Because of his size and muscular build, he'd been directed into the military at a young age.

Padraic tore a page from his journal and passed it to his friend. "I canna read," said Duncan with an apologetic shrug. The youngster pointed towards the field of burning and turned his thumbs down emphatically. Duncan nodded. "Aye, you can say that again."

Murdoch

I am recalling a story told to me by my late father when I was much smaller. I've only just remembered the tale, and it might prove to be of great importance. He spoke of a passage that ran from the limestone quarry to the centre of town.
Portus told me how his grandfather had used it to escape the English. If my recollections are accurate, Father spoke of an entrance in the sub-basement of our church. I feel this story was based in absolute truth and this knowledge should be passed on to Dr. Macleary and the others without delay

—Padraic

Padraic, who seldom left the rooftop, tore the entry from his journal and motioned to Duncan, indicating that he would be back. Chowder leapt to his feet and followed his master.

"Hello, Paddy," said Charlotte. "You've flown the coop, I see." The young woman looked drawn and tense. No one who had witnessed the remains of Willitt this morning felt anything other than gloom.

The mute passed a folded note to her and held up two fingers. This sign, secret except to a few, referred to the second-born Macleary, who was Murdoch.

"Of course, I'll take this to him at once." She knelt and scratched Chowder behind the ear. "You little ruffian, take care of Padraic, and I'll bring you back a treat."

Padraic walked over to the fountain and sat on its edge, scanning the city square. He pulled his jacket tight, tucking his hands into the pockets, and turned towards the church. *I wonder*, he thought. He was intelligent enough to know that not all of his father's stories were factual, and not all had been told, but he found it curious that no one had ever mentioned it. *Well*, he concluded, *some secrets die with the dead.*

"Good old Paddy," said Ronan. "What do you think?"

Tyburn leaned back in his chair. "Well, I've not heard of it, but it wouldn't surprise me. I wasn't even aware of a sub-basement, were you?"

"What is a sub-basement?" asked Murdoch.

"It's a room that lies beneath a regular basement, often the original cellar that is later built over with stronger materials," answered his grandfather.

"Well, what do you say we see what we can find?" suggested Ronan "Go get Padraic, he'll want a look."

Without the benefit of natural light the cellar took on a golden glow. Two lanterns had been brought down and placed on benches. The basement ran the length of the building and broad stone supports came out from the walls on both sides. Columns of dusty books were stacked between the pillars.

The floor was slightly angled towards an iron grate at the back that carried away any water that leaked into the building. It lay flat against a discoloured section of stone similar in size to a loaf of bread. Tyburn called his grandson over. "Tamlyn, bring your canteen here please."

He emptied the water into the drain quickly leaning next to the grate. Close to one second passed before the splash echoed back. "Near to ten feet … I'll be damned!" he exclaimed.

"Well done, lad," said Ronan, pointing to Padraic.

"We need to find a way in," said Tyburn. "There's no guarantee of a tunnel down there, but I'll swear there's a large room below."

Ronan pulled a short blade from his belt and began to scrape at the edges of the grate. No one spoke for several minutes as he worked his way around the drain. Eventually he managed to get a blade edge under one corner, and every eye was on him as he pried out the corroded metal.

A hand's length below the grate was an iron ring. Ronan took hold of the ring and pulled with no result. To the right of the ring was an indentation, wide enough for Ronan to fit his fingers. "Well, this is where the water goes" he said pulling up on the lip. Again nothing moved.

"Look here," said Tyburn, pointing. A thin seam was visible on three sides of Ronan in the dirt that coloured the stone floor. "You can't lift it because you're sat on it." Ronan turned on his knees and began to run his blade along the floor.

Euther was bent over in some discomfort at his desk. "Tell your men," he said to Colette, "that I want the elderly killed. I am offering one gold sovereign for every scalp brought to me." He passed gas loudly and winced. "The young are to be taken alive. See that everything is in place, we've been idle for too long."

Colette assured Faustine that everything was ready. "My one concern is Blunt," she said. "He seems to be falling apart, and I trust him even less than usual."

Euther waved off her remark. "I've spoken with him; he'll do as he's told." Faustine had indeed spoken with Godwyn; he was a master at playing one potential antagonist against the other.

Godwyn Blunt was less than impressed with Dafyd. He banged his gloved fist against the weapons rack. "Sneaking around the village will not win the day! I'm telling you, a full frontal assault under cover of darkness is the only option!"

Dafyd remained calm. "Mr. Blunt, you forget your station. I would like you to go down into the pit and have a little talk with yourself, see if you can't resolve some quarrel that you may have with my authority."

Godwyn stared at the ground, fuming.

"And while you're at it, see if you can't find yourself a nice bottle of wine. Put up your feet this evening and relax, you're far too tense."

Blunt was not a fan of the Welshman's patronizing approach and ducked angrily through the door to the wine cellar. Dafyd couldn't deny that a powerful man like Blunt could wreak havoc amongst the villagers, but he was only one man, and the rest of his makeshift army were ferocious but small. They would creep in at night from several points and kill them in their beds. The Welshman was convinced that within a matter of days Dunradin's cobbled streets would run red with blood. The Teriz who had the advantage of hunger on their side were growing increasingly restless.

Godwyn sat on a wine barrel with his head lowered. His wide hands massaged the knotted muscles of his stout neck. "I know, I know," he said, speaking aloud to the inner voice that was urging him to calm down.

He felt the numerous scars that adorned his shaven head, recalling past battles. Godwyn was a warrior; he wasn't like these animals with their unholy flesh-eating. He would collect his pay like any soldier, then he would return to his own village near the Norwegian fjords. It really was simple, he told himself: *Do what is asked of you; you're a hireling. And don't let the woman get to you.*

At that moment Colette entered the cellar. "What are you doing in here?" she asked Blunt.

Godwyn glanced up and looked into her mocking grey eyes. She thrust her hips forward suggestively. "Give me that bottle," she commanded. Godwyn's whole body went tense.

He reached behind him, gripping the bottle of wine by its neck, and got to his feet in one motion as he swung his arm forward. Guessing that she would duck to avoid the blow, he swung in a low crouch and smashed the bottle across her jaw. As Colette hit the floor he dove forward and plunged the remains of the bottle into her throat and twisted it forcefully. Godwyn didn't need to look closely to know that he had killed her.

Instinct told him to move quickly. There was no need for him to stop and consider his options now. Speed was the only choice. He leaped across the pit and dived into the tunnel. When he had emerged far enough from the armoury, he stopped to catch his breath.

It was foolish to have signed on to this campaign in the first place, he thought. It had been greed that spurred him on. He listened carefully. No sounds of pursuit. *Well, I've no doubt done the citizens of Dunradin a favour by ridding them of that jezebel. I could circle back through the trees and offer my services to the villagers.* He laughed aloud at the thought.

Godwyn was pleased to be outside in the fresh air. He smelled clean, grassy scents and forest pine, mingled with hay and wood smoke. He got to his feet and turned towards the stand of trees behind him. The skyline beyond was coloured with the grey expanse of a new fire, and a handful of snowflakes appeared between Godwyn and the wooded area. *Okay*, he thought, *any direction away from here is good.* He crouched low and made his way quickly towards the smoke, hoping to travel as far as possible before darkness.

"That'll be Mr. Smead's work," he said, gazing at the narrow line of orange in the distance. *Freelancing?* he wondered. *Or just exercising his right to burn whatever he bloody well pleases?* Passing the field, Blunt spotted Tanner Smead far to his left, rocking like a windup monkey. It occurred to him that Smead, the village idiot, was probably the sanest of the lot.

The snow began to fall more steadily, threatening to extinguish the low brush fire that cast a rosy glow across the field.

After he had travelled half a league east to higher ground, he turned and looked back the way he had come. The nightly bonfires along the river looked like a line of stars, and the snow, no longer falling, was lit from above by a full moon that seemed to have torn open the sky.

Godwyn took shelter behind a large stone and leaned back against its flat surface. He was a safe distance from Lilyvine now, and he considered what his next move should be. There would be no more skulking about in the darkness. He would sleep at night and seek his way forward by the light of day.

The big man yawned and patted the lining of his jacket, where he had sewn a small purse. The handful of sovereigns was still there. His pistols were back at Lilyvine, hanging on the wall inside his larger wool jacket. Fortunately his boot sheath carried a sturdy bone-handled knife.

Blunt cursed himself for not taking Colette's pistol before fleeing. It was a woman's weapon but effective at close range. The way Godwyn saw it, he could go south, find a ship bound for Amsterdam, and head north from there, or he could follow an arc back towards Dunradin and enter the village from the woods above the quarry. He decided to sleep on it and make up his mind in the morning.

Dafyd looked down at the body. "All this blood spilled," he said, "and nothing resolved, such an unhappy time. Is there any point going after him?"

Euther put his arm on the Welshman's shoulder. "They were weak—William, Fearghal, Godwyn, all of them weak. The strength is here," he said, pointing to his head. "Forget about Godwyn; we still have Mingus."

"Yes," said Dafyd, "as well as Coyle and Spate. Mingus is less of a hothead than Blunt was, and he is fully blooded." The Welshman considered those who did not take part in cannibalism to be inferior and half-blooded. In his mind they were less effective due to their inability to function in daylight. Nevertheless, only the higher ranks were permitted to consume human flesh. This system made the lower caste Teriz weaker, and easier to kill, but they were controlled with less effort.

Mingus, having been allowed to rise to the ranks of the full-blooded, was a natural choice to replace Blunt. He would not be heartbroken to hear that Godwyn was gone. In fact, the big man would be missed by no one.

The Welshman had always been against hiring anyone but those of his kind. It was so much easier to manipulate someone when they shared the same culinary tastes Commoners like Drake and Blunt only lusted after gold, which was more easily found outside of the Family of Night. "A man with only one vice" Faustine had said "is of little use."

Euther eyed Colette's corpse hungrily. "Would you mind?" he asked half in jest.

"No, go ahead," said Dafyd with no hesitation. "I think I'll join you."

Caymus and Maclean lifted the heavy bow and mounted it into the support. A trench had been built into the hillside and lined with sturdy building stones, on top of which lay an old miller's wheel. Once the bow was in place, it pivoted easily in all directions. The seven-foot bolts that Ronan had made numbered ten and lay on their sides outside the trench.

"Where is Ronan?" asked Caymus. "He should be here."

Across the river the fires had been lit, and a large number of Teriz were visible as the full moon climbed into the sky.

"He's been scratching about in the church all day with your father," answered Branan. "I'll go over and fetch him, I'm curious to know what they may have uncovered."

Tyburn and Ronan had eventually concluded that the only way they would be able to lift the heavy door was with a rope and lever. It had taken the better part of the day to arrange a system to lift the square stone.

When Branan entered the basement, they had secured a rope to the ring in the floor. It was Murdoch who had discovered that, of the five heavy beams in the basement ceiling, the one directly above the slab had a worn track across its centre. The stout rope was looped over the beam and then drawn out to the desired length, determined by a series of measurements. The end of the rope was fastened by both ends to a heavy wooden door that hung at chest height, parallel to the floor.

"Now all we need do," said Tyburn, "is place a weight surpassing that of the slab, onto the door, and the rock will rise.

"Ah, just in time," he said to Branan. "Stoke, you must be close to fifteen stone, are you not?"

"I imagine so" conceded Branan with a grin. The youngsters were dirty-faced and tired. They had spent a great deal of time digging and scraping at the edges of the rock. Branan took in the scene, analyzing what was being attempted, and grabbed a wooden stool from the corner of the basement. "If I step from this chair onto that platform, the stone will dislodge and raise up leaving an opening, but how will you secure it? When I jump from the platform, the stone will drop back in place."

"We've thought that one out too," said Murdoch, pointing to the rope above their heads. "While you are standing on the door we'll put these three logs across the opening" he said pointing. "Then when it's lowered back, we can easily roll it away."

"Very impressive!" exclaimed Stoke, laughing. "Perhaps it could wait, though. I would like the others to see what you've stumbled upon, but Caymus is anxious to demonstrate his bow and would like Ronan's assistance."

Despite their excitement at being so close to discovering if there was a tunnel below the church, the youngsters were even more intrigued at the prospect of actually seeing the enemy set upon. They left the tunnel for the time being as everyone thronged to join the highlanders.

The crowd that had gathered was kept well back from the trench and stood about in a subdued silence, as they stared across the river at the increasing number of Teriz that milled about hollering and shooting guns into the air. This show of force was clearly meant to intimidate the villagers and break their spirits. Five more homes had also been set ablaze, and those who could recognize their cottages from this distance were indeed feeling dispirited and helpless.

Caymus placed one of Ronan's bolts in the large crossbow with help from his brother. "Like this," said Ronan, turning the heavy arrow so that the explosive tin was at the top. "If it shifts during the flight, it's of no consequence, but we don't want it getting caught up on the track." He wound the cord tight and pounded the peg into its slot.

Caymus aimed for a point well above the central fire to ensure that it would lose altitude as it neared the target and drop into the flames. "Ready," said Caymus, and Ronan struck the peg. The bolt ejected with surprising speed and whistled as it climbed into the skies above the river. It seemed to climb forever, and then appeared briefly as it shot across the roof of the armoury to fall somewhere behind the building. Some of the gathered turned to each other and spoke quietly.

"Well, we know it can handle the distance," said Ronan. "I think less tension on the cord. I'll count the turns six instead of ten, and let's try again." The next shot came up short and landed in the river, much to the amusement of the Teriz on the bank, who jeered and howled. The villagers seemed disheartened, and a few turned away.

Charlotte trembled from the cold night air and pulled her shawl tightly across her back. Behind her, Liam stepped forward and wrapped his arms around her shoulders, pulling her close to his chest. He leaned closer and whispered in her ear encouragingly, "Third time lucky."

Ronan counted again—five, six, and seven—and placed the peg. "Ready," called Caymus once more. The peg was struck, and once more a bolt flew from the hill. No one dared breathe. The arrow fell directly in the fire this time. "Excellent hit!" cheered Caymus. The crowd was confused and the howls of derision rose again from the Teriz.

Three of them approached the harmless looking projectile. Two seconds passed as the fire burned its way into the tin. Then with a huge flash and a report like cracking thunder, the black powder exploded. Hot shards of metal and molten silver blew through a half dozen of the creatures, killing them at once. The Dunradians erupted into cheers and applause.

Dafyd and Euther rushed to the window. What deviltry was this? A second bolt was let loose and found its mark in another fire, with the same result. Mingus turned his eyes toward the fourth floor, appealing for direction as yet another deadly bolt landed.

"The fires, you fools!" screamed Faustine. "Douse the fires!" Some of the Teriz had realized that the flames were igniting the deadly spears and ran quickly from the fires.

All told fifteen had been killed on three shots, and two of the bolts had been wasted, with five remaining. Some of the Teriz, braver than they were wise, approached the fires with buckets of water, but Caymus, realizing that the element of surprise had vanished, loaded the bow no more. The bolt's loud whistle as it cut through the air was now a signal of almost certain death. Charlotte would sleep much better tonight, as would a great number of the villagers. With all the excitement the tunnel was abandoned until the next morning.

"Well it looks as though we underestimated these farmers." said Euther. "Imagine if we had placed ourselves in the front ranks, Dafyd. All would have been lost. There is silver in those wounds below; that would have marked the end of a very long silent war that began with my birth. The era of Dorian would have played its last act. It was better for all perhaps."

He stood up suddenly. "What a load of sentimental pissing and moaning. Pay it no heed. Where is Mingus? Send him to me."

Mingus's cheeks and forehead were darkened with wood ash and dirt, and his shoulder was scarred from a new burn. He addressed Faustine: "Sir, there are fifteen lost."

"Yes, very unfortunate. I trust the fires have all been doused; we won't make that mistake again. Clearly this rabble is not easily intimidated; we shall take a new tack."

Faustine paused, considering whether to ask Mingus his advice, then thought better of it. "Fifteen bodies ... well, drain the blood for your men, but of course there is to be no feeding. You and your two captains are the exception." Euther was growing bored with the procedure and dismissed Mingus with a wave.

Dafyd, who had remained seated in the corner, spoke. "Do you really believe that his men will not consume the bodies?"

"Mr. Kendricks, if young Mingus has one half of a brain, he will insure that the bleeding is left to Coyle and Spate, then he will burn the remains. Any captain worth his salt keeps his troops at arm's length."

"And what is to keep, say, Sergeant Spate, from tucking away a piece of arm or leg to be used in barter?"

"Really, Dafyd, you've grown so cynical. If you knew how paranoid you sound."

"I'm a little more cautious," said the Welshman in his own defence, "since Blunt turned on us."

"Caution is a fine thing, but I think you know that Colette pushed the man for her own amusement and probably got what she deserved. I'm surprised that Godwyn didn't have the balls to fuck her first."

Dafyd frowned. "She had a minge like a bear trap, my friend. Did you not notice?"

Euther laughed. "On the subject of your late wife, I have the most wretched case of heartburn, which I can only attribute to the quality of the woman."

"Overconsumption," snapped Dafyd "is oft the cause of such an ailment."

"Perhaps if you would see that the remains are reduced to small packages and locked away we could all relax," replied Faustine. "I daresay we need to put some thought into the situation if we are to live off the fat of the land, as it were. Morning draws near; let's sleep on it and see what solutions a rested mind can offer us."

-65-

Godwyn woke with the first light. He was cold, and his back hurt from sleeping against stone on a winter night. He turned his head from side to side, stretching his neck muscles with an audible click and grind. *This won't do*, he thought, deciding that a long journey was out of the question without supplies. At the very least he required a warm jacket. He would circle back and enter Dunradin from the western approach.

He was also curious as to what may have transpired in the night and what the explosions had meant. He stood up and cursed the cold ground, brushing the snow from his shoulders. A proper meal would suit him as well. The big man was confident that his dealings with Faustine were known only on one side of the river, and he could fabricate a history that would grant him entrance to the village.

He started down the slope in a westerly direction. The snow that had fallen through the night left a blanket of white over the fields, and there was a crisp feel to the air. Soon Lilyvine came into view far to his right. Even from this distance he could see that the white banks of the Sleath were coloured a muddy grey and red. Tiny wisps of smoke were visible from old fires that had defied the weather and smouldered still. There was no mistaking the pink patches of melting snow here and there where a bloodied body had lain. Blunt wondered if he was visible from the roof and put more distance between himself and the armoury.

Fearghal, from his high window, marked the passage of Godwyn as his figure diminished in the distance. He too observed the stains in the snow, though in the grey-white world of the undead there was no colour. It was Fearghal who had whispered into Colette's ear the suggestions of treachery and deceit that had sent her in search of Blunt.

Within thirty minutes Blunt found himself on the dairy road outside Dunradin. On his right two dozen or so sturdy-looking horses grazed in the same field occupied by cattle. A dense barricade lay across the road, guarded by two stern-looking men in highland dress.

As he approached, Godwyn thought it wise to fabricate an injury and limped forward. "Begging your pardon, gentlemen," he called out, "I am in some distress. I have been attacked by creatures of the foulest nature imaginable. I am reluctant to describe them for fear of being thought mad. They have taken my horse and cloak, and I am cold and hungry."

The taller of the two highlanders looked over Blunt's shoulder down the road. "I see no assailants."

"I have walked for some distance," replied Godwyn. "They set upon me under cover of darkness, pale grasping creatures that I shudder to describe."

"Sit you here," said the first highlander, passing him a blanket. "I am compelled to send for my commander before allowing anyone entry."

Hugh Maclean was located quickly. He had slept well after the success of the previous night's encounter.

"There were two of the bandits," said Godwyn, "both with short spears. As I lay asleep they assaulted me and demanded my horse and the cloak I was wrapped in. They asked for no coin and in any event would have found none, except for the money in my boot. These fiends were of a smaller stature than myself and shared my mount. I had no opportunity to pursue them and decided that I was fortunate to have retained my boots."

"Are you injured?" asked Maclean.

"A twisted knee is all, save for my pride. I should have fought the swine."

"I'm afraid it would have taken a much larger man than yourself to subdue the creatures. If my guess is right, they are the same breed that we are currently troubled by. Tell me, though, as I am compelled to ask, how do you come to be on the road?"

"A matter of import with regards to the law," answered Godwyn obligingly. "I am returning from Glasgow, where I testified in the courts on the behalf of a friend. I seem to have been turned about in the snows, and have had a bad coming of it."

"Well," said Maclean, "you have not missed the road by much. I will grant you leave to enter the village, and when you are ready, we will point you. Where do you make for?"

"I was meant to stop in Carlisle the night then through Doncaster to my home in York," he answered.

Maclean eyed the man suspiciously. "If you travel to Doncaster you have overshot your mark. Surely you're aware that Doncaster lies to the south of York on the same road?"

Godwyn, who was not conversant with geography below the border, looked away from Hugh and stared at his boots, momentarily flustered. "I have business in Doncaster as well," he said quietly.

"And what business might that be?" demanded Maclean.

Blunt smiled slowly. "I fear it is a delicate matter involving the fairer sex; for the lady's honour I dare not say more." His voice trailed off suggestively.

Maclean relaxed, apparently satisfied with the answer. "There is a haberdasher in this block," he said, pointing, "who will direct you to a men's outfitter."

Blunt thanked the highlander and turned to leave.

"I suggest you purchase a brace of pistols before venturing onto the north road again, and sleep with one beneath your blanket," advised Maclean. *He walks well for a man with a twisted knee,* thought Hugh as he watched Blunt take his leave. He would keep a close watch on the stranger.

Across the square, Padraic sat on the church steps awaiting his friends. He had slept very little, and that little was haunted by images of bloodied bodies crawling out of holes in the snow. Nevertheless he was excited at the prospect of discovering the tunnel that his father had spoken of.

Eventually Ronan arrived with his children, followed minutes later by Tyburn, Branan, and Liam.

"Padraic says, as he is the smallest and the bravest, he will go first," joked Liam. Twist had admitted to having had enough of tunnels for the time being. The youngsters all laughed, except for Padraic, who just shrugged.

"I think," said Ronan, climbing the stairs, "that that may actually be the best idea. We could well discover that there is nothing more than a small room below filled with rat droppings."

When they got down to their work, the basement was as they had left it the evening before. "Now you be ready with those rollers," said Stoke, "and once they are in place, step away quickly. We don't want any fingers to go missing."

He stepped onto the chair, seized the upper ropes, and placed one foot on the door. "Ready now?" He swung his other leg across and allowed the door to support his whole weight. At first nothing happened, and then everything happened at once. The stone began to rise with a groan, and then as it loosened itself, it came up quickly, dangling barely high enough off the floor for the rollers to be slipped into place. Stoke hopped from the door to avoid being catapulted to the ceiling, and the stone dropped the very short distance to the rollers, sitting aboard them perfectly.

"Good work!" said Branan. "Now don't roll it just yet," he added. "When the stone has come off the third roller, bring that one around in front of the other two." The stone was as thick as three fists but proved easy to move. Once it was clear, what lay below was indeed a small room that was deeper than it was wide. The wall at the front narrowed to the width of a door, and it appeared, due to a pair of rusted hinges, to have been a closed entrance in the past. Beyond the doorway was a narrow stairwell that disappeared into absolute darkness.

Godwyn found no complaint with the food in Ezekiel's Ale House. A triple helping of fried potatoes, eggs, and baked beans vanished quickly from his plate. He would have liked a few rashers of bacon with the meal but was told that meat was in short supply due to the disturbances across the river.

"Beef, mutton, herring, and ale were the standard when my old dad were a boy," said Bardwyck. "There was more meat to be had back then. Nowadays it's oatmeal and potatoes what keeps us on two feet. If you've a mind to hunt, there's quail to be had up beyond the woods, but all that area's off limits at present."

Godwyn nodded politely between mouthfuls. When he'd finished his meal, he questioned the barkeep. "I am told you are a man I should talk to, a man who would provide a fine pair of pistols at an honest price."

"You were given sage advice. I am that very man."

"I'm not in the habit of carrying short arms," continued Blunt, "but as I travel a wee bit, it was suggested to me that it might be wise."

"Always a wise choice," replied the old man. "I have a brace that are worth three sovereigns if they're worth a penny," he claimed, reaching below the bar. "This one is missing a jaw screw on the hammer, and it needs a new flint, but I can repair it tomorrow, if you're in no rush."

"What of the baldric and holsters? They look to be well crafted."

"As good a pair of bucket holsters as you'll find," said the publican, "and I'll throw them in at no cost. You'll find that baldric comfortable for a man your size."

"You are most generous," replied Blunt. "I will give you four sovereigns and call for them tomorrow afternoon." He slipped on his new overcoat and shook the hand of Bardwyck before stepping outside into the sunshine.

It was rare for Duncan to encounter a man that could match him in size and girth, but the stranger, at least from this distance, looked his equal. The man stood above the green, looking out towards the river with his arms crossed below his chest. Then, sensing he was being observed, he cocked an eye towards the rooftop and nodded at Duncan. The big red-headed Highlander mouthed a silent greeting in response.

"Who's that four-acre giant?" asked Caleb Macneil.

"Stranger," replied Duncan.

"That much I knew," chirped the youngster.

"I've nae seen him before," laughed Duncan. "He looks more Viking than Highlands to me though."

"Where's my little friend Chowder?" asked Cardiff.

"Padraic was away with him early," replied Duncan. "They were in need of a ratter at the kirk, I believe."

"Wee Tamlyn said they were having a dig in the cellar," observed Caleb.

"Buried treasure?" asked Duncan, amused.

"Something to do with a tunnel under the village" replied Cardiff.

"It wouldnae surprise me," Duncan allowed. "You have a limestone quarry down the way, and the whole town must be sitting on bedrock. Why don't you lads go down and have a look?—and you can bring me back a loaf."

The brothers didn't require much encouragement when adventure was suggested and happily left the watch to Duncan.

Although Padraic was willing enough to enter the tunnel first, Stoke decided that if the youngster were to fall on the slippery steps, he would not be able to call out. Murdoch was chosen to enter first, and after a ladder was found, he climbed into the pit and reached above his head to take the lantern from Ronan.

"Watch your footing, Son, and not too fast."

"There is a curse written here," said the youngster. Murdoch read for all to hear the words carved into the steps that greeted him upon entering the low doorway.

A curse on thair haids
The English swine
Their blood shall run
Like sower wyne

His reading was met with soft laughter. "These stairs look to go on forever," called Murdoch, more than a little nervous.

Ronan entered the pit and stepped into the stairwell with his son, almost losing his footing on the first step. The air below was cold and damp but easy enough to breathe, leading Ronan to believe that a larger passage must be close at hand.

"The bottom is here," said the younger Macleary. Another doorway opened on his right to a much broader and level passageway. Twenty feet in, Murdoch came to an abrupt halt. "There's a hole," he said.

Ronan drew even with the youngster. The hole was wider than a grown man's shoulders. "I wouldn't be surprised if that pit gave up English bones," said Ronan. "Someone who was familiar with this passageway could flee in the darkness and his pursuers would fall into the hole, or at the very least break a leg." He pointed behind him. "Look, there in the wall is the sign." A brick at hands height protruded from the wall. It was a yard before the hole and would signal a jump to the blind. "It was pure luck that you didn't end up at the bottom of that trap." Another brick was located on the other side for the journey back.

"Please keep your eyes open for others, Son." The passage was wide enough now for them to walk two abreast. It suddenly occurred to Ronan that some of the others might venture into the tunnel, and he decided the two of them should turn back at this point and warn everybody to be wary of holes.

"I wonder if there are bats down here," said Murdoch.

"No, I don't think so," answered Ronan, as he started up the steps. "You are more likely to find rats in such a place; bats prefer large caverns."

"How far does it go?" asked Stoke.

"There is no way to know without further exploration," replied Ronan. "We came back to tell you that the air is breathable, but don't go in without a light. There are holes that a man could slip into and never be seen again."

He went on to explain his theory that their ancestors used this passage as a means of escape, as Padraic's father had suggested. "I feel they must have run from their pursuers in total darkness, knowing where the traps were and how to avoid them."

"The secret of this passageway might have died with Portus, if Padraic had not recalled the story," said Branan, putting his hand on the boy's shoulder. "We had better find the other end before the Teriz stumble upon it, which is a distinct possibility, the way they're chewing up the valley."

After much discussion it was decided that no more than two in number would explore the tunnel, and that a heavy wooden door from above would be brought down and placed over the hole that Murdoch had discovered. This would serve a double purpose, in that it would also prevent anything from creeping up out of the hole.

It had taken some time to determine who should follow the tunnel to the end. Stoke insisted that at least one of the party must be armed and that the other should be small enough to explore any narrow sections that might appear. Eventually it was decided that Ronan and Murdoch should resume their exploration. The younger Macleary was given a leather belt with a sturdy dirk attached, and his father had the loan of a reliable flintlock. Ronan took the lead, and father and son both carried lamps.

Tamlyn was disappointed at being left behind but excited that Padraic's efforts had borne fruit. It was a discovery that had quickly become public knowledge, and the townsfolk referred to it as Padraic's Tunnel.

The two friends left with the Macneils in search of food. Cardiff was determined to find the largest loaf of bread possible for Duncan. Soon they located a half wheel of cheese and a hefty rye loaf, along with a stick of Ceana's raspberry butter. The day seemed to be filled with sunshine and mischief that even the shadow over the river couldn't touch. The lads laid out a fine lunch on the rooftop, when a low rumble somewhere below the valley reminded them that diligence was still required.

Ronan and Murdoch had felt the tremor also. They stopped momentarily as particles of dirt fell from the tunnel above their heads. They both had visions of the walls coming in on them. When it was apparent that they were safe for the time being, Ronan suggested that they carry on.

The tunnel had run for some distance now in a straight line with no change in the width or depth. They had encountered another hole similar to the first. When Murdoch lowered his lamp into it at arm's length, the bottom was not visible beyond the reach of the light, but the intrusion triggered a squeaking and mewling of what sounded like a large collection of rats. "Not a spot I would care to slip into," said Ronan.

Murdoch shuddered at the very thought. "No worries," added the elder Macleary. "They probably only have a taste for the English." After several more minutes of travel in a straight line, the floor seemed to be angling up, and suddenly they came upon a divide in the tunnel which forced them to make a decision. To their left was another passageway that broke off from the main route. Ronan suggested they explore it for a small distance but then return to the main passage. By his reckoning, they had been steadily proceeding in an easterly direction towards the quarry.

They had only taken a handful of steps into the new passage when a low threshold appeared. Stepping over it, they found themselves in a compact room that was hewn out of the rock bed. A low bench had been cut into the back wall, and except for the remains of a broken barrel, the small room was empty.

"This must have been a storage room," suggested Ronan, "and no doubt a fine spot for an ambush." The air in here was less clean and decidedly thinner. "Let's get back to the main passage then."

Before long they encountered another branch that was identical to the first. "Should we look?" asked Murdoch, and they entered the second left-hand passage. "It's the same," said the youngster.

"See here," said Ronan pointing. There was a hole in the roof above the bench, and the air here was much clearer than in the rest of the tunnel. "If you stand on my hands, could you reach your head into that opening?"

"I think so," said Murdoch. Ronan cupped his hands together and lifted the boy up. "There's a ladder on this wall," said the youngster.

"See how far it goes," suggested Ronan, "but be careful."

"Do you think of me when you're serving watch on the roof?" asked Charlotte.

Liam frowned. "Of course not, I've far too many important matters to concern myself with."

"You liar!" laughed the young woman

"Truth be told," he said softly, "I think of little else."

"My mother says you're a good catch," said Charlotte, putting her hand on Liam's neck.

Liam smiled. "How is your mom? She looked a wee bit drawn when I saw her last."

"Yes, this whole business has her very worried, I'm afraid," said the young woman, looking over Liam's shoulder. "She frets about Tamlyn and little Padraic, all the wee ones really."

"Well I wouldn't worry too much about Padraic," said Liam. "He's grown up in a hurry, with what he's had to face."

Charlotte leaned over and kissed Liam lightly on the lips. "I still think of him as a little brother though, and it's no way to grow up."

"I miss my father every day," he agreed. "Everything I know about life I learned from him, but I'm fortunate, as I still have a mother. It hasn't been easy for her this last while."

"She's wonderful with the little ones," said Charlotte.

"What do you make of this fellow?" asked Liam, motioning with his head. A good-sized man sat at the fountain with his chin resting on his knuckles, deep in thought.

"I haven't seen him before, is he one of the Highlanders?"

"I don't believe he is," he answered, "but I'll warrant he could match our Duncan at the caber."

"If you ask me, he looks troubled," said Charlotte.

"Or hungry." quipped young Twist.

Godwyn was neither hungry nor troubled. He was simply undecided. Blunt had done many things that he was not proud of. He'd travelled the length of the kingdom in pursuit of adventure and profit and had never cared which side of the law he was on. In a sense he was similar to the late William Drake, who in the end had tired of looking over his shoulder.

Godwyn differed from Drake in that he had always imagined himself ending up as a family man, growing fat with children at his feet. These Teriz were the most abhorrent band of cutthroats that he had ever been employed by, and their cannibalistic practices appalled and disgusted him. He had intended to leave when the job was done yet realized that there was no way to justify staying as long as he had. As much as Blunt hated Colette, he was nevertheless fascinated by her strength and had been unreasonably attracted to her. Godwyn was not the first man she'd cast her spell on, but was without a doubt the last.

An unfamiliar inclination towards making amends had begun to emerge in Blunt's musings. The more attention he gave it, the more it responded, until, by the afternoon, he had formed an unlikely alliance with his decision.

Euther and Dafyd were the charismatic leaders of a rapidly growing cult. Godwyn had heard talk that there were pockets of Teriz below the border waiting and watching to see what the results of Faustine's experiment would be. If Dorian was able to successfully segregate this little village for his brethren, others would follow his lead and search for villages of their own. There would be fiefdoms everywhere populated by the Teriz and their dictatorial leaders.

Godwyn's observations had helped him determine who the most influential men were in Dunradin. He would speak with the highlander Branan Stoke. He appeared to be the helmsman, along with perhaps the bowman Caymus. Stoke, in his judgement, appeared to be the most approachable.

Branan entered the Ale House, as luck would have it, shortly after Blunt arrived to take ownership of his newly purchased pistols.

Murdoch gripped the iron rungs tightly and continued one step at a time. After having advanced two thirds of the way up the twenty-five-foot ladder, he began to feel foliage under his palms where vines from above had twisted around the ladder which was firmly imbedded in the wall. Daylight peeked through the remains of a thatched cover, fighting to gain inroads against the tangles of ivy that held it in place. "An opening," Murdoch called as he pushed against the circle of vines, which rose briefly and then snapped back into place as though it had been pushed from the top.

He wrestled with the opening until it eventually gave way, and light flooded into the tunnel. He pulled himself up and looked about. He climbed down again quickly and brushed the dirt from his shoulders. "We're somewhat close to the quarry. I could see it up there, near to fifty yards off."

Ronan climbed up the ladder himself and looked from east to west, blinking in the bright light. The tunnel opened onto an edge of the tree line, where small patches of gorse hid it from below. It was not unlike one of the Teriz sinkholes, albeit better constructed and not designed to be fallen into.

Macleary closed the thatch work and re-joined his son. The two sat on the recessed bench and had a pull from Ronan's canteen before deciding to continue. As it happened, they reached the end of the main passage soon after. They had been walking no more than two minutes when the floor of the tunnel angled down at the same time as the roof appeared to angle up, and they were suddenly faced with a dead end.

Murdoch looked up and let out a yell as he stumbled back and bumped into his father, almost dropping his lantern. Ronan looked up while stretching out an arm to steady his son. Above their heads was the skeletal remains of what was once a man. Chains and iron ring works held it with the back of its spine facing the roof. The arms and legs were secured at four corners, and the skull stared down , mocking anyone who dared to gaze too long.

"Bloody hell," said the youngster, "that gave me a fright."

Ronan shook his head slowly. "The poor bugger. God knows how many years he's been here. or how long it took him to die."

"What do we do now?" asked Murdoch.

"Well, Son, I don't think this is the end of the tunnel, but that won't be determined by you and I but by picks and shovels. I wouldn't be surprised to learn that behind that clay there's a wall of bricks that's easily knocked down. We'll go back and let the others know. Are you as hungry as I am, Son?"

"Mr. Stoke and the others are at the pub," said Caleb as Ronan and his son emerged from the tunnel. The Macneil brothers had been left to guard the cellar and listen for any signs of trouble within.

"Have you been to the quarry and back?" asked Cardiff.

"Not quite," said Ronan. "Is that roast quail I'm smelling?"

"Oh aye," answered Caleb. "Miss Charlotte brought a platter of food down, knowing you'd have missed lunch. Cardiff told me five more minutes and he was gonna eat the lot."

"Filthy liar!" replied his brother. "Cold quail and cider for two, as you tell us the tale!" he sang happily.

Murdoch described their findings excitedly, omitting nothing. Caleb whistled, repeating, "And a dead man strapped to the ceiling. I'll bet he were a Yorkshireman out for plunder."

Cardiff chuckled. "Out fer plunder and stuck down under!"

"Whoever he was," said Ronan between mouthfuls, "he met a nasty end."

"A horrible way to die," said Murdoch. "The rats probably chewed at him while he was still alive."

"True," said Caleb, "just like the way you're gnawing on that fowl."

Murdoch stopped eating and threw the quail bone at Macneil. "I don't feel hungry now."

"I want to secure this entrance," said Ronan, "so that we can return later, and I don't want access to the church from within the tunnel. If the creatures were to stumble upon the tunnel, they'd soon find themselves in a building filled with children, and I don't have to tell you—" His voice trailed off. They sat in grim silence pondering Ronan's last thought.

"I know the solution!" said Cardiff pointing to the ceiling. "The highlanders are bedded at the schoolhouse just now, and the wee ones are upstairs here. Make a switch! Big ones here wee ones there."

The others perked up at once. "Cardiff, that's brilliant,!" said Caleb. "Coming from an oaf like you, it's genius!"

"I think you've solved our problem, lad," said Ronan. Cardiff grinned proudly. Ronan was pleased "Sometimes the easiest answers are the hardest to find," he said. "We'll arrange this before nightfall."

"Master Stoke, is it?"

"Yes," replied Branan taking Godwyn's hand in greeting. "You have me at a disadvantage, sir. I don't believe I know your name."

"I beg your pardon. I am Godwyn Blunt, a stranger to Dunradin, recently employed on the other side of your river Sleath."

Branan looked shocked, and Caymus, who had entered behind the Highlander, put a hand to his blade belt.
"Please forgive my directness. I have nothing but your welfare in mind." He continued, "I am a fugitive from the Teriz, having only recently slain one of their leaders."

"Carry on," said Stoke cautiously, pointing him to a chair.

"I am acquainted with Mr. Maclean who gave me leave to enter the city. With apologies to the gentleman, I was less than honest about my business."

"Maclean is not here at the moment," said Caymus, clearly irritated. "Explain yourself."

Blunt recounted his history with the Wraiths, leaving out only the matter of his strange attraction to Colette. "Why then did you not continue south and make for your homelands?"

Godwyn answered Branan in an urgent tone. "You are in grave danger. I fear there is more about these Teriz than any of us can guess, and more are bound to fall into harm's way. You are just one small village. There are men who toil in the quarry by night. Faustine grows tired of his lodgings and is having an underground fortress cut from stone."

Stoke's eyes widened. "That would explain why we've not been assaulted."

"They are just toying with you for the moment, building small fires, and playing at a game of deception. The quarry houses thrice the number that ever entered the armoury, and more are on the way." Godwyn stared down at his boots. "I believe I can only remove the shame I feel by offering my services, and relating to you all that I know."

He placed his newly acquired pistols on the table in a gesture of submission. Branan looked at Caymus and then returned his gaze to Blunt.

"Hang onto your baldric then," encouraged Caymus, "and I hope you're an accomplished marksman; you'll need to be."

Both men were shocked to hear the numbers that Godwyn had suggested. Branan in particular was alarmed. He had been led to believe that only a few Teriz remained. The news of hidden colonies further alarmed him, and he wondered if Her Majesty had been apprised of the situation. He began to question the reliability of what the Queen's liaison had told him. Perhaps he was only one of several agents working to eradicate the scourge.

The more he thought about it, the more he realized that this must be the way of it He had quite frankly been surprised and flattered when he was chosen over Lord Pengrove to manage the operation. It all began to make sense. Pengrove had been chosen for a similar if not more important task elsewhere. His old classmate Griffin was probably involved as well, and none aware of the others' parts. *This is a growing practice within the royalty, I shouldn't be surprised.* Espionage was nothing new to the ruling classes. Walsingham was an example during the time of Elizabeth. Spies had only become craftier and more efficient since then.

Ronan, who had not found Stoke at the grocer's, made his way to the Ale House where he found his companions deep in discussion with a tall stranger.

"This is Ronan Macleary," said Caymus, "my brother. Mr. Blunt here has told us an intriguing tale and swears allegiance to our cause."

Being familiar with Caymus's manner of speaking, Ronan knew that no oath had been sworn and that Cay was pressing for assurances in his own way.

"Godwyn Blunt," said the large man, shaking Ronan's hand firmly. "I am pleased to assist in any capacity," he added with a glance at the bowman.

Although Ronan tended to be more trusting than Caymus he decided not to mention the matter of the tunnel until it was brought up. Stoke did not ask immediately; instead, he relayed all that Blunt had told them, practically in one breath for the sake of expediency. He seemed to gather from Ronan's demeanour that something of note had been discovered underground.

"This is alarming news!" said the blacksmith. "The tunnel …," he began, pausing to read the mood.

"Yes. Go on," Stoke encouraged.

Ronan explained all that they had found and offered Macneil's solution for moving the children. This was met with instant approval, and they decided to make the switch before nightfall. The matter was urgent: Godwyn had made it clear that the Teriz were aware of the placement and number of highlanders, as well as where the villagers commonly gathered.

Ronan suddenly felt less inclined to further explore Padraic's tunnel and expressed his fears. "We might consider using it to our advantage," replied Caymus. "If the tunnel is opened from the other end, we should bury the fiends alive as they pour in."

"If Mr. Blunt speaks the truth," said Ronan, "we are all in peril, and it is imperative that we formulate a plan for our survival. Let us look to the care of the children first, and then I would like to arrange a meeting in the church tomorrow. Every man and woman should have their say on this matter. This beast has become immense."

Before long Charlotte, Ceana, and some of the other mothers in the church informed the children that they were to pack up their bedding because a big adventure was forthcoming. There were to be treats and stories in the schoolhouse along with candied plums and a real juggler. The children were beyond excited and rushed about anxiously gathering their bedrolls and belongings.

Wee Simon Macauley was the lone holdout. Of all the children, it had taken him the longest to feel comfortable in his new home, and now he was the most reluctant to leave. "Nae gonna leave kirk!" he insisted, shrilly defiant. ("Bollocks tae that!" was another useful expression he'd learned from the older boys.) Eventually the little man was coerced into leaving with the offer of a horse ride.

Ronan, as instructed told the women only that the schoolhouse was deemed safer than the church due to the nature of the digging below. Branan had stressed the importance of not inciting mass panic with too much information. Macleary, for his part, was happy enough to not supply his wife with further concerns.

Ceana was not sleeping well, and her poor health was beginning to show. The dark circles under her eyes and the loss of weight worried Ronan more than he cared to admit. "You mustn't take it all on yourself" declared the blacksmith. "We have a very competent force of highlanders in our midst, and soon," he lied, "a further platoon will arrive."

Ceana took off her apron and slumped in her chair. "I know, it's just the little ones. I worry so much for their sakes. We never had to face these things in our youth, and it's just very unfair."

"Think of our grandparents," said Ronan. "Look what they dealt with. The English were just as monstrous, and they came out of it with their chins up."

"Rubbish," snapped his wife. "Look at your own grandfather, a broken man."

"Aye, well, he was broken by the bottle as much as any troubles with the soldiers," insisted Ronan. There were two types of whisky drinkers in Scotland, those who killed the bottle, and those who were killed by the bottle. "I'm just asking that you let others help as well," he continued, taking his wife's hand. "If you destroy yourself, you're no use to anyone."

Ceana dabbed at her moist eyes with a linen. "I know," she said. "Make me a cuppa tea then, and I'll sit here."

"Well, let's not get carried away," joked Ronan. She smiled, tossing her apron at him as he rose to find the kettle. Beneath the laughter Ceana knew that her husband was holding something from her.

As night drew close, Fearghal wondered what further havoc he might wreak on the House of Faustine. In his "undead" state he began to feel somewhat less concerned with matters. To his mind, nothing worse could possibly happen to him. He was beyond harm of any kind. Where was the motivation to remain at the armoury? The result of this little war would not affect him in any way whatsoever. He existed in a form that was without purpose—unless his destiny was to haunt the living.

This form cannot be endless and purposeless, he thought. *Was I not a victim in life, created through an act of violence, doomed from the beginning? How do people make amends for bad decisions after they have entered this void, or do they? Does it change?*
An evening breeze drifted in through the window, nudging him towards the rear wall of the fourth-floor room. He hung like a silk banner suspended in a cloud of ether, a gentle ripple running through the threads of his consciousness. *Perhaps it's time to visit my stepfather.* Fearghal closed his eyes and drew a deep breath. He turned to face the village and exhaled slowly, creating a ghost trail. Opening his mouth wide, he connected to the invisible cord and inhaled. Fearghal had discovered the art of spirit travel quite by accident and found that with practice he could climb to a respectable height, enabling himself to see for great distances.

Some time later he arrived in the village square and was making for the guesthouse. Tyburn had been given a small room on the first floor just at the bottom of the staircase. Fergus's guesthouse was alive with the sounds of its inhabitants, snoring and farting in their sleep. A few of the men who found sleep difficult without the company of their wives paced the floors impatiently.

All the men of Dunradin in good health were being trained daily by the highlanders. They were subject to a regimen of callisthenics and firearm handling. This served a dual purpose. At the end of each day they were tired and less susceptible to the effects of boredom and torpor.

Fearghal peered into the first room that he came to and discovered his stepfather in curious circumstances. The doctor lay on the floor naked beside his bed, sleeping soundly. Fearghal gazed at him, puzzled. The old man, who lay on his side, was drooling from the corner of his mouth, and his left leg twitched. Macleary had all the mannerisms of a canine dreaming of rabbits.

Tyburn sat up suddenly, seeming to sense Fearghal's presence. His eyes flashed yellow for a second, and a low growl escaped his throat. He crossed the floor groggily on three limbs, cocked his leg against the wall to piss against the green wallpaper, and then climbed into the bed and pulled the blanket up to his chest.

The names *Lupus* and *Shape-changer* sprang to mind at once. *Why, you old villain. You've fooled us all.* Fearghal, who had been concerned for Tyburn's welfare, was stunned with disbelief. There was no need to worry about shape-changers as they were generally not in danger from anyone except another of their own kind.

The existence of these marvellous creatures was so rare in these days that two were seldom found within the same county. Tyburn might have developed the skill later in life, and as Fearghal had been informed, the transformation took a number of years to master.

In the early days of the world shape-changers had been more common, and life was very different. Man and beast were more closely linked and in some cases existed in harmony with one another. In later years the shape-changers began to be regarded as demonic aberrations by the churches and were eventually hunted to near extinction. The stories and histories of these remarkable beings vanished quickly as their numbers decreased.

Fearghal felt a need to be with his stepfather for a time and hung in the air like a sentinel meditating on the old man's life while he slept.

A line of Teriz entered the quarry quietly, in single file. The newest arrivals passed through a checkpoint at the entrance and were detained in the selection tent. Dafyd had insisted that a small number tattooed in the palm of one's hand would insure that the armoury and quarry would not be infiltrated by troublemakers.

It was also decided that the weak would not be permitted to carry on. For the immediate future they would be segregated from the others in a separate area. The sickly ones would be given an opportunity to apply for a tattoo when and if they could pass a physical examination. Those whose health deteriorated further would be taken away and bled.

The Welshman believed that fairness and efficiency were necessary to keep the operation from deteriorating into minor power struggles. Flesh-eaters were easily separated from the bloodlings and sent to Dafyd, who would determine himself whether they posed a risk or deserved a position of trust. In short, the Wraiths existed as masters or servers, and a distinct line was drawn between the two classes.

Mingus sat behind the large desk with a opened book of numbers in front of him. "Gaze into the candle, please," he said, bored with the repetition of it all. The next applicant stepped up to the light and opened his eyes. Mingus noted that his pupils remained wide open and he blinked in pain. "Number forty-seven," he said, motioning to his right.

A larger, more confident-looking creature stepped up to the candle and gazed into the light, not waiting for instructions. His pupils shrank to a pinpoint with no apparent discomfort. "To the left, please," said Mingus, motioning the next applicant forward. He stood up and stretched, cracking his back. The man with the ink and needle was slow at his craft. It was going to be a long night.

-66-

It was an overcast day in Dunradin, and clouds threatened rain at any minute. Tyburn had woken up earlier than usual that day. Every muscle in his body screamed as he raised himself from the bed. The room smelled of piss, and the doctor lurched toward the window in search of fresh air.

Macleary recalled most of his prowl, although some of the details were sketchy. He'd climbed the high ridge above the quarry and watched as creatures filed in. The landscape here was changing quickly. What had once been a gathering place given over to wildflowers was now freshly carved into a system of underground barracks.

Clearly Stoke had missed something. These numbers were far beyond what Branan had spoken of. Tyburn would need to put some thought into how he conveyed this news to the others without giving himself away.

Was it time, he wondered to reveal himself for what he was? Macleary had developed his skills over a period of time, but hadn't found a use for the strange abilities until recently. He found the transformation to be a strenuous and exhausting practice.

Doctor Macleary had discovered that he was a shape-changer quite by accident while quail hunting. He amazed himself by leaning over and picking up the wounded bird with his teeth and immediately dropped it in surprise, looking around to see if he had been observed. Tyburn developed grey hair at a very young age but hadn't attributed any special meaning to it. The first time he made the complete transformation, though, he stopped at a pond of still water to drink and was transfixed by his image. He was a powerful, fully grown grey wolf that probably weighed close to ten stone.

He soon found that he could cover great distances at a stretch, but after such exertion, he was exhausted when he took the form of a man once again. For this reason Macleary was reluctant to explore his powers further. In times of war the skill would have been very useful, and some very renowned citizens throughout history had been shape-changers.

"You don't appear to understand the implications of defeat. It's not a straightforward matter of being slain and having your village overrun. The elderly will be killed at once, and their bodies will be left to rot in the square. Your children will be taken from you and blooded; soon they will develop the hunger. Your women will be impregnated repeatedly by these monsters. And you ..."

He paused for effect. "You will spend your days chained to a wall, eaten one inch at a time until nothing is left. Your demise will be a long, drawn-out torture, and the strongest of you may survive long enough to see your offspring feeding on your dungeon mates, if not your very selves!"

Godwyn struggled to control his emotions and spoke again. "Please trust me, this is no storm in a teacup. You risk the future of generations to come. You don't want your grandchildren raised in some subterranean charnel house. All I ask is that you make your decisions based on what is and what may be."

Dunradin's male population had gathered in the church at Godwyn's request, and he spoke from the pulpit. The men sat in stunned silence as Blunt stepped down, then chatted quietly amongst themselves. The graphic details would be spared in the retelling when they spoke with their wives. Some of them shook their heads in disbelief as they left the building. Each of them had a purpose today, and they'd not been given that for some time.

Ronan gathered the men he'd been assigned to, along with Caymus and Branan, who were in charge of an equal number. Tyburn was asked to organize Liam's lads and have them gather at the schoolhouse.

Tamlyn was close to his grandfather and it felt as though he had not had much of his attention lately. He'd spotted the old man entering the church early in the morning with several others and waved to him as he continued to the grocer's.

Duncan was not on the roof this morning, and from the youngster's vantage point the village seemed quieter than it had been for many days. A mist was drifting in from the valley, and there was a damp chill in the air.

Liam and Murdoch were peering towards the river, looking as though they could not possibly be more bored with life. Padraic sat with his back to the wall, with Chowder sitting contentedly in his lap. Even the pigeons seemed to have stopped cooing. Tamlyn glanced up the street towards the schoolhouse and wondered how his mother and sister were getting on.

The youngster walked over to the adjacent wall and looked into the alley between the grocer's and the guesthouse. The passageway was empty and silent. Some of Branan Stoke's men had covered the stones below with shards of broken glass. Trespassers would have a very difficult time entering the alley quietly at night.

Tamlyn was staring at the play of light on the bits of broken bottle when he noticed a moth nestled between the two bricks where his hand gripped the wall on its outer side. He had always thought of moths as the butterfly's poor cousin and marvelled at their ability to remain motionless in one spot for hours. A cloud of lethargy seemed to have descended on the village.

Above the alley, Padraic opened his journal and began to write.

Journal Entry:

Today is quieter than any day I can remember. Almost everyone is in the church for a meeting. I believe Duncan will let us know what has been decided when he returns. I almost feel I could sleep forever.
I will write more when there is news.

—Padraic

Euther dragged his finger across the map. "Here, where the lawn rises, and over here to the left of their watch post. Four columns of men, each separated by ten yards from those in front. Each man will carry a whipsnare and short flogger for the prisoners. Advance with four rapid waves of attack. Kill the highlanders at the guard posts. Roll right over them and take the villagers.

"Mingus and his men will be at the dairy farm taking control of the horses as the horn sounds, so that none of the remaining can ride off.

"The object is to keep alive as many as possible with the exception of the elderly. The cells have been prepared. Just fill them up; we can separate the women and children after."

Euther paused and eyed his captains one by one. "If any of your men fall wounded, carry on, and I don't think I need to tell you that if you are incapacitated, there will be no help for you.

"An injured soldier is a useless soldier and a hindrance, so it would be wise for you to avoid injury. I'm not going to waste any of our men in an attack from the forest. They have it so laden with barbs and spikes that we would never get through, which also means it would prove hard going for those attempting to flee through the woods.

"Make your preparations!" he commanded, rolling up the map. As the captains dispersed, he broke into a fit of coughing and doubled up in pain.

Dafyd watched with no emotion, waiting for Faustine to stop shaking. Eventually Euther looked up "Thank you for your concern" he whispered sarcastically.

The Welshman looked down as if addressing Euther's trembling hands. "Do you want me to bring you some wine?" he asked.

"Oh yes!" replied Faustine, "and several chorus girls, a dancing mule, and all the sands of Egypt!"

"Perhaps two bottles then," said Dafyd, leaving the room.

As darkness fell the Teriz gathered in the quarry and prepared for battle. Their faces were blackened with charcoal, and even the sharpened blades of their weapons had been rubbed dull, to avoid any reflections from their surfaces. To a man, they were clothed in a dark fabric that blended with the very night itself.

In this manner an army of two hundred Teriz filed into the valley and crept across the marshes unseen, waiting for the signal to attack.

On the other side of the village, Sproad and his companions crept into the dairy pasture. An outhouse was visible next to the fence, where a light shone from beneath the door. Captain Sproad hissed at his men, "Guard in the thunder box; perfect." He waved one of them towards the narrow structure and placed the horn to his lips.

On the river side of the village green a column of creatures crouched in anticipation. Thirty yards in the foreground was the main guard post of Dunradin. Three figures were silhouetted in the mist, huddled around a large stationary bow.

To the left-hand side, just visible on the roof of the guesthouse, was the outline of a huge highlander. The blast from Sproad's horn echoed a signal across the square as he leaned over the barricades, and the first wave of creatures charged, screaming, towards the guard post. Their sergeant was first to breach the short wall, leaping across in one bound with a spear, which he thrust it into the belly of the first highlander. The second guard's head was severed by a short ugly creature that swung a sword nearly his own height. The head flew over the wall and rolled under the feet of the second wave of Teriz.

Intermission

Part Two

Part Two

-67-

Sproad's man tore the outhouse door open and froze. He called back to his captain, "The shithouse is empty!" An oil lamp rested on the bench, and the creature struck at it with his club, knocking it into the hole. If anyone was down there, they made no sound.

At the guard post, the sergeant in charge of the first wave swore loudly. His spear had gone in far too easily, and he pulled it smoothly from the straw figure. The highlander's grinning face mocked him, and he swung an angry fist into the face moulded in wax, splitting it in two. "Pull them from their beds!" he screamed.

A roar of thunder was followed by freezing rain which slashed into the forest. The rain turned quickly to hailstones that bounced noisily on the cobblestones of the village. On top of the grocer's roof, the door to the pigeon coop was open. The straw guard on the roof, which bore a striking resemblance to Duncan, tilted under the blows, and hail quickly washed the features from the dummy's face as it toppled over.

The Teriz, enraged to find the village deserted, rushed about in a frenzy, still charged with adrenaline and the lust for blood. One group of larger creatures took offence at a smaller band, and the rain that ran rapidly through the gutters soon took on a new colour. Still others tore through the empty homes, destroying everything in their path, hoping to locate victims cowering under beds or hidden in cellars. Lamps had been left burning, tables set, games of cards abandoned.

On the ridge close to the quarry, the last citizen of Dunradin emerged. Liam scrambled up the ladder. Tamlyn, who was in charge of the tunnel exit, clapped him on the back and trotted after him into the woods.

It had taken some doing to convince everyone to leave, and eventually it had come down to a decision whether people placed more value in their possessions than in their lives. "I assure you, one and all," said Stoke, "these beasts are not interested in your village, your homes, or your businesses. The Teriz want only you, your flesh, your blood, and your offspring. If you leave now with us, there is nothing for them here."

"I have a farm across the river," said Ben Spratt. "What will become of it if I don't stay and fight?"

"You will never know if you remain because you'll not be able to see your farm from the cells of their dungeon," replied Branan. "This is not a matter of standing up for your land and dying a glorious death in defence of Dunradin. You will be a forgotten man, festering away in the darkness!"

The exodus had proceeded without very much trouble, aside from the inevitable cases of villagers wishing to take more with them than had been suggested. Big Jenna, a woman of impressive girth, had worried about the narrowness of the tunnel, but she managed to squeeze through—much to the relief of Squire Stubbins, who had unfortunately been directly behind her in the line-up. "Come along, dear," he'd muttered, "don't make me put the boots and butter to ye."

He had tried to jostle his way out of position, pushing someone else into the spot, but Virgil Mason was having nothing to do with a switch-up and swore at the old man. "She's your bleedin wife. Get yer bony arse in there!" A couple of the more claustrophobic individuals required a great deal of urging to enter the narrow confines of the tunnel and were helped along with reassuring words.

Tamlyn counted as each head popped up and was ushered into the woods. In the end he decided there was one villager missing as the count was shy by one but quickly realized that he had not counted himself. This caused some momentary confusion with Liam, which resulted in Twist being in front of him in the flight through the woods, and being shorter of leg Tamlyn soon fell behind the older boy. Just as Tamlyn was about to call out to Liam, a white hand, long of finger and firm of grip, locked itself across his mouth.

It was Dafyd who had chosen the three scouts to creep along the ridge towards the village. The Welshman wanted a report of the raid from unbiased eyes. Euther was not aware that he'd arranged for a personal report and looked mildly confused when the remaining scout barged into Faustine's sitting room.

Dafyd was disturbed by what he thought he'd seen through a scope on the rooftop. It appeared that a number of Teriz were clashing with each other, but the storm made it difficult to confirm. He was in the midst of relating what he'd viewed from above when they were interrupted.

"Sir, with your pardon, they are for the woods! The villagers have left."

"And how the devil did they get past the troops?" screamed Euther. "What happened!?"

"A tunnel, sir, which opened on the ridge, midway from the village."

"Dirty filthy vermin! And were they pursued?"

"I believe they were through the tunnel as our troops attacked. They could be anywhere in the trees."

As Liam stopped and turned, the hail stung his eyes. "Tamlyn!" he called. A body crashed into the young man and knocked the wind from him. A creature landed astride his back and pulled his arms painfully together in an attempt to rope them. Liam tucked his head in and rolled forward in a somersault, throwing his attacker off and landing on his feet. Then he dived towards where he thought the path might be, pushing himself past a large branch that snapped back and caught his pursuer in the eye.

He had no idea whether Tamlyn was still behind or had made it past him while he was on the ground. Fear pushed him forward as fast as his feet would carry him.

Tamlyn stumbled backwards as he was dragged towards the tunnel entrance, biting into the foul hand that covered his face while trying to wrestle free his other arm, which was pinned behind him. In a flash the creature's scream died as he dropped from sight, having fallen through the door into the tunnel.

Tamlyn would have followed him had he not managed to free his other hand in time. He turned and sped up the path. A wiry-looking Teriz lay across the path clutching his wounded face. Without breaking stride the youngster leaped over the body and raced ahead.

The hail turned to a steady, blinding rain, and in a matter of minutes Tamlyn was off the path, pushing awkwardly through the underbrush. Soon, with no idea which direction he was going and exhausted, he collapsed headlong on the wet ground, gasping great gulps of air.

Branan's highlanders had positioned themselves along the path at intervals and urged the villagers forward. The elderly were helped along by the young, and the procession filed forward quietly through the trees which had grown thicker now as they climbed. If all went well, they would come out of the woods close to Glencairn Bridge and meet the main road to Threstone Castle.

As the last person passed Woodruff, who was the first on the path, he looked back towards the brush. Deciding that they had all made it out, he turned again to join the others. A voice behind him caught his attention, and Liam Twist stumbled from the short trees. "Tamlyn?" he called to the highlander. "Has he passed through?"

"I don't know," replied Woodruff, "you'll have to ask ahead. I thought I'd seen the last."

"Teriz," panted Liam, still out of breath. "I only just escaped by luck, but I didn't see Tamlyn. The rain is—"

"How many?" interrupted Woodruff.

"Just one, I think," answered Liam.

The highlander peered into the gloom behind Twist. "You go ahead, quickly now, and check the line. I'll have a look back towards the tunnel."

Liam made his way to the others, and rushed along beside the procession calling for his young friend. Before long he came to Murdoch and Ronan, who had heard his urgent enquiries. "He is not with us," said Ronan. "We assumed he was behind with you."

Liam described the encounter with the Teriz. "Woodruff has gone back to the tunnel."

"You and Murdoch go ahead and join Charlotte in the front; she's with her mother. I'll find Woodruff, while you let Branan know what has happened," replied Ronan.

Woodruff stepped over the slumped figure bleeding in the path. The creature had a deep gash in his forehead. The highlander leaned forward, pulled his head back by the hair, and quickly sliced across his throat with one efficient stroke.

Ronan arrived just as the forest path filled with blood. "Have you seen the youngster?" he asked anxiously.

"No, I'm afraid not," replied Woodruff. "There is no sign of him. As near as I can gather, there were two of them scouting this area. One of the bodies lies at the bottom of the tunnel."

"Liam made no mention of killing a second Teriz," said Ronan, with a puzzled look. It was very hard to imagine that a boy the size of Tamlyn could have slain one of these creatures.

Branan arrived and was given an account of the findings. "Ronan, we must press on. You know the roads; carry on and I will search for your son."

The blacksmith was extremely reluctant to leave the area. "I promise you," continued Stoke, "I will comb the entire area for Tamlyn."

Ronan realized that Branan was a master tracker and that it was in Tamlyn's best interests to have the highlander looking for him. If anyone could pick up his trail in this weather, it was Branan. He gripped his friend's hand firmly before leaving. "Please bring him back."

At the sight of his mother's tears, Murdoch's eyes filled with water. Charlotte had buried her head in Liam's chest and was sobbing heavily. Ronan tried his best to reassure them. "If anyone can find him, it will be Branan," he insisted. "Please, we must go on; there is little time. When we have cleared the bridge, I will go back myself."

When Ronan had an opportunity to draw Liam aside, he asked him quietly, "You are certain that you saw only the one creature?"

"I'm certain," he replied. "If only I had not left the tunnel so quickly." Liam was filled with remorse. "Tamlyn should have been ahead of me; I should have insisted."

"There is no blame here," said Ronan. "Had Tamlyn been ahead of you, he might well have been attacked by the creature that you wounded. As it turns out, a second creeper lies below the tunnel entrance. I don't believe he fell in there without help. My son is quick and agile, if not very strong, and he must have dodged the creature, and lost his bearings in the rain."

"I pray that you're right," said Liam. "If anything was to—" His throat choked him to silence.

"Tamlyn Macleary!" called Stoke. His voice echoed into the passageway, and after listening carefully for any type of response the big man turned reluctantly towards the quarry. If the boy had been taken in that direction, there was little hope, but the trail along the ridge east had to be eliminated from his search. A search here confirmed that the youngster had not been pulled into the tunnel with the creature who lay at the bottom of the ladder.

The tracker moved quickly through the darkness, alert for any sounds or signs of the lad. The rain had eased to a light drizzle now, and from where he stood on the ridge, he could make out a line of Teriz, just visible below, presumably making their way back to the river. They would have to cross further down by the quarry if they were bound for the armoury. In any event they would remain in Branan's line of vision for some time yet and he in theirs. He crouched to the height of the bushes along the ridge.

The dim lights of the quarry encampment soon came into view, and Stoke perched motionless on an outcropping that afforded him a view of the entire valley. Faustine must be beside himself with rage at this minute.

The returning troops made no attempt at subterfuge in their retreat. A number of them carried bodies from the melee in town. The corpses were drained of blood, but none of the Teriz had been bold or foolish enough to partake of the flesh.

The penalty for illegal consumption was very harsh and not worth the risk. As the Wraiths grew fatter, the Teriz grew thinner, and with the failure of this raid Euther would soon need to be concerned with the feeding of his Teriz.

Branan shifted his weight and unwittingly dislodged a stone beneath his foot. He nearly toppled from the slippery ledge and managed to right himself in time. But he had given away his location.

A large Teriz captain by the name of Durbin lifted his head and glared in the direction of the ridge. The small band of creatures was directly below Stoke on a smaller path through the brush that had hidden them from his line of sight. They suddenly came into the clear not twenty feet from the startled highlander and were upon him in seconds.

Branan crouched low to the ground as if to spring, only to be immobilized when the big one tossed a grappling net over him. He thrashed about and then seemed to realize it was pointless to struggle.

"Move," growled Durbin, pleased with himself. This one would be taken to Faustine for a reward. It was not likely that any of the others had captured a highlander. A cinch rope was placed around Branan's neck, and his hands were bound. "It's the armoury for you, friend," hissed Durbin, pulling the whipsnare, and forcing Stoke to follow.

What followed was an uncomfortable trek along the edge of the river to the footbridge beyond the quarry. Branan kept his eyes on the path but occasionally cast about in hopes of finding an advantage that he might use against his captors.

There was no sign that anyone else had been captured and certainly no indication that Tamlyn had come this way. He prayed that the lad had not been abducted and that he might be able to confirm it one way or the other. Once across the narrow bridge it was not much further to the old mill, and Branan soon found himself being pushed up the stairs to Euther de Faustine's chamber.

"Well, what is this? I believe you would be Branan Stoke, the master tracker who has dogged my footsteps all this long year."

Stoke, who was curious how Euther recognized him, spit out his reply. "Dorian, somehow I expected a larger, fiercer-looking villain."

Euther shrugged off the insult as well as the usage of his forgotten name. "I send my troops out for a village, and they bring me one highlander, but a most prestigious one." He repeated the last word softly: "One."

Faustine seemed to disappear into his cloak as he leaned forward. "Clearly you were warned of our intentions," he remarked, clearly not expecting a response. He sniffed loudly. "You may feel compelled to tell me about that later," he added suggestively.

Faustine had already let slip the answer to one of Branan's questions. Unless the old man was toying with him, it appeared, at least for the moment that Tamlyn had not been taken. Euther perked up suddenly. "Please excuse my rudeness. Branan Stoke, this is my associate, Dafyd Kendrick." The Welshman nodded ever so slightly.

Dorian continued, "You have some knowledge of our ways, Mr. Stoke. If you would care to take a seat, I will speak in my defence. I think you will find that there are two sides to every story.

"You see, we farm the Teriz, and they farm the undesirables. We can raise cattle and the like for the feeding of our Teriz, in fact we can engineer their diets to our taste. Because we consume them, we have the ability to raise them on select foods. Dafyd here can tell you that a Teriz rich in a diet of fine wine is tastier than a corn-fed one. We will have the privilege of being able to assume the title of Gourmands Extraordinaire. I assure you that a garlic-fed Teriz is a rare treat.

"As long as they have their steady diet of blood and conventional foods, they are happy. For every undesirable that is blooded, another member of the food chain is created. There is therefore one less squealing peasant or London beggar taking up valuable space, and everyone is happy."

"And what happens when all the poor and needy are blooded? What then?" asked Branan.

Euther laughed "That's the beauty of it. There are always poor, downtrodden misfits about. They breed like rabbits!"

Lord Wallace Pengrove entered the room next. Euther stood up, enjoying the look of utter disbelief that washed over Branan's face.

"A compatriot of yours, I believe. I'll let you get reacquainted," he said, following Dafyd. Branan was speechless.

"Hello, Stoke."

"Your Lordship?" " You are a party to this madness?"

"It depends how you define madness. You have not spent any time in London recently, it is much changed. The rate of murder and other violent crimes has decreased immensely. Hunger is rapidly becoming a thing of the past. Disease will soon be eradicated. Sewage no longer runs through the streets."

Branan interrupted, "At what cost!?" He was enraged. "And under whose authority? Not Her Majesty's, certainly!?"

"Come, come, Stoke, it's only the poor, the sickly, and the working class that are blooded—the halfwits, the deformed, the sodomites and the lame. Do you not find it suspicious that the gentry, the well-to-do, the rich, and the ruling classes, without exception, have been spared the bite? Cholera is not so discerning. Sit back and watch the resurrectionists grow fat on the sale of cadavers if you like. When you create the disease, you may direct it to your advantage.

"Until last year the population of London threatened to spill into the Thames itself. For the first time in many years the count is equal to that of the previous year. Raw sewage, disease, opium, and madness ... this is the future of England—unless something is done. And something is being done.

"Of course Victoria knows nothing of this. She hides in Windsor, living with Albert's ghost. She is only a pitiful shadow, riding on the lid of a coffin.

"We are building a future; this is the first of many encampments. You see, Stoke," he added in a quieter tone, "the people need an enemy, and we shall supply that enemy, control that enemy, and eventually, when an enemy is no longer required, we will simply eradicate them and close down the camps. It all works like a charm."

"Until Dorian and his army discover what their future holds," said Branan.

Pengrove ignored the remark. "Where are the villagers?" he asked. His question was met with silence. "You know," he continued, "you could do very well were you to change allegiances. You were"—he paused—"considered, but an old friend of yours suggested that your foolishly high morals would be a hindrance. Griffin Hume has become a very affluent citizen. I think perhaps he may have dissuaded me from speaking with you because he wanted the position for himself. Does that sound like young Griffin to you?"

As close as he and Hume had been, Stoke had to admit that Griffin had been incredibly ambitious, but treachery was not one of his character traits. He decided that Wallace was trying to twist his mind about in an effort to secure his trust. Swallowing his anger, he feigned a look of interest. "And just how affluent has Hume become in my stead?"

Lord Pengrove chuckled. "Very affluent indeed, every man has his price, and some are very dearly bought." Branan assumed a pensive air.

"It would be a shame if you were to forfeit your life for a handful of farmers, Stoke." He went to the doorway. "Tell you what, you relax here and chat with Euther for a while. Put some thought into your future, and when I return, name your price."

Branan understood that this would be his only chance at escape and that he would not be allowed to play at this game for long. He had just been handed a reprieve, but he would need all the skills of deception that he possessed to pull off the ruse.

-68-

Tamlyn's teeth chattered, and his legs shook in an effort to fend off the freezing cold. The rain had stopped some time ago, leaving him soaked and chilled to the bone. He knew that he should get up and move about, but navigating in the darkness would have been impossible, and he'd decided to hang on until the first sign of daylight. He rocked back and forth shivering and wondering what might have happened with the others.

Events had transpired very quickly, but as near as he could recall, Liam, just ahead of him, had called his name, then it all happened at once. The creature's strong hands, its foul odour, and then stumbling forward as quickly as he could, followed by the drumming of hail against the leaves.

Why had Liam not returned for him? But what if he had? Was Tamlyn even on the path any longer? He felt as though he were lying in a shallow mossy area with broad-leaved plants above him. After the rain stopped the forest was dead quiet except for the sound of water dripping from the leaves, and the steady pounding of his heart. Something wriggled underneath his wrist, and he pulled his hand towards his face.

Eventually the forest around him began to reveal itself in small details. The centipede lay on its back inches from his face. Tamlyn watched it struggle, tried to count its legs, then pushed it aside carefully. The organism coiled around itself and rolled into a huge raindrop that mirrored its sleek brown back.

Tamlyn rose to his knees and looked around. He got to his feet and tried to wring the moisture from his jacket. He swept the wet hair from his forehead and pushed through the brush, moving towards the area where the light was brightest. The trail lay where the trees were the thinnest and he soon located a path. Unknown to Tamlyn, the trail that had been taken by the others, lay far to his right and he was headed in the direction of Horn Island on a lesser trail.

Twice he thought he heard small noises behind him, like a broken twig or a bird in the trees, and turned. Once he stopped in mid-stride and spun about, but there was nothing behind him—only silence and a rising mist. He continued on for several minutes, and then as he passed a large tree, he slipped behind it and waited.

Before long a figure emerged from the tall ferns and crept forward. The youngster watched as a shadow appeared on the path beside his sheltering oak. It stopped on the other side of the tree and sniffed, then loped forward. Tamlyn had never seen a wolf, and certainly not one so large. As the animal passed, the youngster, not daring to budge, released his breath slowly.

Twelve yards up the trail, the beast turned its large head towards the boy and met his gaze. There was something safe and reassuring in the wolf's look. It turned and continued as if to say, *follow if you wish—and if you dare.*

Tamlyn took a few tentative steps and decided that the wolf had no intention of attacking. The young Macleary kept pace, leaving a respectful distance between himself and the wolf. Occasionally the animal would look back to see that the boy had not wandered elsewhere.

He wondered if it was wise to be following such a large and dangerous animal. Was he being led into a trap? He couldn't explain it, but somehow he felt the animal was acting in a protective capacity. He could have easily turned at any point and been on the lad in a single leap. The youngster found that as he followed behind, his point of focus narrowed, and in turn the imagery that his peripheral vision registered, blurred and darkened, so much so that he felt he was entering a tunnel of light. It was a comfortable channel of soft colours and muted sounds. He felt a slight pressure on his eardrums, and his legs lost all weariness.

He took in a deep breath of air, and the image stretched towards him, distorting in the centre. He exhaled forcefully, and the figure returned to its original spot as if it had been tugged by an invisible string. Tamlyn turned and scanned the trail before him. The wolf was a small speck in the distance. He dashed ahead, not wanting to lose his guide. Hearing his approach the animal turned once more, this time with a scolding look on its gaunt face.

"You understand now?" said Sproad. "We brings back one of them, and his Lordship allows what we keep eating the flesh. If we stands about like the others, it's the quarry and a number scratched in. I know what's happening down there, I weren't born yesterday."

Blacky replied, whetting the blade of his knife, "I'm for staying above ground. It stinks down there, and I don't miss the headaches one bit. I've heard the talk too: if you fall sick, it's the end, you're on the dinner plate. As we stays captains, we stays alive. It's a damn shame about the raid. I was primed for scalps and a pocket of gold."

"What do you think happened?" asked Sproad.

"Treachery!" he insisted. "Someone talked."

"Not one of ours?"

"I have my thoughts on that," replied Blacky, "but I'll keep them to myself for the time being until it's proved out. I'll say this much, though," he added. "I'm for snaring two youngsters, bringing one in and eatin' tother."

"Agreed." said Sproad, as he got to his feet and prepared to move on. Blacky slipped his knife back into the sheath and pointed up the trail towards Caster's Pond.

Dunradin's villagers had pushed through the night in order to reach Glencairn Bridge. They rested now in a meadow one kilometre from the river. A few hours' sleep had done wonders for their spirits, and they'd had a small meal.

Tyburn, despite protestations, had turned from the group and headed back in search of his grandson. Ronan and others had tried in vain to convince the old man that he should take a highlander with him. "Don't worry," he'd insisted. "Nobody will pay any attention to one old man on his own. All I need is some huge northerner tramping along raising the alarm with his big feet." Liam, who still felt guilty, implored the doctor to bring him along, to no avail.

Charlotte had her hands full with Ceana. Her mother was sick with worry and very little use with the children. Fortunately, Liam's mother proved to have the skills required to organize the other women, and Megan Maguire was an endless source of energy and inspiration. Following a short after-meal rest, the group would carry on across open ground towards Threstone, to secure temporary shelter. Ronan, who assumed the role of leader, had refused to second-guess the fate of the villagers and insisted that plans be discussed after they occupied the castle.

"Concentrate on the task at hand," he'd instructed. "Keep your eyes on the road beneath your feet."

Sproad and Blacky saw the boy some ways ahead of them as he disappeared down a dip in the trail. They did not see his guide ahead. "On him!" said Blacky in a coarse whisper. The two creepers charged ahead, not caring if they were heard, confident that they could outrun the boy, who appeared to be on the slow side.

The wolf turned at the sound and ran at Tamlyn with alarming speed. *A trick*, thought the frightened youngster, throwing himself to the ground. The beast's powerful body flew over his head and landed on the first creature, ripping at his face with powerful jaws.

Tamlyn jumped to his feet and ran up the path with no thoughts of looking back. The screams and the tearing sounds from behind propelled him forward. As he closed in on the water, the trail veered to the left and down. He was familiar with this area: it was the eastern approach to Horn Island, and he was very nearly at the boat keeper's hut.

He looked up at the familiar horn-shaped island where the water divided and saw his escape. The rowboat looked sound enough. It was heavier than it appeared, and he had to enter the water, pull it from the front, and then climb around and enter it from the side. He used one of the oars to push off and was rowing across in no time.

The distance between the shore and the island's edge was perhaps twenty boat lengths. This was fortunate for the youngster, as the oars became heavier and heavier as he approached the island. As near as he could tell, he'd not been followed.

He looked back the way he had come as he secured the boat's rope to the iron ring on shore. It was now afternoon, and a fog settled on the water, obscuring the opposite shore. He needed a higher vantage point and headed up the ancient steps that had been cut from the stone long ago. They were broad and slippery, and Tamlyn wondered how one could possibly negotiate the stairs while moving a heavy funerary box.

If he had been more familiar with the island, he would have been aware of the system of pulleys that were mounted inside the centre chasm of the island. From the exterior, Horn Island appeared to be a solid rock mass. A large portion of the centre was in fact hollow. At its top was a flat area that housed its guests, the dead.

The highest pinnacle of rock was in fact a small stone hut that had been hewn from the peak. Large enough to house one body, it offered shelter from the elements. Four shallow crypts covered with slate lay side by side. Three were occupied by bodies in a similar state of decay. Portus lay rotting and headless in the first, and Jubilant Smith was his neighbour, next to Fearghal's body.

The smell of death was indescribable, putting Tamlyn in mind of a time when he'd stumbled across a cat in mid-decay. He held a hand over his face and looked across the short stretch of water in the direction from which he had fled. The fog had thickened again, obscuring everything beyond the shore, and Tamlyn turned away to duck into the shelter in an attempt to avoid the stench. Hungry and cold, his clothing still wet, and his head filled with strange imaginings, he curled his knees up to his chest and slept again.

Threstone Castle lay below the moors on marshland that opened on to the ocean. Built in the thirteenth century, it was a triangular moated castle that had been abandoned for many years. Three of its great turrets remained standing, and although there was no longer a proper roof, it offered fine shelter from the elements, and within the walls were several rooms in an additional lodging. The huge gatehouse was comprised of two turrets with a three-story entrance reached by crossing a moat bridge.

It was this bridge that the weary villagers crossed in the late afternoon. Threstone's walls were coloured pink with the low rays of early winter sunshine. Branan's highlanders were most familiar with the castle and directed the villagers to the most appropriate areas to lay their bedding. Despite the circumstances of having to leave their village, there was a feel of communal satisfaction. They had travelled through the forest in safety and found refuge before nightfall. Many days had passed since husbands had spent a night under the same roof as their wives and children, and the evening's chill was hardly noticed amongst the warm huddle of reunited families.

In any event a large fire was built in the open courtyard of the far end where the wall had crumbled into the moat years ago. Caymus and a group of Highlanders kept the fire fed as they mulled about chatting quietly amongst themselves. A watch was set atop the gatehouse where a large torch blazed, in the hopes that Tyburn and Branan would be guided to the castle.

Godwyn was stationed outside the castle on the other side of the marsh. He would take the first turn at distant night watch and raise any alarm if necessary. A further attack from Euther's troops was not expected; nevertheless, a proper defence would be organized tomorrow.

The men gathered by the fire were discussing the possibility of future attacks at this moment. "They will not attempt a siege of the castle, that is my belief," said Caymus.

"And mine," added Ronan, "is that we cannot afford to make that assumption. However, I also believe that we can develop a defence while planning a spring attack, this will allow us to raise more support while they grow hungry." Ronan turned to Woodruff. "What are the chances that we might obtain further recruits from the north?"

"My cousins will be made aware of the Teriz threat and will be happy to join the fight. I will travel myself in the morning and make what arrangements I can. I'm concerned on Branan's behalf; he should have been back by now."

-69-

Fearghal contemplated what eternity was going to be like, with no purpose. He wondered if he knew what the extent of his condition really was. There was certainly no finality in the form of death that he'd chosen. He craved an ending more than anything and thought it might be worthwhile to seek out his corpse.

Searching the church proved fruitless, naturally. Then he recalled Horn Island and its purpose. It wasn't difficult to find a small opening for his vaporous form, and he entered the crypt easily. At close range he had no sense of what shape his remains were in, but given the time that had elapsed, he had an idea that it wasn't a pleasant sight. *All the better*, he thought, *for the purpose at hand*.

It was as though Fearghal wore a suit of bones and decaying flesh. He was able to lift his hands and make contact with solid objects again. He shifted a hand to his belt and checked the scabbard. The silver-edged dirk was still there. He reached up and pushed on the heavy slate lid, shifting it an inch to his left. The daylight stabbed at his retinas, and he squeezed his eyes closed. This wasn't going to be a walk in the park. He brought a bony hand to his face and found that he could push a finger through a large opening in his cheek and feel his teeth.

The wolf prowled around the old boat shed, searching for signs. The scent disappeared right at this spot.

He circled the shed once more and then moved off to his right at a steady pace. Farther back on the trail, he'd left the ruined bodies of two flesh-eaters. It had been necessary for him to chew through the vertebrae of their necks in order to separate the heads. The wolf had grasped both heads by the hair and carried them in his teeth to the edge of the water. They bobbed along in the foam of the upper river now, on their way to the second set of falls.

After a lengthy struggle Fearghal managed to shift the heavy slate far enough across the crypt that he could emerge from the opening. He stood up unsteadily and stretched his emaciated limbs. He opened his jacket to discard the heavy fabric, and a handful of maggots fell from his shirt in a writhing ball.

"Enough of that," he said, peeling a fat leech from his upper arm. He made his way cautiously down the stone steps and entered the river, where he washed the remaining vermin from his hair. The belt, which normally hung at his waist, dragged to his knees, almost tripping him up. He pulled it high around his waist and cinched it at the last round. His shoes were also too large now and heavy with water. These he discarded as well as his jewellery. The blade was all he required.

The figure that strode through the trees towards the valley bore very little resemblance to the intriguing Englishman that Charlotte had considered attractive. His eyes were sunken deeply into a skull that was framed by a thinning crown of white hair, and his nose was black with rot. Fearghal's teeth were visible behind his narrow cracked lips that were set in a permanent twisted grin. If that were not bad enough, the smell that came from his rotting flesh was beyond description, and his clothing was stained with the numerous fluids of decay that had seeped from his flesh.

Fearghal now had a purpose again, and if all went well, he imagined it might be possible to redeem himself in some small way.

Journal entry:

Today we are all residents of Threstone Castle, with the exception of Tamlyn. I worry constantly for his welfare and hope to hear good news any day.

Branan and Tyburn both search the woods where he vanished. We were able to carry very little from the village, and some of the men will be heading north soon for more supplies. Tamlyn's mother is very ill with a fever and I believe everyone is concerned.

—Padraic

"If only they can find our Tamlyn," said Charlotte. "I'm afraid that mother has given up. She's so very ill."

The youngsters were seated against the low wall with their knees drawn up and their palms on the warm stone floor that still held the sun's heat.

"If your grandfather is not back soon Duncan and Godwyn will go to the woods. They've become quite good friends" replied Liam.

Padraic and Chowder joined the couple. The youngster had a question in his eyes. "No," said Charlotte, "nothing yet. Don't worry, Paddy, he'll be back." The little dog leaped into her lap, and Padraic sat very close to the young woman and placed his hand in hers. Liam winked at his young friend, and the three comrades sat in silence.

"You would take him at his word?" asked Dafyd.

Pengrove sat across from the Welshman and Euther stood to his right. Faustine was in fine spirits. Wallace had brought him a gift of his favourite medicine from the south.

"I know his type," insisted Pengrove. "London is filled with them: social climbing peasants with one finger on the pulse of the common man and another finger in the pie. They actually believe that because they have a social conscience, they are due a reward. Besides which he told me where the villagers are camped."

"Even I could have told you they would head for Threstone," said the Welshman.

"Nevertheless, he has confirmed it," replied Pengrove. "Give him a position in the quarry where he can be observed then." An idea suddenly came to him. "Put our Mr. Stoke in charge of terminations; that will test his mettle."

"That is Mingus's department!" protested Dafyd.

"Well then." replied Pengrove, "Mr. Mingus will be Stoke's first termination. How's that for a test?"

"Perfect," chuckled Euther.

Dafyd threw his hands up in the air in disgust. "Fine" he said turning to leave "But remember your decision when he turns on you like Godwyn."

"If he hadn't killed the harridan, you would have," muttered Euther.

Godwyn Blunt yawned and stretched his back. It had been a long, uneventful night, and there had been no sign of movement from the forest beyond. In the earliest light of morning he stared at the road that led north. Something appeared in the distance; he rubbed his eyes and squinted at the dark shape. It was a horse-drawn coach of some variety. He crouched behind a rock and drew his pistol.

The vehicle, in much need of paint and repair, thundered past Blunt as its driver whipped the horses unmercifully.

Godwyn stood and watched as the rear wheel hit a stone in the road and crumbled. The coach slid to the right as its driver reined in his horses, trying to keep the coach from rolling. It was a remarkable display of skill, helped by the fact that the rear wheel on the left had freed itself and was rolling towards Godwyn. The coach's back end scraped at the road surface and came to a halt in a cloud of dust.

Blunt holstered his pistol and ran towards the wreckage. The driver, who was quite shaken up, was not much older than young Tamlyn. He had a thick head of hair and heavy brows. He dropped from the driver's seat and staggered to the coach window, pulling open the door with obvious concern. Inside the coach were his mother and grandmother.

"You damn' fool," chided Blunt. "You had no business pushing your animals to that pace with this deathtrap attached to them."

"Please, sir," replied the youngster, "my gram!" The old woman looked to have fainted, and her daughter leaned over her with a fan. Godwyn looked into the cab just as the young woman turned and flashed him a menacing look.

"Leave him alone, he's done his very best!"

Blunt was momentarily stunned. He had never seen bluer eyes in his life. The woman was incredibly beautiful, and he found himself entranced at once. "Are you hurt?" he stuttered. "And your companion?"

"My mother is frail," she replied. "I am unharmed. My name is Violet Gamble, and this is my son, Alfred. We have been pursued through the night by a pair of devilish horsemen."

"Forgive me, I am Godwyn Blunt, late of Threstone Castle." He bowed. "What manner of horsemen were these?"

"I believe they were Teriz," she answered, "if you are familiar with the term."

"Yes, certainly, far too familiar. Look here, your mother stirs." Godwyn turned to Alfred "Where did you encounter these Teriz?"

"In Turfmoor, our village is overrun with the monsters. I only wished to get as far away as possible. They pursued us until just now when the light broke."

The big Norseman was not pleased to hear that Turfmoor was overrun. The news would be a great shock to Stoke when he returned. Godwyn was quite certain that the highlanders were unaware of the extent of the danger despite his efforts to convince them of the facts.

Violet helped her mother from the coach with Alfred's aid.

"Do you mean to say," asked Blunt, "that you are the only ones who have managed an escape?"

The young woman answered solemnly, "We saw very few killed; most were taken away. Some villagers fled across the fields to the south in hopes of reaching Dunradin."

Godwyn frowned. "I'm afraid they will find more of the same in Dunradin. Most of the village is here at the castle. We were fortunate enough to have foreseen the attack on the heath and escaped through the forest." He helped Alfred unhitch the horses from the ruined wagon and turned to the women again.

"My mother does not speak," said Violet, "but she and I converse with Parisian hand language." The young woman moved her fingers rapidly making several signs and gestures. The older woman replied in the same manner, smiling at Blunt when she was done.

"Mother wants to know if you have any whisky," said Violet. Godwyn laughed and shook his head apologetically, pointing towards the castle.

Caymus was in the upper window of the gatehouse watching as Godwyn approached with three strangers and a pair of horses. One of the women was clearly older as they took some time in crossing the narrow road that ran through the marshy area that fronted the moat. The younger of the two women looked vaguely familiar in her manner and the way in which she moved across the ground. She looked up for a brief second, and Caymus's heart stopped.

It had been close to ten years since he had gazed on those eyes, and they had not lost any of their beauty. He leaned against the wall as a flood of memories blinded him momentarily. There was no doubt that Violet Gamble had just walked across the moat and into Threstone. For a minute he wondered if it might be best to stay where he was, thinking that she might have business elsewhere and had just accepted Blunt's offer of water for her horses.

Violet had shared her love and her bed with Caymus many years ago, but spurned his proposal of marriage, for reasons he still did not fully understand. It had always been awkward for the couple to meet, due to the circumstances of their upbringing. He was the son of a small village doctor, and she was the child of a wealthy landowner who educated his children in Paris. Violet had a wild spirit and a disdain for the trappings of the well-to-do. Her adventuresome nature had appealed to Caymus from the first time they had met, and he foolishly pursued her affections, eventually being invited into her bed.

They played at love for one season until Violet grew tired of the fantasy. She was a realist who knew that the classes didn't mix without someone being hurt, and she cut off the relationship abruptly. Caymus was shattered and for the first year refused to believe that the separation was anything but a temporary circumstance. For a time his feeling of hatred rivalled his love for her, and he was totally defeated by the rejection. The bowman had listened to advice from friends that suggested all wounds are healed with time, but he was certain that this wound contained poison.

Eventually time did wear away at his misery until he found that he was capable of passing an entire month without thinking of her Season followed season, and Caymus had other lovers who paled by comparison until he came to the conclusion that he was meant to be a solitary hunter, a man who had seen his time and lost his chances.

He would study bow craft and herbal medicine while keeping to himself more and more.

Something held the bowman to his spot, a reluctance to be seen. He stroked at the whiskers on his chin—grey now, and white soon. His tunic was rough and stained. He pulled a heavy hand through his matted hair. All in all he could use a good washing in the moat. He had been a more slender man back then, with suppler limbs and more of a shine in his eyes.

He made quickly for the moat and despite the cold jumped in with a loud splash.

The first thing Tamlyn saw when he arose was the open crypt. His heart thudded in his chest. Nevertheless he stepped gingerly towards it and peered inside. It was empty of course, and he couldn't decide whether this was a good thing or not.

He spun around, half expecting to see some ghoulish spectre. He was sure the lid had not been removed earlier. *Grave robbers?* He wondered.

His thoughts were interrupted by a soft whisper of movement behind him. He froze in place and tried to turn but found that his feet would not move. "Softly now," said a kind voice. "Release the fear."

Tamlyn found himself quite relaxed and casually turned to face the speaker. He was alone, and the voice seemed to hang on the emptiness in front of him like a shimmering mist. "I see an animal," answered Tamlyn, "a large bird, like a hunting bird. It's circling in a blue sky."

"It is a falcon," said the phantom voice. "Study its ways, and when you encounter one, speak to it. This is your guide. The day will come some years from now when you will wish to shift, and it will be easy for you." The haze quickly cleared, and Tamlyn curled up on the spot and fell again into a deep sleep that carried him through until the early dawn of the next day.

The youngster made his way to the boat below, wondering if the last twenty-four hours had been a dream. After securing the craft on the opposite shore, he headed up the trail that led to the edge of the forest.

-70-

Tyburn woke up and attempted to shake off the effects of his confrontation in the woods. The two creepers had proven to be tougher than they looked. He limped from the forest and started across the marshland. There had been a sense that his grandson was somewhere close and out of danger. He hoped his instinct was correct. The old man turned to scan the trees one last time before heading to Threstone and saw the boy emerge from the woods. He waved at his grandfather and then fell exhausted to the ground.

Caymus climbed from the moat feeling refreshed. He took off his tunic and laid it on the grass just as the sun broke from a cloud. He ran his fingers through his hair, sweeping it behind his ears, and checked his breath before deciding to chew on a handful of juniper berries.

Then he sat for some time with his back against the castle wall wondering if it might be best to spend the day out of sight. Hunting, he thought, might be the better option. His crossbow was in the high turret. He wished now that he'd taken it with him to the moat. *This is foolishness,* he concluded. *It was all a very long time ago, so why am I trembling inside like a young suitor?*

The bowman ducked through a low side door and made his way up an inner stairwell to the top of the gatehouse. He retrieved his bow and turned towards the inner courtyard to scan the crowd of villagers that were readying their small cooking fires. He started down the steps, keeping his eyes lowered. A brace of rabbits would be good, or if he went farther afield, he might be fortunate enough to locate some deer. A meal of venison would benefit all.

"Cay, Is it you?"

He turned and was met with a welcoming smile. She looked radiant. "Hello, Violet. It's been a very long time. What brings you to Threstone?"

"I believe we're here under similar circumstances," she replied. "Turfmoor is besieged and burns as we speak."

Caymus knew his concern showed. "Teriz?"

She nodded grimly. "Very many are dead, and so few managed to flee." She motioned in the direction of the courtyard. "My mother and Alfred are with me."

She paused. "I never married."

"Nor I," he replied quickly, avoiding her gaze. Just then a commotion broke out at the gate. Several people including Ronan and Duncan were gathered around Tyburn, who had returned from the woods. Charlotte arrived at a run, passing Caymus with a look of great cheer. Tamlyn entered Threstone with an arm around the shoulder of his brother Murdoch and flanked by his friend Liam. Padraic was skipping about like a puppy, unable to contain his joy. "Look at you, Master Tamlyn," said Caymus, delighted to see his young nephew. "You're just in time for breakfast."

Violet was forgotten in the excitement, as the group made their way into the centre courtyard. Caymus put a hand on Tyburn's shoulder. "Are you well, Father?"

Tyburn nodded, "Aye, but there is no sign of Stoke. I'm concerned for his safety." The old man repeated his concerns to Hugh Maclean. Godwyn and Duncan were anxious for news and explained to the doctor that Woodruff had traveled north again in search of more recruits.

Tyburn was surprised to learn that Turfmoor had been overrun. This was certainly unhappy news. It could just as easily have been Dunradin's citizens that had been lost. According to the young woman, the elders had been killed first, and the others were taken away in bondage. Turfmoor sounded a frightful scene of carnage, and it appeared that Violet had escaped by sheer luck.

Tamlyn was shocked at his mother's appearance. Her hair had greyed quickly since he had seen her last, and she had lost her cheerful, well-fed appearance. She held him tightly and wept for a long time.

Caymus greeted Violet's mother with a nod of his head. He had met the old woman only once, on the occasion of her husband's funeral many years ago. He introduced Padraic who was most intrigued with the way Violet and her mother communicated.

"Mother says it is a pleasure to meet a young person like you, and she would be happy to converse with you if I would be so kind as to teach you to speak with your hands." Padraic smiled and nodded enthusiastically. Alfred, who was close in age to Padraic, volunteered to teach him, and the two boys became instant friends.

Caymus, who was pleased at having made the introduction, sat with Violet and her mother throughout the morning and quizzed the young woman on the events at Turfmoor, all the time doing his utmost not to gaze into the deep blue of her eyes for more than a second at a time. She had not lost any of her beauty, and age had only added to her alluring appearance. Caymus knew if he were to fall under her spell again, he would be lost. He wondered how many other men had been brought to the brink of ruin by her ways. It was clearly possible to love and hate Violet in equal measure, and because it appeared that she was here for some time to come, he was determined to walk her tightrope with extreme care.

He began to recall what he had long forgotten or had driven from his mind. Violet had always desired that which she was forbidden. Once she attained it, she no longer cared to keep it. The young woman feared abandonment, and for this reason she was troubled with men who desired her. She would not allow love to touch her, and anyone who proclaimed their love for her was soon given up. Her methods were cold and impersonal. Many a former suitor passing her in the street was treated like a complete stranger, much to his dismay. Once Violet had given herself to you, and then tired of the game, you were made to feel invisible. Such was the extent of her intentions. She could certainly be referred to as efficient if not kind, and in some cases brave, as more than one man had felt she was deserving of a thrashing.

Caymus, for his part, was deeply hurt to be treated in such a manner, because for a short time he had felt that the woman loved him, and to come to the realization that it was a sham was very painful. Nevertheless, his wounds were healed with time, but old habits die hard, and he found himself wishing for what he knew was impossible. Such is the nature of love.

Fearghal found his progress was slower than he would have wished. He stepped across the cobbled square of Dunradin carefully, looking for the most part like a gruesome effigy of a man that would not be out of place in the centre of a corn field. Aside from a scattering of Teriz corpses, the village was deserted. It was so quiet that he could hear the steady buzz of flies feeding on the congealing blood that stained the dead. It certainly had not gone Faustine's way here, he reflected with a satisfied hiss that passed for laughter. He checked again to reassure himself that the silver blade Ronan had fashioned for him was still in his belt.

A large rat, which had gorged itself on blood, watched Fearghal as he stood in the square. The creature was so fat from the feeding that it couldn't move. Fearghal took note of the beady eyes that looked his way. He stepped forward and swung his foot at the rat, sending it through the air. The unfortunate rodent hit the wall with a splat and slid to the ground beside Green's Guesthouse.

Two more rats appeared in the doorway. Apparently Fergus's Guesthouse was catering to a new clientele these days. Fearghal crossed the heath and proceeded along the marsh trail slowly. Ben Spratt's old dog, Blinder, who was blind in one eye and could barely see with the other, lay across the trail. At his approach the hound lifted his head and sniffed the air.

Blinder had not fared well with the departure of Spratt. Meals were few and far between. The stink that proceeded Fearghal was almost as good as a meal to the dog. He began to salivate, and as the shadow stepped over him, he lunged forward and snapped his jaws with surprising speed, catching the end of Fearghal's foot in his mouth.

The traveller called out more in surprise than pain and pulled frantically away in attempt to free himself, but Blinder's jaws were locked onto his victim, and he had no intention of letting go. He sensed a large parcel of meat was his for the taking and pulled at his prize as if to drag it away. Fearghal slipped to the ground and found himself in a tug-of-war with the brute for possession of his own foot. The hound pulled him closer to the swamp, and Fearghal reached behind for his knife—only to find that it had slipped from his belt and lay out of reach on the path behind him. Lunging desperately, he got his fingers around the weapon and twisted in the dog's direction to swing with as much force as he could muster.

Blinder using the strength in the muscles of his over thick neck yanked his prey an inch further just as the blade came down. Suddenly Fearghal's leg came free. The front of his foot and all the toes remained in Blinder's mouth. "Bastard!" he yelled. "If you'd waited a few hours, you could've had the whole damned thing."

The dog backed away with his prize, satisfied to have earned something for his efforts. Not much in the way of blood remained in Fearghal's corpse, and the stump of his foot looked like a pink mutton joint.

He hobbled along the path for what felt like ages. When he arrived at the Sleath, he stepped beneath the water and walked across the riverbed, fighting with the current. He decided to emerge a ways downstream and then wait until dark before carrying on to Lilyvine. He no longer had the advantage of being invisible and would need to rely on the darkness if he was to get anywhere near Dafyd. When he could no longer wrestle with the water's motion, he emerged and lay on the bank.

Fearghal was unimpressed with the loss of his foot, as it presented a problem with his balance. He had no pain, to hamper his cause, and would be able to sustain most any form of wound, but he would be required to move quietly. It occurred to him that he should have kept the shoes.

Then, as if in answer to a prayer, a pair of shoes came into his line of vision. He sat up astounded. Stretched out on the grass snoring loudly was Tanner Smead; his shoes lay at his feet like a gift. Fearghal crawled within reach as quietly as he could manage and snatched the shoes. He packed both of them tightly with grass to form a good fit and wound the laces around his ankles. He crouched low and passed Smead, smiling as he imagined the boy's confusion when he awoke.

Inside the armoury, Lord Wallace Pengrove had explained to Stoke that he was being assigned to an important post and that a traitor in their midst had to be eliminated. Branan had never met Mingus until this afternoon when he had toured the facilities at the quarry. The highlander was astounded at what the Teriz had achieved in such a short time.

Captain Mingus himself was really a somewhat nondescript creature who could have easily been mistaken for a common Teriz. The tattoo around his neck was the only feature that set him apart from the others. It was a very accurate rendering of a twisted braid of thorns.

For his part, Mingus had been told to train the new man in the business of termination and to keep a careful eye on him. Pengrove enjoyed his little games, and would often wager on one man over the other. He had placed his bet on the highland tracker, promising Faustine a full tin of the white powder if Mingus was the victor.

A tunnel now ran from the old mill to the footbridge by the quarry. It was reinforced with limestone, and at its central point a periscope protruded above ground, offering a full range of view along the river. Branan had seen no sign of Tamlyn and heard no mention of any prisoners, leading him to believe that the lad had escaped capture or been killed in the woods.

Mingus pointed out a new tunnel that veered off along the mill side of the river. "This one is under construction," he explained. "It will eventually reach the town of Turfmoor over the hill."

Branan had been told to learn the business quickly; then he was to bring Mingus's head to Pengrove. There was no question that he was being tested, and the tracker would have left then, had he not been under constant observation. He would take his time to observe as much as possible, and then when the opportunity presented itself he would attempt to escape.

Stoke wondered when and how Pengrove had become corrupted. Lord Wallace was an incredibly influential man, and it was almost impossible to believe that he was under the influence of another. Certainly he controlled Faustine, and if there was anyone more powerful in England than Pengrove, the name was unknown to Stoke.

"There are no women here yet," explained Mingus. "Just men. To your right is the entrance to the sick ward. Those too weak or ill for service are given a brief opportunity to recover, and if they fail to do so, they are moved along to this unit." He pointed to a connecting chamber which was dimly lit.

They entered the area and walked down a short hallway that curved to the right and ended abruptly in the front of a low wall. Mingus gestured towards the stonework and Branan stepped forward and peered over the edge. A cold draft of air hit him in the face, and from very far below came the smell of lye mixed with something he couldn't identify.

"The fat of man is rendered down into soap here," said Mingus. "Just yesterday," he bragged, "I tossed a sickly child into the pit. It seemed an age before I heard the splash." He looked at Stoke as though he had just told him a great secret.

Branan forced the vision of Tamlyn from his mind. "How many lie below?" he asked.

"Hard to say," replied Mingus turning to leave. "There is no count kept." It occurred to Stoke that he had just lost his best chance at freedom. Certainly Mingus deserved to make the descent himself. "With practice" continued Mingus, "you will be able to tip three at a time. There is a trick to it that I'll show you tomorrow. Tuesday is rendering day."

"I would like to see the detainees if I might," said Stoke. He was anxious now to see if any of the unfortunates were of Tamlyn's age.

"Very well," replied Mingus, and they made their way back to the first chamber. The warden of the sickroom was introduced to Stoke, and a narrow window at chest height was revealed behind a sliding panel. A group of approximately fifteen adults were visible, all grim-faced and cheerless. A pair of them appeared to be mumbling to themselves, and the rest were silent. Another lay at the rear of the room on one of the narrow cots that were chained to the floor. To Branan's relief Tamlyn was not a guest in the ward.

Back at the entrance to the chamber Mingus pulled a large book across his desk and opened it at the first page. He laid his open palm on the page and pointed to number fourteen in the list. Beside the number was the name *Mingus*, and in the center of his palm the numeral *14* was permanently inked. "Anyone in these halls with no number belongs in the sick ward. Remember that, if you remember nothing else. Tomorrow you will receive a number also." *Not if I can help it*, thought Branan.

As night began to fall on Threstone, the fires were lit in the courtyard. Someone in an upper window played a mandolin, and cups of liquorice tea were brewed in a large kettle.

Caymus watched the flickering fire that was reflected in Violet's eyes. He had chosen to sit several feet away so he could observe her as he replaced the string on his crossbow. She stared into the fire, lost in her own world of thought. He decided that she had lost some of her softness and that in this light she looked hardened, wearing a hungrier, more dangerous beauty. Who knew what hardships she had seen in the last ten years? She had obviously left Paris after a time to return to the little town of Turfmoor.

He wanted to ask Violet what her life had been like, but still didn't trust his emotions. At present her demeanour didn't suggest that any pleasantries would be forthcoming. In fact she looked mildly ill as well as distracted. He supposed it was the long chase from Turfmoor that affected her and returned his attentions to the broken bow.

Minutes later, when Caymus glanced up again, she was staring at him. Their eyes met briefly, and he looked away first, unable to fathom the look of quiet desperation that he saw. When he had repaired his bow, he decided to test it. He set a bolt on the track and leaned towards the fire to set the tip ablaze. Then he aimed high into the clouds. The arrow climbed far into the air and then began its return, looking much like a shooting star. It hit the water with a sizzle and a puff of smoke that rested on the surface of the moat.

Without looking at Violet, he stepped past the group and took a seat at the cooking fire next to Ronan. "How's Ceana?" he asked.

"She's a little improved, I think, thank you, but she won't let Tamlyn out of her sight. Tyburn is seeing to her now, with his medicines. I fear if neither of them had returned when they did, she might not have lasted the night."

Caymus was surprised to learn of the severity of her ailment. "I'm sure she will brighten up now that Tamlyn is back. Has he said much about his ordeal?"

"Not yet," replied Ronan. "I believe we'll learn more from our father shortly. You are acquainted with the woman from Turfmoor?" he asked, changing the subject.

"Yes, intimately, but it was many years ago … Is it so obvious?"

"It's in the way you look at each other, a certain familiarity."

"It's a long story," said Cay "for another time."

"She is a most beautiful woman. I can see where you found the attraction."

Caymus smiled at his brother "Well, remember, as the saying goes, all that glitters is not necessarily gold." The bowman looked over towards the other fire and found that Violet had left in search of a cot.

"There is another saying," added Ronan with sudden insight. "Don't let the same dog bite you twice."

Tamlyn was reluctant to leave his mother's side. The old woman's eyes were closed, and her breathing was steady and shallow. Tyburn motioned with his head towards the door. He knew the youngster was tired and in need of rest.

The doctor lifted Ceana's hand gently from Tamlyn's knee and placed it in her lap. "You stretch your legs by the fire then come back here and sleep. I'll make up some bedding for you." Tamlyn thanked his grandfather and went in search of Ronan.

"Here's my lad now," said the blacksmith.

"Hello then, Tam, how's your mother?" asked Caymus.

The youngster sat next to his father and placed a hand on his shoulder. "She's asleep now," he said in reply to his uncle's question. "Grandfather is with her."

Tamlyn spent some time explaining to the two men what had transpired in the woods. The youngster wasn't sure why he'd been reluctant to mention his discovery. It somehow seemed an unreal occurrence that was not connected to his adventure, and in any event he had felt it was something that should remain private.

When Tamlyn described the wolf leaping through the air over his head, Caymus glanced at Ronan with an enquiring twinkle in his eye. The brothers agreed silently, and Ronan carefully revealed Tyburn's secret to Tamlyn.

"Your Uncle Cay here is not a shape-changer, and I myself do not have the skill. Murdoch shows no sign of having inherited the ways either. The knowledge emerges at the age you are now and takes many years of development. You may never show any signs, it's a rare blessing, or curse, depending how you look at it."

The two adults sat in silence, half expecting the youngster to tell them something. Tamlyn stared at the ground for a minute, then looked up at his father and smiled. "I was shown the falcon," he said quietly.

"I knew it!" said Caymus, slapping Ronan's knee. "Didn't I tell you the boy has the eyes of a hunting bird!?"

Ronan gestured to the bowman for silence. He tousled his son's hair and clapped him on the back. "Son, tell us no more, but speak with your grandfather when you get a chance. Tell him the details. They mean nothing to Cay and me, but he will understand."

"I don't want to tell anyone but Grandfather," said Tamlyn, yawning.

Ronan nodded. "It's well that you understand the need for discretion. Get yourself to bed now."

"I bloody well knew it," said Caymus again, very pleased with himself.

Now that's curious, thought Godwyn. He had taken his position at night watch in the gatehouse turret and just observed an intriguing scene. The young woman who'd come in this morning was standing against a castle wall out of the light. She was plainly eavesdropping on the Maclearys, who were seated by the fire. Caymus, the bowman, was gesturing animatedly as he spoke. When the youngster departed, Violet vanished around a corner silently. The Norseman was puzzled. What could that wee bit of espionage been about?

On the other side of the courtyard Liam and Charlotte shared a cup of fragrant tea with Murdoch. "Well," said Liam, "it's not a half bad place to be stuck in. I've always fancied living in a castle."

"Oh yes, Your Majesty," joked Charlotte. "It's fine when it's not raining. I prefer the courtyard to those stuffy rooms. The air is not good in there."

"That would be Cardiff!" laughed Murdoch. "He's famous for that."

"Where are those Macneils anyway?" asked Liam.

"Sleeping, of course," replied Murdoch. "That's all they do."

Duncan, the big highlander, arrived with an armful of wood. Padraic and his small dog Chowder were with him. The fires would be tended through the night, as some of the other villagers had chosen to sleep outside in the courtyard as well. Threstone Castle had seen better days, but despite the disrepair, what remained was extremely solid and would no doubt stand for years to come.

"Please forgive my intrusion," said Caymus. "It's been a very long time, and I fear I've forgotten how to talk to you. I wonder if we might learn to know each other again."

"I don't know, Cay," she replied hesitantly. "It has indeed been a long time. I don't know if we're the same people we were."

"I doubt either of us has changed so much." said Caymus, putting his hand on hers. She pulled away quickly. "I'm sorry," he said, "I just think—"

She didn't let him finish. "You should go back to your cot. It's different now ... everything is different." She looked away.

Being this close to her had filled him with a desire that he hadn't needed to deal with for ages, and he remembered what it had been like to lie with her in a passionate embrace. The craving was there again, frightful in its intensity. "I don't think you came back into my life again just to reject me again," he said suddenly.

Her eyes flashed in anger. "I didn't come into your life, I came into a castle for shelter! How was I to know you'd be here? I didn't ask for this!"

"You're right. My apologies—never mind." He left quickly and didn't speak to Violet again for an entire week.

-71-

"Well now, Fearghal, no time to waste," the scarecrow said to himself aloud. "To the business at hand."

It was no longer a simple matter of melting into the woodwork. Fearghal now had a solid form, such as it was, and would need to enter through a door once again. The front door of the armoury was locked securely, so he made his way to the rear where a ladder ran the full height of the building.

Climbing proved to be more difficult than he'd imagined. His muscles had atrophied to the point that they were not much more use than those of a child. It was slow going, but he eventually reached the lip and toppled over the edge onto the roof. He lay quietly in the shadows for some time listening to hear if his arrival had been noticed.

When he was reasonably sure that it was safe to continue, he got to his feet and made for the fourth floor entrance. Unless the situation had changed, Dafyd's room would still be on the second floor to the rear. With the quarry work occurring there were fewer Teriz at the mill, and Pengrove had appointed a portion of the third floor as his own. Fearghal crept downstairs to the third and from there to the second. The curtain separating antechamber from bedroom was pulled aside, and Dafyd sat at a desk, with his back to the entrance. He leaned over a book that lay open in front of him, beside a small lamp.

"Is that you, Euther?" he asked without looking up. He wrinkled up his nose and sniffed. Then he wheeled around suddenly, swinging low with a short sabre. The blade caught Fearghal across the knee and severed his leg, which fell with a clatter to the wooden floor. The assassin fell to his knees reaching for the silver blade at his back.

"Fearghal is it, then?" said Dafyd, squinting. "You are not looking well at all. I'm surprised you have not had the sense to abandon your corpse; it's seen better days."

"Defiler!" screamed Fearghal as he lunged forward. He grabbed his leg from the floor and swung it viciously at Dafyd, cracking him across the knee and sending him to the floor. The sabre flew from his hand and sliced off Fearghal's left ear.

As he fell across the Welshman, Dafyd got hold of his throat with both hands. "You're really going to pieces," he hissed, tightening his grip.

Fumbling again for his blade, Fearghal managed to loosen it. Then, gripping it in the center of his hand, he made a fist and tried for an uppercut. The blade entered the soft area below the Welshman's jaw and continued through to his brain. The effect of the silver was immediate. "Better than you deserved," said Fearghal, heaving Dafyd's corpse off him and to one side.

He lay panting on the floor. It wouldn't be long before someone came to see about the commotion. It was now time to rid himself of this accursed life once and for all. His body had become a cage, and Fearghal had the key in his hand still. He sat up and wrenched the knife from Dafyd's head. Then he wiped the blade clean on the Welshman's shirt. He pointed the dagger toward his own heart where the last few drops of blood still remained, took a deep breath, and fell upon it.

Pengrove leaped up suddenly at the noise, toppling a goblet of wine across his papers. "Blast it!" He grabbed a scarf and attempted to wipe away the red stains from the foolscap. "Damnation!" he cursed. He had worked on the papers for hours, and now they were ruined. He stormed from his chambers determined to affix blame to someone. Wallace assumed that Euther was too far into a drugged stupor to have heard anything and proceeded by himself to mete out his punishment.

He stormed into the second floor room with a heavy walking stick in hand. "How in the devil am I expected to accomplish anything with all of this racket?" he yelled.

Then he froze in his tracks, and his jaw dropped. It appeared that Dafyd had been the victim of an attack. He lay on his back with blood streaming from a gash under his chin. As far as he could tell, the perpetrator, whose body lay next to Dafyd, had succumbed to a wound dealt by the Welshman. His leg lay close by and was curiously devoid of blood.

These Wraiths were beginning to try his patience. They were either dead or alive or somewhere in between. There were the blooded and unblooded, the Teriz and the flesh-eaters to contend with. When this whole thing was finished, there would be one race of man and one only. In the meantime, he would call someone to clean up the mess.

"Oh my," said a voice behind him. Faustine stepped forward and took in the scene. "Dear, dear me. Cain and Abel, the farmer slays the shepherd. What trying times we live in. Four old friends gone in such a short time."

"You don't look very devastated," said Pengrove.

"On the contrary," Faustine insisted. "I have never been one to display my emotions well, but I assure you my heart is broken. I shall grieve for a very long time."

-72-

"In here," said Mingus, directing the Teriz to the pit. Stoke leaned against the wall observing. Resting on the stone edge of the pit were three bowls of food and three low stools. "Meal first, examination later," he said, ushering the sickly-looking Teriz to their seats. They looked pleased to have a full meal provided and sat down and began to eat with no hesitation.

Mingus winked at Branan. Then he walked up quietly behind the center stool. He calmly reached down and grabbed the outer two Teriz by the backs of their belts. Leaning in to pin the third man down, he flipped them quickly over the wall. Then just as swiftly he collared the other one and tossed him over. The screams receded as they fell, and eventually the splash was heard.

Stoke's eyes were wide with disbelief. "And that, my friend," said Mingus, "is how it's done." He smiled smugly as he turned to drop the food bowls into the pit.

Branan saw his chance. With no hesitation, he rushed at the smaller man and pushed him over the edge. Mingus managed to spin and get a grip on the edge with both hands. Stoke picked up one of the heavy stools and brought it down viciously on the flesh-eater's knuckles, again and again, until Mingus finally lost his grip and fell. He made no sound whatsoever until his body hit the deadly soup below.

"That's how it's done," he said softly as he left the room. He had passed the test but did not intend to stay around for the graduation ceremony. He walked straight from the compound into the tunnel, turning up the unfinished passage towards Turfmoor in hopes of finding access to the outside. A quarter of the way down the tunnel a ladder was visible, lit by natural light from above. Without even a glance behind him, he leapt to the ladder and scampered up, peeking carefully from the opening.

The quarry was far to his left, and the tree line behind curved down towards him, offering shelter. He paused for a minute, reluctant to make himself vulnerable. Then with a last look below, he emerged from the hole and made a dash for the forest.

The following week passed with very little of anything changing. Stoke made his way through the woods to Castle Threstone and was delighted to find that Tamlyn had survived his ordeal. He relayed his findings to the other highlanders and learned that Turfmoor had been overrun long before the tunnel could connect it to Dunradin. He asked Violet about events in her town and found the beautiful young woman to be evasive and suspicious of his enquiries. Ceana, who was much improved, had begun to sew a large standard, which was to fly above the castle walls. Caymus managed to down a young buck, and the venison was appreciated greatly.

Disaster struck on the first day of the new week. Caymus, who had given up speaking to Violet, was seated across the courtyard, and while glancing in her direction noted that the young woman's face was stained with tears. She rose and strode quickly for the gatehouse. Then she crossed the moat bridge with haste and ran down the trail to the edge of the woods.

Caymus went after her, and then hesitated as he stood on the bridge. Then he sighed and followed her into the forest. She turned suddenly and glared at him with tear-filled eyes. The bowman backed her against a tree, gripped her shoulders, and pulled the blouse down her arms. "No, Cay, please," she said, turning her head. He leaned forward and kissed her neck. The flesh was cold and uninviting. Her upper lip pulled back from her teeth in a grimace. "I told you, no!"

The bowman felt himself swell with unbridled lust. He pushed his chest into her, pinning her to the tree, and reached down to his belt freeing the blade. Suddenly he brought up his left hand and slashed across his wrist, severing the artery.

The bowman's blood sprayed across her blouse and painted Violet's face with a bright slash of red. She gasped, and then locked her mouth hungrily onto his arm. He pushed her to the ground and fell to his knees as the blood continued to pump from his body. Reaching behind his back, he retrieved his pistol. It was loaded with silver shot, and he worked quickly to prime it. Spots began to swim in front of his face, and sweat dripped into his eyes.

Violet tore open her blood-soaked blouse, exposing her breasts, and writhed on the ground. Caymus forced her mouth open and shoved the gun barrel in. He paused for one tortured second while their eyes locked. Then he pulled the trigger.

The clouds broke as he collapsed against her, and a cold rain began the work of washing the couple clean.

It had all happened so quickly that Godwyn, watching the chase from the upper gatehouse, could do nothing but call the alarm.

Ronan and Branan ran across the moat bridge with several others and raised their weapons in the air. "There." Godwyn pointed through the veil of rain. "Your brother falls."

The men ran up the trail towards the woods, fuelled with adrenalin, ready to battle with the Teriz that they imagined had set upon Caymus. When they reached the couple, who looked strangely at peace in their bloody embrace, Ronan fell to his knees and groaned.

Cay's pistol lay across the woman's arm, and the top of her head was open against the tree behind her. The bowman's lifeless arm was draped on her breast, and blood still drained from the gash across his other wrist.

Stoke drew his conclusions quickly. "This woman was blooded," he said. "She must have fled in order to attend to her hunger. Your brother dispatched her with silver shot."

"And this whore opened his veins?" asked Ronan, choking back a sob. Branan leaned over and picked up Caymus's knife.

"This made the cut, but by whose hand?"

The blacksmith turned his brother over carefully and ran his hand softly across Caymus's face closing the eyes. "Please," he asked Godwyn, who had joined the group, "if you could fetch a cart."

The entire population of the castle was deeply affected by the loss of Caymus Macleary. The bowman had been well liked, and his death left a shadow across the minds of all the Maclearys. It was now Ceana's turn to comfort Ronan. Her husband grieved deeply at the loss of his brother. Almost forgotten in the tragedy were young Alfred and his ageing grandmother.

Young Alfie was taken in at once by Ceana and treated like one of her own. For the sake of the boy and his grandmother, Violet was buried beside the tree where she had died, and the highlanders built a small cairn over her final resting spot. Taking Padraic into account, Ceana's family had increased by one grandmother and two boys.

The day after the tragedy, a large group of family and friends accompanied Cay's remains in a short journey downhill to the seaside. He was laid out in a makeshift craft heavily coated with pitch and filled with birch bark. His bow lay across his chest. Murdoch and Ronan entered the water and pushed the boat out far enough to catch a wave.

The blacksmith carried a long stave that burned at one end. He thrust it into the craft and covered his face as the funeral boat burst into flame. He waded back to the shore with his eldest son, and they joined Tamlyn next to his mother. The gathered crowd stood in silence with heads bowed as the fire crackled and spit. The glowing embers were still visible from the castle walls late into the night.

"I think we can safely assume," said Branan, "that Cay prevented word from reaching the Teriz of Turfmoor, with regards to the nature of our defences." The council were gathered around the fire discussing their next move.

"I think we should remain here for the time being," said Hugh Maclean. "The moat offers protection, and the walls are strong."

Branan continued, "They will strike at some point, I can guarantee you. And I agree, we can fortify our surroundings much better. My concern is our food supply. I propose that we arrange a visit to Dunradin to see what we can salvage. I'm quite certain that the Teriz are now occupied elsewhere. Woodruff is due back here any day, but our supplies are dangerously low."

Ronan spoke up: "We have the two horses from Turfmoor and a good wagon. Let's ride in and retrieve anything of value."

"I'm thinking the same thing" said Duncan. "We should leave on the hour and arrive by nightfall, do you not agree?" It was decided that sooner was better than later, and Duncan volunteered to lead a small group including Maclean and two of the other Highlanders.

Duncan walked the horses into Dunradin, stopping at the grocer's. It was fortunate that the moon was not obscured that night, for the streetlamps had long since burned out, and the darkness was almost total. The rest of the party jumped from the wagon and joined him at Portus's old grocery. Once inside, they lit lamps and scavenged what they could from the mostly empty shelves. Outside, Duncan was amazed to discover that the huge bow built by Caymus and Ronan was still in place.

It took all four of them to lift it onto the wagon, along with the two remaining bolts that had been left untouched.

Flour, sugar, and oats were duly commandeered, along with a sack of potatoes with twisted eyes that would serve nicely as seedlings. Duncan looked towards the roof of the grocer's surprised to see moonlight shining on the chests of several pigeons roosting in the eaves. Although their coop seemed to have been intentionally left open, the birds remained. A shutter behind him creaked and he spun around. It was just a trick of the wind.

Next they stopped in the Ale House at Ezekiel Bardwick's request. He had hidden a bottle of whisky away in a secure spot known only to himself and asked Duncan to retrieve it for him. In actuality he intended to give the fine whisky to the widow Gamble, who he understood was partial to a wee nip now and then. As Zeke would eventually discover, she was more partial to a belt than a nip, but the shared interest in spirits would stand their blossoming friendship in good stead.

Without its citizens Dunradin looked cold and ugly. Rats roamed in the open and although rain had washed the streets, there was a bad smell about the place. Duncan had no desire to get anywhere near the fountain, where a mound of Teriz bodies still lay headless and partially decomposed.

The light of one small fire across the river was the only sign of the enemy. Duncan was somewhat surprised that none of the Teriz had taken up residence here on the hill but supposed it was due to their preference for low, dark places. He decided that the expedition had been fortunate not to have encountered any of the enemy, and it would be best not to test their luck any further.

They left Dunradin quicker than they had arrived and were soon on the high open road that would take them past Tyburn's abandoned home. They slowed the horses to pass the doctor's farm at a walk. A rope hung from the big oak in his yard. Someone or something hung, twisting in the breeze. A closer look revealed that the dangling corpse was in fact a large dog. Most of its skin was peeled back and hung like a cloak below the animal's waist.

Duncan turned from the grisly sight and urged the horses forward. Tyburn would be disturbed to hear that his home had been defiled in such a manner. The highlander didn't dare imagine what lay inside the house, and that was a question best answered by the full light of day. They had chosen the long route back to Threstone for the specific purpose of determining how far that way the Teriz might have encroached. It appeared that they had definitely been this far north of the village but found nothing to keep them there.

As they swung past Glencairn Bridge more signs of incursion were evident. "Good Lord!" exclaimed one of Duncan's companions. A jute rope had been secured across the road at the entrance to the bridge, and sixty or more severed heads were strung together along its length. The most disturbing detail was the absence of male victims. All the heads were those of women and children.

Duncan swallowed hard and swore loudly. "The bastard whoresons!" Turfmoor had paid dearly for its resistance. If this many had been used for a marking of territory, he shuddered to think how many others had been carried away alive.

Florian, the youngest of Duncan's companions, looked ill. His face had drained of all its colour. "Remember this carnage, when next we do battle," said Duncan, turning the horses back to the road. He doubted the young man would ever forget the horror of what he had just seen. The horses were urged on by their driver who was anxious to be as far from the bridge as possible. As they broke into a clearing, the horizon was suddenly filled with stars. They were so low in the sky that Duncan felt they could rain down at any minute, and the road would peel up behind them like the skin of an apple. A giant blue worm of light wriggled behind the castle illuminating it in the distance.

-73-

Pengrove looked over the edge into the pit and covered his mouth. The broken chair with its markings and stains told the story. "And Mr. Stoke is gone as well?" he asked the captain.

"That's correct sir. No sign of either one, and the door left open as such."

"Does that mean he passes the test?" joked Euther.

"For some reason, Faustine, you never quite seem to grasp the seriousness of the situation. More than once it's occurred to me that your sanity is questionable."

"You may have a valid point there," replied Euther. "But that matters little. I'll have Mingus replaced, and we can move on to the matter of troop deployment. Those villagers aren't going to sit up there in that castle forever."

"You have maps I trust?" asked Pengrove.

"Oh yes indeed, the very ones you requested, if you will follow me."

As they made their way through the tunnel, Euther went on, "Tell me something. What would you do if the Teriz suddenly developed a taste for richer foods, say the aristocracy, for example? That would throw a spanner into the works, wouldn't it?"

Lord Pengrove wasn't sure how to answer the hypothetical question. "It's all a little game to you, isn't it, Dorian?" he replied.

Faustine smiled. "Well, I just wondered, you know. After all, we've got to keep on our toes. By the way, how's my counterpart in Deermuir doing?"

Pengrove entered the room first. "He's progressing. He is close to finishing work on a new village."

Euther took a map down and flattened it against the table. "Douglas was here," he said, pointing to the small village south of Turfmoor. "Deermuir has proven to be a different kettle of fish, as the village is not divided by a river as here in Dunradin. Turfmoor, on the other hand, was easily taken. It's such a little piss hole of a village that we just marched in from the east and out the other side.

"Well," said Euther, "I'm told that Ivan Douglas is not a man to be underestimated. I'd much rather have him as an ally than as a foe." He had been nicknamed the weasel, and was as slippery a character as could be found in the entire northern hemisphere.

"As far as Threstone is concerned," said Pengrove, pointing, "we have troops here, and here to the north. If you bring your men in from this angle, we will have them penned in on three sides against the sea."

"The challenge will be taking them alive," said Euther. "If you're at all familiar with these highlanders, you'll know that they prefer a fight to the death."

Pengrove raised his eyebrows. "In that case, I suggest we accommodate them. All in the works, if you take my meaning." He retrieved a briar from his jacket and scooped some tobacco into the bowl. "I've sent for two of my officers to take up a little of the slack, you understand. Nothing against your people, but they don't have much of a shelf life, do they?"

Euther shrugged. "Circumstances."

Wallace continued, "Drake, Kendricks, his wife, then Godwyn, and now Mingus. Not a very good record of longevity. Oh yes, and Fearghal, I forgot about him. But you've survived them all, haven't you?"

"I hope, Wallace, that you won't forget who initiated this little revolution of yours."

"Certainly , but it didn't take long for your high ideals to go out the window, Euther de Faustine, saviour of the Teriz, the one who was going to bring them above ground."

Euther chuckled. "Call it the exuberance of youth. It all meant something to me when Morgana was alive. Recently, I dealt with the fat pig that slaughtered her. I pretended that it brought me satisfaction, but in truth it changed nothing. It made the emptiness feel as deep as that pit in the quarry. I envy your mortality, but I fear my death. I don't want to know when or how I will end."

Pengrove blew smoke rings into the air, looking bored. "Is there any sherry in that cellar of yours?"

Euther stared at Lord Pengrove for a minute trying to decide whether to be insulted or not. "Did you know," he said finally, "that Sir Francis Drake, no relation to the late William, returned from Cádiz in 1587 with nearly three thousand barrels of very fine sherry?"

"Well," said Pengrove, following Euther to the cellar, "I think one bottle will suffice."

An entire case of Amontillado was located at the back of the wine cellar, much to Wallace's delight, and they worked their way through a bottle in no time.

"Did I ever tell you about Doctor Tyburn Macleary?" asked Faustine.

"If you refer to Dunradin's elder, no, I am not familiar with a specific history."

"My first encounter with the good doctor came very early in his study of medicinals. I was spending a great deal of time with a very attractive young woman who had encouraged my advances on several occasions. To say that she was bold would be an understatement, and at times her behaviour was plainly sinful. Vannah was a tease, and I was a young man with plenty of blood in my veins. This was back in the day, you understand, long before I developed the hunger.

"The sly little whore had me on a string, and believe me; my feet rarely touched the ground. Anyway, the point is we had not consummated our relationship, and I was a great walking cock ready to service a knothole in a floorboard, so to speak. I was a military man at the time and should have understood discipline. However ..." His voice trailed off.

"And what does this have to do with the doctor?" asked Wallace.

"I'm getting to it," replied Faustine. "The doctor, in those days, was a snotty-nosed medical student, and he fancied this trollop as a future wife. So one day, down at the edge of the river, I spy her in the reeds bathing herself. She knows I'm watching, make no mistake about that. It's her game, you see."

Pengrove leaned forward and poured himself another sherry.

"Well, there's only so much a young man can take," continued Faustine. "I slipped out of my uniform, and into the water I went. Soon enough we were on the shore, rutting like hogs in the mud, and out of the trees comes young Tyburn, blade in hand. As he sees it, his sweetheart is being defiled by a filthy Englishman, and that's enough reason to run me through.

"So we grappled. I was slick with mud and lust, greasier than a butcher's prick, but he managed to ground me eventually. In the meantime two of my infantry men have arrived and she's run off. Macleary gets his blade into my ribs, and he's trying twist it good. One of my mates kicks him square on the jaw, and he goes down. They drag me off and later in the day confront the Scots and accuse them of murdering their captain. Of course I'm not dead, but never been closer, and my lads are just wanting a fight. It's all solved with a grovelling apology from the family, and the payoff is taken."

Pengrove relit his pipe and put his feet up on a barrel. "And what of the woman?"

"Well, of course she plays the victim, and eventually when she gets a swelling in the belly marries the doctor while carrying my seed."

Lord Pengrove scratched his chin. "So then we end up with the older Macleary as novice doctor, and I assume young Fearghal is raised under the roof of your enemy?"

"Precisely," said Euther.

"And what becomes of the woman then?"

Faustine raised an open palm. "She bears Tyburn two more sons, Ronan and Caymus, gets old, and dies of an intestinal disorder that the doctor can't cure. Macleary, of course, would give a very different account."

"Yes, I'm sure. How would that go?" asked Pengrove, still intrigued.

"The courageous doctor," he began, "finds his virginal young sweetheart—who, I might add, was not intact when I had her—in flagrante delicto with an Englishman. He rushes to her aid and dispatches the villain quickly with his knife, then fights off a score of infantryman, banning them from the village of Dunradin forever."

Wallace chuckled. "But he was under the impression that he'd killed you?"

"Yes, certainly, he was told as much, and as I said, a small amount of money exchanged hands, and everyone was happy. Well, I wasn't happy, lost my load, but it cost me a pint or two of blood and a miserable fortnight of painful recovery. All it cost him was one of nine fingers."

Pengrove looked down his nose at Euther, "And you've made up for those two pints several times over."

Euther shrugged. "I didn't ask to be a Wraith. I had to make the best of it, didn't I?"

"It may interest you to know," said Pengrove after a silence, "that there is an obstetrician in London who has recently performed a transfusion of blood from one human to another with good results."

Euther looked up. "What is your point?" he asked.

Wallace brushed at a stain on his jacket with a concerned look. "I can't help but wonder what would happen if every drop of tainted blood was drained from someone like yourself, and it was completely replaced with fresh blood—what the result would be."

Faustine laughed aloud. "Turning sinners into saints, there's a sideline for you, Wallace. I suppose," he continued, "from a medical point of view it may prove useful." He ran a hand across the back of his neck and stood up. "You might change a man's blood but not his morals."

-74-

"This is not the news I'd wished to hear," said Branan. "I had hoped that we were not to deal with scattered bands of Teriz. I don't like that creeping form of combat, too many variables. Give me an open field and a sturdy weapon."

"They have been at the doctor's, the bridge, and probably everywhere in between," said Duncan. "I would assume that they occupy the woods from here to the river. Apparently the town itself doesn't appeal to them for the time being."

Branan interrupted, "In my opinion it's just a matter of time before they utilize the village. Given what I've told you about Pengrove, I wouldn't be surprised to learn that he intends to eventually use all of Scotland as his dumping ground. I think his plan involves the eradication of all things Scottish. Traitors and dissidents from below the border will be sent to camps in the north where they will be fed upon before facing eventual extinction. Christians to the lions as it were."

Ronan, who had not been very vocal since the death of Caymus, spoke up. "This is no small matter then. You're implying that a full-scale war is in the works. Who else is aware of this?"

"I know in no uncertain terms that Her Majesty is completely unaware of this plot, or of much else for that matter," said Branan. "There has to be some knowledge of the matter within Pengrove's ranks, in order for the practical aspects of this madness to progress.

Faustine, as menacing as he appears, may just be a pawn. I think he may have already outlived his usefulness to Pengrove."

Godwyn spoke up. "Cut off the head of the beast, and the body dies."

"Possibly," said Tyburn. "Until another beast arises." He felt sick with the knowledge that his cottage had been despoiled and was even less inclined than usual to regard the Teriz with any sympathy.

"Woodruff should be on the road back any day now," said Branan. "I wish I had known the full extent of matters before sending him off. Edinburgh should be informed, if not warned."

"How do you imagine anyone in Edinburgh would have the power to do anything about this?" asked Ronan. "I have some contacts, old friends. We can't use politicians; they'd stick out like balls on a dog. Anyway they are too easy to bribe. It has to be people that we trust who won't talk."

Ben Flint was the gentleman Branan had in mind, a member of the Edinburgh constabulary who had employed Stoke on occasion. At this very minute he was out and about in the big city.

Captain Benjamin Flint was not a man to be trifled with, and Cyrus Dwight was not the first to have misread his calm demeanour. The captain was a slight man, who navigated the cobbled streets with the aid of a walking stick. He was comparable in appearance to most men in their fiftieth year, save that he sported a dark moustache that was rapidly turning to silver and that he walked with a very discernible limp. He possessed a handsome brow, beneath which a more than casual observer might note a pair of curious eyes, both of which were the very darkest shade of blue.

The younger Dwight was an accomplished pickpocket and generally a good judge of character, never choosing his prey without a careful appraisal. Flint he judged to be a willing enough victim and, by his manner of dress, a gentleman of some means. A small gold chain, presumably attached to a watch in his vest, hung carelessly from a side pocket.

The captain was positioned a few steps from one of the market stalls with his arms crossed over his chest, bathed in the warmth of a sunny morning. He tilted his head back and closed his eyes enjoying the turn of the season, seemingly unaware of Cyrus's approach.

The thief made directly for his victim, keeping his eyes to the ground as if lost in thought. He carried a handkerchief in one hand, holding it to his mouth to stifle a well-timed cough as his other hand sought the treasure in Flint's vest.

Cyrus leaned into the man and was caught by surprise as Flint stepped back and turned to one side, bringing the heavy walking stick down across his lower arm with alarming speed and purpose. Both bones audibly snapped just above Dwight's wrist, and the young man howled in pain, falling clumsily to his knees. The captain nimbly kicked him full in the face, dislodging several of the man's remaining teeth. Then, turning with his back to the market, Flint brushed the dirt from his trouser leg and calmly strolled with no difficulty in the direction of the Four Sheep, an inn that served particularly fine ale.

By an odd coincidence, Ben was put in mind of his old friend Branan Stoke. A tall highlander had just entered the Four Sheep and ordered a pint in a deep, familiar voice. Flint glanced toward the bar, half expecting to see Stoke, but laughed quietly at the sight of the man, not in any derision but simply because the similarities had ended so abruptly. He was tall indeed like Branan and had a like head of fiery hair, but the man's nose set him apart from Stoke, and perhaps the entire population of Edinburgh. It resembled a large cob of corn, and it was all the man could do to avoid wetting it in his beer.

-75-

Woodruff arrived the following day with twenty-two men and two wagons of goods. They were joined almost within the hour by Duncan bringing supplies from Dunradin. The volunteers set up three large tents in the field beside the castle and before long had felled enough trees to construct an open enclosure for their horses. The occupants of Threstone were pleased to discover that the highlanders had brought a good supply of food basics with them.

Woodruff was filled in with regards to the changing situation and spoke with Stoke in a solemn tone. "The good news is that all of these men have volunteered to aid in defence of the castle. On the negative side, they are limited by time. These men all have families and farms in the north that can't be neglected for long. They're here because of you, Branan. Your name still commands respect and loyalty."

Stoke knew most of the men who had arrived and understood that the highlanders who had made the trip from Dunradin, would now wish to return to their homes. "I am most grateful for their loyalty," he replied. "I've decided to go to Edinburgh at once to speak to Ben Flint."

Woodruff knew the name and had heard of the man's reputation. Edinburgh's criminal population avoided offending Flint at all costs. He was a fair man but also a man for whom the term ruthless might as well have been coined. Some of Flint's superiors on the force considered his methods objectionable but generally looked the other way because he got the job done quickly and more efficiently than anyone else. When there was dirty work to be done, they turned to Flint. His connections to the underworld were numerous, and some members of the ruling class were of the opinion that the line he trod between the criminal community and theirs was a thin one.

"I don't believe this will be a public battle," Branan observed. "It's more like a disease in need of a cure."

"If it's escalating as quickly as you suggest," said Woodruff, "it's bound to be very public in short order."

"Timing is everything," replied Stoke. "Pengrove may be satisfied with three small out-of-the-way villages for the time being, but that's only a building process. I don't understand how he can assume that something won't be noticed in the larger centres. This is what leads me to believe that our precious politicians are already aware of his undertakings. Money and promises go a long way to cover a wound."

After three uneventful days of travel, Branan located Flint in the King and Dragon, located on one of the alleys leading off the Royal Mile at High Street. The bustle of the city was a change of pace for Stoke, and he found it tiring. Industry had begun to expand the city, and although the rate of change was minimal compared to Glasgow, he still found it much changed from his last visit.

The two men exchanged family news and pleasantries until Flint asked Branan what his real purpose was. "You've not come to Auld Reekie just to share a pint with your friends, Branan. What brings you here in such a hurry, with that wee look of desperation about you?"

Stoke pulled his chair closer to the table and told Benjamin Flint all that he knew of the situation. "Imagine this, Ben, Lord Wallace approaches the power brokers and informs them of a growing threat in the form of Teriz blood-drinkers. In truth there are very few of them left, not enough to constitute a major threat, so Pengrove manufactures more of the enemy, thus enlarging a predicament: a frightening enemy that creeps about in the dead of night. His casually dropped hints have the politicians looking under their beds.

"On top of this he promises an end to poverty and disease, which he claims are only rampant because of the ways of those filthy Teriz. Just leave it up to me, he suggests, and there are enough of his cohorts under thumb to swear that the threat is not imagined. Meanwhile Pengrove has the power to regulate and control the Teriz in their numbers and their actions. You see? He controls the disease"—he paused dramatically—"and the cure. His Lordship also stresses the need for privacy and discretion. His dream of a pure race of Britons gathers momentum daily. And who is next after the Scots? the Welsh and the Irish?"

"I see your point," said Benjamin. "But why me?"

"Because," answered Stoke, "a conventional army raises eyebrows. You have access to men with particular skills, men who go about their business in a discreet manner, and if I may dispense with mincing words, this operation has to be tighter than a fish's arsehole, or it won't fly."

Flint grinned at his old friend. "These ventures require capital. I don't have any associates who work on a volunteer basis, as I'm sure you realize."

"I may have a solution," said Branan. "I'm aware of your disdain for gentlemen in the banking profession, one banker in particular."

"Pepperidge?" asked Flint.

"Yes, Athabasca Pepperidge indeed, none other," replied Stoke. "If you were to come across information that would allow you to relieve old Pepperidge of a large portion of his wealth, would you be inclined to use it for the betterment of the common man?"

Flint smiled again. "I would be so inclined, were I in a position to deprive that scumbag of some of his fortune. I would even be pleased to burn his money if that was that the deal."

"Excellent," said Stoke, "I thought that might appeal to you. It appears that Pepperidge has been skimming the accounts for years. Just a little at a time so as to not be noticeable, but I'm told that it's a king's ransom and that he doesn't trust the formal establishments for its safekeeping. Pepperidge and Pengrove go way back to the early days in London. His name was brought to my attention by a former employee of Faustine's who was intercepted on the road to London. This Margus character had far more knowledge than his rank would suggest and had been dispatched south to purchase opiates for Dorian. The name Pepperidge meant nothing to me until I thought of you and made the connection."

"You allowed this Margus to live?"

"Yes," replied Stoke. "I had no quarrel with him, and he'd done me a great service by supplying the information, for a price of course."

"Therein lays the difference between you and me, old friend," said Flint. "I would have taken the information and then killed him. As a practicality you understand. Information like that can be sold and resold, with no guarantee on the quality of customer."

"You're a practical man indeed, and your value to me is precisely a matter of the proper politics and practicality."

-76-

Tamlyn and Padraic watched the highlanders from the ruins of one of the south turrets. It was a bright, sunny spot that offered a good view of goings-on in the field. The rocks which jutted into the moat at different heights were covered with a fragrant carpet of moss and wildflowers. Ceana had baked chicken and biscuits and the two lads felt like kings as they dined in the fresh air.

The widow Gamble was still in mourning for her daughter Violet and her grandson Alfred was equally devastated. However, he had spent some time with Padraic to take his mind off the tragedy, and young Paddy was beginning to pick up the basics of hand speaking. Tamlyn was learning as well, and the prospect of being able to converse this way with his long-time friend excited him.

"Over here," called Tamlyn, waving a chicken leg, when he spotted Alfie heading in their direction. "Plenty for three!" he yelled. The highlanders were building a large pit fire between their tents, and two of them looked up and waved at the youngsters.

"I wonder if there are any fish in the moat," said Tamlyn. The water closer to the shore from the castle side, was thick with bullrushes.

Alfie pointed to the reeds. "I bet there's a few fat trout hiding under there. Do you wannae make some fishing rods?"

Padraic nodded enthusiastically, and Tamlyn grinned. "We can find some saplings over by the tents." Tam let Ceana know what they had planned, and the three youngsters made their way across the moat bridge. It was a castle rule that anyone passing through the gatehouse was required to sign in and out with the gatekeeper. The rule had been suggested by parents who worried if their children were out of view for very long, and it was decided that everyone would abide by the terms.

Padraic borrowed Tam's knife and cut himself a length of sapling. "What are we gonna use for line?" asked Alfie.

"Dunno, shoelaces? We could ask that Highlander."

Big John Macintosh was at the edge of the camp, splitting wood with a hand ax. "Hullo there, lads. Where would you be off to?" John stroked his handlebar moustache and spit into the dirt. Big John was somewhat on the short side, but he was a muscular man, with a pleasant attitude.

"We're thinking there might be some trout in that moat there, but we don't have fishing line," answered Tamlyn.

"Well," said Macintosh, "not sure I can help you. You might ask my brother Donald over there. He has something he patches the tents with."

Donald gave each boy a coil of heavy thread from a large spool in his tent. "Now then," he said, "I don't suppose you've put any thought into what you might use for hooks."

The boys realized that they really had rushed off half prepared. "Uh, we thought we might use these," said Tamlyn, pulling some bent nails from his pocket.

Donald looked at them and scowled. "Those are as much use as a one-legged man in an arse-kicking contest." The youngsters laughed at his description. "Look here," he continued. "I've a wee tin of proper hooks, and you can have one each, but only one, so don't go getting them snagged in a sea monster. I hear there's one about this area."

The boys were thrilled. "Padraic says thank you, sir, and if there's anything we can do for you, don't hesitate to ask us."

Donald laughed loudly, "I'll tell you what. If you catch more than one fish apiece, then you bring one to me."

As they walked back to Threstone, Alfie spoke with Tamlyn. "Was you scared when you was lost in the woods?"

"It was the Teriz I saw that were the most frightening," said Tam, "and being on the island with the dead." He realized his mistake and apologized to both his friends. "I'm sorry, I didn't mean to—"

"Nae worries," said Alfie quickly, "Ahm nae bothered, not that I didn't love me mam, but it was all for the best." Tamlyn was confused. "You see I was mostly took care of by my gram. Mam was sick for a long time, in a different sort of way. It's best," he insisted again.

Tamlyn put an arm around each of his friends as they continued along. "Sometimes life is shite," he said. He himself had just lost an uncle, and the three boys were bonded in a friendship of familiarity and circumstance that would last a very long time.

Tam recounted some of his adventure in the forest but omitted any reference to voices or visions. "I'll tell you this much," he said. "I don't ever want to see those Teriz again. Twice is two times too many." He claimed to have given them the slip in the fog and that they hadn't seen the boat that carried him to Horn Island. It was plausible enough, and there was already a mystery and a climate of rumour around the island of the dead, so the story was accepted as factual.

Tamlyn had felt an odd sense of comfort while listening to the voice and wished to explore his discovery further. He knew it would have to be in a very private moment, away from the castle, and the opportunity had not arisen yet. It was not as though he had a specific question, but the general feeling of being surrounded by wisdom and learning was a pleasant one that he wanted to experience again.

Murdoch spent less time with the younger boys and more time with his father. He was very close to Caymus and identified with Ronan's loss. It was almost as if the older son had taken the place of his uncle in the way of things with family. Murdoch and Ronan were seldom out of each other's sight these days.

Charlotte was occupied with Liam, and the couple spent a great deal of time entertaining the small children while their parents went about the work of trying to contribute to the betterment of the castle.

Ceana joked that they often acted like an old married couple and referred to them as mister and missus.

Lara Twist, Liam's mother, had become quite close with Ceana and Charlotte. Ronan attributed his wife's return to health in part to the friendship that had developed between the women and their shared interest in the young couple. The widow Gamble moved her cot to an alcove adjacent to Lara's room, and the pair of them often brewed tea together.

-77-

In the meantime, through the woods and across the river, Pengrove was greeting his two officers, Griffin and Gareth Hume. The brothers were both quiet spoken by nature and slow to anger. More than once this attribute had fooled adversaries into believing they held the upper hand in dealings with the Humes, until they showed their real face. Gareth in particular was like a snake that lulled its victim into a comfortable state of hypnosis and then struck with a venomous bite in the tenderest of spots.

Neither man was very large or physically imposing. Their father had been a tiny man who they claimed couldn't pull the skin off of a custard. He was blessed with a brilliant mind for tactics, which had allowed him to rise to a respectable rank in the military. Colonel Hume had unfortunately aged in mind before body and now passed his days in Bellscove Sanatorium.

"It might interest you to know," said Pengrove to Griffin, "your old friend Branan Stoke was a guest here briefly."

"Oh, indeed," replied Hume, "and how is Mr. Stoke?"

"Mr. Stoke looked well, but I'm afraid to say that his sympathies don't lie with our cause, quite the opposite, in fact."

Griffin smiled. "Yes. Well, I would have been very much surprised if Stoke had come aboard. He was never much of a joiner when it came to the more radical affairs. Am I to assume that Stoke has been eliminated?"

"Oh no, on the contrary," said Pengrove. "He appears to have done away with one of my men and made good his escape."

Griffin's eyebrows rose. "Pity that he didn't see the way forward; we could have used him."

"He was in a different class from me," said Gareth. "I don't recall meeting him."

"No, you never did," answered Griffin. "We chummed about for a bit, mostly on the drink. Nice fellow, but a bit of a dreamer. I could have told you he'd be opposed to what Wallace has achieved. I wouldn't want to meet him on the field without backup though. He's a hard man."

"I haven't told you about Netherfield," said Griffin, turning back to Pengrove. Wallace looked puzzled. " It's Ivan Douglas's project."

"Oh, I see he's put a name to it. How is it working?"

"Well, it's early days yet, but the entire town is populated with the cream of the crop, as it were. No slackers, none but well-to-do upright and white. All new buildings of course, and a central rehabilitation centre for those who might lose their way. No darkies or feeble-minded. Not a pansy or a whore for miles. It's very refreshing, I must say."

"Good," said Pengrove, "it's the way of the future. I'll have to see it for myself. How's the security?"

"No one gets in or out without a pass."

"How does he weed out the Irish?" asked Wallace.

"With paperwork, pedigree, and the like, there's even a great number of English, of course, who don't make the cut. It's a very tight operation; he's following your instructions to the letter."

Netherfield was situated on a sunken plain on the moors north of Carlisle just below the border. It was a new village built with no fanfare or visibility. In the unlikely event that a stranger came across the town he would naturally assume that he'd arrived at a factory of some sort. All the buildings looked much the same, and the centre of the town was dominated by a large building that housed all services for its citizens. From the outside it resembled a church, but the interior was much larger and more complex, reaching far below the ground level. The rear of the building spread out for a full block and contained every manner of supplies required for a comfortable living.

A narrow road behind the village carried on uphill to a coal mine that had recently been put to use. The villagers themselves did not work the mine. The Teriz were used to bring the coal out, and they themselves never left the mine. Netherfield's inhabitants tended their small vegetable gardens and milked their cows, happily unconcerned with the miners above the village. A school was under construction for the children, and before long classes would move from the centre complex.

No one living in the town had any relatives residing elsewhere. They had been chosen carefully, and received no news other than what the town's paper felt was appropriate to print. Dunradin's modification would follow Deermuir with the success of Netherfield being so apparent. Citizens had already been screened and selected for both villages.

-78-

"What do you think of the plan?" asked Branan.

Flint looked thoughtful. "You can't know for certain that he will or will not be at home. I would suggest that we arrange a liaison between Pepperidge and a woman of my acquaintance who is more than able to hold his attention for an afternoon. If we can have that assurance, then I feel it is a very good plan."

Pepperidge was in the habit of visiting a certain dwelling in Leith every Wednesday. While there, he was offered the services of a variety of women. Flint and Stoke came to the conclusion that Benjamin's whore would entice Athabasca to join her for a full afternoon of pleasure, allowing the would-be burglars to enter and leave the banker's premises with no interruptions. According to the informant, a large brass replica of Lord Nelson housed the treasure. They would dress as tradesmen and be in and out of his home quickly, providing the money was located in the statuette as they had been led to believe.

"Then we're in agreement," said Branan: "we will relieve the banker of his ill-gotten funds and recruit a few irregulars."

"Yes, and *irregular* is the appropriate term, as you will see," said Flint with a chuckle. "Very good men, of course," he added. "But a few of them will take a little getting used to. The common man comes in a variety of forms.

"I'll begin to make contact before our Wednesday date with destiny. Athabasca's punishment is long overdue, but maybe it's better this way. The longer he's hung on to his fortune, the larger it's become, so the loss will be grander."

Branan nodded in agreement. "He's been a thorn in your side for many years."

"The man repels me," said Flint. "He destroyed a friend of mine, forced her into prostitution and separated her from her children. She is no longer in her right mind and is confined to an asylum. He has much to answer for. I shall relish his financial demise."

Ben changed the subject abruptly. "These flesh-eaters, if I understand you properly, are very difficult to kill. What, in your opinion, is the most efficient manner of termination?"

"In my experience the best way to ensure you are not bothered by these creatures is to separate them from their heads. There is a little-known piece of history dating back to Spain in the 1200s: hunters gathered a group of twenty in one place, and a competent swordsman was hired to do the chopping. The heads were carried off and buried far from the bodies but not before one of them dashed forward and made off with one. He wasn't fussy and grabbed the nearest to him. As the story goes, it belonged to his father, and when he returned home to his wife, she would have nothing to do with him." Branan smiled. "And I assure you, there may even be a fraction of truth to the story."

Ben laughed softly. "What about live burial?"

"Effective in some cases," replied Stoke. "But they have incredible strength and can dig like badgers. I don't know that they can ever be completely eradicated, but if they can be decreased in number to where they are no longer useful to Wallace Pengrove and his henchmen, then something will have been accomplished. In all seriousness, I have found that silver mixed with lead shot is in fact the fastest way to kill a Wraith."

-79-

Tanner Smead limped across High Street barefooted and stopped in the middle of the square. He stood in one spot for several minutes, thinking. He had made his way into town in search of shoes and was not drawn to the footwear worn by the rotting Teriz piled up by the fountain. He turned in all directions, reassuring himself that there was no one else about, and then entered the first house on his right.

"Hello," he called as he stepped through the door. "Shoes," he said, finding a number of them in the dark hallway. There was nothing his size. He peered up the narrow staircase and decided to explore further.

He ascended one flight and entered the first bedroom. In the corner was a dressmaker's dummy wearing a smartly made red corset. Tanner's eyes lit up, and he approached the model with reverence, running his hands across the silky material. "Good for Tanner," he said, falling to his knees and fumbling with the hooks. "Mine," he said, tucking the garment under his arm.

The next house was well locked, and a horrid smell from somewhere inside drove him away. The third house was open and appeared to contain no shoes, until Smead entered the sitting room and found a pair of slippers that fit him well.

He peeked through a pair of double doors into the larger room and dropped the slippers. There in the corner was a pair of beautifully polished men's hunting boots. Putting down the corset, he crossed the room quickly and snatched up the boots. They were a perfect fit and came all the way to his knees. He sat in a chair and admired the footwear, crossing and uncrossing his legs.

Then with little trouble he wrapped the corset around his torso and clipped it tight. He rubbed his hands across the top of his chest enjoying the feel of the curves that were created. The rigid fabric dipped in the centre, forming two breasts. Tanner laughed out loud and continued on through to the kitchen. Here he found a colander with shiny brass handles. Perfect for a helmet but a little wobbly when he tried it on his head. A necktie from one of the bedrooms looped through the handles and passed under his chin worked well to steady the new headgear.

Feeling very pleased with himself, he stepped out into the square in search of a weapon. Being attracted to shiny objects as he was, he chose the brightest, cleanest-looking sword. He leaped about in his new boots, spinning and waving the weapon about while growling like an angry dog. After tiring of this, he entered the grocer's and made his way to the roof with a large cheese he'd found. The rind was tough, but the centre was soft and tasty.

Tanner sat across the back wall and dangled his feet. "His Majesty!" he yelled across the valley. In Smead's mind the town was now his, and he was the king of all he surveyed. All that the oddly attired lackwit required now were more fields to burn.

-80-

Wednesday arrived in Edinburgh with grey clouds and a light rain. Stoke and Flint dressed as gardeners with simple trousers, suspenders, and caps. They approached their destination in a wagon pulled by two horses. As they passed a cemetery, Branan commented, "Did you see the look that woman gave us? Perhaps we are a little too dishevelled."

Ben Flint laughed, "She'll probably be off to the nearest station, claiming to have seen the two Williams at work." Flint referred to Burke and Hare, the notorious grave robbers. They made their way up the long drive to Pepperidge's home and stepped down from the wagon. The front garden was home to an assortment of statuary.

A menacing gargoyle grinned at the pair as they passed. "He could use a gardener," said Branan, noticing the unkempt lawns. Flint easily sprung the small lock on the side door, and the two burglars stepped inside. They stood in the back room for a full minute listening for any signs of occupancy and then stepped quietly forward into an upper hall. Pepperidge appeared to be in need of a housekeeper as well. A good dusting was long overdue, and an airing out needed. There was a musty smell about the old place, and it was obvious that Pepperidge spent a great deal of his time elsewhere.

Benjamin spotted the brass statue at once by the window in the main sitting room. He turned the heavy replica over on its side, and Stoke worked at the base with a small knife, eager to locate the alleged fortune.

The wooden capping came off easily and with it a tiny object wrapped in fabric, which he handed to Flint. Branan reached into the hollow statuette. "Not a bloody thing!" he swore.

"Not quite," said Flint, unwrapping a small key. He held it in his palm and looked at Stoke. "Well, I don't suppose we were going to be so lucky as to find Old Nelson stuffed full of banknotes. Now we have to find a lock that fits this key. It could be anywhere in this clutter." The pair searched the room, being careful not to disturb anything. "Of course," said Flint, "it could be in any room. This could take days."

They were about to move to another room when Branan froze, his eyes locked on a painting on the far wall that depicted a sailing ship. He pointed to the canvas. "Is that not the HMS *Enterprise?*" he asked. The two men crossed the room and looked at the small plaque which read hms enterprise admiral nelson. Branan carefully took the painting down and discovered in the wall a small wooden door that opened easily. Inside the hidden cupboard was a tin box with an ornate lock. "Give it a try," he said to Flint.

Ben put the key into the lock and snapped it open. Inside the box were several stacks of British currency.

Stoke whistled softly at the number of packages. "There's a fortune here," he said. "According to this ledger, the balance is £227, 000," said Flint. Both men just stared at the money dumbfounded until Ben broke the silence. "For the sake of trust and expediency," he said, dividing the stacks roughly into two bundles, "we should carry one half each."

"Agreed," said Stoke, watching with curiosity as Flint pulled a note from his shirt and placed it in the tin. Then, seeing Stoke's expression, he took it out briefly and read aloud, "Bad luck that." Placing it back into the tin and closing the cupboard up, he went on to explain.

"Many years ago I confronted Pepperidge after he had my aforementioned acquaintance put away with the infirm and his reply at the time was - *bad luck that*- I would dearly love to see the bastard's face when he reads it. In any event, this is a good piece of work done today that has been long in coming. I thank you."

"My pleasure, Ben, now comes the planning."

Flint grinned. "I think we should retire to the pub at once and only then save humanity."

Branan had taken a room on the top floor of the Four Sheep, and the men went up first so he could find a temporary home for his newfound wealth. Before he could tuck it away, Flint stopped him. "Look, you better take all of it. I would be tempted, I'm afraid, to put it to other uses. Just knowing that Pepperidge has been deprived of the money and that it will go to a good cause satisfies me. Too much money changes a man, you know. I've seen it happen."

Branan patted his friend on the shoulder. "I know what you mean. Don't think I haven't considered the possibility of life on a small beach far from all this madness. It's certainly a temptation."

"Well, I think we can squander some of our ill-gotten funds on a pie and a pint," replied Flint, and they headed downstairs to discuss their plans further.

The Four Sheep was popular on High Street due to the quality of its meat pies, and Stoke was halfway through his when he noticed the dark stranger in the corner with the broad-brimmed hat pulled low. "Do you know that fellow in the back corner?" he asked.

Flint lifted his mug and looked into the mirror on the post to his left, examining the man's reflection. "I've not seen him here before," he answered, putting his ale back on the table.

"He's been watching us since we came downstairs." said Branan.

"Did you notice him when we first came in?" asked Flint.

Branan shook his head. "I can't be certain, but he has the looks of the Moorish people."

"He's black?" asked Flint.

"Yes, I think so, if you want to put it that way."

"Well, he either is or he isn't," said Benjamin.

"There are degrees," replied Stoke.

Flint leaned forward. "Is he armed?"

"I can't tell," answered Branan. "What are you proposing?"

Flint leaned down and loosened the buckle on his boot knife as a precaution. "I may just have a word with him."

Branan watched as Ben Flint crossed the room and slid into a chair beside the stranger.

The dark man lifted his head to reveal a face that was a patchwork of colours. The left half was black, while the rest of his face was pink. The stranger's left hand was black, and his right was brown. Aside from the odd pigmentation, he seemed human enough to Flint.

He offered the man his hand. "Benjamin Flint."

The big man shook his hand limply. "Toulouse Auberge," he offered.

Flint continued, "Well, Toulouse, my partner over there was wondering what interests you about us."

"I am a entrepreneur," he replied. "Word has it that you may have come into some money and might be looking to invest it."

Flint was dumbfounded, and it showed on his face. How could this man know of the small fortune they had only acquired this morning.

The man cleared his throat. "Let me begin by telling you that I am—or more precisely, I was employed by Mr. Athabasca Pepperidge as his gardener. I was intending to collect some of my tools this morning when I observed a pair of gentlemen arriving at the property. I asked myself if these were the new gardeners. They did not look to me like the types who would tolerate any dirt under their nails, so I stood in the trees watching. Now then I asked myself, *Toulouse, if anything goes missing from the banker's home, who will be blamed?*"

"I see your point," said Flint.

"And Mr. Benjamin Flint, I know who you are. I also know that you are familiar with Thomas Tull."

Tull was a shady character in the business of importing opium, and Flint knew the name. However, he had never met the man. "You would be referring to the opium trader," he said.

Toulouse nodded. "Big Tom has an associate who knows just how to cook the stuff to his customer's liking. Tull himself ain't bothered with the pipe; it gets in the way of business, and a very lucrative business it is. It means nothing to him if those twats in

Parliament decide to make a law to ban its import. That'll just drive the prices up and make us all richer.

"Shanghai Red cooks up his muck on the south side of the docks. I have no difficulty locating the cooker. There ain't but one red-haired Chinaman in the city, and he's sought after by many. A cook with Red's skills can turn a bit of coin these days. There's some cleverness involved in transforming the raw goods into gold, and Shanghai possesses the required skill. It's fascinating to watch Red toast the opium. An amazing process.

"Toasting the opium properly is no less important than choosing the proper clients. The best customers are your well-off professionals, your lawyers, and your lords. They have the most money and the most stamina. It often starts out as a doctor's prescription for laudanum. A little something to ease the pain of a riding accident perhaps, or even a flesh wound acquired while duelling. Servants are sent to the apothecary for the milder concoctions, but before long a liking grows for the powerful sedative effects found in the more potent derivatives.

"I ain't like the usual customers, who are happy to have a bowl cooked up and handed to them, perhaps as many as four times in an afternoon, paying for the privilege of a straw mat and a tobacco cigarette to follow their pipe. I'm just small-time, you understand—a bit here and there for the rheumatism."

Flint nodded patiently.

"But to make a long story shorter, I'll get to the point. Tommy Tull can be had for a price, and he's out of business if the cooker goes down too. It's an easy scheme: I delivers the man; you delivers the money."

"Mr. Tull has not broken any laws that I'm aware of," said Flint.

"Exactly, none that you're aware of, but I might make you aware of some aberrations in his behaviour that propel him beyond the borders of legality, such as the procurement of young men for activities of a carnal nature. I believe that sodomy is offensive to the courts."

"That depends on the circumstances," said Flint, taking out his pipe. "If it were that clear-cut, half the pages in England's Parliament would have a case, and we all know buggery is rampant in the navy."

Ben went on, "I understand your offer, sir, but I have much larger fish to fry at the moment. Mr. Tull, and the business that might find its way to you if he were to be incarcerated, will have to wait." He paused. "However, if you are inclined to earn a piece of this alleged fortune, we may have work for you. Have you ever killed a man Auberge?"

"Wever I killed a man or were responsible for his death are two different matters," replied Auberge. "Let's just put it that I 'ave the capability."

"I'll be frank with you," said Ben. "I am in the process of hiring assassins. Are you interested in the work?"

"I will not kill a man who is deserving of life," answered Toulouse, "regardless of the wage, and some men I would kill for free."

Flint nodded, pleased with the answer. "Subterfuge, efficiency, and discretion are the trademarks of anyone wishing to be in my employ."

"The very qualities I admire," said Auberge. "Would Master Pepperidge be on your recipients list?" he asked, somewhat hopefully.

"No, certainly not," answered Flint. "We would prefer that Athabasca have many years to experience his new standard of living. To put your mind at rest, I might add that he will be aware of whence his downfall originated. I left my card, in a manner of speaking, and a former gardener will not be suspected."

Auberge smiled. "You have my thanks and my loyalty."

Flint shook his hand. "I count on it."

-81-

"Do you think there are any tunnels in this castle?" asked Tamlyn. Padraic shrugged.

"There's a dungeon," said Alfie, "Bottom of the east tower, I seen it through a little window."

"I don't think there's any fish in this moat," said Tam.

Alfie looked thoughtful. "Maybe we're in the wrong spot. We might try t'other side."

"What's Turfmoor like?" asked Tam "Did you fish there?"

"Sure I did, real good fishing, but now it's filled with the creepers. They're all over, and their holes are everywhere too." Alfie suddenly looked downcast. "It'll never be the same," he added sadly.

Padraic scribbled a note in his journal and held it up. *Teriz are Horseshit!* it said. The young boys broke into fits of laughter.

"Hey, down there! The boys looked up at Cardiff Macneil who was leaning over the top of one of the southern towers. "Catch any fish, lads?" All three boys shook their heads at the same time.

Caleb, who had joined his brother at the wall, called down to the would-be fishermen. "What's that?" he asked, pointing into the water.

-82-

Euther, who could tolerate daylight to a degree, decided that he would accept Pengrove's invitation to join him while he inspected the compound at Netherfield. He had heard of Ivan Douglas and wanted to meet the man. They travelled overland by horse, with Faustine hiding under a hood and wide-brimmed hat. Both men wore pistols and tall boots.

"It must be nice," commented Euther, "being at the top of the chain of command, with no one to answer to?" He was sounding out Pengrove. He had no idea if His Lordship reported to a superior or not.

"Yes, well, there's no one to complain to either," answered Pengrove. "Ten men, including yourself, answer to me. I consider Griffin Hume a second in command, and five of the ten answer to him. It's not very complicated. You all know very little about each other, but that will change before long."

Faustine still felt it was unlikely that Pengrove had masterminded the entire plan. He began to wonder, not for the first time, where he himself fit in. He had emptied Dunradin and organized the processing center at the quarry, but his failure to capture the citizens had not gone unnoticed. It suddenly occurred to him as they rode along that he might have seen the very last of Dunradin and the old mill.

Putting all sentiment aside, he judged the situation from Wallace's point of view and quickly concluded that perhaps his days were numbered. Now that he pondered his fate, it all made sense. He was of no use whatsoever. He probably wasn't even good eating. A stiff breeze penetrated his cloak and chilled him to the bone.

He began to consider his options. The wisest choice would be to kill Pengrove at once, leave his body out here on the moors, and carry on to Netherfield to inform Douglas of the change in command. This didn't appeal to him as he would have to deal with the Humes next. Too much bloodshed, so much energy expended. Perhaps it would be easier if he was a younger man.

Another option was to flee and be done with the lot of them. *Where do retired Wraiths go?* he wondered. Maybe he could open a rest home for toothless flesh-eaters. He suddenly felt very weary. The terrain began to get rockier, and the two travellers pressed on in silence. Eventually they came out of the scrub and began to cross the high moors. The sky in front of them was bright with billowing clouds, and the air was warmer.

Faustine's horse followed close behind that of Pengrove. He reached behind and felt for the pistol at his back. It would be simple enough, he thought, to load and prime his weapon without being noticed. He could easily blow the back of His Lordship's head off. But why bother? Another maniac would rise up and take his place.

"Wallace, a break!" Euther called. His bladder needed emptying. He slid down from his horse and groaned. "I'm getting too old for this."

"Just over that rise," said Pengrove, pointing ahead. "You could probably piss that far." As they continued the last leg of their journey, Euther reflected on the nature of treachery. It really was a part of life, he decided. As well as making it his practice, he'd certainly seen his share of it. The trick was finding a balance between power and subjugation. He decided to put off any thoughts of his future until after the trip to Netherfield.

Within five minutes the town came into view. The buildings were similar in appearance and all painted the same shade of white. Netherfield had a pristine, well-ordered look about it. Faustine was surprised that the streets were empty. A hill rose east of the settlement, over which loomed a dark cloud of smoke.

The only sound was that of a lone dog barking in the distance. "Where is everyone?" asked Euther, hitching his horse to a post beside Pengrove's.

Wallace answered "Probably at a meeting this time of day. In the centre, there are many meetings." It turned out that the entire village was at a prayer meeting, a common event at which Douglas presided twice a week.

As Euther and Pengrove approached, the doors of the centre swung open, and a crowd began to file out, smiling and laughing. The sounds of organ music brightened the air, and several children ran about the legs of a tall, white-haired man who was dressed in a flowing robe. He smiled at Pengrove with bright flashing teeth. "Your Lordship!" he said happily, gripping Wallace's hand with both of his. "What a pleasant surprise. And who have you brought with you?"

"Ivan Douglas, this is Euther de Faustine."

Douglas shook Euther's hand energetically. There was nothing about Ivan that suggested the nickname "Weasel." This didn't appear in any way to be a man responsible for countless deaths. Euther supposed that his ability to maintain this saintly facade contributed greatly to his success.

"How's business on your side?" asked Douglas.

"I hope to pick up a few pointers from you while I'm here," answered Faustine politely.

"Certainly, my pleasure, please come in and have some tea first; you must both be weary." He ushered them into the chapel and directed them through a door to the left. They entered a modest room with table and chairs that was filled with sunlight streaming in through tall windows. "Make yourselves comfortable, I'll just put the kettle on."

Douglas stepped through a curtained door at the back of the room and returned quickly in trousers and jacket. "I'm not an ordained minister, of course," he explained, "but I find the townsfolk require some guidance from time to time, and God's word has been spoken by smaller men than me, sugar and milk with your tea, gentlemen?"

As Douglas went on to explain the importance of Christianity in Netherfield, Euther was drawn to the man at once. Douglas practised a subtle form of hypnosis with his voice and charismatic manner. He spoke quietly and clearly with no pauses and punctuated his phrases with graceful movements of his hands. Euther found himself looking away occasionally to keep from succumbing completely to the man's charm.

Pengrove's voice broke the spell like footsteps on dead leaves. "We had hoped to have a look at the mine."

"By all means," replied Douglas. "I would be most pleased to show you about. I must caution you, though," he added. "The workers can be somewhat crude. We deal with them as best we can, but on occasion it's necessary to apply a firm hand. If you're at all squeamish, it might be better to remain behind."

"We are all men of the world," insisted Euther. "I'm sure we share a common appreciation for discipline."

"Fine," said Douglas, obviously pleased. "My dear old father, rest his soul, flayed the skin off my back on more than one occasion, and I'm a better man for it today."

After they'd drained their cups, Douglas led them from the room, and the three men walked out to the mine. Faustine surveyed the terrain as they trudged up the slope. To his right a richly tilled field was tended by young women dressed in practical white robes and conservative headgear. They raked the dark soil in silent unison, like a line of puppets. One looked much like the other, and Euther marvelled at their similarities.

Ivan Douglas smiled, noticing Faustine's puzzled expression. "They are bred to be workers," he explained, answering the unvoiced question. "Your eyes are not tricking you. These girls are gardeners for life and very happy indeed with their situation."

"Absolutely astounding," said Pengrove.

Douglas continued, "Their children will follow in the line and replace them as they age and are no longer useful. If you're interested, we can tour the clinic later."

"You've achieved a great deal in a very short time, Ivan. I knew you would impress Euther, and I'm hoping he will be encouraged to follow your lead."

Faustine began to understand the real reason behind Pengrove's visit to Netherfield. The old villain was approaching a strange twist in the ribbon of fate that tied the three men together. He saw all at once that he'd been played like a fiddle but also took note that there was a part for him, if he was willing to stick to the script. Euther's problem was that he had always been the author of his own destiny, and he wondered if it was possible at this point to follow another's lead. Douglas clearly had his own agenda, and it remained to be seen whether an alliance was in the old Wraith's best interests.

Faustine admitted to himself that his priorities at this point were in an unusual state of flux. He had not looked far beyond the domination of the small village of Dunradin for some time and realized now how far the ideals of his youth had slipped into the past. It was very perceptive of Pengrove to have seen that Euther's commitment was flagging, and he was suddenly flattered to be thought worthy of inclusion.

As they entered the drift mine's wide adit, Douglas directed them to a wooden walkway on the left of the first chamber. Euther felt considerably more comfortable being out of the light and removed his dark eyeglasses. The air was cool and damp here, and Pengrove drew his cloak across his chest.

"The entrance is just here," said Douglas pointing ahead. "The workers are housed in the mine itself, due to the fact that they are more comfortable underground." Ducking through the short opening, Euther saw that the second chamber was much larger than the first and lit with a very modern system of gas lamps. The housing development was to the right-hand side of the large cavern and was defined by a massive set of heavy doors that fronted an extremely long staircase that descended into the murky darkness beyond.

To the left, an expansive opening to the work areas was framed in sturdy, hand-carved oak. The carving resembled two thick trees whose twisted branches met in the centre. The effect was that of the entrance to a forest, and above the handsome archway was a simple sign that read freedom. "After you, gentleman," said Douglas, ushering the visitors into the noisy interior of the mine.

Neither man was prepared for the blast of heat or the massive panorama of industry that lay below them. The unassuming exterior of Netherfield's mine offered no hint of the vast enterprise beneath the ground. Rails and carts, workers and ovens, pick shovels and digging machines stretched into the distance beyond the limit of both men's vision.

As they looked out over an area that could have been no less than a half kilometre in length and half that wide, Pengrove said, "There must be fifteen hundred or more workers in view here."

From where Euther stood even the smallest workers appeared larger than any of Dunradin's Teriz. He was struck dumb at the numbers of workers. He stood there speechless, clearly aware now what a small player he had been in the game.

Douglas smiled at Euther's response. "I won't bore you with details," he said, pointing directly below, "but these are the coking ovens from which we are able to draw gases from the coal, which in turn provides our lighting, both here in the mine as well as the village. The coal is heated at a very high temperature until virtually all volatile constituents have been driven off, leaving a residue that is chiefly coke or carbon. We will very soon have the capabilities to heat and light several villages with the resources from this one mine."

One of the larger Teriz, presumably a foreman, glanced up from the pit and squinted at Pengrove. Like the rest he was clad only in a loin cover, and his body shone with perspiration. He reached up with his whip hand and wiped the sweat from his brow, nodding quickly at Douglas before turning back to his charges

"How many hours do they toil?" asked Euther "The pace appears rather brisk."

Douglas answered, "It varies. They work in shifts, and the ovens are seldom allowed to cool. The departure point for the product is at the other end, beyond where your line of vision extends," he added, pointing towards the back of the cavern, having anticipated Euther's next question. He placed a large hand on Pengrove's shoulder and shifted him gently towards the door, indicating that there was nothing more to be seen. Wallace and Euther were at this point both happy to leave the sweltering confines of the mine.

Once in the fresh air again Douglas made a welcome suggestion. "I'm sure you gentleman would care for a bit of a rest after your journey, when we get back, I will have my servant make arrangements. Then perhaps you would care to join the populace for our evening service." It was less an invitation than a summons, and Euther was beginning to get a sense of Ivan's ways.

Faustine's room was small but comfortable. He removed his boots and stretched out on the bed, folding his arms behind his head. Weary but preoccupied with recent revelations, he stared grimly at the ceiling, deep in thought.

How many Teriz remained in Dunradin under his power? His chief commanders had either abandoned him or met their deaths. Here in Netherfield dwelt a leader of thousands who in all likelihood considered Euther a miserable failure.

The more he thought about it, the more it became apparent that Dunradin was intended to be the feed basket for Douglas's larger operation. While Euther had assumed that his Teriz would feed upon the citizens of Dunradin, it began to appear that his own Teriz were merely a link in the food chain that would supply Douglas's miners. It had all been thought out carefully. Dunradin would be a large meat processing plant, an abattoir or slaughterhouse to fulfill the demands of Ivan Douglas's elite, and the gradual realization that he had become redundant began to congeal into a palpable fear.

He now saw that he had no choice but to play along for the time being until some other options arose. The revolution that he had originally sparked was well under way and had gained a momentum that threatened to trample him under. Pengrove had played him like the old fool he was, and now it appeared that Ivan Douglas was the one fucking the cow, while Wallace held its tail out of the way.

How much time, he wondered, did he have left, or was he even regarded as a threat? Was now the time to start over? A sudden weariness came over him at the thought, and he closed his eyes.

He would hang on here and learn what he could before making a decision. Something told him that Douglas was arrogant enough to want to rub his nose in the shit a little before disposing of him, and that he had enough time to weigh his options.

-83-

Caleb pointed again. "No, not there, more to the left."

Tamlyn dragged the shepherd's crook in the other direction and connected with something solid. "I see it, it's a box," he said. "I can get the handle." He leaned forward and pulled in the rusted container, dragging it on to the grass.

"We're coming down!" yelled Cardiff. By the time the Macneil brothers arrived, Tamlyn had his knife angled into the edge of the box and was hitting the hilt with a rock.

"What do you think is inside?" asked Alfie.

"Gold coins!" said Caleb, laughing. The boys circled Tamlyn and leaned in as he snapped the catch on the box and the lid sprang open.

"Just a bloody book," exclaimed Alfie.

"And this," said Tam, lifting a pendant from the box.

Padraic took the book out and began to leaf through the pages. The first page was titled "Incantations."

"It's a book of spells!" said Tamlyn.

"Maybe we shouldn't touch it," said Alfie quickly.

"Nae, it's just a book. Let's have a look," said Caleb, holding out his hand.

Padraic passed the book to him and motioned to Tam for the pendant. It was an oblong crystal that came to a point. The mute held it up, watched it spin in the light, and then placed it back in the box.

353

Caleb passed the book along to Tamlyn. "A big trout wouldae been more interesting." he snorted.

Liam and Charlotte, who had passed through the gates, noticed the boys on the banks of the moat and headed in their direction. "Oh my goodness, where did you get that?" exclaimed Charlotte.

"Twas in the moat," said Caleb "Coulda been there years."

The young woman leafed through the pages carefully, and towards the middle of the book was an entry in a different hand. It began with a notation of the year: August 1430. "Good Lord, this is hundreds of years old. It's a wonder that the water hadn't gotten into the tin and ruined the book."

"Well, Tam fished it out, so I s'pose it's his. Not that it's worth nuthin'," said Caleb.

"It doesn't interest me," said Tamlyn with a shrug. "You can have it if you like," he said, passing the pendant as well to his sister.

"So that's all you've caught?" said Liam. "No trout for supper tonight?"

"Let's try the other side," suggested Alfie.

Charlotte remained behind with Liam. They sat in the warm sunshine enjoying the play of light on the water. "Do you realize?" said the young woman. "This is a book that was carried about by a witch. Look here, there's a name in the back. It says Katherine Hollis. I wonder who she was and what happened to her."

Liam leaned over her shoulder and kissed her cheek. "She must have wanted someone to find this book," he said. "Read some of it aloud."

She returned his kiss. "There are several pages of spells, but then here she's written a sort of diary."

Munday:
I fear they will come for me soon. Anna's child was born with deformations of the face and the council will be certain to place the blame with me. As Midwife I did all I could to deliver the child peacefully, but the little lad was born to pain and they have buried the poor creature alive. I

write this that my descendants will know my fate at the hands of the citizen's council.

Tewsday:
The Lord Mayor entered my cottage today and offered me his protection in exchange for services of the most depraved nature imaginable. I turned him out at once and have been given the remainder of the week to reconsider my refusal.

Wednesday:
I fear greatly for the safety of my young son Axel and have sent him to his Aunt's on the moors. It was almost more than I could bear to say good-bye. I would attempt to flee myself but am watched both day and night.

Thorsday :
I have laid every curse upon the head of Lord Mayor Harper that I can imagine. He has threatened to lock up my father John Hollis widower of Evelyn Hollis in Threstone Dungeon.

Fryday :
Too weak this day to do other than sleep.

Saturnday :
I fear they shall come for me soon. My father John Hollis has been taken against his will to the castle. Had my mother Evelyn not been buried these three years I believe they would have taken her as well. They have charged Father with passing demon seed to Mother who they claim bore a witch child.

These mourn for the hanging tree
Seven sky clad in circle to sea
They were where the cloven hoof
Had left its mark of fire on thee

"Oh my Lord, the poor woman!" exclaimed Charlotte. "What a monster of a man this lord mayor must have been."

Liam held the pendant up and turned it in the sun while Charlotte continued to read. He squinted into the light trying to peer through the quartz. "It's amazing how nature can create something so beautiful from rock," he said. "Will you put it on a chain and wear it?"

"What?" asked Charlotte absently, still absorbed in the diary.

"The crystal," responded Liam. "Will you wear it?"

"Oh, I'm not sure that would be wise" she replied, looking up from the book. "It certainly didn't bring Miss Hollis any luck, by the sound of things."

Liam stretched out on the grass. "Well she must have valued it, or she wouldn't have left it with her diary."

Charlotte shook her head. "I think she sank it in the moat to be rid of it, and I wouldn't be surprised if it was cursed."

"Indeed," said Twist. "Look how disagreeable it's made you already."

Charlotte laughed loudly and took a playful swing at Liam, who pulled her across his chest and pressed his lips to hers. He reached for her hips and allowed his hands to pull her close, enjoying the feel of the fabric that covered her flawless skin.

Charlotte let the book drop and pushed her lower body against Liam's growing manhood. The young woman's skirt moved in his hands as though it covered fine porcelain. The young man gasped. "You wear no underclothing. Are you not cold?"

"Yes indeed, very cold," she answered in a silky voice. "I count on you to warm me, sir." She reached for the book and tucked it under her arm. She swung the pendant playfully in front of Liam, in pretence of hypnosis. "You will follow me to the trees, sir."

Liam responded in a monotone voice, as though he were under a deep spell, "Bloody right I will."

Alfred and the Macneil brothers tired of fishing and decided to investigate Alfie's assertion that there was a dungeon in the east tower. The boys entered the base of the tower in single file through a low narrow door, stepping carefully down the six stones that brought them to a flat dirt floor. A draught of cold air chilled them as their eyes adjusted to the darkness.

A stairwell led to the level above, and Alfie stepped behind it into the dark and disappeared. "In here," he called. The alcove behind the stairs was well hidden in the dim light, and Tamlyn imagined that it had served to conceal on more than one occasion.

There was a small window no larger than a man's hand on the heavy wooden door. Alfie slid the panel open, and a pale light shone from within. They could see that the source of light was a small window just above the water level on the outside of the castle.

"There's a keyhole here," said Tamlyn, "so somewhere there must be a key."

"Could be anywhere." suggested Caleb. "It could even be inside."

Tam was surprised that no one in the castle had thought to look behind the stairwell before.

"I wonder what we can use to jig that lock," said Alfie.

Tamlyn tried the handle, and the door swung open easily. The other boys laughed loudly. "It wasnae locked," said Alfred in disbelief. "I feel a right clown now."

"And you look like one as well," added Cardiff, smiling as he pushed past the smaller boy and entered the room. The chamber did in fact have chains and shackles attached to the wall, which one would expect to find in any respectable dungeon.

Tamlyn found himself feeling very reluctant to enter the cold damp room, for reasons he could not explain. When he did enter the dungeon, he was gripped with an overpowering dread that had him backed against the wall in a cold sweat. His eyes were drawn to a low closet with no door at the back of the room. The floor of the small closet had a square compartment from which pure evil seemed to emanate like invisible smoke. "Don't open it!" yelled Tamlyn in panic as he bolted from the room.

His stunned companions turned in shock, not having seen the small trapdoor and alarmed by the young lad's sudden reaction. Their concern for Tamlyn's well-being quickly displaced any curiosity at the closet's contents, and Tam was soon surrounded by his puzzled friends. "There's death there," said the young boy, wiping tears away. "It's horrible, horrible."

"It's okay," said Alfred. "There's nowt there," he added, turning to re-enter the dungeon.

"Nooo!" screamed Tamlyn, leaping forward to grab his friend by the lapels of his vest. Buttons flew as Alfie was pulled forward. And the two boys cracked heads painfully. Tamlyn brought his hand to his forehead and apologized.

Alfie felt his head for blood. "Okay, don't go crazy, fer god sake."

The incident brought an end to the day's adventures. The Macneils wandered back to where they had left the fishing gear, while Tamlyn and Padraic wandered off to see if they could locate Murdoch. Alfred, who would have joined them, held back, still smarting from his confrontation with Macleary. As the boys made their way towards the courtyard, Padraic glanced back inquiringly, and Alfie waved him on sullenly and turned his back on the two youngsters.

Despite Padraic's concern for his old friend, the mute understood that Tamlyn was somewhat embarrassed by his outburst and would prefer to be alone for a short time. He conveyed his thoughts by raising his whistle in the air as if to say, *If you need anything, just signal me.* Tamlyn nodded and headed for the moat.

Because the castle didn't offer a great deal of privacy, many of its occupants took advantage of the outlying fields and trees for more clandestine matters such as introspection or romance. Tamlyn had found a large fallen tree in the deep grasses close to the woods that no one else appeared to have discovered.

The youngster sat here now and thought about his uncle Caymus. He missed him very much, and was not sure how deal with the feelings of grief that arose as his previous sense of fear vanished. He sat on the tree with his legs crossed and closed his eyes.

Placing his hands at his sides Tamlyn tried to imagine himself taking the form of a bird. Nothing happened at first, and he felt a little anxious. Then all at once the clouds seemed to spin in the sky, and the sunshine filled his head like fibres of spun gold, and there it was.

This time the mist appeared to take the shape of a young woman. The figure placed her palms together and bowed. Tamlyn instinctively copied her actions. "You are troubled," she said.

"Yes," he replied, somewhat astonished to find that the spirit had indeed not been a part of his imagination brought on by his ordeal in the woods. He went on to describe the passing of his uncle, and how it had affected him.

"When you think of your uncle," said the apparition, "don't ponder his manner of death or his suffering. Be aware that he is at rest now, and remember what you admired most about him. Take the best of his actions, and make them yours. In this manner, he shall live on within you."

Tam nodded. He liked this idea, and it gave him comfort to think of Caymus continuing on as a part of himself.

"Also," continued the voice, "as you live in this way, be certain that you pass those aspects of your uncle on to someone younger than yourself, such as a child you may bring into the world. Can you see how this will give your uncle's life some worth?"

"Yes," he replied happily. "Yes, I understand."

"It all depends on how you perceive matters, whether you will be happy or not in this life. You must look at anyone's passing as a learning experience. You must also accept pain and suffering as part of life. They are inevitable. How you react to them is what will define you."

Tamlyn nodded as she spoke to him in her soft, otherworldly voice. "Look to the unseen, the space between you and the trees. There is strength in the trees, but also there is energy in the spaces between. Above all, remember this: the tall oak will crack and fall in a heavy storm, but the supple reeds and grasses will bend with the wind and survive it. Be like the grasses." As her image began to shimmer and fade, the vision waved farewell. "I am with you always."

Tamlyn had been transported so far from his earlier feelings that he had forgotten to ask his spirit about the frightful nature of the dungeon or the manner in which he might effect a transformation to the form of a hunting bird. The warm breezes that danced across his face began to lull him into a comfortable, dreamlike mood. He noticed a few flakes of snow that suggested a change to come in the agreeable weather.

Alfie was completely confused by Tamlyn's strange behaviour. The youngster from Turfmoor had felt nothing close to fear when they'd approached the small door. On the contrary, he'd experienced a strong desire to enter the opening in the floor of the closet, which was quite ludicrous, as the opening was only wide enough to accommodate a man's fist.

Even now, standing outside the room, he felt as if drawn by a cord and found himself walking slowly towards the dungeon. He stepped into the tower room a second time and felt a warm welcoming sensation at once.

The air inside was heavy. Countless tiny dust particles were visible in a shaft of sunlight that shone from the narrow window, pointing like a finger of amber towards the open closet. Alfie approached the alcove wondering how Tamlyn could have been that violently repelled by something so beautiful. The lid of the compartment, if that was what it was, could only have been made of the most expensive marble, and surely the lift ring at its centre was gold. Alfie couldn't understand how the others had failed to notice what a precious treasure had lain at their feet.

He got to his knees and gazed at the stone until an overwhelming desire to lift it took hold of him. A faint buzzing seemed to be coming from below, and he rested his head against the chamber listening carefully. A tiny worm wriggled from the seam and made its way into Alfie's hair. In time it would move unnoticed along the edge of his ear and continue, burrowing silently through the waxy outer portion of his eardrum.

As his hands met the top of the compartment, a surge of energy passed from the rock through his fingers and up the length of his arms. The sensual vibrations caressed his shoulders and wound about his thin neck, travelling across and around the top of his skull. The essence of pure radiant power raced down his spine, climaxed in his groin, and then exploded through his feet. Alfie's hands rose from the stone as though opposing magnetic fields had met, and the hairs on the back of his neck stood up. His entire body felt as though it was wrapped in a soft garment of the most pleasurable fabric imaginable.

The sensation lasted for some time after he'd made his way from the room, and Alfred decided almost at once that this was his and his alone. It was not to be shared or spoken of. There was a forbidden aspect to his discovery that suggested to him that there would be shame and judgement should he reveal this experience to the others.

As the day progressed, the sensations abated, and Alfie re-joined his companions but said nothing of the incident.

-84-

"I won't need you any longer today, Jewel, thank you." Flint handed the young woman a robe. His eyes took in her full brown nipples as she reached for the garment. *Perhaps next time*, he thought, Stoke was on his way upstairs.

Ben placed his brushes in the solvent and shifted his easel away from the window as the model continued to dress. He approached her from behind, placing his hands gently on her hips and kissed the side of her neck softly. "Thank you. I'll be out of town for some time. I'll send for you when I return."

She gathered her hair in a ribbon and pouted seductively. "You better had," she declared, "if you know what's good for you."

"Yes," he replied, opening the door for her, "and I do know what's good for me."

Turning, she bumped into Branan, who smiled and stepped carefully aside, visibly resisting the urge to follow her perfume trail down the hall. "That's a very fine hobby you have, Mr. Flint. Are you sure you want to go adventuring?"

"I think," suggested Flint, ignoring the remark, "that perhaps you and I with Auberge shall be the unholy trio. I suggest we keep our number at three."

Branan stared at the toe of his boot thoughtfully. "I agree, given that he who knows nothing can reveal nothing. Ben, I want to thank you for your help. I am surely in your debt."

Flint laughed. "Surely you are an old friend. Don't think I haven't calculated a third of the funds into my offer of help, a most lucrative use of my time. I will enjoy investing Pepperidge's kind contribution to our cause."

"The most expensive piece of tail old Athabasca has ever purchased, I'll warrant," chuckled Stoke. "I think Auberge will see things our way."

"Certainly," agreed Flint. "As fond as he is of his criminal connections, he is fonder still of a full purse, and I always maintain, money aside, that the more parts you incorporate into a piece of machinery, the higher the odds of a breakdown.

"Do we travel by carriage or saddle?" asked Flint, anxious now to make a plan.

Branan laughed again at his partner. "Saddle, of course, assuming you tender-arsed city dwellers can handle it."

Flint grinned widely and pointed below, towards the pub. "Toulouse should be downstairs. I think he can afford to buy us both a pint now."

Auberge had arrived at the Inn and was seated in his customary corner behind a frothy pint of ale. He was feeling somewhat pleased with himself and his good fortune. Several names went through his head as he considered whom he might suggest for Ben Flint's employ, as well as who might be recruited at a reasonable price.

The Gimp was probably the most talented, but far too greedy, and William Snitch was very useful, but not very hardy due to his diminutive size. He puzzled over his choices, still unaware that Flint had not turned to his own men for recruits. By the time Ben and Branan came down the stairs, Auberge was no further ahead with his decisions.

He was glad to learn that the alliance would stay small. They decided that Toulouse would be well paid but would receive the bulk of his wages when the job was done. The dark man was agreeable, and plans were made to gather supplies for the journey back to Threstone. They decided to hold council with the others and suggest a six-man command consisting of Ronan, Maclean, Godwyn, Flint,

Stoke, and Auberge, each with two dozen men. (None of these six were yet aware of the hordes of Teriz at Netherfield.)

Branan clapped the table. "Fresh horses, silver shot, and some packets of jerky, then we make for Castle Threstone." Auberge and Flint nodded in agreement.

"You have enough of the white powders to buy your way into Dorian's confidence?" asked Flint.

"The very finest available, as well as a satchel filled with pure opiates just off the boat, and a pretty penny it cost me."

Branan turned towards Auberge. "Well done, Toulouse. Just remember to keep your nose out of the feedbag."

"I assure you," he replied, "you may count on me in all matters. I anticipate a fine return on my investment." The conspirators decided on an early dawn start, in hopes of covering half the distance on the first day.

-85-

The next morning proved to be cold and cloudy. The three men travelled at a brisk pace for close to two hours and then walked their animals for a further hour before coming to a halt next to a crooked side road. A bent figure approached them casually. "You'll be after water, I suppose?"

"Yes please, if it's not a hardship." replied Stoke.

"You young fellers are welcome tae join me and the missus fer a midday meal." The farmer was without a doubt the oldest gentleman that Stoke or either of his companions had ever come across. A broad-brimmed hat sat astride his unusually small head and covered a full growth of white hair that fell to his shoulders, which appeared to begin just below his ears.

Every wrinkle on his parched face had been earned toiling on the soil of the small farm where the trio had stopped for water. The pupil of his right eye was white and ruined where an errant branch had blinded him years ago. The farmer's hands looked impossibly large for such a tiny man, as he gripped a wooden fork with apparent strength, half leaning on the implement as he motioned with the other hand to the road beyond. "'Taint much down that way for quite a spell. Best your horses drink deep, and fill your skins if you have'm then.

Branan offered the old man a coin, which he refused. "The good Lord don't charge me nuthin' fer water, so's I give it free. Are you sure you don't want to stay fer some beans?"

"Many thanks to you, sir," said Flint," but we are in great haste."

"No harm, travel well, but your friend might want to clean those expensive-looking boots," he said, pointing to Auberge's feet. "He's been stood in a fair-sized round of cow shit fer the last while."

The dark man looked down at his feet and swore quietly.

Back on the main road, Ben Flint paused. "How is it," he asked, "that these Teriz have not been seen even at the outskirts of, say, Glasgow or Edinburgh?"

Branan rubbed the muscles at the back of his neck and frowned. "If we don't eradicate them now, it won't be long before they are at your doorstep, or in your basements."

"How many are we talking about?" asked Toulouse.

Stoke looked troubled as they remounted their horses. "In my mind the number changes daily. I had thought we were making progress until we spoke with this Norseman Blunt. I see no reason why he would have exaggerated his claims." He reined his horse back towards the road. "I trust the man as much as I trust anyone, which is to say; with reservations I can't see a motive for treachery, at this point."

Flint nodded, apparently satisfied with Branan's answer. He looked to the sky and narrowed his eyes. "We had better ride hard if we want to cover any ground before it rains."

Stoke smiled. "Well, all right, let's see if you and shit heels can go a little faster this time," he joked, spurring his horse on. The powerful animal thundered forward, quickly gaining speed. Flint leaned into his horse's neck, gritting his teeth as the scenery sped past. Turning once to glance behind him, he noted that Auberge was gaining on him and would soon draw even. The three riders raised a cloud of dust as they made their way south in haste, and the skies began to darken with approaching rain.

After an hour's travel, Branan began to wish that they had taken the offer of a meal from the strange old man. Flint's horse whinnied as a sudden flash of lightning illuminated the road before them, and Stoke raised his arm to signal a halt. It had become too dark to continue.

The stone foundations and two walls were all that remained of the small church that marked the midpoint of their journey. Branan was familiar with the old building and pointed to the half cellar that would shelter them from the rain. Stoke soon had a proper blaze lit in a circle of stones that he'd used for cooking many times in the past. There was a store of firewood to the rear of the cellar and a warm, dry area for sleeping. Before long, the highlander had a rich soup of lamb and potatoes simmering in a pot on the cooking rocks.

"Well, it ain't the King and Dragon, but I'll be damned if that don't smell heavenly," said Auberge, rubbing his hands. After they'd eaten their fill, Flint settled back and fished through his jacket for smoking material. He was fond of the tobacco cigarettes which had come north from Walworth in London, unlike Auberge, who preferred a pipe.

"This is a tidy little hideaway," he remarked "There are so many strange types in the city, that I'd imagined there were none left in the country. Our wee friend up the road was odd but helpful. Are there stranger folks yet in the countryside?"

"None stranger than yourself," joked Branan. "I've met a great many of the farmers along this road, and they're all good people for the most part. The woods are where you'll find a queer lot. Those with more to hide tend to dwell amongst the tree; the thicker the forest, the stranger its inhabitants. Not that they all belong to the criminal element, but some are shunned by society, and others are sickly and deformed and wish to keep to themselves."

He paused to relight his pipe. "If you spent very much time in the woods you'd find that there is still an ancient kind of magic there that hasn't completely vanished from the earth. Some of it is good, and some is unbelievably dark. No offence to Mr. Auberge," he said with a laugh.

Toulouse grinned. "There are some as runs from this face and others what desires it beneath their skirts," he replied with a leer.

Flint laughed loudly. "Indeed, I imagine the gardener's tools are well suited for the tilling of Edinburgh's virgin soil."

"My deformity brooks no hiding," said Toulouse quietly.

Eventually the trio tired of conversation. Auberge yawned. "This rain suits me well for sleeping gentlemen. Good night."

Branan arranged his bedroll carefully in an area where the storm would not enter. "We'll start at first light; sleep well."

-86-

Sitting at the fire, Tamlyn glanced over to where Alfred was seated and pondered the blank look that had settled on his young friend's face. Padraic was showing Caleb how to tie a double hitch with a length of leather cord, and Cardiff was laughing with Murdoch, who had come down to the main fire to spend some time with the younger boys.

Alfie got to his feet without a word and vanished into the shadows. Tamlyn found his behaviour very curious but thought no more of it, deciding that Alfie was still upset with him for the earlier altercation. Given what the three younger lads had dealt with recently, it was surprising that their emotions were not more ragged.

"I'm tired of this cold castle," said Tamlyn, moving closer to the flames.

Murdoch spoke up. "Duncan told me that there is no one in the village, save for a few dead Teriz. He said they had been killed by one another, or something that finished them permanently."

Tamlyn shook his head. "Home at the top of High Street—wouldn't it be nice?"

"Nice, yes," replied his brother, "but things will never be the same. I think we've left our childhood back in Dunradin, and it seems very long ago right now."

"I wish we was back home just fer the sake of Mom and Dad," said Caleb. "I don't so much mind the castle, but they ain't young anymore, and it's a hardship."

"Aye, it don't seem fair," answered Cardiff, "but truth be told, there's no bleedin' house left there anyways."

"We're all safer here in the castle then we would be back in Dunradin." said Murdoch. "Word is that the quarry is filled with creepers now, and more each day. I think it's going to be a very long time before any of us can return. Godwyn was amongst them and says that we wouldn't recognize the east valley anymore, what with tunnels and sinkholes everywhere."

"He killed one of the leaders and run off; that's how close he was to the top." Caleb turned to Murdoch. "I hope he's not a spy. Who says he killed anyone?"

"He says he did, and if Stoke and Father trust him, that's good enough for me," replied Murdoch quickly. "I never liked the looks of that Welsh bastard. I just knew from the start that something wasn't right."

Cardiff picked up a stick, the end of which glowed hot from the fire. "That bearded wanker ... if he shows up here, I'll burn his feckin' eyes out!"

The other boys laughed at his comical attempt to look fierce. "Will that be after you ride his arse or before?" said his brother. The rest of them laughed all the harder as Cardiff grabbed Caleb by the shirt and began to wallop him across the side of the head. A boot struck the fire, and sparks flew high into the night sky.

They stopped grappling and brushed the ashes from their knees before sitting to catch their breath. A gloomy sort of silence settled on the group until Padraic, forming a circle with thumb and forefinger raised his arm and pushed the finger of his other hand in and out of the hole rapidly, sending the lads into another fit of uncontrollable laughter.

Ronan, who was beyond the castle wall in the Highlander's tent, heard the laughter within Threstone and smiled to himself.

Tyburn, to his right, took the stem of a long clay pipe from his mouth. "The young ones have been through a lot, but they're hardy. We'll need their strength in days to come."

"It's not so bad here," said Godwyn. "There is much yet that could be done to make the castle comfortable against the winter, but it is very achievable. I will stay and work. I'm not fond of travelling in the snow."

"Snow!" blurted Macintosh. "We're a far way from that yet."

"I'm not so sure. I think an early winter is on the way. There was a dusting to the east when I circled along the edge of the valley, and a few flakes here just yesterday." Ronan leaned back in his chair. "I would prefer that. The Teriz digging will be slowed by the frozen ground."

All at once Macintosh stood up and placed a finger to his lips. He reached for his bow and quickly nocked an arrow. Ronan rose carefully as the big highlander stepped from the tent. The arrow whistled through the night air and found its target. The large Teriz dropped to his knees grasping at his neck, while a horrible wet sound rasped from his pierced throat.

Macintosh pointed at Macleary's belt, where he knew the Dunradin kept a silver blade. Ronan understood his task and approached the beast, who had fallen forward. He approached the Teriz reluctantly, telling himself that it was no different than what one does while hunting. Gripping the hair he pulled backwards and quickly drew the blade across the intruder's throat while Donald Macintosh joined his brother John in a search of the area. Within minutes a number of armed highlanders had determined that no one else was in the encampment. A half dozen men searched the perimeter of the castle to ensure the safety of its inhabitants.

"My compliments, John, you have a finely tuned ear."

Macintosh bowed in the direction of Tyburn. "To be honest, my hearing is rather poor, but my sense of smell told me something was out there that didn't belong. I'm surprised you didnae smell the bastard yerself. What a stench. Had we not been downwind from the spy it might have played out differently."

Ronan spoke up. "Do you reckon he was alone then?"

"We can only guess," he answered.

"His size surprises me greatly," added Godwyn, who had entered the tent. "I saw no Teriz in the valley as large as this one, and he has a healthier look about him than most."

"Not anymore," laughed Macintosh.

Ronan asked, "Do you really think he's from elsewhere?"

"It's hard to say," replied Blunt. "I should like to have a closer look at him in the daylight."

Tyburn spoke. "Help yourself, but let's carry the body off to the woods quickly, lest it frighten the youngsters."

Ronan returned to his family's small sleeping area and found that Ceana was already asleep. Charlotte looked up from her reading. "Hello, Father."

He smiled into the candlelight. "You'll ruin your eyes reading in that dim light," he scolded. "What do you have there?"

"It's a diary of sorts that the boys found," she answered. "Tell me, Father, were there ever burnings in Dunradin, of witches I mean?"

Ronan thought for a moment. "I don't recall hearing of any, but I'm sure it happened there in the past. Times being what they were, people were more suspicious of woman healers then they are now."

Charlotte nodded and returned to her reading, satisfied with the answer.

"Is it a witch's book you have there?" Macleary asked.

"Yes," answered the young woman. "I think this poor girl must have had a very sad life."

"Well," replied her father, "I remember when I was very small, a calf with two heads was born in the next farm to us, just down in the valley across from where Corb Macneil's farm is—or was," he corrected himself. "There was more than one that blamed your great grandmother's chantings for the bad birth."

"Chantings?" said Charlotte.

"It was just her way of singing in the old tongue. Her family had come over from Ireland, and she knew the original songs of her people. Goidelc was very similar to what we call Gaelic, but those thick farmers thought she was cursing their herd."

"She wasn't—!"

"Of course not," answered Ronan before she could finish her question. "I recall she was thought of as a bit of a shrew, but she passed in a natural way." Ronan changed the subject. "How was your mother this evening?"

"She had the chills again, but improved, I'd say, as long as she doesn't try to do too much."

Ronan did not conceal his concern. Ceana was fast asleep already, and covered well in blankets. "We need to make some improvements very soon," he said, referring to their living conditions. "I'm afraid we shall need to winter here. The castle offers the protection we require, but it's too cold for most, and others will become sick if we don't shore up the draughty rooms and arrange for more comfortable bedding. Our supply of food may be a concern before spring also. I'd hate to resort to living on horse meat."

Charlotte frowned at the suggestion, more disturbed at the thought of one of the horses being killed than the menu selection.

Ronan made no mention of the intruder beyond the walls and wondered if his sons had been informed. The boys were very adept at tracking the movements of the small settlement. "What are your brothers doing to amuse themselves?" he asked.

"Probably sitting by the big fire and seeing who can spit the farthest," she said. "Liam was here until a few moments ago and went to fetch them."

-87-

Ivan Douglas rolled over and squeezed the young girl's arse. She had bled heavily in his bed sheets, and he just now became aware of the sticky mess. He pulled the sheets from her and cleaned himself briskly, tossing them into the corner when he was done.

"Little whore," he muttered. Reaching for the bell cord he summoned Greaves. The elderly manservant arrived quickly. Douglas picked a thread from the mantle of his robe. "Take it away," he commanded gesturing towards the sleeping girl. "Clean it up and bring it back tonight, and for God's sake bring clean linen as well." The young girl was awakened rudely and whisked away, having had no opportunity to complain.

Ivan stood in front of the mirror and examined the pouches under his eyes. Frowning, he reached for a pot of oily face cream and applied it liberally with one hand while aiming his cock towards the sink with the other. The pain in his scrotum was worse this morning, and he spat noisily into the sink and then washed the mess away with what remained of the contents of the water pitcher.

He was anxious to treat his guests to a very impressive service this evening, and it would require special preparations. He decided against waking the pair for breakfast, assuming they would sleep late while he made arrangements. The large man strode quietly past the closed doors of the two guestrooms, and exited the building.

Despite the chance for a few hours of extra sleep, Pengrove lay awake in his bunk. Ivan had not indicated whether Faustine was to be utilized or not. He had just been told to bring the old Wraith to Netherfield for an orientation and evaluation. Perhaps Douglas would show his hand later today.

He knew that Ivan would base his decision in part on what Wallace told him, and he hadn't decided whether to endorse Euther or not. The old fellow had certainly made a mess of things in Dunradin. The town was secured, it was true. However, the citizens had outwitted the Teriz and fled into the woods. Food would have to be brought in to feed the quarry troops soon, and this hadn't been planned upon. The truth was, the old villain seemed a bit soft. He'd allowed all his generals to either run off or kill each other, and he did seem a little too dependent on the powders.

I could easily handle Dunradin myself, thought Pengrove. Griffin Hume was capable enough to oversee Turfmoor if need be. So there it was, an easy decision. His father had always told him that a conclusion was simply the place where you got tired of thinking. In a short time he had convinced himself that Euther was of no use, but he would wait until after the service to speak of the matter with Ivan. Having made his decision, Wallace lay against the pillow and allowed himself to drift back to sleep.

-88-

In the heavily wooded hills north of the mine Dorian Euther de Faustine tied his horse to a stout branch and settled into the dark recesses of a richly scented pine grove. There was little point, he'd decided, in returning to Dunradin, and Netherfield certainly offered no future.

It was clear that Douglas was a maniac, but the old man could clearly talk a dog off a meat wagon and Pengrove was obviously intent on following him. This left no choice for Euther other than to vanish into the mist. An unusual feeling of relief washed over Faustine as he pulled his cloak closer and nestled into the dark bed of pine needles. The old creeper felt a boyish sense of freedom in his ancient limbs and rested pleasantly with a smile on his face. He would stay here until the sun went down, and ponder his future much later while travelling by moonlight.

-89-

Ivan Douglas was not particularly surprised to discover that Euther had taken his leave. "Let us imagine," he suggested, "that de Faustine was intimidated by our numbers, which in all truth far surpass his troops in count and quality. Or that he came to the conclusion that his flock were meant for our dinner plate. Do you really suppose that he would return to Dunradin in the belief that his meat factory could muster up some form of defence against the inevitable?"

Euther's sudden departure confused Pengrove. The Wraith had been up at a sparrow's fart and out the door without a word to either man. Wallace had incorrectly assumed that Faustine was grateful for the opportunity to redeem himself after the botched operation in Dunradin, and now he reluctantly found it necessary to shift the blame to himself.

It gave Douglas a psychological advantage over him that left a bad taste in the Londoner's mouth, and Pengrove tried to trivialize the matter, by speaking of it in a dismissive tone. "Dorian has outlived his usefulness. These affairs are best dealt with in the company of men who are assured of their mortality."

Wallace continued. "Hume and his brother will not disappoint us."

"They cannot afford to do so," replied Douglas. "It would be best that the Humes come to believe that de Faustine was dealt with harshly. I'm very certain that we will not cross paths with

Dorian again. Given the circumstances, I suggest we make plans to accelerate our actions in Dunradin. Captain Nash will accompany you back with a score of my best Teriz. They should more than adequately replenish the disappointing Welsh contingent."

-90-

Ceana woke up from a troubled dream, pleased to find that she was next to her husband, Ronan. Damp air in the castle had brought on a recurring ailment of the lungs, and she felt frail and weak. She wished that it were possible to slip away and return with a large breakfast for her husband and children, but she had barely the strength to feed herself, let alone others.

Charlotte spent her nights with Liam—an arrangement that would have been frowned upon were they still in the village. There were a number of social customs that were impractical in their new environment, and both Ronan and his wife appreciated the fact that their young daughter was in safe hands. A marriage had been discussed, and it was unlikely that the youngsters could have been kept apart at any rate.

Young women were, however, discouraged from socializing with the highlanders beyond the wall. Tamlyn had to this point not shown an interest in girls, but his older brother Murdoch, who Ceana felt was growing up far too quickly, appeared to be very interested in more than one of the young women in Threstone.

Ronan opened his eyes and found himself facing the back of his wife who had maneuvered herself to a seated position. Reaching up, he noticed that her hair seemed to have greyed considerably over the last month. He ran his hand down the curve of her back affectionately.

"How are you this morning?" he asked, and she turned towards him with a smile.

"Good morning," she replied. "I must have slept like the dead. I don't recall you coming to bed"—she cast a look about the room—"such as it is."

He sat up beside his wife. "We're going to do something about that" he said, drawing her close for warmth. "It's only going to get colder, and since we are to winter here, preparations must be made."

"If you want to know what I think," Ceana said "I can't abide the dampness, and I would choose a dry shelter over a warm one any day."

"Well," said Ronan, kissing his wife's cheek, "let's see if we can't arrange for both."

She rubbed her hands together for warmth. "What I wouldn't give for our old downy quilt right now. It's a shame that Duncan hadn't the time to bring back more than these thin horse blankets."

He ran a hand across the stubble on his chin. "Yes, well, we all stink, and most of us have looked much better than we do at the moment, but for the time being, at least we are safe."

Ceana wrinkled her nose. "You could use a quick dip in the moat, you know," she teased, poking him playfully in the ribs.

"Indeed," he agreed, getting to his feet. "What is it, women to the left and men to the right?"

She laughed out loud. "Good try, old man, you know the rules." For the sake of privacy it had been agreed that the women would bathe on the right side of the moat furthest from the encampment. However, this hadn't stopped a few of the younger boys from finding a tree that grew close to the far wall from which they could gain a view of the proceedings.

This practice ended when wee Simon Macauley, who always managed to find himself dangling at the edge of misfortune, fell from a branch and landed with a splash in the midst of three very startled and very naked women. The poor lad might have drowned had Mrs. Green not been intent on getting him to shore so she could thrash him on and about the head.

Tamlyn and his young friends had taken to sleeping around the large central fire which was open to the elements. They had been awarded the title of firekeepers which meant it was their duty to see that the blaze was never allowed to grow cold. The great stone circle that encircled the fire was hot to the touch but perfectly comfortable for the boys who slept with their backs to the blaze.

This morning Tamlyn lay wrapped in his horse blanket, aware of the smells that mingled in the light fall of cooling rain … a smoky scent flavoured with the odour of damp wool that had been singed with more than one errant spark.

Murdoch nudged his brother with his foot. "Hey, Tam, wake up, your head's on fire." His head, the only part exposed to open air, appeared from a distance to be smoking as the escaping heat turned to steam.

"I'm warm," he replied. "I don't want to get up."

The older lad took a seat on the ground. "You'll steam yourself and end up three inches shorter. I've already noticed that you're getting smaller."

"You're daft!" said Tamlyn sitting up.

"Father's called a council for the afternoon, and he wants the boys' defence league there as well." Murdoch glanced about. "Is everyone here?"

Tamlyn rubbed his eyes. "I think so … no, wait, Alfie's not here, I'm not sure why."

"It's been hard for him, I imagine," said Murdoch "losing his mother. I'm told that the troubles in Turfmoor were quite grisly compared to what we saw in town. They were the only ones to make it out." His voice dropped. "You know, his mother was infected with the blood sickness."

Tam's eyes widened. "Really?" he asked.

"That's what I've been told, but for Alfie's sake, don't mention it to the others. I don't believe he's aware himself."

"Whazat?" said Caleb, raising himself on one elbow. His hair stuck up at odd angles, and his face was smudged with ash.

The Macleary brothers broke into a fit of laughter. "You look a right clown!" chuckled Murdoch.

Caleb smoothed his hair down, looking mildly insulted. "Piss off. Oy, did Alfie come back then?" he added.

"No he didn't," replied Tamlyn, growing concerned. "We had best look about for him. I'm afraid I may have hurt his feelings."

Murdoch got to his feet. "When he shows up, bring him along with the others to council. I'm off to let Liam know."

Alfred Gamble leaned against the stonework of the dungeon wall. The young boy had not slept and only now had managed to drag himself from the glowing orb that dominated the narrow alcove across the room from him where he had spent the night. He was completely drained of energy and emotion, and his eyes felt raw and bloodshot.

It had not taken long for Alfie to become powerless against the stone's seductive pull, and he felt at some point during the night that perhaps he would never leave the room again. It was such a comfort against the cold reality of a motherless life outside. Eventually his eyes closed and he drifted off to sleep.

"Alfie, come out, come out, wherever you are." Caleb's singsong invitation echoed down the full measure of the tower stairwell.

"He isnae here," said Cardiff, scratching his head.

"There's only one place we haven't looked," suggested Tamlyn.

"Oh aye, it's the dungeon then," said Caleb. The trio had searched the castle top to bottom. With no clue to their companion's whereabouts, they now filed down the stairs of the second tower, confident that they had examined all but one corner of Threstone. Padraic had remained behind with instructions to signal with his whistle in the event that Alfred returned.

Journal Entry:

A rainy morning in the castle and nothing of much importance has happened here for what seems a very long time, until this morning. Alfred Gamble appears to have gone missing in the night. The others are searching for him, and my guess is that they will find him curled up asleep in some corner. Like myself he has lost a parent, and there are times when such a tragedy is best dealt with in a solitary manner.

Everyone in the castle is anxious to discover what Branan Stoke's anticipated arrival will mean in regards to a possible return to the village, but few hold out hope for a homecoming before the end of winter. I am very interested to know how much the rest of the country has learned of our plight and the dreadful events in Turfmoor. We are two commonly overlooked villages, small in size and of very little importance to the rest of the world, but I find it hard to believe that there is not help on the way. Branan Stoke was very vague about the politics of the situation and unless the Teriz threat is only centred in our out of the way valley, I wonder at the lack of response. Is it possible that the creatures have infiltrated some large cities and we are neglected due to battles elsewhere? Only time will tell.

—Padraic

-91-

The town of Deermuir was situated off the main road from the north behind a small forest. The entrance to Deermuir Road was marked with a tall post upon which two signs were mounted. One directed readers towards the town, whose population was double that of Dunradin. The other sign read threstone castle and pointed the same way Stoke and his companions were travelling.

As the three men approached the sign, Toulouse pointed to the clouds, where a number of buzzards were circling high in the sky. Branan looked up and then forward as his horse reared suddenly, almost unseating him. Something in the distance towards the castle, perhaps a bad small, had spooked his animal. He spun towards Flint before regaining control of his mount.

Ben was motioning towards the signpost in the distance. "Something ahead of us at the crossroad is attached to that sign. It looks like a man from here."

Branan dismounted and turned towards the south. The others followed suit. "Very carefully now," he said, taking a pistol from his baldric. He primed the weapon and began to walk towards the sign, leaving the horses tied together.

"Good feckin' Christ" exclaimed Auberge. "What the bloody hell is that?"

Flint wiped the road dust from his brow. "I take it that this handsome fellow is one of our aforementioned Teriz."

Branan nodded his head slowly. The corpse appeared to have been strung up as a warning with its throat open from ear to ear. One leg was missing, and carrion birds had already taken away the eyes. Apparently they'd found the rest of the creature inedible. "Not much of a meal there," said Auberge.

"This is bad news," said Stoke. "On the one hand it means that Deermuir has been targeted. I don't know why we were not made aware of this. Unless they are already overrun, but our friend could also have been placed here by the citizens as a warning to the other creepers.

"I think it won't be long before news filters north to Glasgow and then on to Edinburgh. The ensuing panic will not be a pleasant scene to witness. It would have been much better if we had been able to contain them in the south. I fear now that Euther de Faustine may prove to be the least of our problems." The Highlander holstered his weapon. "Nevertheless we have no time to linger here, we must press on."

Auberge took a last look at the creature. "Never again," he muttered, "shall I curse my pretty face. Tell me," he asked, climbing into the saddle, "how do you imagine that three of us can possibly stack up against a slew of those spooks?"

"We shall have a small army of highlanders at our disposal and the advantage of daylight," answered Stoke. "Not to mention two of the most tactically brilliant minds in the history of warfare and crime fighting."

Flint laughed at his response. "Aye, there's no substitute for optimism."

"All joking aside," said Stoke, "the highlanders stationed at the castle are very special individuals, and once they're trained with the explosives we've brought, they'll be all the more valuable."

-92-

Alfie stumbled from the entrance to the dungeon and tripped over the top step, falling on his face in the dirt. "Here he is!" called Tamlyn, much relieved.

Alfie regained his footing and put an unsteady hand to his face. Blood trickled from his nose, and the youngster's eyes began to roll back in his head. Tamlyn stepped closer just in time to prevent the youngster from falling a second time. "Here, tilt your head back, and pinch right there," he said, positioning Alfie's fingers along the bridge of his nose, while supporting his friend against his chest. Caleb handed him a rumpled handkerchief, and soon Alfred was able to sit up by himself and wipe the blood from his face.

"What were you doing in there?" asked Cardiff.

Alfie answered in a weak voice, "I suppose I fell asleep."

"I should say so," the older boy replied. "You spent the whole night in a dungeon and gave us all a scare, you wanker."

Tamlyn glared briefly at Cardiff. "Come on; let's get him to his granny for now."

"Sorry," offered Macneil, "I'm just glad yer nae' harmed."

Tamlyn helped his young friend to his feet with a glance towards the entrance of the dungeon. "I think we should all steer clear of that place for now on."

Alfie mumbled something incoherent, and the boys made for the centre of the castle.

High above on the walkway between the two towers, Godwyn smiled at the recollection of his own boyhood.

He turned from the scene below and scanned the horizon. Far to the north he seemed to discern a dust cloud that might indicate a small group of travellers. The big Norseman watched it for some time, and when he was sure that it was approaching the castle, he decided to call for another set of eyes. Blowing into one of Padraic's whistles, he caught the attention of John Macintosh in the field below and motioned for him to come up to the watch post.

Big John put his axe into the stump and rolled his sleeves up as he made his way across to the drawbridge. Upon his arrival at the stair top, Godwyn pointed to the hills. "What do you make of that?"

The highlander worked at the waxed corners of his full moustache, twisting them to a fierce point before speaking. "Those are large animals. My money's on Stoke. If that is him, he travels with fewer men than we require." He looked at his surroundings as though seeing them for the first time. "This would be a fine spot for a small catapult," he commented, mentally taking in various measurements.

"Aye, a small one," agreed Blunt, "with a good aiming device, a pistol is not much use at this range."

Macintosh looked thoughtful. "Leave it with me, I'll come up with a design." He clapped Godwyn on the back. "In the meantime I'll go tell Ronan we have visitors."

Ronan was deep in conversation with his father Tyburn when John found him. "If this is Stoke arrived, he has phenomenal timing," exclaimed the doctor.

Branan slowed his horse at the top of the hill and stood up in the stirrups. "There it is, gentlemen." He pointed towards the sprawling fortress below. "No need to announce ourselves. We will have been seen as we crested the hill."

"I don't suppose there's an ale house within," asked Toulouse hopefully.

"I'm afraid not," answered Stoke.

"I certainly wish you'd told me that before we left," complained the dark man. "I would have stayed home. I feel I've been deceived, and now I'm unhappy."

Flint laughed. "You might make a search of those tents yonder for an errant keg."

"You can count on it," replied Toulouse.

"Everything looks fine from here," said Branan, "but be on your guard nevertheless."

-93-

Padraic remained behind with Alfie's grandmother to explain what had happened, using the sign language that the old woman had taught him. Tamlyn and the other two made their way towards the big fire, with Caleb in the lead. "Alf doesn't seem quite right in the brain" exclaimed Caleb. "What's with that?"

"All I know," said Tamlyn, "is that I wouldn't stay overnight in that dungeon for anything. There's something haunted about it."

Liam Twist's sudden appearance put an end to the conversation. "Just the lads we're after," he said cheerfully. Murdoch was behind Twist, talking earnestly with Duncan and Hugh Maclean.

He looked up and waved to his brother. "Find Paddy and whoever else belongs in your group and meet at the large tent right away."

Tamlyn asked, "What's the event?"

"Branan has returned," came the answer, "and just in time for the council."

There was a rare excitement in the air as the boys left the castle and crossed the field to the highlanders' encampment.

Inside the tent they saw that Branan and Tyburn fronted the council table along with two men they were not familiar with. The taller of the pair, who wore a heavy cloak, possessed the oddest skin pigmentation, unlike anything they had seen before. He had a faintly frightening demeanour, accented by a sly, self-amused grin. The other stranger looked stern in a dangerous kind of way.

The tent itself had a comfortable smell of waxed canvas and tobacco that wafted through the warm structure. A palpable air of anticipation bristled the hairs on Tamlyn's neck as Tyburn waited for everyone to be seated.

"Well, I think it's total rubbish," said Charlotte to Megan Maguire. Lara Twist and Ceana Macleary looked amused. "I'm very serious," she continued indignantly. "We're good enough to carry their bloody meals over there, but we're not welcome to join the discussion on matters that clearly involve us."

"Oh, darling, you don't really want to be over there with a bunch of hairy men arguing about who can piss the farthest."

Charlotte was surprised at her mother's crudeness.

"Well, I wouldn't mind to be a judge of that," said Megan, blushing. The young widow wasn't pleased with the off-limits status of the highlander encampment. "I'll wager that young Duncan could fill the moat by himself." The four women broke into gales of laughter that only subsided when Lara Twist, who had not laughed so hard since her married days, spilled a cup of tea into her lap.

Charlotte was cheered at her mother's laughter. It seemed a long time since she'd seen the older woman in such a buoyant mood and decided that it was a fine evening after all.

Branan had begun to speak to the crowd. "My original estimation regarding the number of Teriz"—he paused—"has altered greatly. Even in the last few hours. It's not my intent to alarm you but to forewarn you that matters will not be resolved as quickly as we may have imagined. This is not good news, of course, to those who are anxious to return to your homes.

"We don't presently know what the situation in Dunradin is, except that a force of Teriz is digging in there, literally, and presumably expanding in numbers. What is more worrisome is the question of whether Deermuir to the north has been infiltrated. We believe that something may have happened there, which would indicate that a plan of sorts is gathering momentum.

"However, Edinburgh and Glasgow, as far as we can tell, are completely oblivious to the growing threat, and it's unlikely that the Teriz have multiplied in numbers sufficient to attempt incursions into larger cities." Branan's audience had grown solemn, and no one had questioned anything he had said to this point.

He continued, "Before I get too long-winded, let me introduce my companions, please: Constable Benjamin Flint and Mr. Toulouse Auberge. Both gentlemen have been apprised of our situation and have graciously offered their assistance. For those of you who may have expected a small army to arrive from the city, I apologize. But let me assure you, a full-blown assault is now out of the question." A few men grumbled audibly, not convinced that a show of force wasn't favourable. "Ben and Toulouse have been instrumental in procuring resources for us. We have purchased a sizable cache of silver and explosives, which will prove to be invaluable, as I will eventually explain."

Hugh Maclean, who had perfectly grasped the situation, fed Branan a question. "Are you suggesting covert action, raiding parties and the like, to eliminate a conventional battleground?"

"Yes, exactly that!" replied Stoke. "I propose that Threstone be the base of operations, given its strong defence features that we will of course begin to bolster immediately."

John Macintosh stepped forward. "I'm nae one fer creepin' around the woods and mincing about in tunnels. I like a field where I can swing an axe freely. Youse can sign me up for defence, and I'll stay fer the duration."

His suggestion was met with scattered applause. "Thank you, John," replied Branan. "You gentlemen can all express your preferences over the next few days. Keep in mind as well that I will be requesting a small party of men to go through to Deermuir as early as tomorrow. I want Dr. Macleary to speak to us for a minute please."

Tyburn stood up and leaned on the table. "Thank you, Branan," he began. "If you'll bear with me, I want to clear up some misconceptions regarding the creatures that have overrun our homes. I have a knowledge of these beasts that surpasses that of even Master Stoke, with due respect."

Branan looked up, surprised.

"First, pay no attention to the claim that they cannot be killed except with the use of silver. Silver speeds the process better than anything else. These Teriz have an uncanny ability to regenerate quickly when wounded in any other manner, but they will still die eventually. They don't prance about exchanging heads! They have no aversion to garlic or mirrors or the sight of a crucifix! That's foolishness, old wives' tales.

"Euther de Faustine himself is not a five-hundred-year-old vampire!—despite his claims, although he may believe them in his own mind. Euther is an eighty-year-old flesh-eater who, along with his followers, has extended his existence by ingesting blood. They do not possess fangs with which to suck their victims' blood." Tyburn paused and reached across the table for a wooden stake, which he lifted above his head. "This is of no use unless you are pitching a tent.

"I have no knowledge of what happens when one of the Teriz is killed. I can tell you that it is a difficult task but not impossible. So if you face one of them without a weapon fortified with silver, you had better be prepared for a very harrowing time. We have silver at our disposal and talented smithies on hand. Be prepared, but please, don't take foolish superstitions into battle with you."

There was a general air of relief in the tent after Tyburn spoke, and several of the men chatted amongst themselves, the main topic being how they might improve the castle's defences. The young boys in the crowd puffed out their chests, proud to have been included with the adults.

"How did you come by these details regarding the Teriz?" asked Branan, when he found a quiet moment to draw Tyburn aside. "I have to say I find some of it contradictory to what I have learned."

"Oh, don't worry about that horseshit," replied the doctor. "That was for the benefit of the general public. Some of it was true, and I made up the rest. We can't have everyone running about the castle chasing bats. They'll go back and tell their wives what I said, and everyone will sleep better. For all I know, Dorian could be the antichrist himself, but I rather doubt it. In the end he may be just like you and me, a rotting pile of flesh."

-94-

"I want no more than two scouts," said Maclean. "Padraic and Tamlyn are the smallest but not too young. If you lads are willing, you would be my choice, with Ronan's permission of course."

It made sense. The two boys could easily skirt the boundaries of Deermuir unseen. It would take them a full day's trek by foot to arrive and another coming back. If a large force of Teriz were within a day's march of the castle, they needed to know it, and if all appeared to be well, a rider would be sent from the castle to warn the citizens of the possibilities of invasion.

Tyburn shook his head at the irony of the situation. Fearghal and Dafyd had not so long ago arrived in Dunradin with the same dire warnings.

Ronan, who appeared troubled, spoke up. "I think perhaps I should go with Tam instead. As far as anyone could tell, we would just be a father and son out for a day of grousing."

Hugh Maclean's eyebrows rose. "I see your point, and if you should find that nothing is amiss, you will have the opportunity to speak to someone in charge sooner."

Tamlyn grinned up at his father. "Go ahead," said Ronan. "Smile now while you can. We've not told your mother yet. That'll be the most dangerous part of the whole thing."

The youngster straightened his collar and brushed the hair from his forehead, hoping the adjustments would make him look older.

"We could just tell her that we're going hunting and might camp overnight."

Ronan gave his son a serious look. "Now that wouldn't be terribly honest of us." He punctuated the statement with a conspiratorial wink of the eye, which Tamlyn returned. "I hear," he continued, "that the pheasant hunting is particularly good this time of year across the moors close to Deermuir."

-95-

Euther was no longer hungry. He gnawed absently at the calf muscle for a minute more and then returned the remains of the leg to his backpack. He was quite certain that any who might be following him would be deterred from coming any closer to Deermuir by the creature he'd strung up at the crossroads.

He looked up at the sky dreamily as the first stars began to come out. *I really should have done this years ago*, he thought, deciding that solitary travel was one of the most peaceful pastimes one could indulge in. His musings were tinged with regret that he had not made more friends in his lifetime. How pleasant it would be to travel about, staying with old friends and recounting forgotten adventures. He imagined a long-lost comrade greeting him with surprise. *Dorian, my dear friend, how long it's been. Please come in and sit down. It's an absolute delight to see you again. What in the world have you been up to? Tell me everything.*

But truth be told, a great number of Euther's acquaintances had ended up on his dinner plate. It couldn't be said that he had not enjoyed his friends. *Ah well, if we don't learn from our mistakes, we learn nothing.* As he started down a long, gentle slope covered with heather, he noticed a wisp of chimney smoke reflected in a distant pond. The pasture between Dorian and the pond was coloured the deepest shade in midnight's palette. It seemed a logical destination, so Euther made for the dimly lit shapes, slithering across the wetlands like a mirage.

Gradually a small crofter's cottage began to take shape, similar to the stone houses which were commonly found in the northern areas of the country. The cottage would have appeared abandoned, had there not been a small blaze inside. Euther soon reached the building, approaching it at an angle. He slid across the grass and crouched beneath the narrow window. Gripping the windowsill with his long fingers, he slowly raised his head and peered through the pane.

A young woman was just visible beside the dying embers of an evening fire. She was wrapped in a blanket, on a coarse mat, which had been pulled close to the fireplace for warmth. At her feet was a wooden cradle. The word *unwed* came at once to mind *How sad*, he thought. *What a tragedy.*

He slid down the wall with his back to the window and wiped away the tears that ran down his porcelain cheekbones. He pulled at his hair while his hands shook uncontrollably. Slowly he gained control of his racing mind, and a smile began to replace the grimace that had distorted his pale face.

Finally he placed his hands behind his head and decided to rest there. His legs stretched out almost to the short stone fence that housed the woman's sheep. A single ewe approached the fence and stared at Euther while he seemed to fall into some type of trance. When morning arrived, the sheep, who had not moved all night, spoke to Euther in his dreams. "Are you through with the past?"

-96-

"We have a great deal of work ahead of us," said Branan. "John and Donald will see to the increased fortification of the castle, while Hugh and Duncan construct warmer living quarters. I propose also that we talk about the possibility of underground housing for the highlanders and beat these bastards at their own game."

Tyburn pointed at Branan. "You have a point there. The castle cannot house everyone, and these tents will burn like tinder."

"For my part," continued Stoke, "I would like to make Ben and Toulouse familiar with the lay of the land. We'll go through the woods and see what's happening at the quarry." Stoke was of course unaware that Faustine no longer held sway over the pale menace that had infiltrated the valley, but before long the Queen's agent would have a much clearer picture of the situation. Victoria had been apprised of many of the plots and subplots that had arisen since she went into her period of mourning, and it had been a very long time since she had any word from Branan Stoke concerning the Teriz rumours. He would have asked for an audience with the Queen while he was in Edinburgh, except that she had recently left Balmoral for Osborne Castle on the Isle of Wight.

Branan was painfully aware that his communications with Her Majesty had lapsed dangerously, but in his own defence, he trusted no one to deliver an accurate report to the Crown aside from himself. He was eager to know more about the origins of the plot so that he might better justify a request for military intervention. The order could only come from the Queen, and no one could be trusted, right up to her closest advisers, who all appeared to be capable of treachery The only exception was his fellow Scotsman, the Royal Gardener, John Brown. Brown's dedication to Victoria, and her acceptance of him as a confidant, had sparked a flurry of ugly rumours that appeared more and more frequently in the London papers.

"When will you leave?" asked Tyburn.

"Very soon, I think perhaps tomorrow."

Dr. Macleary nodded, "I will suggest to Ronan that he and Tam time their hunting trip to coincide with your departure, eyes to the north and the east as it were."

Padraic was disappointed to have been replaced but was at the same time reluctant to leave the castle while young Alfie was so bothered. He sensed that his friend needed immediate care and attention to deal with whatever malady had afflicted him. The change in plans reinforced his decision to stay close to Alfie.

John Macintosh, standing outside the big tent, spoke with Duncan. "Any opportunity we have to increase the distance between ourselves and the forest is good. We'll take the trees down over here, and there," he said, pointing to the edge of the woods closest to the castle. "Those younger trees will come down easily and will fortify a bunker if we mean to build one."

"Your brother has a design in mind that looks very workable," said Duncan. "I'm going in to study his plan just now."

John looked concerned. "You mean Donald?"

Duncan was confused. "Yes, Donald."

"Oh, ya dinnae want to spend much time wi' brother Donnie. Just make sure he keeps his hands to his self. He's a man's man, if you take my meaning—a little light in the boots, as they say."

Big Duncan looked even more confused. "I don't follow you."

"Oh, fer Christ's sake, do I have tae spell it out? He's an arse bandit. I kid ye not." Duncan's eyes widened as John turned and walked back to the tent. "Just don't say I didnae warn you," he mumbled.

John held a hand to the side of his mouth as he approached Donald and spoke quickly in a hushed tone. "Duncan is here. Be on yer guard. I think he's attracted to you."

The Macintosh brothers often set each other up in humorous ways, amusing themselves as well as their friends. The mood in the encampment remained lighthearted as the highlanders went about the work of planning improvements, pleased to have some respite from the boredom of guard duty.

-97-

Just as Ronan and his son prepared to begin their hunting trip across to Deermuir, a gentleman by the name of Crispin Fortune was on a journey from London that would take him far north across the Scottish border.

Fortune, who was often described as portly, was an articulate man of fine breeding, not unaccustomed to travel, and an admirer of the pleasant aspects of a country hike. His preferred mode of travel included a good pair of boots and a stout walking stick. It He had planned to travel by coach to Carlisle and carry on from there by horse. It was rather daunting task, given that Crispin was not comfortable in the saddle due to his longstanding fear and mistrust of horses.

It was, however, imperative that he locate and speak with an agent of the Queen by the name of Branan Stoke. Stoke's lack of communication and the need to relay to him news of great importance had prompted the Queen to search him out. It was assumed that Stoke was somewhere in the vicinity of an out-of-the-way village by the name of Dunradin, and this was Crispin's destination.

-98-

The memory of his brother's violent death still haunted Ronan; He ran his hand across Cay's crossbow. Then he hefted it to judge its weight and quickly hung the weapon across his back. Each hunter carried a whistle and a sharp blade, and Tamlyn included his hunting sling. They had dressed in the muted hill colours of green and brown and carried skins of water and packets of jerky.

Tamlyn's excitement at the prospect of hunting with his father was edged with a sense of danger that had him catching his breath at the sight of his uncle's powerful crossbow. "It's time you learned how to use Cay's weapon," said Ronan; "he would have wanted you to have it."

The youngster nodded silently, not wanting to betray the emotion in his voice. They left the castle quietly, speaking to no one, and within the hour were warm enough from the steady march to remove their outer jackets. The morning proved to be uneventful, and before long Ronan suggested that they stop to rest and take some nourishment.

"Up here" said Ronan, deciding to take to the high ground where they would be able to see anyone's approach. He took an apple from his backpack and sliced it in half, offering some to his son. "Are you okay, Tam?" Tamlyn smiled in response. "Frightened?"

"No, I'm okay. Dad, will we see any pheasant?"

"Well, anything is possible."

"Will we see any creepers?"

Ronan met his son's gaze. "If we do, I don't think it will be until we get closer to Deermuir. We'll have to be more careful from here on as it starts to get dark."

They decided to skirt the town along the woods, keeping close to the tree line in case it was necessary to hide quickly. For a time there was no sound other than the wind in the trees and their own footfalls on the crisp ground. Colourful leaves and frost covered the woodland floor, and the forest edge, open to sunshine, was somewhat drier than its interior. Ronan and his son had not come across anything worth hunting for the entire day, and as the light showed signs of quickly waning, they decided to camp for the night.

"Deermuir is just beyond this corner of the woods," said Ronan. "We'll be glad of these blankets tonight; we can't risk a fire this close to the town." Before long they came to a small clearing where two large trees had fallen, creating a natural mossy shelter. Fiddlehead ferns and black mushrooms grew alongside the larger of the two trees, while the other fallen giant reached deep into the woods running parallel with the evening's long shadows. High above, a hunting owl took in the scene below, intent on tracking a fat field mouse that had scampered from beneath a log upon the arrival of the hunters. Deep in the forest, another pair of eyes, no less sharp, had also spotted the travellers.

-99-

In another forest south of Threstone, Branan Stoke travelled by foot with his companions, hoping to gain some insight into changes that had occurred in the woods surrounding Dunradin. He had decided they also needed to know whether the town had been occupied by Teriz and, more important, whether the tunnel which led to the church was still clear.

After walking for much of the morning, the trio concluded that none of the creepers had made advances towards the castle from the high woods. They had not come across any sinkholes and decided to veer to the left as they approached the location of the church tunnel exit. Branan decided that they should have a look at the quarry area before attempting to negotiate the tunnel.

As the light of day grew weaker, they decided to retreat into the deeper bush for the night. A fire was out of the question, so they sought out dry ground. When they were settled for the night, Branan addressed his companions. "Well, Toulouse, Ben, I suppose that this is a very different type of adventure than you had imagined."

"It's not exactly the docks of Leith," said Flint, pulling a large pine cone from beneath his bedroll. "I am used to a more visible adversary. I like to get a read on my enemy before he gets very close."

Branan passed a pouch of tobacco to Ben.

Toulouse winked at Branan and passed him a small flask of whisky that appeared from his jacket. "In the meantime, get a read on this."

-100-

Ronan, drifting towards wakefulness, became aware of the smell of smoke, somewhere behind his other senses, which told him that snow was falling lightly. He opened his eyes slowly and sat up with a start, reaching for his weapon: they were not alone.

A youngster no taller than Tamlyn himself, dressed in dark colours, sat atop the fallen tree. A sharpened stave lay across the child's knees, and beneath a peaked cap, a round face, either through neglect or intent, was covered in dirt.

"Good morning," she said. "I am Salem Brightfoot and we are the defenders of Deermuir otherwise known as the Citizen's Brigade" Other voices behind the fallen tree broke into childlike laughter, and Tamlyn woke up, rubbing the sleep from his eyes.

"Defenders of Deermuir?" said Ronan, pulling Tam close to his side.

Salem smiled broadly. "Please forgive my little joke, and put your weapon aside. You have nothing to fear from me or my collection of merry misfits."

Ronan relaxed his grip on the weapon. "My name is Ronan, and this is my son, Tamlyn." He glanced at Salem's right hand. It was gnarled and twisted like a claw. "You are all citizens of Deermuir?" he asked.

"Indeed some of us are, or were. I myself am lately from Netherfield."

"I am not familiar with that name."

"I'm not surprised; the village is not yet mapped. Perhaps you might tell us from whence you came and what would be your business in these woods. But first, come to the fire and warm your hands."

Ronan spent the next while explaining his purpose to the young girl and her companions, who all, he could not help but notice, appeared to be burdened with some form of affliction. Tamlyn gazed about wide-eyed. One youngster possessed an unusually small head, and another approached the fire on one leg. Yet another made his way through life with empty eye sockets, and one small lad's affliction appeared to be a damaged mind. He sat with the others mumbling and drooling into the snow; however, he was not so limp of brain as one would imagine.

When Ronan finished speaking, Salem removed her cap and shook the snow from it. "As you may have gathered, we are not the guardians of Deermuir as I earlier introduced us we are keepers of this small forest, bound to each other by our history. We have all been rejected by society, a society that is daily more frightened by differences." She waved her withered arm in the air and gestured towards the others. "We are outcasts, who pool our skills for survival. Oddly enough we find that it is in our best interest to be aware of anything that changes in the city beyond that has rejected us.

"We've not seen the Teriz that you speak of in Deermuir, but I myself am familiar with the miners of Netherfield, as I think you might call them. My parents were recruited to become participants in the grand vision of a new settlement to the west. As my hand began to curl upon itself, Mother tried to hide it, even from my father. Before long a fellow student saw that I was not the same, and I was reported to the committee. I was ejected from the community, taken here, and left in these very woods. Out of sight is out of mind. I believe my mother's heart was broken, but my father, who was very strict, seemed totally unmoved."

Tamlyn stared at his own hands, not knowing where to look amongst the group.

"None of the present company are bitter about our circumstances. We are a happy family of wood dwellers and would rather be where we are than in the rigid, unforgiving societies that cast us out."

Ronan shook his head in disbelief, and Tamlyn looked deeply concerned. If Dunradin or Castle Threstone had been guided by these archaic rules, it would not be unimaginable that Padraic and Alfie's grandmother would have been banished to a life in the wild. Most certainly Tanner Smead would have been one of the first sent away, not to mention Fergus Green, who had five fingers on his left hand in addition to his thumb.

"How is it," asked Ronan, "that we have gone backwards on the matter of acceptance of others' afflictions?"

"I think perhaps the reason is that very view of differences as afflictions," replied Salem. "None of us here feels afflicted. We care for each other in a manner that leaves us each with our pride and dignity intact."

"And you are certain that Deermuir has not been overrun with Teriz, everything operates as normal?"

Salem smiled again. "*Normal* is a subjective word, and the only monsters in the village are those who were born there." Pointing to the gentleman with no eyes, she continued, "I am told by some of my companions that Deermuir is undergoing a time of change, brought on by outside influences."

The blind man spoke up. "I do not see, but I hear very well, and nothing escapes my ears. I was aware of your approach an hour before you arrived here. Until I was sent away, I heard many things. There is a disease of society at work in Deermuir, poisoning the minds of its citizens. Mistrust and treachery are widespread and increasing, and I would not return to the village, even if it were possible. My family is here."

In the midst of their conversation a small, dark-skinned man stepped from the woods carrying a sack which he dropped at the feet of Salem. "There we go, Missy Brightfoot, rabbits from the traps." He switched his gaze to the strangers suddenly.

"Jack, this is Ronan and his son Tamlyn from Dunradin, come to visit."

"Oh aye," replied the black man. "And how be life in Dunradin?"

"We were chased out," answered Tam. "Castle Threstone is our home for the time being."

"That's a pity," said the sad-looking man, who stood no taller than a seated Tamlyn. "But it's a fine castle; I've seen it myself. In the meantime we will lunch on rabbit, hey?" Young Macleary, who was quite hungry, agreed readily, and the dwarf went about the business of cleaning and spitting the rabbits.

Salem introduced the rest of those seated around the fire as the food cooked. Tam found that Colin the mumbler, whom he had initially assumed was very simple, was in fact terribly entertaining. Despite his constantly running nose and his crossed eye, the young man was amazingly adept at rope tricks and immensely pleased to have found a new and appreciative audience.

Dennis, the lad with the tiny head, had a surprisingly deep voice and seemed amused at everything that Salem had to say.

Ronan mused and then said, "We had it in mind to search for any signs of Teriz in the village, but I now suspect that would be a waste of our time. We've already determined that there are no creepers between here and the castle, and I'm inclined to take you at your word. You are aware, however, that these creatures dwell beneath the ground and could be lying in wait beneath the village right now." It was as much a question as a statement.

"Don't caaare so much for the villagers anyhow," bleated the one legged youth, whose wisp of a beard gave him the look of a goat. He had been introduced as Old Donny, despite his obvious age.

"Donny boy," chided Salem, "you know as well as I do that they exist in various degrees of temperament, and there are some that have also been good spirited towards us."

Donny stroked his beard. "Very feeeeew and faaaar between," he brayed.

"This forest rings the village on three sides," said Salem. "No one comes or goes without our knowledge, above or below the woods."

"And what of the open fields to the east?" asked Ronan.

"The road into Deermuir seems an unlikely entry point for invaders," insisted Salem, "given that it's surrounded on both sides with open farmland."

"One of these creatures was hanged and disembowelled on the sign at the entrance to that very road not long ago," said Ronan.

Salem looked surprised. "We are grateful for the warning. You may wish to take the main road back in order to draw your own conclusions, but we very rarely leave the safety of the woods ourselves." The young leader motioned towards the dwarf. "Jack here sometimes goes down to the village to trade mushrooms and pine nuts for tobacco, but he hasn't done so recently."

"If you're willing," asked Ronan, "I would like to talk with you further regarding Netherfield."

-101-

Felicia stared at the window, puzzled. The pane of glass was frosted over but for the lower section, where some source of warmth had melted the ice crystals in a semicircle. Outside below the window something or someone breathed heavily.

The young woman got to her feet and instinctively glanced into her child's cradle. The baby was fast asleep on his side. Perhaps, she thought, one of the sheep had escaped from the pen and was resting below the window. Her dog was nowhere to be seen, and it occurred to her that Duke might have settled outside below the window to gnaw on a bone. She gathered the thin sleeping gown around her legs and stepped lightly across the room to the window. Nothing was visible through the steamy cloud of breath that rose from below in the frigid morning air. Felicia stretched her back and reached for a blanket, which she quickly wrapped around her lithe body with a shiver.

"Duke, what are you doing out there?" she called weakly. She took hold of a poker and shifted the hot ashes in her fireplace while adding more wood to the embers from the previous night. She swung the mounted hook over the gathering blaze after attaching her kettle and warmed her hands in anticipation of a hot cup of tea. Her blanket fell open and the warmth crept into her gown.

She held her hands close to the blaze for as long as she could and quickly pushed them into the neckline of her garment where she caressed her small, firm breasts, enveloping them with delicious warmth. A creak from the door startled her, and she quickly pulled the blanket once more around herself and turned in the direction of the sound. The door swung slowly open. She swore quietly, "Damn wind." She must have not have caught the latch last night, and the dog had pushed it open. She approached the open door quickly, anxious to bring the animal in and to shut out the cold. Nothing could have prepared Felicia for what happened next.

-102-

Branan crept forward through the underbrush and peered about before signalling to Flint and Auberge. Below them lay the Dunradin quarry, buried in a haze of dust and sunshine. The digging had expanded since Stoke's previous visit, and as the three men gazed silently into the valley, he noted that even the burned homes that had previously stood out black against the yellowing grass had been flattened and buried under mounds of gravel from the quarry.

"Here and here," he said, pointing, "were the small farms of the valley, and over that way is the armoury which is connected to the quarry by underground passages." Back towards the town, he noted that the bridge had been rebuilt over the river, and a wide unfinished road was extending towards the rise of the village common. Apparently the Teriz had plans for the town itself. "It looks as though the town centre is still deserted," remarked Branan, turning again to the quarry. A pall of smoke hung over the sky in that direction, coming from several chimneys that Stoke had failed to notice earlier.

Although they saw no sign of anything alive and moving in the town, it was obvious that a great deal of work was being accomplished during the night. It was impossible to gauge the number of workers while they hid from the daylight, but in view of how the landscape was changing, Stoke inferred that the population had grown. There was an unhealthy smell to the air here, and Branan suggested that they return to the tunnel exit to investigate the possibility of examining the town square from within the church.

When they arrived at the tunnel, they could see that Dunradin's Teriz had not deemed it necessary to block the entrance. Clearly they thought the villagers would have been mad to attempt a return to their homes. The three men made their way carefully through the passageway after stepping gingerly over the festering corpse of a long-dead creature. "Follow my lead" said Branan, "I'll make you aware of the drops as we approach them."

Flint held a handkerchief to his face against the overpowering stench.

"Good Christ!" exclaimed Toulouse. "This smells worse than a pair of French whores in a heat wave."

"Are you speaking from personal experience?" joked Flint.

"Ah, nothing can match the charms of Paris," he replied. "If it gets much worse I'll throw myself down one of those crevices for a breather."

Eventually they reached the church basement and emerged cautiously from the passageway. All three of them blinked in the sudden light of the main floor and carefully sidestepped an area where some manner of being had defecated more than once. The foul air was abuzz with flies, and Branan quickly directed his companions to a room at the front of the building that benefitted from an open window.

Then he froze in his tracks. A pair of boots protruded from the anteroom that was connected to the front room through a wide doorway. Branan raised a finger to his lips and motioned for his companions to wait while he crept quietly ahead, crossbow at the ready. Someone was seated against the wall with outstretched legs. The highlander leaped into the room to land on one knee with his weapon raised.

The man before him had been dead for a number of days. His grey, lifeless eyes stared straight ahead. Branan was astounded. Before him was a relatively young man wearing a rich-looking pair of boots and a colourful corset. He was naked from waist to knees, and one of his hands was idly cupped around his very ample scrotum.

His lips and cheeks were heavily made up in red, and there were wilted flowers behind both his ears. Smead's prominent nose was an unhealthy shade of blue, and from it a substance had leaked down his chin and across the ruffles of his ill-fitting blouse. A crude attempt to apply mascara had added a chilling touch to his overall appearance.

Stoke's companions approached the corpse, shaking their heads with disbelief. "Who the devil is this?" asked Flint.

Branan laughed. "Your guess is as good as mine, He's certainly not Teriz, but what he is or was baffles me."

"And where are his breeches?"

"Were I to hazard a guess," said Branan, "I believe we would find his trousers somewhere beneath that mountain of shite in the other room."

"It takes all kinds to make up a world," added Auberge. "I've seen some that are similar back in Leith, but none quite like this clown. Look at that," he added suddenly, pointing between Smead's legs. "I wondered where I'd left my purse. Flint, would you mind bending over and retrieving that for me?"

"Not on your life," chuckled Ben. "Looks more like a saddlebag from here."

The trio's attention was drawn to the sound of a horse whinnying outside on the street. They clutched their weapons while keeping close to the walls. Stoke edged closer to a torn curtain and stared out into the square. The town centre certainly appeared to be empty.

The highlander waited for several minutes, listening to the beat of his heart, before deciding that it was safe to emerge from the building. "Keep low and to the shadows until we are certain that we're by ourselves."

Branan risked a quick glance through the partially open church doors. Across the street in front of Treacher's Grocery, a man was seated on the steps. He was loosening the collar about his neck while wiping his brow with a large handkerchief. His horse was hitched to a post on the right.

Stoke watched him for a few seconds and, deciding the man was alone, opened the door quietly and stepped slowly down the stairs and onto the street. Flint remained behind on the steps with his pistols at the ready, and Auberge positioned himself at the window. "Good day, sir," said Stoke, announcing himself.

The stranger, who was visible startled, scrambled to his feet. "And to you as well," he replied. "Do you live here sir?"

Branan replied, "I might well have asked you the very same question. I assume you are from elsewhere. May I ask your business in Dunradin?"

The short man paused and glanced toward the church. "I'm looking for someone."

"And who might that be?"

"A gentleman by the name of Stoke, Branan Stoke, "he replied.

Branan tried to conceal his surprise. "Indeed. What is your business with this Stoke fellow, and who are you?"

The stranger frowned and toyed with a pendant that hung from his neck. "My name is Crispin Fortune, and my business is of a private nature."

Branan's eyes were drawn to the medal at the end of chain around Fortunes rather fat neck. "Well, Mr. Crispin Fortune, I believe that were I to examine that trinket around your neck, it would prove you out as an agent of Victoria."

Crispin gasped. Stoke had reached into a pocket of his vest and produced a similar token. Each man had been given a small cross in royal blue with the letter V emblazoned at its centre. The highlander gripped Crispin's pudgy hand in a firm grip. "I am the man you seek."

-103-

Tam stayed by the fire while Ronan stepped away from the group with Salem. "Mark my words," she warned, "this man Douglas has his hand in everything. Deermuir is becoming a sterile factory of a town where individual expression is discouraged on a more regular basis than ever before."

Ronan nodded. "How is it a girl your age can be so well spoken?"

She grinned. "Education is very high on the list of priorities in Netherfield. Unfortunately so is a creeping form of subliminal brainwashing. The village has been populated by the brightest and whitest. My own parents suggested to me many times that one day all villages would be like Netherfield. Had I not developed a deformity, I'm quite sure that I would have bought into the big lie myself."

"So it's your contention that the Teriz miners number in excess of fifteen hundred?"

"Yes of course, it's common knowledge that the mine is filled with them," said Salem. "The mine generates a large income for the community, and the citizens are basically drunk on the promise of personal wealth and social status."

The young girl shook her head slowly. "I see the beginnings of it in Deermuir. They're being groomed for a similar fate. Netherfield was the model, created from nothing other than a hillside rich with coal and an understanding of the nature of greed. Ivan Douglas is a genius, but he's also a misguided bigot. He's brought prosperity to many, yet to many more he has brought only pain."

Salem felt a measure of relief, having been able to inform Ronan of the pestilence that was being visited upon them.

"I'm just one small person," she said. "What can I do?"

Macleary placed his hand on the young girl's shoulder. "It's possible that you may have just done more than many twice your size. I assure you that this news will open the eyes of some highly placed individuals who answer to the Queen herself."

"I will take some comfort in that knowledge," said Salem.

Coneys were not Tamlyn's favourite food, but he tucked into the hot meal enthusiastically. "You understand," commented Ronan as he sat to eat, "all of you would be welcome to shelter at Threstone, if you were to grow tired of these woods."

Young Brightfoot laughed. "I can just imagine the looks if you marched into your castle with all of us in tow. Ronan and his lad have gone off hunting, and look what they've returned with."

She laughed again, slapping her knee. "Pardon me," she said eventually, "we do appreciate your invitation, thank you, but we've grown very comfortable in these woods. Having said that, the day may come, and it's a comfort to be welcome anywhere."

Dennis applauded enthusiastically, while Old Donny rocked back and forth happily. "You can't have too many friends," said Jack, taking a piece of meat from Colin. The group sat by the fire chatting easily for the next hour, until Ronan suggested that he and Tamlyn take their leave. Both he and his son hoped that someday soon they would have the opportunity to return to Deermuir Forest, but for the time being Ronan felt particularly anxious to return to Threstone, given Salem's disturbing revelations. Salem walked her new friends to the edge of the trees and watched as they retraced the previous day's steps.

As much as he was inclined to hurry back to the castle, Ronan decided that he would show Tam how to use the crossbow. With any luck the pair might locate some autumn grouse or even pheasant before the day was done. The blacksmith was less concerned now with the odds of encountering any creepers, having covered the area once.

-104-

The group of four travellers decided to enter the parlour of Green's Guesthouse for a discussion. Green's was none the worse for a protracted period of neglect and remained comfortable despite the fact that it needed a good dusting. "Please," prompted Branan, "you can speak openly. My companions are completely trustworthy."

"As you are of course aware," began Crispin, "Her Majesty lost her husband to typhoid. Earlier this year the Queen was faced with the very tragic news that her son, Albert Edward, had fallen ill with the same disease. Miraculously, the Prince of Wales did not succumb to his illness and today enjoys good health. We have been blessed with the skills of a wonderful physician, a man with whom our gratitude shall be eternally linked."

Branan's eyes narrowed as Fortune continued. "What the public does not know, nor do many others beyond myself, is that the Prince was not and has never been ill with typhoid. Edward was indeed very ill, but the nature of his illness was beyond the understanding of the Queen's subjects, and had the details of his malady been divulged, the result would have been mass confusion and mayhem."

Flint leaned forward, intrigued with the conversation's direction.

"Being men of the world, I am sure you have been aware of the rumours of Edward's infidelities and appetites." Edward was in the habit of visiting a woman by the name of Alice Kendall. "If you will excuse my bluntness, I must refer to their affair in common terms, as there is frankly no way to be delicate. Mrs. Kendall, who often entertained the Prince at her home, planned a surprise for her lover one evening and procured the services of a prostitute, who was invited into their bed. The three"—he paused, searching for a word—"shall we say, participants, spent the night together. At some point during the evening, Edward had carnal knowledge of both women and was bitten on the side of his stomach by the prostitute, in a rather playful but fierce manner."

"Perfectly acceptable," remarked Auberge, smiling until Fortune shot him a disapproving glance.

"Blood had been drawn, and within days the Prince fell ill." Stoke began to see where the story was going, and shook his head in amazement. Fortune continued, "Later, Edward's physician was witness to a most bizarre incident in the gardens of Buckingham Palace, which involved, on two occasions, the Prince consuming live animals, first a ground squirrel and then a pigeon. You can imagine the horror of the situation and the difficulties faced by the good doctor, who was put in the position of having to explain Edward's sickness to the Queen. Her Majesty simply refused to believe that anything so dreadful as this disease of the blood was possible, and it took a great deal of discussion to convince the Queen otherwise.

"Edward was cured with a procedure which involved the replacement of his blood. It was a dangerous experiment that saved his life, but not practical on a large scale. It was also very costly.

"The prostitute was located and taken to a private sanatorium where she could be observed. The observations were astounding. The young woman had a voracious appetite for raw meat and appeared to suffer greatly when she was deprived of it. It was clear that she had infected the Prince with her bite. Furthermore, by her own admission it was discovered that she was not the only one of her kind. The truth of these miserable creatures' existence was finally revealed to the Queen, who, it would prove, had enough compassion to set in motion a search for solutions to deal with the problem. This is where you came into the story."

"Yes," agreed Stoke, "I was contacted and hired on behalf of Her Majesty to eradicate what was believed to be a relatively small number of what came to be known as the Teriz."

"Her Majesty has been desirous of learning your whereabouts and whether your task is being accomplished. You understand, London is a city filled with rumour and intrigue, and there are suggestions in some circles that the situation may have gotten out of hand. There are few men that the Queen still trusts, and quite frankly I believe she is at her wits' end with worry. In short, I expect that nothing less than a full report from you will suffice."

"I'm afraid," replied Branan, "that what I intend to relay to you will do nothing to lessen Her Majesty's concern. Through no fault of my own, the situation has deteriorated at an alarming rate, and in all likelihood, it may prove necessary to involve the army—despite the risk of inciting panic."

Branan pointed a thumb over his shoulder. "I have been on the other side of the river, where there are perhaps a thousand of these creatures. They emerge at night, building road and tunnel, which will eventually connect Turfmoor, a neighbouring village, to the very hill upon which this guesthouse sits."

Crispin Fortune paled at the suggestion and cleared his throat nervously.

Branan continued, "There have been virtually no rumours in Edinburgh regarding what is afoot, but very soon I believe the news will filter through to Glasgow and points north. My men at Threstone are already missing their families and we will need replacements before the end of winter. I urge you to speak with the Queen and implore her to consider marshalling all the available soldiers. It's time that this scourge was eliminated with force."

Crispin chewed his knuckles thoughtfully, pondering a response. Branan gave Auberge an odd smile. "Toulouse, would you be willing to escort our friend Crispin here to London?" he asked.

"If you wish," he replied, looking mildly flattered.

"It's very important that he reach the Queen as quickly as possible and in perfect health."

"Yes I can understand why."

Toulouse turned to Crispin. "Is that nag out there capable of any speed?"

"Yes, I suppose," answered Fortune, "but there is one horse, and we are two?"

Branan interrupted. "There may be a wagon at the smithy. We have no time to retrieve an extra mount from the castle." The highlander took note that Crispin looked rather ill at ease. "Don't let Auberge's manner put you off. He looks bloody strange, but he has a heart of gold. You may find his dangerous appearance useful in intimidating your enemies." Fortune still looked apprehensive. "For God's sake, put the man to some use while he's at your disposal," he added.

-105-

A cold fog was rolling in from the moors as Felicia stepped from the door. Then she froze in fear at the sight that greeted her. She dropped her blanket, and at the same instant lost control of her bladder. Steam rose up from the hot urine that ran down the inside of her thighs.

Duke, her large hound lay beneath the window chewing on the remains of a human leg. Blood had trickled from the dog's mouth and was congealing between the toes of the foot. Below Duke, in the morning frost, footprints were visible leading towards the barn. The young woman began to shake uncontrollably.

She snatched up her blanket and whispered in a voice hoarse with fear, "No, Duke!" As she spun back into the room and bolted the door, she realized what she'd seen. The intruder had left the prints of two feet. She leaned with her back against the door and continued to shake. Whose leg was Duke making a meal of, and who was in the barn?

She could hear the big animal ripping meat from the long bone, and now the baby was stirring in the cradle, a small pink arm waving uncertainly in the air, with a gurgle and a morning grin appearing on its small face. Felicia, suddenly fearing for the safety of her little girl, ran to the cradle and picked up the baby. Then she nestled her close as she crossed the room quickly and dashed up the short staircase to her tiny attic. She lay down on the wooden floor and curled into a ball, pulling the baby within.

She needed time to reason things out. There was presumably a dangerous stranger in her barn, one who had possibly killed and dismembered another person, all while she slept. And why had she not heard Duke sounding the alarm?

Beginning to panic, she did a quick mental inventory of anything that might pass for a weapon in her home. There was a pitchfork in the barn, leaned against the inside of the door. In a kitchen drawer below, she had a sizeable knife, and there was the poker by the fireplace. Perhaps if she stayed right where she was, the intruder would simply leave. She imagined entering the barn with a knife in one hand and a poker in the other. Perhaps, she pondered, if she had Duke with her—but he would be very reluctant to leave his feeding, unless of course she was in obvious danger. On the other hand, she considered, it might be wiser to coerce Duke into entering the house, where he would guard baby Katherine.

Finally, she screwed up her courage and decided that there was only one answer. She had no options outside of a confrontation. Felicia took a deep breath—and remained frozen where she lay. *This is foolish,* she thought. *I will count to ten, and then I will act.*

At ten, she decided to continue counting to fifty. At forty-nine she rose to her feet, carefully tucked her baby into a corner of the room, and crept down the stairs to the front door. Duke's tail wagged as she approached. Fighting the urge to run back into the house, she stepped rapidly to where the dog lay and gripped the errant leg around the ankle. Then she turned, dashed through the door, and threw the gruesome trophy across the floor. Duke, hot on her heels, followed his prize inside with equal speed.

Felicia wiped her hands on her skirt with disgust. She retreated to the kitchen and located the large knife, then made her way to the door, before remembering the poker. As an afterthought, she slipped on her heavy coat. Duke, imagining that it was time to go walking, rose from his feeding and ambled toward the young woman.

"No, Duke, stay!" she commanded and latched the door behind her. Katherine would be safe now, with the big dog on guard in the front room.

Her eyes lifted to the barn and she hesitated again, gripping the poker tightly. The fog had thickened, and the air had grown colder. She held the large knife behind her back and went forward. Reaching the door, she paused, listening intently for any sign of movement within. Then she mustered up enough courage to place her eye at the gap in the door.

It was a small barn, built mainly to house one horse, with an area for hay storage. The rear section opened onto a fenced exit to the pasture where two cows wandered. In stormy weather, they sheltered in the back of the barn.

Felicia saw nothing unusual about the interior. Both the cows and her horse seemed to be at the back, as the stall was empty. She looked backwards over her shoulder, and hesitated, wondering if she should approach the barn from behind. The view to the inside would be better, but she would be exposing herself to anyone that might be watching from within. If her animals were standing about in the fog, they might be spooked as she crept invisibly towards the back of the building.

She would have to risk sliding the front doors open as quietly as possible. She knew that it wouldn't be soundless, but her heart still stopped as the creak seemed to register like a scream across the dry ground of the interior. She froze for a full twenty seconds, listening for any sound within, before sliding the door open another two inches. Still nothing was visible inside, so she opened the door further and slipped into the building. She crouched close to the ground, failing to notice that the pitchfork was absent.

The open door threw a beam of daylight across the floor, and Felicia wondered if it would be wise to close it behind her. No point in complicating an escape route, she decided. Nothing foreign broke through the smell of fresh hay and manure to indicate an intruder, but she was aware of her own scent, a pungent mix of body odours that spelled intense fear. Surely man or beast hidden in the shadows could smell her approach. She stood up and raised the poker to her shoulder. There was no loft in the barn to be concerned with, and the only area that offered concealment was on her right-hand side.

She tucked the knife into the belt of her coat and raised the iron poker above her head with both hands. Stepping shakily around the corner, she stopped suddenly. A large black shadow was visible through the fog.

It moved into the mist and vanished quickly. Felicia spun on her heel, staring at the empty spot where her saddle was usually kept. Her fear vanished with the onset of anger as she threw down her weapon with a curse. The bastard had stolen her horse. Somewhere in the distance, across the meadow, a lonesome church bell tolled, adding to the emptiness of the barn, and her eyes filled with tears, a sign of both frustration and relief.

Leaving the barn, she noticed that the pitchfork was not in its accustomed spot either. As the sun began to burn away the fog, she remembered that someone out there was still missing the leg which lay on her kitchen floor. With an innate sense of practicality, she decided it had to be taken from Duke and left as far away in the moors as possible. She would find some fresh treat to bribe him with, before disposing of the rotting limb. Her first priority of course was Katherine, and she quickly returned to the attic. The baby wrinkled up her nose as she arrived and began to cry. "Yes, yes, Mother's here. Let's feed you, my little darling."

Baby Katherine had been named after Felicia's great grandmother Katherine Hollis. All that she knew of her ancestor was what her mother, Lizzy, had told her. Grandmother Katherine was rumoured to have been a witch, whose husband had died in some long-forgotten war. The family supposed that she was regarded as such merely because she lived by herself on the outskirts of town with a child whose father could not be accounted for.

Felicia, on the other hand, who identified with her great grandmother's romantic story, had been abandoned by a very live husband who bolted at the suggestion of fatherhood. She preferred being by herself and had considered his leaving a blessing. Felicia often imagined that her great grandmother, as a single woman, had faced many of the same challenges that she had, and in all likelihood life had been much more difficult for her.

Felicia's mother, Lizzy Drew, had been taken from her parents at a very young age. She was told by a young woman in the orphanage that her father's name was Axel Hollis, but that was all she knew of her own parents. Later in life she made the discovery that Axel's mother had been named Katherine. Lizzy never spoke of the orphanage in any detail, only referring to it as "that place," and Felicia understood that she must never ask about it.

After Baby Katherine was fed, Felicia located a length of fabric in her front room and searched her kitchen for a treat that might entice Duke. She decided a piece of bread with honey spread on it would be appealing enough. The hound was more than happy to follow his nose to the door after the young woman wiped some of the honey on his snout. "Off you go, boy," she commanded, closing the door behind him quickly.

She hesitated before, the leg, transfixed by the grisly sight. It was unnaturally white and barely resembled anything that had once been attached to a living being. Duke had devoured most of the flesh, leaving bone, sinew, and a foot with five horrid toes. The nails were long and filthy, and she held her breath while wrapping the leg up and placing it above her fireplace.

The moors were not a safe place to wander in the fog, especially when there was someone out there carrying a pitchfork and riding a stolen horse, so Felicia waited until the skies cleared before starting out. Little Katherine was happy enough, with the rhythm of her mother's stride, as the young woman made her way across the fields. She had strapped the baby comfortably to her chest, while carrying the other bundle under one arm. Duke, who had not been invited along, remained at home behind a latched door.

When Felicia was far enough from the cottage and close to the river, she scrambled down a rocky embankment and heaved the leg as far into the water as she could manage. "That's that," she said quietly to the baby, who giggled in response. A muskrat rolled over at the splash and sank beneath the water to investigate.

Felicia pondered the loss of her horse as she returned home. The pony was her only link to Deermuir where she occasionally travelled to trade in the market. This probably meant she would have to sell one of the cows for another horse. The prospect of walking all the way to Deermuir with a cow tired her. *Damn that thief,* she thought. *Of course I could have been murdered in my bed or worse.*

She would mention the theft to the constabulary for all the good it would do. For some reason the officials in Deermuir seemed to have adopted a chilly attitude towards outsiders, and she felt that there were fewer familiar faces in town lately.

The matter of the leg was somewhat more disturbing. She could not imagine a rational explanation for it. There was always the chance that Duke had stumbled upon a fresh burial, but it was very unlikely. Maybe it came up from the bog down by the lower creek. Someone may have fallen in, but in that case an entire body would have surfaced, not just a leg. In any event she had disposed of it now and wouldn't mention the matter to anyone.

-106-

"The trick lies in managing the pull on this bow. Once it's cocked, you can carry it across your shoulder, primed to fire."

Ronan handed the weapon to his son. "The most important thing to remember is to not point it at anyone or anything that you don't intend to shoot. Try for that tree trunk, Son." The youngster levelled the weapon and sighted the tree. Ronan reached over and adjusted his aim. "Remember to aim a little low. The bow will kick up as it releases the bolt."

The arrow whistled through the air and struck the tree with a thud. "Good shot!" Tam grinned widely, as his father twisted the bolt from the wood and examined its point carefully. "Always retrieve your ammunition when possible." He placed the bolt back in the quiver. "Also, if you're shooting for distance, aim an arm's length above the target. The arrow will arc high as it starts and drop down to the level of your prey."

Tamlyn looked up at his father with concern. "It's not very good news, is it?"

"What's that?" asked Ronan, fairly sure of what his son meant.

"What Salem spoke about."

Ronan took the crossbow and slung it across his own back. "No, it's not good news. This Netherfield business is very disturbing. It would probably be best if you didn't share any of this with the others just yet. Branan will find it very interesting, and I'm sure he'll have some advice as to how we should proceed. Let's not concern ourselves with it for the time being. Look here, the sun is coming out. Let's keep our eyes open for birds."

Despite the sunshine, it was a cold day. As they crossed the fields towards Threstone, there was less snow on the ground. The air was crisp and still, etching the landscape with a clarity that allowed every rock and blade of grass to stand out on its own. Ronan had decided that they should return by a different route where the land rose and fell along an old creek, in the hopes of encountering wild game.

It wasn't long before they came across a thicket filled with ringnecks. The brightly coloured males were feeding along the edge of a stand of gorse. Tamlyn reached for his sling and downed one almost at once. They stalked the large nye of pheasant wordlessly as the prey took to air and settled a number of times. Four was a very good number for an hour's hunt, and Ronan soon strung the birds to a sturdy cutting of poplar that he carried across his shoulders. He passed the crossbow to Tamlyn and the pair headed again in the direction of the castle.

After travelling for a while, Ronan suggested they stop and rest. He laid the birds on the ground and lifted his arm to shield the sun from his eyes. Something in the distance glinted for an instant as the sun bounced off its surface. Far across the plain a small black form moved quickly. "Can you see anything over that way, Tam?" asked Ronan, pointing to the west.

"It's a horse," he replied, "moving very quickly."

"And a rider?"

"Yes, there's someone in the saddle all right, with something bright like metal. Whoever it is, they're not heading towards us, but it seems they're going in the same direction we are."

Later as they approached Threstone, just as the sun was vanishing behind the far hills to the west, Tamlyn spotted another animal briefly silhouetted in a circle of light. It was difficult to tell how far away the wolf was, and the mournful howl echoed from hill to hill confusing the listener who may have gotten the impression that several of the creatures prowled the area.

-107-

A wagon was located at Ronan's stable and hitched to Crispin's horse, who looked mostly uninterested at the prospect of pulling a cart. It was loaded with empty barrels to give the two gentlemen an appearance of normality on the road south to Carlisle.

Before setting off for the castle, Branan took Toulouse aside and reiterated the importance of seeing that Crispin Fortune be delivered safely to the Queen. "A great deal depends on it," he said. "I'm most anxious to know Her Majesty's response, so please don't dally on the way back. Buy a fast animal and apply the whip. I'll take it out of my own wages."

Stoke bade them farewell, and they left Dunradin at once, going out past the old barricade. They came at once to a dairy farm on the right which appeared to have been completely pillaged with not a cow in sight.

Before long they were out in the rambling lowlands approaching the coastal road to the border. The air was different here, perfumed with a salty mix of breaking waves and kelp beds. Soon they would have to turn inland again towards Carlisle, where they could arrange passage to London.

Eventually, Toulouse suggested to Crispin that he hand over the reins and try to rest. "You can spell me off when I tire," he offered.

"I am fine," Fortune replied. "Take the reins if you wish, but I can't sleep on this bumpy road." In truth, he didn't trust this man of colour and was afraid to let his guard down.

"As you like," said Toulouse. "I am bound by my word to protect you, even at my own risk. If you didn't regard me as a heathen black devil, you would probably be more comfortable."

Crispin frowned. "I assure you sir that your colouring is of no consequence to me. Your manner of dress and your distinct odour also have no bearing on my opinion of you. Your Scottish and French descent and your speech peppered with profanities, none of that matters a whit either. I am simply unaccustomed to travelling with strangers."

"You don't trust me," said Auberge.

"Only as far as I can throw you," came the reply.

Toulouse broke into laughter. The image of this fat little man throwing anyone was ludicrous. "I'll tell you what," he laughed. "You keep a close eye on me, and I'll watch you like an eagle."

-108-

The black horse climbed the hill easily. Its rider was bent over in the saddle, gripping a devilish trident in his claw like hand. His gaunt, unshaven face was pale and shiny with sweat, despite the frigid air that swirled about him. The dark eyes, resting deep in their sockets, belonged to a man in the throes of a heavy fever.

The dark spectre raised his arm in the air, thrusting the pitchfork toward the clouds. "I am Dorian Euther de Faustine, and I command you to rain!" A flashing vein of white broke the clouds and struck a large branch above Euther's head, setting the limb ablaze. His horse reared, almost toppling him from the saddle.

Euther laughed crazily as he struggled to regain control of the beast., then slid from the mount and fastened the reins to a lower branch. Falling to the ground, he tore at his hair and began to sob uncontrollably. Clearly he was teetering on the brink of madness. The old villain was thirsty. Thirsty for water and companionship, but mostly thirsty for the relief he had found with the white powders. His body heaved with cries of despair, and his knuckles pounded at the dry soil covering the roots of the big tree.

The clouds finally broke, and an icy curtain of rain fell across Dorian's wasted body, quickly soaking his clothing through. He opened his mouth wide and closed his eyes as the heavy drops of water broke against his forehead.

Brother Michael, feeding his chickens, had seen the flash of lightning across the moors and heard the frightened horse. As he peered through the sudden rain, the young monk could make out the small hillock where the animal was sheltering and decided that the beast was in need of rescue.

His small cottage was home to a number of rescued animals, including dogs, cats, birds, and rabbits. In his manner of thinking, they were all God's creatures, and there was always room for more, even if there was very little more than a tiny sleeping area left for himself.

He tightened the rope around his robe, and pulled a hood over his shorn head. He picked up his long staff and set out towards the big tree in the distance. Brother Michael's sandals were not well suited for walking any distance, and he soon scolded himself for being so impulsive.

As he drew closer to the hill, the monk realized that someone lay beneath the tree next to the horse. He picked up his pace, despite objections from his aching feet, and was soon climbing the slope that led to the large tree. An emaciated-looking individual lay on the ground, with his feet stretched out in front of him, and his hands in his lap. He appeared to have been ill for a long time. Brother Michael wondered if he had arrived too late and stumbled upon a gentleman who would very soon require burying.

He reached down and lifted the limp body easily, then turned it over and laid it across the saddle. The horse snorted and stamped one foot. "There, there, my friend, we must all do our part." He stroked the animal's mane in a comforting manner.

The young monk was concerned that the old man's body would slip from the horse as they left the hillock, so he removed his rope belt and tied one end around Euther's hands, then pulled it beneath the animal's belly and wound it securely around his boots. In this fashion he led the animal back over the stony ground towards his cottage. As they approached the small building, the rain slackened and soon halted altogether.

-109-

Murdoch and Liam had taken a post on the landing above Threstone's entrance and were scanning the darkening hills, when Liam suddenly pointed into the failing light beyond. "There they are. Let's go greet them."

"Well, hello," said Ronan, lowering the brace of pheasant to the ground "you're just in time to relieve me of this burden." He stretched his back and groaned. "My shoulders are sore."

"The hunting was good," said Tamlyn excitedly. "We bagged two each, three ringnecks and a female."

The two older boys lifted the birds, admiring the fine take "All is well then?" asked Murdoch.

"We are fine," answered Ronan. "There is much to be discussed, but it can wait until morning. Has Branan returned?"

He has," replied Liam, "and will wish to speak with you as well, I'll warrant."

Ronan turned to Murdoch. "And your mother; how is she?"

Murdoch smiled. "Mother is fine and hopes that you've brought something to cook."

Tamlyn stuck his tongue out and poked his older brother in the chest. "Pheasant pie and wild berries for you, my lad!"

Then he suddenly remembered what he had wanted to tell Murdoch all day. "I've learned to use Cay's crossbow," he boasted.

"And he's not a bad shot," added Ronan.

"Well, I guess you will have to school me in that matter," replied Murdoch, taking a mock swing at his brother's head. "I'm glad to see you both back safe."

The hunters were pleased to be home and, despite being hungry, were chiefly in need of warmth and sleep. Ceana had, with forethought, seen that a pot of hot cider was waiting by the fire and reacted excitedly when Ronan and Tam were escorted in with their take of game. She insisted that they have a hot drink with black biscuits before they slept.

They spoke of the hunting and the rider that they'd seen in the distance, and Tamlyn recounted the tale of his bowmanship, but neither of them mentioned Salem and her odd friends. Charlotte was pleased to see her father and brother and made Tamlyn swear that he would take her along next time.

"There is more snow on the ground to the east," said Ronan. "It won't be long before we feel the lash of winter here. We must make preparations very soon, and I think we'll need to hunt more often now. We could have brought more game back had we thought to take a packhorse with us. Tam and I could have bagged twice the number, but we couldn't have carried them the distance."

Not much later, as Ronan joined his wife in bed, she ran her hand across his chest and spoke softly. "So tell me now, how are the citizens of Deermuir doing?"

He was flabbergasted. "You knew! Then our subterfuge was pointless?"

"Don't you men know that we women talk amongst ourselves? I appreciate that you wanted to spare my feelings, but I'm going to worry regardless of what you keep from me."

"Well, I feel a little foolish now," he admitted.

"And so you should," she teased.

"Everything will be fine," he lied. "I'll tell you more after I've slept." Within ten minutes Ceana was digging an elbow into Ronan's back to silence his snoring.

On the other side of the castle, Alfie sat by the fire with his head in his hands. "I'm not angry with you Tam, really. I'm sorry, I've just been feeling very odd lately, I canna explain it."

The young boy appeared seriously remorseful, which confused Tamlyn, because as far as he knew Alfie had done nothing wrong. As he put his arm across the youngster's shoulder, and attempted to comfort him, young Gamble broke into tears. "I told them your name," he sobbed.

"Told who?" asked Tamlyn, confused. Murdoch looked up from the fire, very concerned.

"I don't know who they are, but I hear them in the dungeon, talking. I'm sorry." Tamlyn looked over to his brother, shaking his head slowly.

"How about you both go to sleep," suggested Murdoch, "and in the morning we'll go speak to Grandfather about it."

Tamlyn's eyelids had grown heavy, and he pulled the blanket close and edged closer to Alfie. Murdoch got to his feet and arranged his own blanket around the two youngsters, then stood by the fire and warmed his hands. He would speak to Tyburn in the morning.

-110-

"Take a look at this map," said Douglas. "Here is Turfmoor, where presumably your Teriz in Dunradin have almost finished tunnelling. Here is Deermuir, and we are here in Netherfield."

Pengrove noticed that the four villages formed the corners of a square.

"Everything is as it should be here in Netherfield. Deermuir is being cleansed, and Turfmoor has been emptied and readied for repopulation. Dorian's high ideals got in the way in Dunradin, and he didn't succeed with his plans. In fact he failed miserably. Had he managed to contain the citizens, there would be feed for the growing number of Teriz marshalled at the quarry. Instead, our man Dafyd was killed before he could turn Euther to our way of thinking, and every citizen of Dunradin has escaped. God only knows whether any of them have raised the alarm elsewhere.

"This must be our chief concern. Right here," he said, tracing the walls of castle Threstone which lay at the centre of the square. "Every man woman and child must be captured and brought to the Dunradin quarry. There is absolutely no room for error this time. The very youngest will be brought here for re-education, and anyone capable of a complaint will be repackaged as food." Ivan Douglas paused to collect his thoughts.

"Are you suggesting that I postpone my return to Dunradin?" asked Pengrove.

"Yes, but only briefly, leave Hume and his brother in place there for the time being. I want you here one more day. I'm going to ask you to help me select three hundred of the most powerful miners we have, for an assault on the castle." He pointed to the map again. "There's a great deal of open ground on either side of Threstone, and it's protected from the rear by water. The most logical approach would be here from the forest, wouldn't you agree?"

"That's just where they would expect an attack, and they will build their defences at the front. What if an attack was mounted from the trees followed by an attack from the water?"

Douglas sized up Wallace before answering. "The frontal attack as a diversion, or perhaps an assault from the water, followed by an advance from the forest might work."

"Yes," answered Pengrove enthusiastically, "a boatload or more of archers, but are there bowmen at our disposal?"

"We would not require many. An attack under cover of darkness, with flaming projectiles, would be very effective, driving them from the castle into our arms."

"What sort of timeline are you thinking of?" asked Pengrove.

Douglas rubbed his hands together. "I will introduce you to the council this evening, and we'll put it to a vote. Everything in Netherfield is democratic, you understand."

Yes indeed, thought Wallace, *unless of course you disagree with the leader*. He didn't labour under the illusion that freedom of speech was the foundation upon which Ivan Douglas's town had been built. He was sure that the council members were well versed in the leader's dogma and wouldn't dream of straying from the path. The entire town consisted of well-bred, highly educated sheep who were convinced that they were the best that society had to offer the new world.

"Wallace, if I appear somewhat histrionic at times, it's because we are on the brink of massive changes for the better. And please understand, I bear no ill will against the people of Scotland. It is merely their misfortune to be located in the geographic position that is most beneficial to our cause. All the riffraff and unholy scum that dwell beneath the border can be relocated here and made into one of two things. They can be reborn into the glory of God, or they can simply become grist for the mill. The choice will be up to them. The law of nature will once again be balanced.

"Certainly some individuals, indeed hundreds, will be beyond hope of redemption, but just imagine you were one of those poor lost souls, who was told you no longer had to suffer in this lifetime, that you were finally being offered an opportunity to be involved in real positive change. When they are assured of a place in heaven, they'll leap into the pits!"

Ivan remained fired up at the council later that day. Pengrove was astounded at the size and modern look of the chapel. The room was designed like nothing he had ever seen. The ceiling was angled from the three entrance doors, rising to a high peak above the simple white lectern. Ornate trappings, such as one would find in churches or cathedrals to the south, were nowhere in evidence. Everything was clean, white, and very straightforward. Behind the podium and spanning the width of the room was a long table upon which a single row of lit candles stretched from wall to wall.

Douglas was dressed in a simple white shirt and cream-colored trousers. He sat to the side of his lectern in a relaxed manner, as though he were addressing a small group of friends. Row upon row of curving church pews filled the rest of the room, and every seat appeared to be occupied.

The buzz of conversation ended abruptly as Ivan rose to speak. This was not a church service, so Douglas stood before his chair, one hand on the table as he spoke.

"Hello friends. I ask you to imagine the future tonight, to imagine, if you can, a great storm." Douglas bowed his head and put his palms together. He remained that way for seconds. The room was silent with anticipation.

"Envision a great wave building in the English Channel, a massive wall of water that rears up and smashes against the coast, pushing its way across England, taking with it all the dirt and refuse of London and all the other large cities—all the centuries-old filth and corruption that have settled into the very soil of Britain, mile upon mile of vermin writhing in a vile discharge of crime and sin, all washed forward over the border to the centre of a massive strainer."

Douglas spun his wrist in a circular motion, mimicking the sound and motion of a drain. He paused again for effect. "As the storm abates, everything is bathed in a golden light of sunshine and prosperity." He clasped his hands behind his back, bowed slightly from the waist, and lowered his voice. "This is your future, and all it requires are three simple things." He counted them off on his fingers: "Diligence, trust, and faith."

He continued on for some time in this fashion, raising his voice to drive home an important point, and lowering it to insure that he had his audience's complete attention. Pengrove watched as Douglas moved his hands through the air like a conductor directing the thoughts of his citizens in a fascinating display of charismatic power that bordered on mass hypnosis.

-111-

Branan and Ben had made it back to the castle with no further incident, deciding that it would be best to return without exploring Dunradin any further. They rose early, anxious to speak with Ronan. Murdoch, who had been present more and more often when matters of importance were discussed, joined Tyburn and his father in the large tent.

After Branan recounted their journey to Dunradin and the chance meeting with Crispin Fortune, Ronan described the woods outside Deermuir and the startling revelations that Salem Brightfoot had shared.

Stoke was extremely alarmed. The disclosure of events in Netherfield meant that the number of Teriz was easily thrice his recent estimations. He briefly considered intercepting Crispin and Toulouse, or perhaps travelling to London himself. "Damnation!" he exclaimed. "I should have gone myself to the Queen, had I only been aware of this sooner."

Tyburn reminded him that, had Ronan and his son not been discovered by this Brightfoot person, they would yet be unaware of this buildup of Teriz, let alone the very existence of Netherfield.

"This is most disquieting," said the doctor. "The individual who controls this phantom town Netherfield surely is aware that an entire settlement cannot go unnoticed for long, which leads me to believe that we are in grave danger. I would not be surprised to find that an attack on other villages, and perhaps even ourselves, is being mapped out at this moment."

"I suggest we redouble our efforts in the matter of fortifications!" shouted John Macintosh.

"Aye!" agreed his brother.

All present were in accord, and Ronan proposed that every able body be put to the task. "But let's not run about digging holes everywhere; we need planning."

Donald Macintosh coughed crisply. "What think you of tunnelling into the woods, far enough that if we are to face an assault from the trees, we might rise up behind them for a counterattack?"

"In my opinion, we can use the forest to our advantage in several ways, such as pit traps and snares," answered Ronan, shedding his jacket. The blacksmith rolled up his sleeves and took a seat at the table where Macintosh had laid out maps.

Murdoch turned to leave, under the impression that Tyburn was tied up in important matters. "Murdoch, what do you think of all this?" The old man placed an arm around his grandson and steered him towards the exit of the tent.

"I'm not sure what to think. I suppose it's both frightening and exciting at the same time."

"Well, it seems these matters come around every third or fourth generation, and we're in the unhappy position of having to indulge in the act of warfare. It certainly seems inevitable now." Murdoch shrugged. "You have something else on your mind, unless I'm mistaken?"

"I do, Grandfather. I wonder if you might have time to speak with our young friend Alfie. He's acting incredibly strange. Tam and I are really quite worried about him. He talks about voices in his head, and he's certainly not very cheerful."

Tyburn looked concerned. "He's the wee fellow who lost his mother, as I recall. Yes, I'd be happy to have a look at him right now. Just let me get my bag, and we'll see to him." Macleary located his satchel and they headed back across the field to the castle.

Once they were inside, locating the youngster proved difficult. He was not at the fire, nor was he with his grandmother.

"I think I might know where he is." Tamlyn had joined the search, and hoped his hunch was right. There was no reason that the small room at the base of Threstone's third tower had not been used as a sleeping quarter, aside from the fact that it was a dungeon. Superstition about such rooms kept the castle's occupants from contemplating the practicality of using it for lodging. Otherwise, it would make a very private area to spend the night.

Tam was the only one who had expressed a serious aversion towards entering the room, but he guided the others there in the hopes of finding Alfie. He stood back from the group, nervously wringing his hands while Murdoch led the way.

Padraic's little dog Chowder stood at the door growling, the hackles rising on his narrow back. Tam whistled for him, and the animal backed away from the steps with his tail between his legs. Paddy, who had heard that dogs were particularly sensitive to the presence of ghosts, picked up his frightened pet and gave him a comforting hug.

"It's empty!" called Murdoch from inside the dungeon. He and Liam emerged and closed the door behind them.

"No sign that anyone's spent any time in there," said Twist. "I would've placed coin on that call, Tam. Where could he have gone?"

The doctor ran his tongue across his teeth, and took a deep breath. "I think I had better send some highlanders into the woods right away."

Murdoch had a thought. "Liam, come with me, we'll have a quick check in the moat, in case he's just bathing." The two older boys went off to circle the perimeter of the castle.

"Here's hoping he hasn't drowned," said Liam when they were out of earshot of Tam and Paddy.

"I'll wager he's gone mad and run off," Murdoch conjectured. "Grandma Gamble will worry herself sick, I'm afraid, just like my mom did when Tam was missing."

"You should send your mother over to sit with her," suggested Liam.

-112-

A group of thirteen former villagers entered the council tent. Amongst them was Virgil Mason the dairyman, Corb Macneil, Raine Waters, and the barkeep, Ezekiel Bardwyck, who appeared to be the group's spokesperson.

Ronan, who had just been apprised of the situation with young Alfie, looked up from the table, with concern etched on his face. "Hello, Zeke, Virgil, what can I do for you?"

"Well, I'll tell ya," said Ezekiel in his familiar slow drawl. "Me and tother fellows here, speaking for our kin as well, are a little anxious to know when we might be getting back to town. From what we hear, the creepers have left the town empty, and with winter moving in, we're all of us inclined to be taking our chances back in our own homes."

Ronan looked disappointed. "Threstone is not a prison. I'd be happy to discuss your concerns, but please, gentlemen, if I might ask for your assistance on a very pressing matter, we're missing one of our children, and your help would be much appreciated."

Macleary went on to explain how Alfred Gamble had vanished and went on to remind the group that Alfie was an orphan living through very difficult circumstances, just as they were. Ronan knew that his visitors were all reasonable men who would put their concerns aside for the time being.

There had obviously been some dissent among the villagers, and they had settled on Zeke as their voice. It was only natural, after a time span in which they had lived shoulder to shoulder with little or no privacy, to feel that returning to their homes was a better option.

Some or all of the thirteen had forgotten that a large percentage of Threstone's population, who had lived below the town, no longer had homes to return to. Ronan reminded them of this point before asking for their help in scouring the fields around the castle.

"The highlanders are combing the woods now, and seeing as you are able-bodied gentlemen, who are apparently well organized, I would be most grateful if you would search the banks along the water to the rear of the castle." After some shuffling and murmuring, they all came to agreement.

Virgil Mason stood with the trace of a smirk on his long face. He had questioned on more than one occasion the ease with which the Maclearys had acquired a leadership role in the community of misplaced Dunradins. Portus Treacher had been the closest thing to a mayor for many years, and after his murder, the Macleary clan had more or less dictated what manner of voice sufficed for law in the village.

Virgil had never been overly fond of old Doc Tyburn, and not so quietly suggested that the doctor's past had contributed to the situation that he and the other townsfolk faced. To his way of thinking, had these Teriz leaders not been acquainted with Macleary, they might never have targeted Dunradin.

Virgil, more than any of them, now resented what he considered a delay in the hearing of their concerns. The little nuisance of a child was from Turfmoor anyway and no doubt was having a bit of fun at their expense.

He left with the others, who didn't perceive Ronan's tone as dismissive, the way he did. Virgil's cousin placed a hand on the back of his neck, which Mason shrugged off. "Okay let's look for the boy, but this isn't over."

Godwyn and Duncan both decided to speak with Ronan about Mason discreetly. For the time being they decided to stay close to the castle in the event that Alfie's disappearance was an orchestrated move to draw the troops off, leaving the others unprotected,

Such was the growing sense of imminent danger amongst the men that the seeds of paranoia had taken root and were unwittingly being nourished by overactive imaginations.

This was not the first time that Godwyn had been aware of the dairy farmer's mood. He knew very well that Virgil mistrusted him because of his former affiliation with Euther. The big Norseman had tried to ease Mason's concerns by being friendly towards him, but this only seemed to deepen Virgil's mistrust and Blunt soon left things as they were.

For the most part Godwyn was regarded as an enemy of the Teriz by everyone, but he understood that some would always wonder to what degree he had been responsible for the obvious atrocities committed across the river. It was generally believed that he had left in protest of the wrongdoings, and most were now aware that he had slain one of the leaders in the process. For this, he was afforded a small degree of respect, which translated into tolerance; still others close to him had come to regard Godwyn as a genuine friend.

For this, the big man was most grateful and quite humbled. He felt as though he had been adopted by the community, and had some time ago made the decision not to carry on towards the south and beyond. He felt a kinship with the burly highlanders and had become fast friends with Duncan and Woodruff.

"Virgil is becoming troublesome," said Duncan.

Godwyn agreed readily. "Mr. Mason puts me in mind of a weasel with his shifty ways. How would you suggest we deal with him?"

"Keep the man busy and close at hand," suggested Duncan. "A man with a modicum of power cannot easily hide."

"I'll speak to Ronan," said Godwyn. "We could place Virgil in charge of horse milking!" he added with a loud burst of laughter.

Duncan grinned broadly. "I respect Mason less than my horses; perhaps he and his cousins should form a mobile guard unit to patrol the water."

"Good idea. I wonder if he can swim."

-113-

Auberge tilted the hat to the back of his head. "I propose we make for Leeds."

Fortune looked irritated. "And why would we wish to do that?"

Toulouse placed his hand on the little man's shoulder. "The sleeping car! The GNR runs a line from Leeds to London. Just imagine sleeping and travelling at the same time."

Crispin had to admit that sleep would offer a delicious escape from Auberge's constant chatter. It seemed as though the big man from Edinburgh had an opinion on everything and felt compelled to put it forward at every possible opportunity. "I suppose ... after all, Branan did stress that speed was crucial. Very well then, lead on."

"Good," said Toulouse. "When we get to the city, we can sell the horse and wagon and use the money to purchase fare. It should be more than enough."

Auberge wet his lips which were chapped from the dusty road. "I'm for a pint. Can I buy you a drink, Crispy?"

Fortune's eyebrows crept up the expanse of his forehead. "Did we not just agree that speed was imperative?"

"Aye, but we'll save time by train, and besides, I drink quickly. I'll even treat you to a Carlisle crust, one of the finest meat pies in Northern England." Auberge appeared to have it all figured out, with drink, food, and sleep as his priorities.

"Tell me, Mr. Auberge," said Crispin, after they had found a table at the Black Feather Tavern "before you came south from Edinburgh, what vocation put coin in your purse?"

"Vocation?" asked Auberge through the froth of ale that coated his whiskers.

"Your job," sighed Fortune patiently.

"Oh yes, well a bit of this and a bit of that, but chiefly I was employed as a gardener. However, I make my coin as I can."

"From gardener to mercenary, there's a leap," said Crispin, sipping on a glass of port.

Auberge slapped his palm on the table. "Or in this case a soldier of fortune," he replied with a wink. Crispin allowed himself a smile at the play of words. He was not entirely comfortable with Auberge's manner. The odd-looking Northerner already drew enough attention with his mottled colouring and tall, rangy bearing. Patrons of the Feather had been sizing up the pair from the moment they walked in, and Fortune, never the most outgoing of individuals, chewed nervously at the corner of his thumb.

Toulouse lowered his voice. "I don't like the sound of these creepers, Fortune. No sir, not one bit. But if you're wondering what motivates me to lend a hand, look no further than my purse. I am being very well paid. Otherwise, I would be just as pleased to be back on Princess Street with a flask of whisky in my coat and a pinch of snuff handy. In the meantime, having never ridden on the Great Northern Railway, I find that I can barely contain my excitement."

Fortune yawned widely, a reaction that was related more closely to his nerves, than it was to fatigue.

"There ain't nothing for you to be concerned about," claimed Auberge, reading his companion's mood. "The message what you carry is in yer haid only. The creepers would have to tie you down and pull yer toenails out before they'd get you to spill."

"Thank you so much for your sentiments, Mr. Auberge, but I am most confident that it will not come to that." Something outside the window caught Fortune's attention, and he pointed silently, first at his eye and then outside.

Toulouse turned and scowled. An unkempt-looking ruffian was removing a barrel from their cart, and another was in the act of examining the horse's teeth. He leaped up, almost upsetting the table, and dashed outside.

"That would be my barrel," he said, approaching the first thief.

"They's nuthin' in it," said the man.

"Aye, just like yer haid." agreed Toulouse, lifting the heavy barrel above his shoulder. He brought it down hard on the unfortunate thief's skull, laying him out unconscious. "Might I interest you in purchasing a horse and rig?" offered Auberge, stepping towards the other thief, who had suddenly gone quite pale.

"Jes' lookin', thanks," he replied, taking off his hat passively.

Toulouse leaned into the man's face. "Then keep yer bleedin' hands to yourself, shite-fer-brains!" As the frightened man scampered away, Auberge grinned. "Horse for sale," he sang in a cheery voice for the small crowd that had gathered.

Crispin, standing in the doorway of the tavern, shook his head in wonder. *So much for not bringing attention to themselves.*

-114-

Padraic and Tamlyn sat on the edge of the low wall to the rear of the castle, absently tossing pebbles into the water. Threstone backed onto the Solway Firth via a wide lake that fed the castle moat. At its narrowest point inland, the lake could easily be mistaken for a river, and the resulting marshland was where Virgil and the others were slogging through the weeds in search of Alfred Gamble.

Paddy and Tam were both slumped with head in hand, staring at the ripples. The disappearance of Alfie weighed heavy on their hearts, and Tamlyn wished that the group of them had never entered the small room at the base of the tower. He was sure that something horrible dwelt in the dungeon and believed that very something had a great deal to do with Alfie's mystery.

Padraic's eyes were red-rimmed and sorrowful. *"I wonder if Alf went back to Turfmoor,"* he wrote.

"I don't believe he would do that," replied Tamlyn. "There would be nothing but danger and grief to welcome him there."

Paddy shrugged and pointed to the water.

"I pray not," said his friend. "We must keep our hope up, Paddy, he can't have gone far" It was then that Tam saw the first snowflakes. "I hope Alfie is dressed warmly, wherever he is."

Ceana strode up behind her son and scanned the sky. "I think we have a great deal of snow on the way. Some of the men who are not out searching have begun to build a shelter of boughs over the big fire."

Tam didn't know how she could forecast the weather, but mothers, it seemed, were very skilled at determining what the skies would offer. Ceana credited the soreness in her back for her ability to sense the changes.

"We need a dry place to store firewood and some strong boys to haul it. Perhaps you two could recruit the Macneils and whoever else is about."

Her son's face lit up. "I know just the place," he said. Clearly Ceana knew that Paddy and her son would come out of their doldrums when an important job was offered to them.

Before long Tam was at the end of a line of boys who were passing firewood hand over hand across the square and into the dungeon at the base of the tower. Young Macleary's stroke of genius served two obvious purposes, and his spirits rose as the pile of lumber climbed the walls, making it impossible to enter the dungeon.

Back at the fire, poles were lashed together in a strong framework, and long boughs of fir were stripped and woven into a covering that rested high above the flame. The big fire was now sheltered from the elements.

Wooden hammers rang out as the workers, who had moved on, continued to modify the high east wall of rooms. There were three stories of high windows that needed to be renovated in order to keep snow from piling up inside on the stone floors. Straw was being hauled up to each room, which would be allocated to families first.

Most of the highlanders were searching the woods and had abandoned any thoughts of tunnelling into the frozen ground for the time being.

Charlotte joined her mother at the fire warming her hands. Along with Lara Twist, Megan Maguire, and the rest of the young mothers, she took it in turns to supervise the young children. The older children were more or less left to their own devices for the full day, and boredom inevitably led to mischief.

"That little bastard Cam Gordon!" complained Charlotte to her mother. "He took one of the girls aside and told her that if she didn't lift her skirt for him, he would tell the creepers, and while she was sleeping one would crawl into her bed and cut her throat." Ceana looked up. "And by God," continued Charlotte, "I came this close to slapping that little bully across the head!"

"Well you were right not to," replied her mother "Young Campbell is nothing but a big blowhard like his father. He'd have gone whining to the old man, who in turn would have raised a huge stink. Those two are cut from the same cloth. And yet his mother is such a nice woman."

Charlotte calmed down. "I warned him if I heard the same story again, he'd be wearing my shoe on the inside of his arse."

After the two women stopped laughing, Ceana put an arm around her daughter. "We'll have to put up with them for the time being, though. I think this snow is going to keep us in close quarters all winter."

Charlotte sighed. In her fancies the young woman imagined herself in a fine little cottage down in the valley, with Liam outside cutting wood and a baby on her hip.

It was a difficult time to be in love, and she worried constantly that a slip-up would push her into motherhood before she was ready. Liam appeared to be less concerned at the prospect, but she had no desire to raise a child in this draughty castle.

And there was the matter of privacy. She knew very well that some couples occasionally left the castle for a walk in the tall grasses and was shrewd enough to understand what was meant by a "quick walk." In fact some quick walks lasted longer than others. Now that the snow was gathering on the ground, other methods would have to be devised to accommodate Threstone's frustrated lovers. Megan Maguire had asked Charlotte more than once to watch over little Nelly so she could keep a date in the woods with her highlander. Duncan risked a strong dressing-down from his peers if the relationship was discovered, and the change in weather would make it particularly difficult for them to see each other.

As day ran into evening and the snow continued to fall, the highlanders returned to the castle. It was obvious even from a distance that they had not come across the missing lad. They returned to their tents, with the exception of Hugh Maclean, who sought out Ronan to let him know that their attempt to locate Alfie was fruitless. Virgil and his cousins had discovered nothing in the swampy mud flats by the water, and the large castle had not given up this secret to those who had explored every nook and cranny. Grandmother Gamble was inconsolable and spent the day praying silently.

-115-

The fact that Alfred Gamble had arrived in the woods of Deermuir simply by following his nose was nothing short of a miracle. Alfie, who had overheard Tamlyn discussing the strange family of wood dwellers with Murdoch, decided that he was a misfit also and that he belonged with them.

The youngster's judgement had been clouded for some time now, and he'd brushed off the loss of his mother far too easily. Now his failure to deal with those emotions and the strange events in Threstone's dungeon left him mired in a worrisome state of psychological tunnel vision. He had set out across the moors with a single purpose, to find this Brightfoot person that Tamlyn spoke of in whispered tones.

Young Gamble had enough wits left to recall that by keeping the afternoon sun to his left, he was certain to be proceeding in a northerly direction, and he plodded along determined to achieve his goal. It didn't occur to him that he might not be accepted by the wood folks. He regarded himself as somehow broken, and this quest was as much about accepting the punishment that he believed was his due for not protecting his mother, as it was about finding a way to become whole again.

The horrors he had witnessed in Turfmoor were always with him. Alfie was there when the Teriz had forced old ones into the smoke pit. Live burial was deemed to be the quickest way to dispatch the aged, who were exhumed later for consumption. The cured meat was considered to be quite flavourful in this smoky tenderized form, or so he had overheard the creatures saying.

Alfie was astounded at the strength exhibited by some of the elders. Not having succumbed to the smoke, they managed to scramble up the side of the pit, only to be pushed and pulled back into the cooker with poles and gaffs. He'd told no one what he had seen, and he had carried the sounds in his head since the day he and his mother had fled the village. In a manner of speaking, Violet had not really escaped, and her young son, along with her mother, was the only one to have physically survived, although at this point the quality of that survival could certainly be questioned.

At the same time that the Highlanders had emerged from the woods by the castle, Alfred was several miles away in the direction opposite where they had searched. It was cold and dark now. The small boy was curled up next to a large tree that grew from the centre of a high, grass-covered mound. He drew up his knees, pulling the long cloak around his feet, and quickly fell into a deep sleep.

Sometime just before sunrise he suffered from horrific dreams in which his grandmother clawed her way from the smoke pit. The old woman had glowing coals that burned in her forehead where eyes should have been. As she dragged herself through the ashes, fat crackled and withered skin peeled.

Alfie's skull filled with the greasy smoke, and he pounded his fists into the sides of his head until the images vanished, allowing him to leave the world of dreams. The snow had nearly stopped falling in the night, leaving a crisp blanket of white on the downs.

Something rigid was pressing uncomfortably into his back. He shifted around and reached behind, sitting up straight. His hand came in contact with the tines of a large pitchfork. No wonder his back ached.

His stomach grumbled for food which would not be forthcoming. He scooped up a handful of snow and slaked his thirst before scanning the sky for directions.

-116-

Tyburn was more tired than he'd been for a long time. The old man wondered if he would survive the war, for surely that was where they were headed. Some generations were born to peace and others to warfare. It was only a matter of numbers. It seemed unfair to the doctor that he had avoided it all his life, only to have it thrust upon him in old age.

The elder Macleary was positioned in the uppermost turret of the castle. He sat at Threstone's highest point, gazing out the small window. He knew that he should be out there on the snow-covered moors, bounding across the white fields on four legs, in search of the missing child. The shift was such a powerful drain on his system that Tyburn still felt weak from the last time, when he had only undergone the transformation in order to act as Tamlyn's guardian. It occurred to him, not for the first time, that life was certainly short.

One hoped to have attained wisdom in a lifetime and, before senescence closed in, that it might be put to some use. Tyburn knew that he had not lived his life well in the early years but believed that he had been of some use in the last decade. He'd studied the medicinal properties of plants for most of his lifetime and put his knowledge to good use improving the health of others. That had to count for something. Macleary knew that he'd made his way through the world with good intentions, and maybe even that was good enough.

His eyes strained to pick out the men below in the fading light of the encampment. They were just colourful forms, moving in and out of the larger shadows. He rubbed at his eyes in an attempt to clear his vision. More and more lately he'd suffered from periods of blurred sight and extreme fatigue.

Suddenly he came to the realization that his death was close at hand and made a wordless vow to take down as many creepers as he could on the way out. More than anything he wished to return to his house of garden and stone, and that alone would be something worth fighting for.

The doctor had never remarried, having adapted to the loneliness of a solitary life, and doubted that anyone could put up with his odd way of life. His children and grandchildren were good company and had made life in the castle bearable. Tyburn had spent more time with them lately than in the previous ten years, and this closeness made the prospect of war even more frightening, as there seemed to be so much more to lose now.

Tyburn often wondered what life would have been like had Vannah not passed away. He couldn't recall her face as easily now, as she faded from memory, and he tended to remember her in a fonder light than she deserved. She would without doubt have retained some of her great beauty, and her wild nature might even have softened to some degree. He imagined it was the young woman's excitement that he missed, for she was in truth not the best of company, being prone to fits of self-indulgence.

The onset of disease had been rapid, and it was relentless in its intentions to devour the woman. The illness was described by her doctors in vague terms, as a failure of the blood. The speed with which Vannah passed was in some terms a blessing, as Tyburn was spared the horrors of a lingering death. The loss of Cay had brought the past back. Macleary considered it a cruel irony that his son had lived to be no older than Vannah.

He had outlived two of his sons, and now his grandchildren's lives were at risk. Tyburn sat by the tower window and told himself he needed a way to find some optimism in the situation. Otherwise the heavy and morose storm clouds of hopelessness would crush him completely.

In the last month he'd found sleep difficult and had little interest in even feeding himself adequately. The old man placed his head between his knees and began to weep. He was roused from his miserable state by the sound of several men yelling from below. Wiping a sleeve across his eyes Tyburn leaned towards the window, and saw at once what had raised the alarm.

-117-

The massive locomotive came to a halt with much fanfare, accompanied by a loud clanging of bells. Thick black smoke spewed from the funnel in bursts, as steam shot across the platform, giving it the look of some otherworldly realm of clouds and demons.

The whistle blew long, threatening to knock the hats off men's heads with the force of its volume. Women in bustles and colourful hats held their skirts down to keep them from revealing ankles or even calves.

Toulouse literally pulled Fortune up the step into the passenger car. "Come on, Crispy, put some effort into it. We're in for a treat now. Did you see that Chinaman with the long pigtail?" he asked "You've got to watch them. They all carry big curvy knives under their shirts. They'd slice yer nose off as soon as look at you. Did I ever tell you about the—"

"Please," interrupted Crispin, "I'm so very tired, perhaps we could just forgo the stories for a little while."

"Well!" replied Toulouse indignantly "If you want me shut up, just say so. I'm not one to prattle on over and over when it's not appreciated. If you want quiet, just say the word. I know when to shut my mouth; you don't have to tell me twice. If you'd have said so, sure, I'll be quiet. You look a little tired. You should try to get some sleep. I won't say nothing. I'll be quiet now, it's not like I need to talk."

"Tickets, please," bellowed the conductor. Fortune took advantage of the opportunity to close his eyes while Toulouse dealt with the tickets.

A very attractive woman took the seat across the aisle from them, much to the relief of Crispin. Perhaps now Toulouse would turn his attentions to the young lady.

As predicted, Auberge suddenly went silent as his eyes danced up the hem of her skirt, stopping briefly at the top of her corset, before settling on her full lips. As she turned towards him, Toulouse's eyebrows jiggled, and the corner of his mouth turned up in what he hoped was an inviting smile.

She turned away at once and stared out the window, visibly restraining a smile. *Ah well, she's playing coy, I see. Fine then, I shall play hard to get.* He arose from the seat and, turning on his heel rather dramatically, made for the dining car in hopes of locating an alcoholic beverage.

"Thank goodness," said Fortune under his breath. The woman across the aisle giggled and pulled out a fan. She glanced over at Crispin and winked knowingly. He smiled and closed his eyes, deciding that if he couldn't fall asleep he would at least feign sleep for a little silence.

As it turned out, he needn't have worried. Toulouse had found a new home in the dining car and abandoned Crispin to his dreams. The tall stranger was taking the opportunity to enjoy some of his wage. *Let the little fat man sleep,* he thought.

His mind was centred on a brace of stiff drinks and a plateful of lamb chops. Auberge was quite pleased with himself. He had gone from unemployed gardener to highly paid bodyguard in what seemed the blink of an eye.

"To Athabasca Pepperidge," he toasted aloud, much to the waiter's consternation. *Wonderful,* thought the nervous Irishman, *just what I need: a big coon that talks to himself.* His outlook changed quickly when the man tipped him handsomely and asked for another whisky. *Good, a halfwit drunk*—his favourite type.

Lester Grimes mixed the drink double strong. This darkie looked like an easy mark and obviously had a heavy purse, probably stolen from an honest, God-fearing white man. He paused to briefly contemplate the odds of a large score, and then reached into his vest for the small packet of powder. The diminutive waiter loosened his tie as the porter passed by. This was a signal for his burly cohort.

-118-

Pengrove lit the torch from his own and passed it to Nash, who in turn passed it to the Teriz underling. The flame followed this course along the line of creepers until all of them possessed the means of ignition.

Wallace turned to the Teriz captain. "Your shirt stinks of petrol. Don't hold that flame so close, unless you plan to cremate yourself."

The big man grunted, presumably intended as thank you.

Nash extracted a horn from his jacket in a ceremonious manner and signalled the hoard of arsonists, who clambered across the cobblestones of Dunradin's town centre, making for the abandoned building with much enthusiasm.

Far across the river, at the quarry, a huge cheer went up as the first buildings exploded into flames.

Green's Guesthouse was the first building to come down. The blackened framework crumbled to the ground, leaving nothing but the stone foundation. Next door, the grocer's was fully ablaze, and Padraic's remaining pigeons took to the air, their underbellies coloured orange against the dark blue of the sky.

The petrol-soaked captain ran from the door of the church in flames. As his shirt quickly burned off, the howling monster beat his wide palms against the remains of his smoking hair and scrambled across the square to dive into the fountain with a hiss. One of the last homes to be razed stood at the top of High Street, where the smoke rose into the sky well above the top of the tree line.

It had been decided in advance that prior to an invasion of the castle, Dunradin would be burned. The demoralizing effect would benefit the Teriz and fill the inhabitants of Threstone with fear.

Despite the fact that Pengrove was sacrificing the element of surprise, he believed the action would go a long way in weakening the enemy by forcing them to react emotionally. In Wallace's experience, battles were won with cool determination and planning. Furthermore, he planned to march the prisoners back through their ruined village to break their spirits further before processing them at the quarry.

The Teriz miners, pleased to be away from the coal pit for a change of scenery, went wild, uprooting fences and anything else that could be tossed into the all-consuming flames. They were like maniacal children on a school outing to hell, laughing and cheering every timber that came crashing down. Just as Pengrove had hoped, the wind was absent, allowing the pall of heavy smoke to rise higher and higher into the air.

Those at the castle who were unable to see the smoke had no trouble smelling it. Tyburn leaned from the window, pointing to the darkening sky. From his vantage point tiny tongues of flame were visible beyond the high woods.

Godwyn Blunt; positioned on the landing above the drawbridge turned and called up to the doctor "Are the woods burning?"

"No!" replied Macleary, shaking his head. "It's the village, Dunradin burns!"

As the word spread quickly amongst the spectators, cries of disbelief and anger echoed from the encampment to the central courtyard. Several townsfolk made their way to the higher reaches of Threstone for a clearer view across the roof of the forest.

At this point the snowfall, which had abated briefly, made its return, accompanied by strong winds. Tyburn pulled the cloak tightly across his chest and made for the stairs. He had no idea what he would say to Ronan and the others but imagined they would expect some words of wisdom. There was nothing he could say to offer comfort.

He realized spirits would be crushed as the Dunradins realized that there were no homes to return to. Most of them had been able to bear the recent hardships by clinging to the belief that one day their village would be liberated. Now it appeared that all was lost, and to add insult to injury, a huge blast from the direction of town suddenly shook the ground.

The treacherous finale had not gone exactly as planned. The explosion that had been arranged to obliterate the large familiar fountain in the town square was far more powerful than expected. Stonework flew in all directions, and Captain Nash's assistant took the force of one of the larger stones square in the face.

Wallace, who had been standing close to the victim, found his jacket coated in a vile pudding of grey matter as the brain shot from the man's opened skull. As Pengrove attempted to brush the sticky mess away, the bile rose in his throat, and he vomited up the contents of his stomach. Nash, who appeared unperturbed at the loss of his second in command, watched him with detached amusement.

-119-

"And you say you are originally from Turfmoor?" asked Salem. "How do we know you're not a spy sent here from Deermuir?" Brightfoot thought it was highly unlikely but continued her questioning nevertheless.

Alfie, who stood in the center of the circle, looked offended. "Because I know who youse are." His fists were clenched, and he stepped back a pace. "You're Salem Brightfoot, and you are Jack, and this is, er, Dennis. I've come to live here in the woods."

The woodfolk all laughed in a loud but friendly manner. "How did you come by this decision, Master Alfred?" asked Salem.

"I don't belong at the castle; I'm a misfit with nae mother or father."

Brightfoot tucked her chin into her neck and frowned. "You're a misfit, are you? How do you imagine that? Come, sit down here and tell me."

"It's ma haid," he explained, taking a seat by the fire and eyeing the quail hungrily. "It don't work proper. I hear voices when no one's about and sometimes I see things what aren't really there."

Salem smiled. "You don't say. Well, tell us, do you have any skills or talents?"

Alfie lowered his head and chewed at his lip. After what seemed a long time, he brightened and reached into his pocket. "I can throw a blade most accurate," he claimed, showing Salem the well balanced knife that was his only possession.

"Suppose you show me," said the young girl. "I'll place this apple over there on the stump" she offered.

"Nah, too easy, toss it in the air," he replied.

"Okay then, let me know when you're ready."

Old Donny rocked back and forth enjoying the show. Salem stepped away from the fire and readied herself.

"Toss it up high," said the young boy, placing his hand behind his head.

"Okay." She lofted the apple underhand as high as she could, stepping well out of the way. Alfie's arm was close to invisible as it snapped forward. The blade sliced the apple clean in two at eye level and thudded into a tree beyond.

The group, struck dumb for a moment, suddenly broke into applause. Salem retrieved the knife and examined the apple pieces with a low whistle. "Most impressive, Mr. Gamble, most impressive, grab yourself a piece of that quail, and come with me into the hut."

Hut did not adequately describe the underground living quarters. What at first glance appeared to be a large mound of earth covered in grass and snow turned out to be a deep circular excavation in the ground, covered with branches and packed clay supported by a strong wooden frame that resembled the workings of an umbrella. The interior was lit with a small fire that burned beneath an opening in the top.

They entered the hut through a hinged door in the roof via a wooden ladder. A low sleeping platform circled the interior next to the wall leaving several feet open to the centre of the hut where a round table was located. Natural light from the open door revealed a flat, level floor of hard-packed earth.

"When we close the door and extinguish the fire," said Salem, "we are virtually invisible. It's all quite safe and comfortable."

-120-

"This is far too cruel," sobbed Charlotte. "I thought I understood how you felt when your cottage was burned, but this is beyond terrible." 4

Liam held her head against his chest as she cried. "This will be difficult to overcome, but we'll find a new home together, just you and I." He doubted his own words but knew he had to put on a brave face.

Charlotte felt as though she had lost her childhood to flames, and there was a large hole in her heart that would fill with hardness over time, enabling her to survive future hardships.

"Why did this happen to us? Mother doesn't deserve this. It's already been so difficult for her."

"I know," replied Liam. "It's not just us. The entire castle must be strong now. Whether we like it or not, Threstone is home, and surely more help will arrive from Glasgow and beyond. The rest of the country has to learn that what's happening here will happen elsewhere. Murdoch has told me that Branan will stay here but has sent word to the Queen herself."

This last bit of news seemed to offer Charlotte a tiny glimmer of hope, and she sat up, lifting a handkerchief to her eyes. "Oh dear, I've soaked your shirt with my tears." She dabbed at his chest with the linen and laughed a little. "Sometimes I think we should just go to my aunt's in Inverness and try for a new life."

Twist shook his head. "But then the creepers would have won, and what would stop them from moving northward? I have seen their ghastly appetites firsthand and never want to witness that again. We have to stand up to them here in the castle where we have a chance of survival."

"If they don't starve us out first." suggested Charlotte. "And where is our poor wee Alfie in all this snow?"

"Indeed," said Liam. "They say bad luck comes in threes. First I vanished, followed by Tam, and now Alfie. We can only hope that good luck follows suit. In any event, we must concern ourselves with those who are here. Your mother's been getting stronger every day; let's hope this doesn't prompt a relapse of her illness."

Charlotte swept her hair back and twisted it into a knot. "Mother is much stronger than any of us imagined. I can see it now, and I think this will make her fighting strong."

An attitude was beginning to take form amongst the castle's inhabitants that Pengrove would not have foreseen. The destruction of Dunradin would only prove to have further united the villagers. He had unwittingly lit a fire in the heart of every man and woman in the castle. Now Threstone was truly their only home, and they would defend it with every device at their means. Food had been rationed for some time now, and all but the very elderly were lean and angry. The temptation to give in to despair was replaced by hunger and determination.

-121-

Branan was very alarmed at the turn of events and again regretted that he'd not gone to London himself. If the weather were not threatening to unleash a blizzard, he might have decided to follow Auberge and Fortune.

It was imperative now that the Queen be made aware of the rapidly deteriorating situation above the border. There could be no argument against army intervention, and the highlander had lost sleep trying to second-guess Her Majesty's response. If only he had known about Netherfield before sending Fortune away.

He was prone to stern self-criticism at the best of times and struggled now to avoid branding himself a failure. He had certainly not managed to eradicate the Teriz, but the fault did not lie with the men around him. Hugh Maclean, Woodruff, Duncan, and the others were all capable men who had done their jobs well, and many of the Teriz had been eliminated. There was no way they could have known of the vast numbers rumoured to be at work in Netherfield.

It might be wiser now to raise the alarm in Edinburgh and Glasgow in hopes that an army might be recruited. The Queen could try him for treason if he overstepped his bounds by involving others, but he doubted that she would be inclined to do that.

Branan lit another pipe, beginning to imagine that he might be unwittingly involved in what amounted to a mass cover-up. He wondered briefly if her Majesty was already aware of the extent of the damage. Had he been duped by a very clever monarchy? Perhaps there had been a call to have matters dealt with, and Victoria had sent him north to keep up appearances.

Stoke had wondered, on more than one occasion, how the emptying of villages could go unnoticed, despite their size and location. The fact that the citizens of Dunradin had managed to occupy Threstone with no questions asked was also suspicious. The castle was out of the way as well, and Threstone's upkeep had been neglected for many years, but still Branan imagined that there must be some historical interest in the location, *unless the roads surrounding the area have been closed by official decree.*

He shook his head and took a deep breath. "I'm becoming paranoid," he said aloud. The closeness of the weather and his inability to accomplish anything while the snow fell had left him with an excess of time to entertain too many wild theories.

The wind whistled and howled between the tents, blasting anyone who had foolishly remained outside. The horses huddled together with their heads close to one another. It was going to be a long night.

-122-

Auberge rubbed his temple. The dining car seemed to have stopped shimmying to the left and right as though it had come to a stop. However, the scenery still sped past the window.

He glanced at the drink in his hand and watched in fascination as it slipped to the floor, shattering without a sound. As he tried to stand, two strong arms from behind circled his chest and lifted him.

"Are you all right, sir?" The waiter's voice didn't synchronize with the movement of his lips. Lester had a look of concern on his face. "We had better get you back to your seat."

The porter steered Toulouse to the dining car's exit, preceded by the waiter, who opened the door between the carriages. "Perhaps a bit of fresh air." he suggested.

Auberge felt the vibration from the train now as they paused between cars. The porter's hands travelled lightly across his body, giving the big man a very strange impression that he was being played like a stringed instrument. "Got it," said the stout assistant in a muddy voice that echoed in the narrow chamber. A rush of cold air raised the hairs on the back of Auberge's neck, and four hands shoved him out the open door.

Toulouse grunted loudly as all the oxygen was driven from his body. The impact, which broke several ribs as well as his left arm, instantly registered a pure dizzying pain that increased as his body spun over and over and finally coming to rest at the bottom of the hill.

Seconds later, Crispin entered the dining car, just as Lester re-emerged, straightening his apron with a smile. "Good day, sir, were you wanting a meal?" He reached for a broom, and Fortune glanced at the broken glass in front of a table which had yet to be cleared.

"I'm looking for my travelling companion. Was a tall darkish fellow here recently?"

"Indeed he was," said the waiter with a smile, pointing to the door behind himself. "He went out that way, just a minute ago."

Crispin shivered as he negotiated the unsteady landing between the two cars, glancing briefly out the windowed door at the deteriorating weather. He searched the two cars ahead before deciding that the waiter had been mistaken in his directions. Of course, Toulouse may have passed back towards the rear of the train, unseen by the waiter.

It was a damn nuisance having Auberge along in the first place, and now the bloody fool had him searching the train when all he wanted was a hot meal.

-123-

When he was not situated in front of a canvas, Ben Flint was a man accustomed to action. He grew restless when circumstances dictated that he remain in one spot for long. Policing the halls of Threstone was very different from his duties back in Edinburgh, but he'd come to know the vast expanse of the castle like the back of his hand and settled into a routine of patrolling every step and corner, often stopping to chat with the inhabitants. It was not long before he became familiar with every tenant and every room.

He took a longer time this evening with his rounds, doing his best to insure that everyone had what they needed against the freezing temperatures. "Evenin' Mrs. Twist, y'aright then?" he asked

"It's very cold tonight, isn't it, Mister Flint? I thank you for your care; the extra blanket helps."

"My pleasure; let me know if you have any trouble." Ben smiled and turned down the hall. Under the archway and three steps up, was a larger corner room. As he negotiated the steps quietly, Flint caught the sound of a hushed conversation from within. He paused to listen carefully.

"This Netherfield that we've heard spoke of doesn't sound all that bad to me, probably a damn sight warmer than the castle. I'm of a mind to look for it when this weather leaves off. Sounds tae me like new families are wanted. For my part, I'm sick to the guts with these Maclearys telling me what to do. If big Portus were still about, I'd wager that Ronan would be put in his place quick enough."

The voice belonged to Virgil Mason, who stood in the corner of the room with a blanket around his shoulders. "If you lads have any balls, you'll join me, along with your families, and anyone else who cares to get out of this slag heap."

Ben had heard enough to know that his intervention was warranted. He stepped into the room. "You there, it's Mason, isn't it?"

The dairyman hid his alarm behind a smirk. "That's right; Virgil to my friends, but you ain't one of my friends."

Flint stepped forward and pushed his walking stick into the soft area beneath Virgil's chin, forcing his head back. "I think you'll find, *Virgil*, that you can't 'ave too many friends, and you don't really want me for an enemy."

Mason attempted to swallow his saliva, and the result was a wet gasp.

"Don't say anything. I'm going to do the talking," continued Flint. He lowered his walking stick and rearranged the blanket on Virgil's shoulders carefully. "It is really in the best interests of everyone here at the castle that we stand together, united as one. It is in fact imperative that we do not slink about poisoning each other's minds with our shitty little self-serving plans.

"I couldn't help noticing what a particularly nasty piece of work you are, Mason, so be forewarned. If I hear even a whisper of you inciting divisions amongst the villagers again, I'll shove the full length of this stick up your arse and snap it off. Are we clear?"

Mason dropped his gaze from Flint's and turned to his three companions wordlessly.

When Ben turned the corner out of earshot, Virgil spoke again. "Can you bloody believe it? That little prick doesn't even come from the village, and he's telling us what to do. Someone should put him straight."

His cousin spoke up, "Someone other than you I suppose."

Mason declined further comment on the subject of Flint. He'd looked into the man's eyes and seen something deadly. *That twat must have balls of iron. He wasn't even feeling the cold.*

Virgil knew one thing. As soon as this weather improved, he was out of here, to see what was left of his dairy farm. After all, it couldn't snow forever.

Flint continued down the hall, deep in thought. He had plenty of snitches on pay in Edinburgh and was formulating a plan to employ one or two of the castle lads to keep an eye on Mason and his cousins, when around the corner, as if by fate, arrived the brothers Macneil.

Cardiff and Caleb were wrapped tightly in blankets, looking red-nosed and miserable as they shuffled down the hall mumbling to themselves. Cardiff held a large taper, which he almost dropped as they encountered Flint suddenly.

"Careful, stupid!" snapped Caleb. "Uh, not you, sir," he added quickly, "me brother."

Ben Flint bowed slightly. "My fault entirely, however, this is a timely meeting. Would you lads care to earn a bit of coin?"

Caleb laughed, "Beggin' yer pardon, Mr. Flint, but what use would we 'ave fer coin 'ere in the castle?"

Ben smiled. "An intelligent question but let me ask you, do you plan to reside here forever?" Cardiff blinked in the dim light and made no comment. "A sovereign to each of you for a wee bit of detective work" suggested Flint

When it was put this way, Caleb visibly warmed to the proposition. "What would you 'ave us do then?—keepin' in mind that we doesn't do criminal-like work."

"Nothing of the sort," continued Flint. "I would just like you to keep an eye on the daily movements of a Mr. Mason and his cousins and report anything odd to me."

"Old Virgil and his inbred cousins, that's nae problem. The milkman always struck me as a dodgy character, a little too fond of his cows, if you take my meaning."

"I don't understand," said Cardiff.

"Never mind," replied Caleb. "We'll take the job, Mr. Flint, sir."

-124-

To a man, Pengrove's troops were armed with whipsnares and slashing blades. One hundred and fifty Teriz were gathered in orderly lines in the centre of the Dunradin quarry. Strict orders were being issued on the use of their equipment.

"Gentlemen," Nash began, "—and I use that term loosely—your blade is to be used as a last resort. It's there for intimidation only. The whipsnare is used in this fashion."

He held the modified bullwhip above his head. The end had been looped back and woven through the length to the end of the handle. As a volunteer stepped away, Nash reached across and dropped the leather loop over his victim's head, then snapped it back quickly while cinching it tight in one movement.

"You can now control the prisoner with one hand. Do not exert too much pressure on the snap back, or you will strangle your prey. Do not get greedy and attempt to retrieve two villagers. The reward will not double, and be aware that anyone found eating villagers will be destroyed at once." He paused briefly letting this last point sink in.

"As well, keep in mind that we have a long march back through the woods and down into the village, so don't waste time kicking the shit out of your prisoner. If they require a little encouragement to keep marching, then kicking them in the legs would defeat your purpose, would it not?"

Nash crooked his thumb and rested it against his temple. "If you should have a particularly resistant companion, I suggest you remove an eyeball. There is nothing more effective than the prospect of blindness to bring even the largest of men into line. Again, don't get carried away: only one eye, or you'll have to carry your catch the distance." The snow had stopped now, and the air in Dunradin was perfectly still.

Above the forest near Threstone, the change in weather had come through. Tamlyn stood beneath the arch of the main entrance to the castle marvelling at the silence and the sparkling drifts of snow that reflected moonlight against the rapidly freezing moat.

He squinted into the darkness, trying to make out a shape which suddenly stood out in the snow by the tree line. Something or someone had definitely moved. He took a few steps toward the movement and then glanced behind to reassure himself that an escape route was clear should it be required.

There was nobody on watch from the high landing at the moment, for one reason or another, and Tamlyn knew that he should turn around and make a report of his sighting, but what indeed had he sighted? In any case he had no sign that the visitor represented any danger.

He stepped closer. As the distance behind him increased, it became clear that the mystery was a four-legged one. It was a small, stout pony, cream in colour with a tangled white mane. It stood on a level area looking for grass beneath the snow. It raised its shaggy head and seemed to smile at Tamlyn.

He suddenly had a chilling thought, which stopped him in his tracks. What if this was a shape-changer sent to lure him away from the castle? But no, he decided, this animal had a peaceful welcoming nature.

The winds began to return as Tam approached the animal and reached out to stroke its mane. "Well, who are you now, out here all by yourself, looking lost and hungry?" The pony stepped towards him and rubbed the boy's chest affectionately with its forehead. He placed his arms around the animal's thick neck and gave it a hug.

The beast trembled now as the wind gathered force, blowing snow into the air from the tall drifts. Tamlyn looked behind him across the plain and saw that the castle was now a dim shadow in the swirling clouds of white night. The moon no longer lit the way back, and his footprints were rapidly filling.

"You had better come with me," he said. "It's warmer in the castle." He loosened the jute that held his jacket in place and looped it around the animal's neck. Turning to lead the pony back, he saw with alarm that the castle was no longer visible. The storm had returned so quickly that he was now disoriented and somewhat panicked.

Tamlyn located his footprints with some relief and struggled to follow the faint markings. He pulled on the rope but the animal would not budge. "Please hurry, come along!" he urged "There's no time to be stubborn." When it appeared that the wind would completely eradicate all signs of the way back, Tamlyn did panic. He let loose his grip on the rope and raced back along the fading footprints. As he staggered forward, leaning into the wind, his heart began to race. Where was the next print, and where was the castle? In his haste he tripped over himself and fell into the white abyss.

Once back on his feet, he had lost all sense of direction. "Help!" he yelled in desperation, but his voice carried no further than his lips and was blown back down his throat by the storm. His fingers were starting to freeze, and his teeth began to chatter as he forged ahead. The snow was stinging his face now, and his forehead ached. He tried to pull the jacket close but the relentless wind snapped it from his hands. No one would see him and nobody would hear him.

Soon he found it difficult to distinguish up from down and felt as though he had been buried alive. He fell on his side and curled into a ball with his hands between his knees. The constant roar of the storm was all he could hear, and before long his ears became so accustomed to the sound that it worked itself into a frozen silence. He was encompassed by utter emptiness and soon lost consciousness.

-125-

Somewhere in England, Toulouse Auberge was waking up. He was surrounded by blackness and didn't have the luxury of a blizzard to numb him from the pain. Every nerve in his body seemed to scream in agony, especially his left side, where most of the damage had been done.

He no longer had the benefits of the alcohol or the drug he had ingested to dull the searing pain, and the dark man from Edinburgh slipped in and out of consciousness as he tried to puzzle out what had happened. One astounding fact was clear to him: he was no longer on the train. He had no recollection of how this might have come about, but he felt certain that he was in grave danger.

It was obvious that he had been sorely hurt. His arm was broken badly, probably in more than one place, and the side of his body, somewhere beneath the pain, had a soggy smashed feel to it. There was certainly no point in attempting to move, even if this was a possibility. He tasted blood in the back of his throat, and he was sure his head would have ached had it not felt completely numb. This was the only blessing, he supposed, as everything else seemed to hurt.

I wonder where I am. He had always imagined that he would know when his time had come. How strange to not know where you were as death approached, and what about his charge? He couldn't recall Crispin's name. Had he met with the same fate?

Auberge could not recall any reason for the journey by train or where it had been going. As he struggled to remember the events of the day, something liquid inside bubbled up and his throat filled with blood again.

-126-

Journal Entry:

The weather for the last week has continued to deteriorate. It's very cold here in the castle. The snow has been falling steadily, stopping briefly only to return with more force. The winds are becoming stronger, and all activity has ground to a halt. We are all keeping warm as best we may, but the main fire in the courtyard has gone out and everyone has retreated with candles to the many small rooms in the upper levels.

I can only imagine that the highlanders are not very comfortable below in their tents. Surely they will join us in the castle soon. They have stood by us the entire time and everyone admires their strength and generosity. My hands are too cold to write now.

—Padraic

-127-

Charlotte's teeth chattered as she wiped at her runny nose. Liam had just removed a large rotting tapestry from the wall of the small room and hung it across the window. He wrapped his arms around the young woman and pulled her closer.

The flame in an ornate wall sconce stopped flickering and burned steadily, giving the room an orange glow. Liam wondered what would happen when all the candles were gone. The candle provided no warmth, but its tiny flame seemed to offer hope. He would extinguish the light soon to preserve it for the next evening.

"The storm will abate," he insisted, trying to comfort Charlotte, who was feeling more miserable than she had ever felt. The young woman was ill with the cold and fever that was sweeping through Threstone during the coldest week of the year. "You and I will walk in the sunshine again. We'll find a proper home and make babies, strong healthy baby boys."

"Girls," snuffled Charlotte.

Liam chuckled, "both, and lots of them."

"Not too many," she replied. "Two of each, and we'll live in a large house with fireplaces in every room that will burn the year 'round. Our children won't ever be cold."

The young woman tucked her hands into Liam's jacket. He pulled her close and kissed the top of her head. "Leave the candle burning," she murmured sleepily. "I don't want to be in the dark."

Despite the cold, the young couple managed to make love, passionately stealing and returning each other's heat.

-128-

Ronan raised his voice above the howling winds. "There is room in the castle!" He was addressing Branan and the Macintosh brothers. "Your tents will not hold. At least stonework repels the wind."

Branan nodded. "Yes, you're right. Tell Tyburn we will be there right away." He turned to John Macintosh. "It appears you were correct. Gather your men, and bring your weapons with you"

"It's about feckin' time," grumbled John. "I cannae find my bollocks, never mind the weapon."

Ronan leaned into the blizzard and stepped through the deep snow towards the castle. The footprints he'd made walking from Threstone to the encampment were already filling with new snow. As he approached the entrance, He saw a small form from the corner of his eye. Glancing to his right, He could see a shape in the field at some distance that was rapidly being covered with snow. The icy blast of winter stung his eyes, and he turned away. *It could be anything*, he thought, rushing through the archway. *Certainly none of the enemy would have ventured into this storm.*

It was Godwyn Blunt who later reminded Ronan that young Alfie was yet unaccounted for. "Good God!" exclaimed Macleary. "It hadn't occurred to me that it might be the wee lad out there!" An hour had passed since his return, and all the highlanders had trudged into the castle, having sighted nothing unusual.

"We had better have a look," suggested Godwyn, "even if it means we are to retrieve a victim of the storm."

"Let us pray that that's not the case," said Ronan, wrapping a scarf around his face.

The winds were weakening somewhat when the two men stepped from the castle, and visibility had improved. They stopped at once and scanned the tree line. For every tree visible there appeared to be a Teriz warrior. They were emerging from the high woods from as far to the left and right as either man could see. "Feckin' hell," said Blunt, groping for his pistol, which was behind him in the castle.

"There must be a thousand of them." Ronan grabbed him by the shoulder and turned the big man around. They both fled into Threstone, instinctively lifting the huge caber to bolt the wide door behind them. The drawbridge itself was never lowered, due to the fact that a sturdy footbridge had been built across the moat. The times when it was necessary to draw the bridge for defence had passed many years ago. "We are under siege!" yelled Ronan, no longer caring if panic ensued. "To arms!"

-129-

Perhaps the train had stopped while he was asleep, and Auberge had gotten off. The waiter may have seen someone else, but the odds of two gentlemen on the train matching Toulouse's description were slim to say the least.

Eventually Fortune concluded that a riddle with no answer was a waste of time. Since Auberge's absence really had no bearing on his mission, he would simply have to dismiss his curiosity. It was time to get on with the task at hand.

He had not bothered with the sleeping car and had slept in a seated position for the rest of the night. As the train came to a stop, he rose from the seat, wincing with pain as a spasm shot through his lower back. He cursed himself for not taking advantage of the comforts of a mattress and moved towards the exit.

The short man glanced about Victoria Station, half expecting Auberge to emerge from one of the train cars. After crossing the platform, he hailed a carriage and made for Greenwich, where he would spend the morning before carrying on to Buckingham Palace. The Queen was staying there briefly. She much preferred Windsor but found that it was occasionally necessary to travel to the palace.

On the other side of the Thames in Greenwich, William James, the shoemaker, answered the bell at his door. To be more precise it was Joseph his young son who ushered Crispin into the shop front.

"Well, hello, young man," said Fortune, "and how have you been?"

"I am fine, thank you, sir." He smiled.

William shook Fortune's hand. "Good day, Crispin. I finished your boots just this week," he said, retrieving them from behind the counter.

Crispin took a seat and removed his old boots. "Tell me something, Joseph, are you going to grow up to be a wonderful cobbler like your father?"

"Why, no sir. I'm going to be a carriage driver and drive very, very fast all over London, but I will be careful so that nobody gets hurt."

Crispin chuckled. "You're a bright boy, Joseph, and these are fabulous boots." The road-weary footwear that the Queen's emissary had discarded was not up to Buckingham standards.

Fortune wasted no time crossing back into Westminster and was soon using the pendant around his neck to gain entrance to the palace. Winston Parker, the Queen's doorkeeper, was a tall, balding man with heavy jowls and deep-set eyes. He had a voice an octave deeper than anyone Crispin had met before, and the old gentleman always spoke in a slow, deliberate way.

"Good afternoon, Mr. Fortune."

"Hello, Winnie. You're looking well. How is she?"

Winston replied carefully. "With regards to the Queen's appearance, Her Majesty would seem much improved." He paused, "In all honesty, sir, if I may speak plainly, it's Her Majesty's state of mind that concerns me."

Crispin frowned. "That's worrisome, and unfortunately I doubt that my news will offer any solace. We are living in difficult times, Winston."

"Yes, sir," replied the servant, stepping ahead of Crispin to swing open the large oak doors. "Your Majesty, Mr. Crispin Fortune."

The Queen wore a healthy look of opulence that Fortune was unfamiliar with. She beckoned for him with a curve of her finger.

He crossed the floor and went down on one knee with a flourish. "Your Majesty," he said, lowering his head.

"Please Mr. Fortune; take a seat so that we may hear what you have to say for yourself. I am most anxious to know if you were successful in your quest to locate Mr. Stoke."

Fortune took the seat beside Victoria's large ornate desk. The Queen leaned forward across a stack of letters, meeting the emissary's gaze with an intensity that prompted him to look away.

After an uncomfortable silence, she brightened. "Forgive us, Crispin, we've not enquired after you. How do you fare? Was your journey enjoyable?"

"Oh, I am very well indeed, Ma'am," he stammered.

"Good, then," she replied, looking about the room absently as though searching for something. "Indeed, and what of Stoke?"

"Yes, Stoke," began Crispin. "I was able to speak with Branan, due to an exceptional turn of fate. By the oddest of coincidences we intercepted each other in the small village of Dunradin." He went on to recount the meeting and the circumstances surrounding their discussions. "Stoke is of the opinion that the severity of the situation warrants the use of martial intervention."

The Queen pursed her lips and sighed while tapping her fingertips on the surface of the desk. "And why did Stoke not accompany you?"

"Mr. Stoke felt it was imperative that he remain with the villagers in the event of an attack." Crispin went on to explain how the tall northerner sent in his stead had vanished from the train, espousing his belief that the bodyguard had succumbed to the lure of an attractive woman and abandoned him.

"We wonder what knowledge went with him," replied Victoria quietly.

Crispin's attention was diverted briefly when a striped cat boldly trotted into the room. "Oh, Stella, what have you brought Mommy?" enquired Victoria. The feline leaped onto the table and proudly dropped the plump mouse in front of the Queen. Fortune's mouth fell open, as the monarch casually picked up the little rodent by its tail and turned her back to the stunned gentleman.

What happened next turned his spine to jelly. As he watched in disbelief, Victoria's hand went to what he imagined was her mouth. The muffled squeal was followed by a horrible sucking noise, before she dropped the creature into a wastebasket at her feet.

-130-

I awoke the next morning with the rising sun shining into the window of my bedroom—the room I shared with my older brother Murdoch. I rubbed my eyes with disbelief. Had I died and entered the afterlife? It was as though I'd been transported back through a portal that led to the distant past.

I sat up straight. There was Murdoch lying asleep beside me, and on the chair beside our bed was my old backpack, which I had lost some time ago. My mind raced furiously. Had I gone mad? How the devil could I be back in Dunradin when the entire town had burned to the ground?

I leaped from the bed and looked out the window. The snow had vanished, and across the valley towards Lilyvine a plume of smoke spiralled lazily from one of the cottage chimneys. It was all too incredible. The last thing I recalled was lying in the snow, in the midst of a howling storm, with nothing but whiteness surrounding me, praying that I could go back in time to the point where everything had been warm and safe.

Murdoch woke up just then and scratched his head. I smiled at him brightly despite my confusion. "What are you grinning at, you clown?"

"Good Lord," I said. "I've just had the most incredible and frightening dream imaginable, it was all so very real."

"Bloody hell, I'm not surprised, you greedy sod!" He had noticed my open backpack. "You've eaten every last mushroom. What did you expect?"

And so I had. I recalled now how I'd lain in bed munching the tasty morsels until the lot was gone. I'd had a stomach-ache later in the night towards morning, and gone outside to relieve myself. The sky was cast in purple, and I remembered feeling somehow that I was floating, but I didn't recall returning to my bed.

"But the dream was so vivid," I continued, "a story worthy of a novel, all in one night."

Murdoch just laughed and pulled the covers over his shoulders.

I suddenly thought of something. "But what about the English soldiers?" I asked.

Murdoch scowled at me. "Don't be thick," he said. "Those men were hunters, and the one daft bugger had fallen from his horse and hurt his self. Father took them off to get patched up by Tyburn. It looked to me like both of them were pretty deep in the whisky."

After dressing quickly, I rushed outside and gazed down at the centre of town. Even from this distance I could make out the hefty frame of Portus Treacher sitting on the steps in front of his grocery shop, with a morning pipe of tobacco. Padraic would be upstairs sleeping still. It was almost too much to take in at once. I reached for my head and stared wide-eyed at the ground.

I suddenly had an overpowering urge to rush along the path that wound down the hill on High Street to look for Uncle Cay. Everything was going to be perfectly fine. I sat down in the grass, dizzy with joy, and lay back with my arms behind my head smiling at the blue sky.

EPILOGUE - 1943

Twenty-year-old Tammy Macleary threw the handful of rice high above her brother's head as he descended the steps of the small church with his new bride. The young girl had been named after her mother's favourite grandfather, Tamlyn. "You get over here, Tam Macleary," she would say "You've got a mischievous way about you, just like my grandfather had. He was always playing little tricks on me."

Many of the bride and groom's family had motored out to the country church for the wedding. It was a beautiful old building that stood halfway between the city of Deermuir and the ancient ruins of castle Threstone. Tammy's father often made the trip up from Dunradin with her brother to this area for the pheasant hunting, and Patrick had always admired the quaint little building, with its beautiful turn-of-the-century chapel.

As the guests clapped and cheered the young couple, Tammy noticed that an old man was on his knees in the little graveyard beside the church. He was cleaning moss from the engraved letters on one of the headstones. As she continued to stare, he turned his face towards her and smiled sweetly.

He looked incredibly old, with an unbelievable map work of wrinkles. Thin wisps of long snow-white hair were visible beneath his battered straw hat, and a pair of dark sunglasses rested on his beaklike nose. The gentleman returned his attention to the headstone and continued to work the moss away carefully.

As the guests began to file back into their motorcars, Tammy approached the minister, who remained on the steps. "Thank you so much, Father Mackenzie," she said politely. "If I may ask, who is that old gentleman taking care of the stones?"

The preacher replied with a smile, "Oh, you mean old Dorian. Yes, he's been with us for many years; started here long before I did. No one is quite sure of his age."

Tammy nodded in thanks.

"I'll tell you one thing," added Mackenzie. "The old boy has an uncanny knack for preparing the departed for their journey into the afterlife. Very delicate he is with his hands, and a nicer man you'll never meet."

Finis Author's note: Tamlyn Macleary's adventures continue in volume 2 entitled

Where Dreams Lie